*O*verhead, something dragged  the floor, sound-mattress or a big bag of laund: it was. Hannah stopped to look ba scattering her tears. Mom said th: Anna tried to stop crying so he v ..., but her sobs turned into hiccups. They felt like something that was trying to escape from inside her – something she couldn't fight.

Will he notice the panel? Will he know we are here?

She heard Travis cross the length of the living room, from the far corner of the house, heading to their mother's bedroom with swift and determined footsteps. Anna was sure he was still looking for the money, and she wondered why her mother hadn't just given it to him. Furniture moved, drawers and doors slammed, and Travis bellowed in anger. A huge crash followed, glass shattered, and Anna was positive the floor would soon collapse on top of them.

Acknowledgements

"Feeling gratitude and not expressing it
is like wrapping a present and not giving it."
—*William Arthur Ward*

A mammoth *Thank You* to:

Roberta Colasanti—my fiancé, first draft reader, professional adviser, sometimes therapist, and love of my life, who makes waking up each morning a joy, and going to bed every night even better. *'S leatsa mo chridhe gu bràth.*

Christopher Golden—for all the advice, line edits, endless answering of stupid questions, but most of all for being my friend.

Rick Hautala—for the same. I miss you, my friend. You left us far too soon.

Linda Nagle—for the hawkeyed editing skills, pinpoint observations, and goofball antics. (See what I did there?)

Madelon "Mad" Wilson and **Marianne Halbert**—for last-minute proofing heroics.

Haverhill, Massachusetts (my hometown)—for letting me use you so liberally in my novel.

Elm Creek, Nebraska—for letting me invade your unique little town.

Crossroad Press—for the obvious.

Macabre Ink is an imprint of Crossroad Press Publishing

Copyright © 2015 By John McIlveen
Cover by David Dodd
Design by Aaron Rosenberg
ISBN 978-1-941408-61-2 — ISBN 978-1-941408-62-9 (pbk.)

First edition

HANNAHWHERE

JOHN McILVEEN

For my daughters
Heidi, Heather, Kayleigh, Kyrie, and Lara

Daughters are like flowers; they fill the world with beauty, and sometimes attract pests.

—Author Unknown

"Your memory is a monster; you forget—it doesn't. It simply files things away. It keeps things for you, or hides things from you—and summons them to your recall with a will of its own. You think you have a memory; but it has you!"

—John Irving *(A Prayer for Owen Meany)*

PART ONE

MONDAY

March 10, 2008

CHAPTER 1

Elm Creek, Nebraska

Anna sensed the ugly on him the instant he came in the door. It wafted from him and surrounded him like fumes from gasoline. With Travis, it always involved the senses, from the vibrations of his movements to the loudness of his voice, from the heat of his temperament to—worst of all—the stench of his addiction. The reek of the alcohol he drank and the pungent chemical smell of an even darker dependency—the one that turned him from regular mean to savage mean—made him ugly, and turned home into a house of dread. It assailed Anna's nostrils, her eyes, her ears, and her every nerve.

Travis was no more interested in the children than he was in the cat. He treated both in much the same manner, which was with minimal contact except to occasionally kick them aside with a dirty beige work boot should one happen into his path.

Anna, with the fairness shown by most seven-year-old children, would admit to two things she *did* like about Travis: the bold musky scent of his cologne, which saturated the small house after he showered, and his deep and soothing singing voice. Both were completely out of character for a man who existed on a level of frenzy similar to that of an alarm clock buzzer. Even though they were twins, Hannah wasn't quite so forgiving.

When the demons of Travis's addiction grabbed ahold of him they multiplied, and it was safer to stay clear. Anna's mother called the ever-increasing occasions when her boyfriend got high *getting ugly*. During these times, she would tell Anna and Hannah to play in the bedroom or go outside. She called this *staying out of harm's way*.

Travis had never physically harmed Anna or Hannah, but neither had he ever displayed the slightest hint of affection. He wasn't their father or stepfather, and neither of the girls desired or even considered the possibility of him being such. Physical contact did not exist between Travis and the sisters outside of him occasionally pushing them away with a long bony arm or the aforementioned boot. Anna was fine with that. She would rather he never touch them, yet she did feel that someday he might hurt them, or worse.

Thus far, Travis had only hurt their mother Elizabeth, which was primarily why Anna and Hannah did not like him and avoided him whenever possible. When he would come home, ugly and smelling bad, those were especially dreadful times. And *in* those especially dreadful times, Anna felt as if he could hurt anyone and everyone— but it was always Mom who got hurt.

After his outbursts, Travis usually took off, ranting and raving and subsequently leaving Mom with a swollen cheek, a weepy eye, or some other flavor of injury. Once Travis was gone, Mom would come into the bedroom to comfort and reassure them. *Everything is fine* Mom would lie through swollen lips. Afterwards they would sing. They always sang.

The heavy stomp of Travis's work boots across the rear deck had become the warning system, but today it sounded different. It was rushed, and frenetic. His boots hammered up the deck like thunder and the door slammed open before Anna had time to react. It barely missed her, swinging hard enough to blow the hair back from her face. Anna dropped her doll and staggered back as an intense combination of bad smells washed over her. She didn't dare look up. She retrieved her doll and ran for the safety of her bedroom.

She listened from within her bedroom as Travis stormed about the kitchen flinging open cabinet doors. She heard the sound of fluttering papers, plastic cups spilling, and containers bouncing off the countertop and onto the floor. The shattering of plates and glasses filled the house as Travis screamed incoherently. Mom ran into the kitchen and tried to settle him down, but it didn't work. It never worked. Anna wondered why her mother even tried when they all knew he was just going to hurt her. "Be quiet," Elizabeth angrily hushed Travis.

Anna heard Hannah's and her names spoken in a hushed tone,

and then Travis started saying horrible and atrocious things to her mother, threatening her and swearing at her.

"Where's the fucking money!" he yelled.

"Watch your language!" Mom said.

"Fuck you, and fuck *them*!" yelled Travis.

"It's my money! I put it where you can't get it!" Mom yelled back. "I'm sick and tired of you expecting me to support you. You keep getting worse and worse. You've hardly worked since I met you and you haven't worked in nearly a year. You haven't even *tried* to get a job! All you do is drink, get high, and steal my money! You're a goddamned drug addict!"

Travis hollered something Anna couldn't understand.

"You're a piece of shit!" Elizabeth yelled. "You're worse than shit! At least shit can be useful!"

Anna seldom heard her mother say bad words, and she had never before heard her call anyone names. She did once tell Anna and Hannah that sometimes you just needed to swear or you'd explode. Mom's anger scared Anna.

"Get out! I want you gone!"

A scuffle ensued and Anna heard the sound of numerous things skittering across the linoleum and realized that the spice rack had fallen. There was a sharp and familiar cracking sound and Mom cried out in pain. Travis had slapped Mom. It was a familiar, ugly sound, and always left her mother's face red and swollen.

Anna started crying. Even though her mother told her that staying strong helped you to stay safe, Anna couldn't help it. How could she stay strong when her Mom was being hurt?

Sitting on her bed, squeezed into the corner, Anna screamed, "Leave my mom alone!"

"Shut the fuck up!" Travis yelled back.

Anna knew he was yelling at her so she jumped up and closed the door, but not all the way. She wanted to help her mother, but she didn't know how. He was too big and frightening. A heavy concussion rattled the whole house as her mother hit the kitchen floor.

"Ow! Let go of my hair!" Mom screamed, her voice weighted with anger, but Anna recognized the fear, too.

Anna slipped silently through her bedroom doorway and

inched her way up the hall. She peeked around the corner and into the kitchen, hoping she could do something to help, yet knowing she probably couldn't.

Travis had Mom's hair wrapped around his hand and dragged her across the kitchen floor by it while she kicked and fought. It was all a tangled mess, not long, lovely, and golden like usual. He kept demanding the money, his voice raspy and loud, almost growling. It was the worst Anna had ever seen him. She knew she was supposed to get away from him when he was like this. She needed to go into her room, into her hiding place, and sing it away. Sing so loud you can't hear anything but your song, Mom had told them.

Anna tried to sing, but she was too terrified. Her sister Hannah had always been there to make the singing work. They always did it together. She'd never done it without her.

Anna's mom grabbed at a drawer handle and yanked it free from the cabinet. It crashed to the floor, scattering silverware, steak knives, and utensils, trailing behind her as Travis dragged her across the linoleum. Mom blindly patted the floor, seeking desperately for anything to protect herself. Jerking her body toward the island, she lifted a long knife from the floor. It was sharp and serrated with many teeth, but was not pointed . . . a bread knife.

She swiped at Travis's hand, but he evaded her and started yanking her back and forth violently by her hair, so hard that she slammed into the cabinets and chairs. He bent over the counter, never letting go of her hair, and pulled a large, chef's knife from a wooden block. As he did this, Mom swung *her* knife upward with renewed intent, but the rounded end hit Travis's jacket sleeve and did no harm. He slashed Mom's hand with the chef's knife and her own weapon fell to the floor. Mom covered her right hand with her left as blood seeped from her knuckles and ran down the length of her raised arms, soaking through the sleeve of her sunny yellow shirt. Seeing her mother's blood, Anna changed direction. Her fear for herself transformed into a fear of losing her mother.

Anna ran into the kitchen and screamed at Travis with every bit of her being, "Stop hurting my mom!"

All motion stopped. Travis held her gaze with dilated, savage eyes, and breathing as if he'd just run a mile at full speed. A silence descended over the house.

The wooden screen door at the back of the house slammed with a crack as Hannah came into the kitchen holding Shrek, their cat. Seeing the disarray in the kitchen and Travis standing over her bloodied mother, Hannah's eyes widened in alarm and she shrieked. Travis lunged for her, but Mom wrapped her arms around his legs, tackling him to the kitchen floor.

"*Run!*" she yelled to her daughters. "Run! Hide like I showed you!"

Mom snatched the bread knife from the floor and swung at Travis, scoring a mean slash across his cheek. Anna wanted to cheer.

"Fucking bitch!" Travis bellowed. He swept the chef's knife downward, driving it into Elizabeth's breast. It sank to the handle, making a horrible, wet noise as it went in.

Shhcck!

Frozen, Anna watched her mother's face contort with pain. Elizabeth took a whistling breath and screamed her anguish and fear, a sound like Anna had never heard before. "Ruuunnn!"

Thawed by her mother's voice and Hannah pulling at her, Anna turned and sprinted for the back door. Her mother's shrieks turned to sobs and the sound of her agony followed them . . . and the sound of the knife, too loud in her ears.

Shhcck. . . Shhcck. . . Shhcck!

Anna vaulted from the back steps and ran alongside the house, following Hannah. They passed the living room windows and Mom's car and then Hannah dove into the crawlspace under the house where Mom had said to go if things ever got *really ugly*. It was their secret place.

The hinged access door, built from wooden planks, stood slightly open with its hook and eye lock unlatched. Anna could see the bottoms of Hannah's pink and white sneakers, and her hair, so long and so impossibly white in the darkness, as she scuttled under the house on hands and knees. Wishing she had her own sneakers on, she hesitated, but then followed Hannah under the house barefoot.

She could hear Hannah whimpering in the dimness ahead of her, which made her aware that she could no longer hear her mother crying. This was a bad thing, she knew, but she also knew she had to obey her mother. She closed the wooden panel behind her, sinking them into near darkness, and crawled after Hannah, who was scrabbling over small mounds of dirt toward the barely discernible outline of the chimney at the far side of the house. Anna realized that if she could see *that* well, it was too light, which meant the door hadn't closed properly. A look over her shoulder verified that the panel was slightly open.

Overhead, something dragged across the floor, sounding like a mattress or a big bag of laundry, though they both knew what it was. Hannah stopped to look back at Anna and shook her head, scattering her tears. Mom said that they had to stay down here. Anna tried to stop crying so he wouldn't hear her, but her sobs turned into hiccups. They felt like something that was trying to escape from inside her—something she couldn't fight.

Will he notice the panel? Will he know we are here?

She heard Travis cross the length of the living room, from the far corner of the house, heading to their mother's bedroom with swift and determined footsteps. Anna was sure he was still looking for the money, and she wondered why her mother hadn't just given it to him. Furniture moved, drawers and doors slammed, and Travis bellowed in anger. A huge crash followed, glass shattered, and Anna was positive the floor would soon collapse on top of them.

Overcome by the certainty that Travis would notice the slightly opened hatch, Anna turned, shambled forward, and pulled it closed, but it popped open again when she released it. She tried holding the panel in place by the edge of the crosshatch, but her fingers just weren't strong enough and the panel kept resisting.

"Anna," Hannah hissed from the far under the house. "Come on, we have to go!"

"The door won't stay shut," said Anna. "He'll see it."

Panic blossomed within Anna when she noticed the silence, and that the crashing and shattering above them had stopped. Travis was not stomping around anymore. She listened, motionless, trying to hear something, anything that would tell her where Travis was, but all was absolutely still.

"C'mon!" Hannah repeated in an urgent hush. "Let's go!"

Anna's fingers were now hurting and shaking with the effort to hold the defiant panel in place. She grabbed beneath the panel, her hand squeezing through the gap and above the pavement on the outside. She released her top hand and flexed it against the pain.

Hannah was making furtive noises, trying to tell her something, but it interfered with the concentration she needed to hear.

Hear what?

A little tinkling sound floated to her ears. It was familiar, but she couldn't quite place the jingling sound. The jangling sound of . . .

Keys!

Anna saw a shifting of shadows beneath the panel as something moved past, and she had the sinking realization that Travis was right outside the crawlspace. The panel fought her and she prayed her fingertips didn't fail.

She heard a scraping on the other side of the access door, and then Travis's foot stomped down, trapping her fingers against the pavement. Panic seized her and she tried to pull free, but Travis pressed harder. The pain was terrible. Tears flowed as she fought her need to cry out. The pressure finally disappeared, and the relief was so enormous that Anna couldn't move. Basking in her reprieve from the pain, she unthinkingly slid her little hand from under the door, allowing it to spring open.

Travis stood just outside, towering over her and glaring at her. He had Mom's car keys dangling from a hooked finger, pinging and dinging as he pulsed under the spell of his drug-fueled frenzy. On the largest key she could see a large red thumbprint, and could see blood all over Travis, thick on his shirt, his pants, splattered on his hands and across his gaunt face. Their eyes locked. His were bugged and so dilated that they appeared completely black. Anna held her throbbing fingers to her chest and backed away.

"Where—is—the—money?" Travis whispered in an ominous staccato.

Terrified, Anna held his hypnotic gaze while still inching backwards.

"Where is the money?" he screamed.

It thawed her and she sprang backward, away from the little doorway and toward the darkness under the house. He dove through the opening, landing on his belly right in front of her.

"Where is it, you little shit? Tell me!" he growled, spittle running over his chin and blending with her mother's blood.

Anna backpedaled, trying to increase the gap between them, but he lunged again and grabbed her ankle in steely hands. A small set of arms wrapped around her from behind, trying to pull her deeper into safety, but Travis was too strong, *insanely* strong, and he yanked her, shrieking, across the dirt surface and back to the opening. Reaching out, trying to clutch onto anything, Anna grabbed for the traitorous door. She embraced it and her arm jammed beneath it, lodging between the wood and the asphalt. He yanked her free with a feral growl, and the pain was brutal, blinding, and complete. He dragged her to Mom's car across the searing, crumbled surface of the hot driveway.

Mercifully, slipping into darkness, Anna lost consciousness.

TUESDAY

March 11, 2008

CHAPTER 2

Riverside, Massachusetts

The night nurse ran her hand gently over the boy's head. The child gave a somber smile and then closed his eyes. It had been a long night and the child was tired but too anxious to sleep despite the sedative. Midnight had come and gone two hours ago, but the eleven-year-old boy's legs still pedaled and his arms still twitched.

Debbie Gillan watched him for a few moments, met the nurse's compassionate eyes, and then closed the door, leaving only a three-inch band of the subdued hallway light swathing the child's legs.

Ricky Lourdes was the boy's name. He had been rushed to Riverside Hospital earlier that evening. His frantic mother had called 911, reporting that Ricky had been playing in the living room and "just collapsed." The paramedics found Ricky lying on his back, non-responsive. He had suffered a cardiac arrest, caused by the blunt force of a fist to the chest, bestowed by his mother's boyfriend. The chest also bore a constellation of cigarette burns, also courtesy of the owner of the fist. Fortunately, they were able to revive Ricky. Unfortunately, the lowlife who had inflicted such pain on Ricky Lourdes had dodged a murder conviction.

In Debbie's six years as a caseworker for the Massachusetts Department of Children and Families, she had seen many situations. Many of them were bad—drug-addicted parents, neglect, prostitution—but the physical and sexual abuse cases were always the worst.

Debbie started down the hallway, her soft leather flats scuffing mildly along the vinyl-tiled surface. At the dimly lit nurse's station, a pretty nursing assistant with tired eyes looked up from a computer monitor and smiled. Debbie returned the gesture and a silent nod. A second nurse, thoroughly caught up in a John Irving novel, didn't appear to notice her pass. Debbie repositioned the strap of her laptop bag to a more comfortable spot on her shoulder and continued to the bank of elevators. She rode alone to the second floor and made her way through quiet hallways to the outpatient entrance. It was the only public point of egress not alarmed after 9 pm.

She paused at the doorway, her apprehension keeping her from pushing her way outside. In the parking lot, her blue Honda Accord—looking brown beneath the alien aura of sodium lighting— seemed miles away. An empty ambulance idled in the rotary with open rear doors and pulsing red and white lights, its occupants now unseen somewhere beyond the emergency room entrance. The clicking of the diesel engine was muffled, but audible through the thick glass of the doors.

"Shit," Debbie muttered.

At the far end of the rotary stood a dreadfully thin man wearing loose, faded jeans that somehow clung to his nonexistent hips. His tacky printed tee-shirt promoted his beer of choice, though Debbie doubted choice mattered much to him. He lifted a cigarette to his mouth, inhaled, and staggered, barely managing to regain a semblance of balance. He released a huge smoke cloud skyward and she followed the ascent until it dissipated into nothingness.

A skunk emerged from the shrubbery on an island between the hospital and her car, sniffing along the lawn edge, seeking grubs. The skunk didn't concern Debbie or cause her anxiety. Skunks were docile creatures that took great measures to avoid conflict and only used defensive measures in dire situations. *Humans could learn a lot from skunks,* she thought.

What did concern Debbie were the dark, ambulances, and drunkards. Tonight she had all three. It was the triad, the troika, the big trifecta, and the bitch of it was, she didn't know why the last two concerned her so much.

Fearing the dark was credible. That's when the bad shit happened, and where the monsters hid and the predators roamed. Millions of people were afraid of the dark. She supposed fearing drunken men was understandable, too. Besides being obnoxious, they could be intimidating with their emboldened, crass attitudes, and their lack of restraint and discretion. What baffled her was her fear of ambulances. Fear of hearses seemed more valid than fearing a vehicle created solely to benefit people, but there it was. It mocked her with its ticking time bomb engine and its doors a gaping maw into an overly bright interior. Her fear was unprecedented. She'd never ridden in or been hit by an ambulance, yet she dreaded even walking near one.

This was one of the drawbacks of being single . . . having no support system. No teammate who had your back when loneliness became most palpable, and concerns that were invisible during daylight loomed huge and ravenous at night. At two o'clock in the morning, everything became threatening. Shadows turned into stygian caverns, and rows of trees became primeval forests. The absurdly immortal psychopaths of so many teen *slasher* flicks suddenly didn't seem that ridiculous anymore, and a blade hacking at your heels from beneath your car didn't just seem possible, but inevitable. The mere thought of it sent a cold rush right through her.

Debbie searched through her laptop bag and found her keys. Bracing herself, she left the safety of plate glass and entered the balmy night. The cloying stink of cigarette smoke and diesel fumes accompanied by the significantly amplified rattle of the ambulance's engine assaulted her senses. As the night surrounded her, she fought the temptation to make a mad dash for her car. On weak legs, she stepped forward.

"Hey," called the inebriated man, speaking around a dangling cigarette.

He was about thirty feet from her, but near enough for her to see that he was most likely homeless or a vagrant, and thoroughly smashed. His beard was matted, greasy, and dark brown with a few strands of gray, matching the thinning chaos on his head. He was of indeterminable age, but furrows of exposure and addiction tracked his hollowed cheeks and sunken, sparsely toothed mouth, harshly aging him to anywhere from forty to sixty. Debbie expected him to ask for a cigarette, money, or maybe even a ride, so she began formulating a friendly but direct rejection in her mind.

"Hey sweet-stuff, where you goin'?" he said more purposefully. He pitched toward her, trying to add an arrogant swagger to his swaying body. He was probably five-eight, and considering his stick-thin form and his condition, Debbie found him non-threatening . . . until:

"Hey, Red!" he said.

Debbie froze. Hearing the name sent a torrent of dread through her, though she wasn't sure why. It was just a name, and she was a redhead after all. It was something that most—if not all—redheads were called eventually, and a name she'd been called before, but coming from him, and with that intonation of his, it jolted her.

"I got a redhead right here," he drawled, grabbing at his crotch. "Why don't you put your pretty freckled face right here and give 'im a little kiss."

Even from twenty-five feet away Debbie thought she could smell his breath, rancid with beer, cigarettes, and rotting teeth. His cheap cologne seeped into her nostrils and set up camp, getting stronger and so cloying that she couldn't breathe. She could suddenly taste his cologne and his putrid breath in her mouth as he tried to force his tongue between her tightened lips.

"No!" Debbie cried and stepped back, astonished that he was still twenty-five feet away. It had seemed so vivid and so authentic that it made her gag.

"How's that sweet little pussy of yours, honey?" he slurred. "Is it tight? You just as red down there, or do you shave it?" He flicked his tongue over the crook of his middle and index fingers, tottered, and gave Debbie a knowing smile. "Will it taste like cherry *Jell-O* if I lick it, or is it spicy? Will it burn my tongue? How 'bout givin' me a little taste?"

Debbie suddenly envisioned him above her, her little hands warding off his scrawny, naked chest as he thrust wildly into her, driving her into the rough surface beneath her. She backpedaled from him, revulsion enveloping her.

"Stay away from me!" she said, hating herself for the fearful display. It would only encourage him. She looked back to the outpatient entrance, desperately hoping she could signal someone for help, but the room was empty, as she expected.

"How can I resist a piece of ass like you?" he slurred and took another few steps towards her. "You and your little strawberry pie pussy. Got some nice tits on you, too . . . those real?"

"Leave me alone!" she shrieked, feeling exposed and small.

"What's wrong, didja close up shop? Get religion?" he said and took a few more steps in her direction.

The emergency entrance doors opened and two hospital employees jogged out and took in the situation.

"Did someone scream?" asked a short but solid woman with a stern voice.

"Henry, you don't be troubling people out here or we'll get the police on you," said the second employee, a tall and handsome black man with huge biceps that threatened to split the sleeves of his lab coat.

"Just talkin' with her, doctor," said the drunkard, raising his hands defensively.

"He's harmless," the big man told Debbie. "Just gets a little mouthy once he's been drinking."

"Which is *usually*," added the unyielding nurse.

The words did little to console Debbie. She wheeled and hurried for her Accord, her earlier concerns of predators in the trees and under her car now forgotten.

"Wait! Are you okay?" called the doctor. He started after her, but the nurse halted him with a word and a hand on his back.

Debbie triggered her door locks with her remote, scrambled into her car, and hastily relocked them. Clutching the steering wheel, she stared through the windshield, waiting for her heartbeat to settle. When her panic started to subside, she leaned her head back on the headrest and closed her eyes. "What the fuck was that all about?" she said into the silence.

She could not recall ever having a reaction like that before, and she'd met some unsavory characters since putting on her caseworker shoes. Some of them she felt were dangerous and some she *knew* were, but she never felt total depravity as deeply as she had tonight. Now she felt as if *she* were the dirty one.

It didn't add up. Scrawny, trashed, and ignorant equaled pathetic, and persons like Henry the vagrant had never warranted anything more than her pity and concern for their well-being, but the terror that the man instilled in her tonight was unusual and illogical. The difference tonight was that Henry wasn't just looking for a handout like most itinerants, Henry was perverse, obstinate, and aggressive, and his abuse was directed at her. Debbie had never seen him before, as far as she could remember, and she was quite sure she would have remembered him. He was a deviant and dangerous, without compassion or conscience. Of this, she was certain, though she didn't know why. Debbie suddenly pictured the drunken beast staggering into a child's room and a new level of alarm spilled over her.

Can he get inside? The children are so helpless and vulnerable. The things he could do to them!

She understood her fear was probably irrational, and the likelihood of Henry actually making his way inside was near to nil, but she couldn't drive the image from her head. She didn't want to *think* it wouldn't happen; she wanted to *know* it couldn't. She looked at Henry who stared right back, afloat in his intoxicated arrogance. The nurse and the doctor had since made their way back into the hospital and it was just him and her again.

Debbie started her car, shifted into gear, and gunned forward, pulling to a stop before the outpatient entrance. As she climbed out, Henry started stumbling in her direction, a smug, conquering smile playing over his gaunt face. Debbie wanted to dive back into her car and flee, but she knew she must stand up to him. The man posed no threat to her, she could knock him over with a wish, but in her mind, he represented a threat she could not identify. To defeat her fear she must not only face it, but stand up to it without wavering.

Debbie locked eyes with Henry over the roof of her car and spoke in as menacing a voice as she could conjure. "Take another step closer you piece of shit, I'll put a bullet right between your fucking eyes."

Debbie had no gun. She had never touched a gun in her life, nor did she plan to, but ol' Hank didn't know that. With her heart rattling like a jackhammer, Debbie glared at him, unwavering, trying to convey a bravado she didn't feel. She feigned reaching back into her car.

"Hey, don't you go all psycho-bitch on me, I'm just trying to be friendly," Henry said, backing away, his hands raised in a compliant display that still struck Debbie as condescending.

"You wouldn't know friendly if it bit you on the ass," Debbie sneered.

She sensed the nervous tic twitching under her left eye and

prayed Henry couldn't see it. She triggered her car door locks and re-entered the outpatient area. She felt as if her shaking legs would betray her and cause her to collapse at any moment, yet she was oddly invigorated. She intended to tell her fears to the admissions attendant, hoping she could assure her that Henry would not enter the hospital, but Debbie got a better idea. Pulling her iPhone from her pocket, she dialed the Riverside Police Department and waited for the dispatcher to answer.

When they picked up the line, she steadied her voice and said, "Hello, my name is Debbie Gillan. I wish to report a belligerently drunk man who is being aggressively vulgar and making inappropriate advances towards people outside the Riverside Hospital Emergency entrance. I'm afraid to leave the building."

In less than ten minutes, a cruiser pulled up. Two officers stepped out of the car and began questioning Henry. It was clear they were familiar with each other and Henry even tried to pat one on the back, but the officer pulled away. Emboldened, Debbie returned to her car, flashing Henry a self-righteous smile. Since the police had their backs to her, and reassured by the presence of her car between her and Henry, she flipped him the bird.

"You fuckin' bitch!" Henry yelled, lurching away from the officers. "You called the fuckin' cops on me? You whore!"

This was exactly what Debbie had hoped he'd do. In a matter of seconds, they cuffed Henry and stuffed him into the cruiser.

The older of the two officers turned to face Debbie. "Probably not the best idea instigating him like that, ma'am, he's already confrontational and stupid drunk . . . not that he's all that bright when he's sober." He had a hint of a brogue and a voice that could lull mosquitoes. He was shorter than his colleague was, but squat and solid like a bulldog.

"I didn't . . ."

"Ma'am, I saw your reflection in the cruiser's window. You gave him the finger . . . and a rather long finger at that."

"Yeah, I did," Debbie sheepishly admitted. "I'm sorry."

"I'm Sergeant Condon and this is Officer Maplewood. Are you the woman who called?"

Debbie nodded.

"Figured as much. Is he your husband, ma'am?"

"Dear God, no!" Debbie said, flabbergasted.

"Boyfriend?" he asked. His expression had a smug know-all edge, yet there burned a boyish gleam in his eyes.

"No!" said Debbie.

"Never know. Had to ask, ma'am. Did he attack you or hit you, or anything of that nature?"

"Only with words. I was more concerned for other people," Debbie said.

"What other people, ma'am?"

"Well, in case others came out."

"Did you prompt the attack, ma'am? Did you hit him?"

"What? No!" Debbie nearly shouted, not believing her ears.

Henry pushed his lips to the small gap in the cruiser window and hollered, "You're a twat!"

"Shut up and sit back!" Officer Maplewood barked at Henry and slapped the window with a heavy, thick-fingered hand. The glass, in turn, connected soundly with Henry's face. Henry obediently sat back looking baffled and quite pissed off.

"Would you like to file charges, bury me in more paperwork, and make my already miserable night even worse?" Sergeant Condon asked.

"No. I'd just like him gone."

"Believe me, ma'am, you're not alone. We'll give him a place to dry out, though he never stays that way for very long."

"Does he do this a lot?" Debbie asked.

"Yes, ma'am. Too often. He'll probably be back tomorrow night."

"Is he dangerous?" Debbie asked.

"Only to himself for the most part, but you'll never see me asking him to babysit. I'd advise you not to either."

"Wasn't even a consideration," agreed Debbie.

She noticed that the younger officer was suppressing a smile as he climbed into the passenger's side of the cruiser and Debbie wondered what was so funny.

"Will you be collecting him in the morning?" Sergeant Condon asked as he slid into the driver's seat.

"Collect him? You know this guy!" Debbie nearly yelled. "Why would you ask if I'm his wife? Are you kidding me?"

"Yes, ma'am, I am," said the cop. He closed his car door and with a wink and a wave, they drove away.

Debbie rested her arms on the roof of her car and watched the cruiser's taillights fade. A sudden fluttering sound startled her and she quickly climbed into the car, her limbs battling the pins and needles of fear as her imagination ran the gambit from bats to vampires. As she slammed the door, a large cardinal settled on the hood of her car, did three quick hops, and positioned itself directly in front of the driver's side of the windshield. It was vibrant red, beautiful, and somewhat majestic with its peaked crown and regal, attentive stance. Debbie couldn't remember ever seeing a cardinal after dark before. *Are they nocturnal?* she wondered, impressed by the bird's audacity. *Was it rabid? Can birds get rabies?*

"*Chirby-chirby-chirby-djou-djou!*" the bird said, looking straight at her. It cocked its head to the side as if expecting a response. The action appeared intentional and surreal, which seemed appropriate.

"Are you chirping at me?" Debbie asked. She pictured De Niro using the line in *Taxi Driver* and smiled slightly.

The bird took two hops nearer to the windshield, ruffled its feathers, and re-established eye contact with Debbie. "*Djou-djou . . . djou!*" The bird seemed to assess her for a moment and then took flight, quickly vanishing into the night.

"That was bizarre," Debbie said aloud, trying to alleviate the unease she was feeling. She started the car and shifted into gear. *At least he didn't shit on my hood like every other bird in town,* she thought wryly. Her attempt at humor did nothing to lighten her mood.

CHAPTER 3

Elm Creek, Nebraska

Anna cowered in the back seat of her mother's car, pressing herself into the corner where the seat and door met, keeping as far away from Travis as possible.

She remembered Travis dragging her from beneath the house, but little more until she came to, lying on the rear seat. She had been using her left arm to push herself into a sitting position, but collapsed when a blinding pain shot through her, robbing her both of breath and all thought. She had screamed out in agony and started sobbing, the sound of which caused Travis to shout and lash out at her. Fortunately, he had only managed to graze her forehead, but his intent and effort were clear and Anna knew his rage would only elevate if she didn't remain silent. She forced herself not to cry and moved as seldom as possible so as not to get Travis's attention, and because even the slightest movement made her arm throb excruciatingly. A deep gouge marked her arm where it had jammed beneath the crawlspace door, and the flesh around it was now an expanding black and purple bruise. When the bouncing of the car wasn't sending searing jolts through her, the bottoms of her arms burned from the patches of road rash, angry red and seeping like the time she had wiped out on her bike. She eventually managed to sit up, gingerly supporting her arm, but with little relief.

Even in the darkness of night, and tucked into the trees as they were, she recognized the moonlit dirt pathways of Sandy Channel, an embarrassingly primitive state-run campground on the south side of Elm Creek. Her mother had once said that Sandy Channel was the big park with little-to-nothing to offer. Still, when there was little money and little-to-nothing to do, Sandy Channel was a place to walk and share a picnic. They had gone there regularly.

The memory of her mother's words reawakened images of Travis stabbing her—carried back from some safe well in which she had been hiding them. Anna wanted to know that her Mom was okay and all the blood and screaming didn't really happen. She wanted to be with her mother and Hannah. Anna couldn't help herself. The longing, the pain, the fear, and the unknowing had become too much to hold inside, and it had oozed out of her in a sob.

"I want to go home," she pleaded. "I want my Mom!"

Travis, who had been sucking a lighter's flame through a little metal tube, turned sharply and looked at Anna. He had clearly forgotten about her. His eyes, barely visible in the car's moonlit interior, juddered back and forth sporadically as he tried to focus on her.

"Shut the fuck up," he choked out, spitting out his hateful words with little plumes of smoke. He released a pungent cloud at her face. Anna pressed back against the seat, hoping that he'd soon forget her again.

"You know where it is," he drawled. "You know where she keeps her money, don't you, you little shit wad?"

Terrified, Anna shook her head.

Travis pointed to one of Sandy Channel's numerous ponds. Its icy surface reflected the moonlight, leaving no question about the coldness of the water beneath.

"You see that? If you don't tell me where she put her money, I'm going to tie your arms and legs together like the little pig you are and drop you right through that ice."

Anna couldn't respond. She didn't know what to say.

"Do you think you'll drown or freeze first?" Travis cruelly mused. He pinned her with a wolfish smile, but his attention soon wavered and returned to his pipe and the shadowy world beyond the car's windshield.

If Hannah were here, she and Anna could sing and together they could go to their secret place where it was always beautiful and where the sun always shined. Instead, Anna's mind carried her to a solitary place inside of her where it was dark and cold, but where her pain and fear was muted and held in check.

They had been at Sandy Channel for quite a while. Travis would start the car periodically to generate some heat, but the car had since lost its warmth and Anna, with neither a coat nor shoes, was feeling the effects of a cold so intense it had brought her back to the present. Anna's mother kept a blanket they had used for picnics on the rear shelf of the car, and Anna had wrapped it around herself. It was thin, but it did offer some comfort in the increasing cold. She wondered why Travis wasn't starting the car any longer and thought he must have fallen asleep, comfortable in the insulated warmness of his Carhartt jacket. She waited, too afraid to move, but despite the blanket, the cold became almost unbearable. She considered her chances of getting out of the car without Travis noticing. If he was truly sleeping, her chances were pretty good.

She shifted carefully, reaching for the door handle, and her left arm slid from her lap to the car seat. The pain flared, but it seemed a little less severe than earlier. Encouraged, she took ahold of the door latch with her right hand and slowly pulled it toward her. With a mild *click*, the door popped slightly open, teasing Anna with the promise of escape. *Just a slight push and . . .*

"Go ahead," said Travis dismissively from the darkness of the front seat. "You'll freeze to death before you get to one-eighty-three."

Anna had no idea what he meant by one-eighty-three, but his indifference was promising. She pushed the door open and was assailed by a numbing arctic blast that instantly turned the car into an icebox.

"Close the door, you fucking idiot!" Travis raged.

Terrified, Anna vaulted back into the car, pulling the door closed behind her. Travis struck out at her as she dropped onto the seat, trapping her arm beneath her. The pain returned in its full magnificence and Anna tried to push herself off her injured arm, but her long hair was also pinned between her arm and the seat, hindering her from rising. She fell to the floor between the front and rear seats, her body petrified in its need for relief from the blinding agony that completely embraced her.

Too anguished to sob, Anna expressed her distress with a long, quavering plea. "Mmmmmmoooooommmmmmmm!"

"She's fucking dead, already!" Travis yelled at her. "You open that goddamned door again, I'll slice Hannah up the same way I did your momma. And I'll make you watch! You fucking hear me?"

Fighting the waves of pain rushing through her, she pulled the thin blanket from the seat and laid it over her. She remained on the floor, out of Travis's reach and hopefully his sight. He started the car again and allowed it to heat up. Anna welcomed the warmth despite the pain coursing through her and somehow managed to return to the safety of the solitary place in her mind.

CHAPTER 4

Riverside, Massachusetts

*I*t was nearly three o'clock in the morning when Debbie arrived home from the hospital. She entered the kitchen by way of the garage and punched in the alarm code on the keypad. She could hear the strains of music coming from the radio in her bedroom, giving her a small sense of familiarity and comfort. She had not changed the station since Kenny's departure, nor had the radio been powered off, except for random power outages from lightning storms or blizzards. For more than three years, WODS 103.3 FM—Boston's oldies station—was Debbie's constant companion when she was home, and the house's companion when she wasn't. Steve Miller begged empathy from a *Big ol' Jet Airliner* as Debbie set her laptop bag onto the island countertop that divided her kitchen from the small but cozy dining room. She draped her blazer over one of the stools, ignoring the keys that fell from the jacket pocket onto the floor.

The kitchen was the first and last area in the old house on which she and Kenny had splurged . . . as much as their budget had allowed. They had agreed that the kitchen was the heart of their home, so they'd given it a transplant.

Debbie wasn't particularly hungry, despite not having eaten since lunch. She knew if she didn't put something in her stomach, she'd soon be suffering a mean bout of acid reflux, which occurred whenever she neglected her nutrition. She scanned the contents of the refrigerator, wondering why she bothered. The only items lining the lonely shelves were a half-empty quart of lumpy milk, raspberry jam, Kraft parmesan cheese, a half-dozen eggs that were probably laid by Jurassic chickens, salad dressing, a half loaf of bread that could be an experiment in moss growth, and a few condiments. *Time to pull out ol' dependable.*

From the cabinet over the refrigerator she retrieved a large container of whey protein powder. Although the label proclaimed vanilla, its taste was indefinably bland and in grave need of flavor enhancement to be considered even remotely palatable. Unfortunately, she had no fruit or Ovaltine to sweeten the mix, only water and ice.

Delish! Nothing beats an ice-cold glass of liquefied dust.

She added two scoops of protein powder, a handful of ice, and a glass of water into the blender jar, covered it, and pressed the button. The room fell into darkness as the betraying *click* of a circuit breaker rang out from the basement. It was a lesson she'd refused to learn. More often than not, all was well, but if the compressor on the refrigerator happened to gasp and wheeze to life while she was using the blender or microwave, things got quiet.

"Oh, come on!" Debbie cried. "Shitty-fuck!"

She blindly felt her way along the kitchen counter, past the refrigerator, and through a doorway. Patting the dining room wall, she found the switch and flipped it, bringing two brass wall sconces to life.

When she and Kenny had remodeled the kitchen, they hadn't the funds to gut it to the studs and upgrade the horsehair wiring, though that would have been the preferred route. Replacing the cabinets and tiling the floor had strapped them, although at the time, seemed like a monumental step in the right direction. That was one of the downfalls of owning a circa 1900 home with a history of do-it-yourself homeowners. Old homes had charm, with their elaborate accents and moldings and unique fireplaces, but modern homes adhered to building codes and refrigerators now had dedicated circuits . . . *and modern refrigerators didn't cause small cities to brownout.*

The simple fix would have been to move the blender to the left side of the stove, where the outlet was on a different circuit, but the blender looked awkward there and it made the kitchen seem unbalanced.

Screw aesthetics, thought Debbie. *I want my flavorless, nutrient-filled sludge.* She moved the offending blender to the left side of the stove, intent on delaying her trek into the creepy basement until later . . . maybe even tomorrow.

Debbie plugged in the blender and pushed the *Crush* button. The blender growled to life, making light work of the ice while whipping up a colorless mush. She poured the contents into a glass and took a large swallow.

"Oh God," she gasped, cringing at the pasty concoction. She forced down two more gulps and then dumped the remaining dreck into the sink, rinsed the glass, and took a drink of water to cleanse her palate. As she rinsed the sink, a thought occurred to her. *The refrigerator has no power.*

"Sssshit," she hissed.

A peek in the freezer revealed a two-pound bag of jumbo shrimp, a pot roast, Delmonico steak, a pound of haddock, and a four-pack of Angus burgers; all foods she could and would eat if she ever remembered to thaw them.

Well, here's your big chance!

"Damn!" Debbie huffed and shut the freezer.

She walked to the basement door, opened it, and pressed the old push-button light switch. Another negative of most circa 1900 homes was that square, vacuous, and therefore dry basements, had been exclusive to the elite who could afford large granite block foundations. The average Joe had to settle with stacked fieldstones with cracks and crevices to allow in copious amounts of moisture along with a generous assortment of crawling and slithering critters. Anything with more than four legs freaked Debbie out, and her basement was a critter metropolis.

The basement was very well lit. She had insisted that Kenny replace the four incandescent bulbs with six four-foot fluorescent fixtures, but it did little to make the idea of descending the stairway less foreboding. She thought about all the leggy slithering and skittering critters that would have a well-lit view of her from their comfortable little fissures in the fieldstones and along the rafters, and nearly reneged.

Steeling herself, she descended the stairway, studying the railing for spider webs or any telltale movements. A few cobweb strands taunted her from the ceiling at the bottom of the stairway, softly swaying like antennae trying to sense her presence or lull her into obedience. Steering wide, she locked her sights on the breaker panel at the far corner of the basement and stepped onto the uneven concrete floor. She wondered why it had to be at the furthest reaches of the cellar, and why it wasn't installed somewhere smart, like near the stairway or in the kitchen.

The basement always felt damp, which was part of the reason the critters thrived. A small dehumidifier—long defunct—sat on an old workbench to her right. A long plastic tube ran from it like a catheter into a sump pit cut into the cement floor. From the pit, a black garden hose ran up to a pipe trap, which connected to a waste line hanging just below the ceiling. She wondered what manner of vermin might reside in that pit, and it gave her a severe bout of the willies.

At some point in the house's history, someone had made an unfortunate attempt at painting the fieldstone foundation white. The paint had since peeled extensively, leaving the walls water-stained and scabrous, which only added to the already ominous atmosphere.

Debbie tiptoed gingerly across the basement, stopped before the breaker panel, and scoped it out for any evidence of arachnid habitation. The panel had *Pushmatic* breakers . . . the breaker of the future—fifty years passé. She ran her hand gently over the breaker caps, feeling for and finding the slightly raised crown of the one that had tripped. She pushed it firmly and the little black "off" indicator switched to a little white "on" one. She was rewarded with the rumbling vibration of the refrigerator overhead.

A loud *whoosh* erupted from behind Debbie. She squealed, spun, and darted for the stairs, chased by the awareness that it was only the hot water heater igniting. She halted, feeling a little embarrassed even though no one was present to enjoy her humiliation or the drum solo her heart was performing.

She stepped towards the stairs again, and paused, hating how the backs of the steps were open to the darkness beneath. Anything hideous and feral that hid there could easily reach her feet . . .

"I don't want to go!" she said, her voice fearful and childlike.

It was uncomfortably hot in the basement. The floor had somehow transformed into packed earth and a smell of fuel oil and coal hung heavily in the air. To her left rumbled an old monolithic furnace. It was set on large granite blocks, with asbestos wrapped pipes sprouting from it at various angles like tentacles on a giant octopus. Brilliant red flames swirled in a vortex beyond the damper slots on the iron hatch. The more modern furnace that Kenny and his brother had installed was nowhere to be seen.

It wasn't the same basement.

A lean, red-haired boy with wide, urgent eyes stood near the stairway. He looked about thirteen years old.

"Help! Hide me!" she begged in her frightened little voice.

"Here!" said the boy, his voice alarmed and breathless. He motioned underneath the stairs. "Hide under here!"

He looked familiar, but she couldn't place him. Another boy, blond and younger, maybe eight, stood silently near the older boy. He wore jeans and a flannel shirt, both soiled and loose fitting, maybe hand-me-downs from the older boy. It looked as if he'd been playing in the coal bin.

She shook her head, not wanting to go beneath the stairs . . . not where the spiders and millipedes lived!

"Red! Where are you!" a man's voice called from somewhere outside the basement's windows, strong enough to be heard above the roar of the furnace.

"No! Please hide me, but not there! I don't want to go there!" she pleaded.

"Come on, Little Red, you have chores to do!"

"You have to hide here!" said the boy, his words hushed. "It's the only place! It's too late to hide anywhere else!"

He took her by the arm and pulled her forward, closer to the stairway. He pushed her downward, a hand on her head, the other on her back, and directed her under the stairs.

"Now stay there and be quiet, or he'll find you."

He moved away from the stairs, leaving her in the sweaty, damp, darkness.

"Get back in the bin," he directed the younger boy. "Pretend we're playing."

"What?"

"I don't know . . . anything. Coal miner. Get in there!" he said, and climbed into the little stall after the younger boy.

She watched them from where she knelt in shadows beneath the stairs. There had to be a million-trillion bugs sharing the space with her, she imagined. She was sure that she felt them moving on the floor beneath her legs, those little black pill bugs that the boys called roly polies, with their little armadillo bodies and countless millipede legs, making a home under her as they did in the moist earth beneath stones and rotting boards.

"Come on, Red! We don't have time for games," the voice called.

The man was in the house, walking the floors above them. She watched the two boys as their eyes followed the progress of the man's footsteps above them. They all started as the basement door swung open, spilling custard yellow light over the stairs.

"You down there, Red?"

After an elongated silenced, the younger boy conceded to an inner struggle and blurted out, "No, it's just us."

The older boy jabbed him with his elbow, a look of inflated contention on his face. There was another quiet moment, and then the man started down the stairs, each step creaking in protest as he descended.

Dread spilled over her when his beige work boots appeared through the opening before her. She carefully shifted closer to the old basement wall, forgetting the creeping insects and spiders. Being found was far more frightening. The two boys remained motionless, watching the man as he stepped onto the packed-dirt floor and faced them.

"What are you boys doing down here?" asked the aged man.

"Playing," said the older boy. "Playing coal miners."

"Hmmmm, quite industrious," said the man, with forced appreciation. "Now, you boys wouldn't know where Red is, would you?"

"That's not her name!" blurted the younger boy, earning another glare from the older boy.

"It's just a nickname, kiddo, nothing to get up in arms about," the man said with a disarming chuckle. His eyes studied the boys as if looking for a hidden symbol. "She's forgotten a very important appointment. I need her help and I'm running short on time. Are you sure you don't know where she might be?"

The younger boy's eyes unconsciously shifted to meet hers for a fraction of a second and then instantly returned to focus on the old man. It was hardly perceptible, but it was enough. The man's eyebrows rose as if intrigued, and the young boy's face lit as the realization of his error hit him. The man leaned forward slightly and peered under the stairway, meeting her frightened eyes.

"Well, hello, sweetheart," he said. "What in the world are you doing under there?"

"She doesn't want to go," the older boy pleaded, nearly whining.

"Nonsense! She'll have a good time just like you do." The man said, glaring at the younger boy. He reached under the stairs and took her by the wrist. "Come on, honey. You're all filthy now and that will never do. That isn't attractive at all, is it? How about if we go for an ice cream after? We can get you a new dress."

He led her to the stairs and she knew better than to resist. Once they were away from other people, he changed. He would pull off his belt and beat the defiance out of her. He always did.

"Please don't," she whimpered. "I don't like it, it hurts!" She looked at the two boys beseechingly.

They only watched, frightened and confused as the friendly old man led her upstairs and out of their view.

Debbie knelt beneath the basement stairway, sobbing and staring through the gap in the risers. She frantically crawled out and across the dusty floor, too aware of the cobwebs that crackled in her hair. She had no recollection of crawling under the staircase and knew that she would have never crawled there willingly. A cricket skittered along the base of the wall not a foot away from her. Still on her hands and knees, she backpedaled, landing on her ass in the center of the basement floor. She knew crickets were harmless, but she was still terrified of them.

She rose from the floor and wiped her hands on her pant legs. She ran her fingers through her hair, feeling the intermingling of cobwebs . . . or were they spider webs? Ken had argued that they were one and the same. More shivers wracked her body and she rushed upstairs, killing the lights and slamming the cellar door. Her nerve endings were crackling with the fear of a reoccurrence.

Who were the boys? Who was the baleful man? What was going on with her lately?

It was late. Maybe she was too exhausted. It had to be close to four in the morning and she needed to be out of bed by eight, but she needed to shower and clean the webs and dirt from herself. She figured sleep would not come easily, if at all, so she took a quick shower and popped a Tylenol PM. She brushed her teeth, closed the bedroom door securely, and then climbed into bed. Jefferson Starship assured her that *if only you believed in miracles, baby, you'd get by.* Despite her fears, Marty Balin's crooning voice soon caressed her into oblivion.

CHAPTER 5

Elm Creek, Nebraska

"Fuck," Travis said. He sounded frightened. "Jesus, what the fuck is this?"

Jarring movements from the front seat brought Anna back to the present. She had been lying on her right side, still nestled on the floor in the rear of the car. Trauma, severe fatigue, and the cold had disoriented her thinking and she had settled firmly into her fugue. It took her a few moments to remember where she was, but when she did, all the terror of the previous day came rushing back to her—the blood, her mother's cries of pain, and the sounds. *Shhcck . . . Shhcck . . . Shhcck!*

He stabbed her with the big knife! Is Mom dead, or did Travis say it just to be mean? Is Hannah okay? Mom can't really be dead, can she?

The panic built in her and she started to rise, but her mind alerted her . . . *Don't! Don't move your arm and don't let Travis know you're here!* She settled down and the front seat shook again with frantic jolts that made the whole car convulse, followed by more juddering and exaggerated movement.

"Oh fuck!" Travis cried. "Oh God! What did I do?" He sounded as if he were about to cry.

It was still dark outside, and so cold that moving her toes even the slightest bit was painful. She tried pulling the edge of the blanket down with her feet, but they were too numbed to feel anything except the icy pain when she moved them. She drew her legs up, pushing her knees partway under the seat, and tucked her feet against her bottom.

She thought Travis was coughing at first, but it intensified and then the sounds coming from the front seat were unmistakable. Travis was crying big, mournful sobs and Anna hoped he stabbed himself with the big knife, but then felt guilty for thinking like that and took it back. It was hard for her to comprehend how someone who yelled, hit, screamed, and stabbed huge knives into someone, had the capacity within themselves to cry. It was short-lived, and soon all Anna heard from Travis was heavy breathing, almost like a panting dog.

Travis started the car and Anna willed the heat to find its way to her. Once the car warmed, Travis lit a cigarette, but when the smell—kind of sweet, but a little like cat pee—made it to the back of the car, Anna knew it was pot, the stuff Mom made Travis smoke in the shed. Anna actually preferred this smell to that of cigarettes . . . but not much. The more Travis smoked, the more he mumbled to himself.

"You really screwed up this time, Ulrich," he said. "How the hell will you get out this?"

The heat of the car mixed with the sweet cloud, seeming to thicken it and make it heavier. Within half an hour, feeling slowly returned to Anna's extremities. The painful numbness in her toes had ramped up to excruciating before finally reverting to nearly normal. She dared straightening her legs, but another sense of urgency registered with a sharp jab in her lower abdomen, causing her to wet her pants a little. She seriously had to pee, which was especially troubling to her because she knew that pee was liquid and if she peed her pants and it got really cold in the car again— and she was pretty sure it would—she'd have a real problem on her hands.

"Shhhit!" Travis complained. He popped the car into gear and the familiar crunching of the tires on the dirt pathways vibrated up through the carpeting of the car's floor and against Anna's delicate cheek. It might have been comforting if not for the tremors it sent through her tender left arm and distended bladder. Mercifully, the dirt surface soon transitioned to the welcomed smoothness of Route 183. The car picked up speed, adding a lulling hum that combined with the comforting heat, and within a few minutes, Anna felt like she was floating. The pain in her arm and feet was still there, but seemed distant and gauzed over. She felt Hannah was nearby, calling her, and Anna thought things would be better if she sang . . . the same way she, Mom, and Hannah would sing when things got ugly. Things were definitely ugly, so Anna sang.

The car jerked to the shoulder, decelerating with the blatting of the rumble strip. Travis must have heard her singing. Anna knew she had messed up, but it had seemed all right at the time. Dread washed over her as the car came to a jolting stop and the dome light flared to life, bathing the car in a blinding haze. Travis's head appeared over the back of the seat, his expression changing from confusion, to alarm, and then to irritation.

"Which one are you?" he asked with slow, thick words. He'd never been able to tell them apart.

Her answer was barely audible, her voice hiding behind her fear. "Anna," she said.

"How the fuck did *you* get here?"

His eyes were squinty, not wide and crazy like yesterday, but Anna was still petrified. Her chin started quivering as she tried to speak. "You made me . . ." A tractor-trailer sped by, buffeting the car in its wake.

Travis stared at her, his top lip curling in distaste. "What the hell am I going to do with you?"

Anna held his gaze, too frightened to look away or to speak. Travis spun back around and sat in silence for a moment, then slammed the steering wheel with his open palm, startling Anna. The urgency in her bladder increased and she released another quick stream. She managed to stop it, but the pain and her desperation got too much.

"I have to go pee!" Anna blurted in agony.

"Fucking-A!" Travis bellowed.

Another truck hurtled past them. Travis turned the dome light off and pulled back onto the highway, the tires squealing and the engine roaring. Anna willed her bladder to hold, but the pressure overwhelmed her and her resistance failed. She surrendered to the sweetness of release as a warm rush of urine escaped her. Overcome by shame and dread, Anna pressed her face to the carpet and wept. Again, she retreated into the darkness within herself.

They didn't drive for long before Travis swerved off Interstate 80 so swiftly he nearly had to lock the brakes at the end of the exit ramp. Anna braced herself with her free arm, reigniting the pain.

"Hey," Travis suddenly said. Anna almost replied before he continued, "I'm in Kearney. I need a favor. Yeah, I know what time it is . . . midnight." The interior of the car flared as Travis lit a cigarette and exhaled loudly. "Three-forty-five? Fuck . . . sorry, man, but it's important. Yeah. I need you to front me a little." A short pause followed and then Travis's voice elevated. "Come on, you know I'm good for it."

Anna could hear the tinny response from Travis's phone, though the words were incomprehensible.

"What do you mean, *no go*?" Travis replied. A sense of urgency colored his words. "What do I owe you? Four hundred? I'll have six hundred for you next week . . . guaranteed, man! It's only been a month!" Travis was desperate and nearly hyperventilating. "Seriously!" he nearly whined. "The Bitch just got a tax return for more than five thousand. I promise you'll have six hundred dollars by Wednesday! I'm right in town . . . I'm going to hole up at the empty work shed on Coal Chute Road."

Anna heard a few more tinny words that elevated Travis's agitation to a new level. "Shit. Fuck, no! I ain't squatting there again. No . . . she didn't kick me out!" It was silent for a while, and then Travis went into a frenzy. "FUCK YOUUUUUU!" he roared into the silenced phone.

He floored the gas and the car lurched onto the street as he repeatedly bashed his phone against the steering wheel. The car swerved dangerously, and then corrected.

"WHERE'S THE FUCKING MONEY, YOU WHORE?" Travis bellowed at the top of his lungs.

Anna had no idea what a whore was, and didn't know if Travis was yelling at her or at nothing tangible, as usual, but the insanity in his voice was unmistakable. Anna pushed against the floor of the car, wanting to disappear into the weave of the carpet and as far away from his craziness as possible.

They barreled around a few more turns before the car slowed, left the pavement and drove onto gravel. Anna had the dreadful impression that they had returned to Sandy Channel, but the car pulled to a stop and Travis got out. He swiftly closed the door, but not before frigid air churned through the car, instantly sucking the heat away and turning Anna's sopping pants glacial. Anna heard the sound of something metallic moving outside, and then Travis was back in the car. The buffeting wind faded away as he drove forward and Anna had the sense that they were pulling inside somewhere, like when Mom drove the car into the stall at Jet Wash. Travis turned off the engine and jumped out of the car. The metal rumbling occurred again and Anna recognized it as one of the large roll-up doors, like the ones on the buildings where Mr. Janakowski kept his tractors.

Travis returned to the car, climbed back in and closed the door. He growled in frustration as he lit up and the more and more familiar smell of marijuana filled the car. He reclined the seat back until it pressed painfully against Anna's left arm. She repositioned herself and the aching ebbed.

Travis's snores soon resonated through the car and Anna found an odd—if minimal—sense of comfort in the confines created by the reclined seat. She pulled the blanket tighter to herself, and for the first time considered the probability that she may never see her mother or Hannah again. She returned to the only safe place available to her—within.

THURSDAY
March 13, 2008

CHAPTER 6

Riverside, Massachusetts

Debbie needed to be present for the discharge of Ricky Lourdes, who was looking a lot better since his mother and her beau no longer had access to him. She had set up temporary placement in Amesbury with a very nice family named Massey. Ricky was quiet during the ride and upon meeting his new hosts, as is expected in such cases, but the introductions went well despite his caution. Ken Massey, a jovial and ursine man in both stature and furriness, had actually coaxed a couple smiles and one genuine laugh out of the boy within minutes. Debbie left feeling good about the match, temporary as it might be.

Feeling uplifted but famished, she surrendered to the lure of shrimp with lobster sauce and pork fried rice, so ordered takeout from Lo King, even though it would mean an extra hour on the elliptical. At some point during the ride home, the smell of the food had lost its appeal and become cloying. By the time she pulled into the garage, she was nauseated—even with the windows rolled down.

She triggered the overhead door and climbed out of the car, pulling the bag of Chinese food after her. Keeping it at arm's length, she entered her house, switched on the kitchen light, and quickly stuffed the offensive bag into the refrigerator, where it would probably remain untouched until a formation of culture forced her to throw it away.

She closed the door and her stomach rebelled loudly at its rejection. She would have to appease it in some way other than the mere addition of lobster sauce and pork fried rice. A second look in the fridge presented her with the same nothing as the previous night . . . only a day older. She opened the bag of Chinese food and removed two fortune cookies.

She removed her coat, draped it over a chair and went into the living room. It was the largest room in the house, the hub of her existence, and home to her corner desk, couch, recliner, two haphazardly loaded bookcases, and a twenty-seven inch Panasonic television that had probably existed before she did. She couldn't recall the last time she had turned it on.

Debbie had designed the room with autumnal colors and decor, which lent it warmth even on the coldest nights. The couch was a rust-colored, microfiber catchall buried beneath dozens of case files, a half-full—or half-empty—laundry basket, and a forgotten *Market Basket* shopping bag that hopefully contained nothing perishable. She could have used the huge coffee table as her work surface, but instead piled everything on the couch. She hated when the couch was visible, yet she'd never been emotionally strong enough to get rid of it. It had belonged to her and Kenny, who had insisted they buy it because it agreed with Debbie's coloring, almost exactly matching her hair, eyebrows, eyelashes, and even complementing her pale, densely freckled flesh. When lying on the couch, she had blended into it, yet stood out.

Bare perfection, Kenny used to say.

Barren imperfection, it turned out. Damaged goods.

Prudence would suggest that if she hated the couch she should get rid of it, but it was her most intimate connection to the man she had been with since her sophomore year in high school. They had made love on that couch regularly. They had made love on it the night before he walked out. Swan song sex. A memento fuck to store in his memory as a keepsake, or maybe to simply show her how little it meant. One final fuck you and the only man she ever fully trusted was gone.

It was a slap in the face. No, that didn't even come close. For Debbie it had been a full assault; a flying kick to the solar plexus that had knocked her dreams and hopes from her with one blunt, insufferable act. She supposed there was a psychological contradiction at play here, maybe a little self-abuse or mental masochism. She refused to lie on the couch and had even denied it to Brian, her three-month, whirlwind rebound relationship that had been doomed before it even started. On the floor, in the shower, in the bedroom, even on the counter if you must, but never on the couch! That was sacred land and accursed land . . . *no man's land.* The only male to lie on the couch after that ill-fated final night with Kenny had been the cat, and now the cat was gone, too.

While she didn't like the quiet and loneliness, she had become accustomed to it. However, at nine at night, after a highly emotional day, the empty rooms became cavernous and even the cat would have made nice company. On the radio, Boston insisted it was *More Than a Feeling.* She agreed.

To Debbie, it seemed the modern mindset regarding broken relationships was *the best way to get over one man was to get under another.* That might be so, but not for her. Getting another man to fill her empty places wasn't the problem. She still looked good—so she was told—especially if you liked fair-skinned redheads, and there'd been no shortage of interested suitors. Her problem lay in getting past the pain, rejection, and the continual feeling of inadequacy. Kenny had sworn that her inability to conceive would never matter, but in the end, it had. She feared it would always be that way, being traded in for someone better . . . someone who could procreate?

Of course, there was more to the story, but Debbie would rather not dwell on *those* points. How Kenny, on his way out the door, had called her *the beautiful android* . . . physically and sexually alluring, but devoid of real passion in her programming. She had all the right moves, but mentally or emotionally disappeared when it mattered. When it was time to perform, the curtains closed and the heat turned off. Debbie had heard him loud and clear and she knew the translation: she was a barren, soulless fuck. It was a confirmation of her pre-Kenny conviction that she was worthless and undesirable. She was impaired—a misfit on an island of one.

Debbie had no desire to wade through the relationship cesspool again. She no longer wanted to be a disappointment—not to others and especially not to herself. Instead, she buried herself in children, spending nearly every waking hour at work and at school . . . cases and classes. If she kept busy, she wouldn't have time to be lonely . . . or she wouldn't notice how lonely she was. She instead focused on the pain of others, the mistreated little boys and girls.

Hey Red!

The voice reverberated like a klaxon, vibrating from the depths of her memory into her present mind, sinking a spear of anxiety into Debbie's shoulders.

No, not again!

It wasn't the taunting drawl of Henry, her intoxicated tormentor from the hospital the previous night. This was lower, syrupy, and far more threatening. It brought with it a sense of dread, turning Debbie's home into something alien and menacing. She wanted to hide, to become small enough to burrow beneath the floorboards.

But that's where the basement is, Debbie . . .

"Who's here?" she called out.

Her nerves were shot by what had transpired between the hospital and her basement, and the urge to call 911 was strong. What if they sent the same officers that had picked Henry up at the hospital? What would they think if they found nothing? The alarm was active when she got home. She remembered punching in the code . . . or had she? Now that she tried to remember, she wasn't sure.

Had they released Henry?

Christ! He doesn't even know my name, or where I live! Pull yourself together!

Debbie went to the kitchen and glanced at the alarm keypad, assuring it was set. She drew a large carving knife from a magnetic strip mounted to the cabinet near her sink. She headed through the dining room to check the bathroom, which was purely procrastination since the threatening feeling emanated from the living room. After verifying what she already knew, Debbie returned to the living room. If she could get him to talk again, she'd know where he was.

"I'm here!" Debbie said. Her voice was thin, raspy, and brittle as hoarfrost. "What do you want?"

"You know what I want, you sweet little bitch," hissed a tinny, fluctuating voice. It was a phantom, swelling and fading like a feed from a vintage newsreel, yet it sounded familiar. "You know you want it, too."

In the right corner of her living room, the doorway to her spare room waited ajar, promising only darkness within. It used to be an extra bedroom, but now served as a store-all, Debbie's warehouse for things not remembered and memories best forgotten. In numerous boxes, amid old files, unread magazines, stashed candles, and cheap souvenirs, lay the dregs of her marriage to Kenny. Boxes of pain in a room full of relics . . . *and a ghost.*

He was leaning against the doorjamb. Her desk and her Dali print were gone, replaced by a rusted Keystone beer sign, nailed to faded, red pine boards. He was eyeing her lasciviously and laughing. His grossly fat, jiggling belly protruded over the front of his jeans, which were unbuttoned and unzipped. Sour smelling, filthy, and repugnant, beads of sweat ran profusely into rivulets and fell from his corpulent jowls. He entered through the doorway and she obediently followed him inside. She had no choice. Being with him, pain was a possibility, but to resist, pain was definite.

Her spare room was no longer. They were now inside a rundown shed. Someone latched the door behind them, and a crunch of footsteps receded on the gravel outside.

It was nighttime, but light from some unknown source—maybe the moon—slanted through cracked panes in the higher reaches of the sole window. The lower section had been covered by cardboard and duct tape. Dust motes traversed the room at chaotic angles amid the reek of alcohol, cigarettes, and betrayal.

The fat man sat down upon a small cot, the springs shrieking in wild protest under his substantial girth. The thin mattress was spattered with a legacy of stains. Innumerable and grotesque, they covered the single worn pillow as well. There were no sheets.

Unsure what kind of depravity he would force upon her this time, and what level of pain she would have to endure, she started crying. Crying was bad. It would result in fierce disciplinary action, but one fear trumped the other and she could not hold back the tears. Fear of the searing, splitting pain always prevailed, and then there was the bleeding.

"Come here, Little Red," he said. Red was what they all called her. None knew her real name, and she was forbidden to tell them, or she'd get the belt across her legs and back.

She didn't move.

The fat stranger stood again and dropped his pants to his ankles, exposing his erect hideousness. He grabbed her arm and sat back down, almost falling and dragging her after him. She shook her head, her eyes pleading and awash with tears. He put a massive hand on either side of her head and directed her, and she was almost relieved that it was this he wanted, and not the thing that hurt so badly.

Her teardrops left small circles on his bunched up pants and she saw the contrast of her coppery hair on pasty white legs. She stared at the rainbow-colored winged unicorns on her sneakers and closed her mind to the sour smell of the vile stranger. She concentrated on the unicorn's noble wings and thought . . . fly away. Just fly away from here.

The floor swayed and swooped beneath Debbie and she fell to her knees, landing on the braided carpet in her living room. The fat man's pungent odor still surrounded her, and the demanding pressure of his hands still felt present on the sides of her head. The taste . . . his taste . . . she felt she would vomit. She scrambled on hands and knees to a small trash basket beside her desk, barely making it before losing everything. She gagged and retched until her tears flowed freely and she thought her abdomen would rupture.

"Oh my God, what's happening to me?" Debbie gasped.

A few remaining dry heaves rattled her body, and then she rolled to her side and pulled herself fetal, needing to shrink and to disappear. She lay unmoving and stared into the woolen weave of the rug wishing she could hide inside the braiding like a flea or a maggot, so vile and unwanted. She drifted off, thinking she would be content knowing that no one wanted her.

Her eyes refocused on the rug. How long had she been there? An hour? A day? She didn't know. She pulled herself shakily to her feet.

The doorway to the spare room still stood open and sinister, mocking her. Stepping forward to close the door, she saw the carving knife lying on the floor, well inside the room. She couldn't recall leaving the living room.

Had she been inside the room? Had she thrown the knife inside?

She yanked the door shut, hoping to close the images inside.

She dealt with cases like this daily—neglect, child abuse, sexual abuse, and incest—and as horrendous and utterly heartbreaking as they were, she'd always kept an emotional barrier between herself and her cases. It was a requirement for her career and a means of emotional survival. Like a high wire act balancing between compassion and professionalism . . . lean too far to either side and you might fall. Debbie had trained herself early in her career to keep a buffer between her and her children. It might be a thinner buffer than most caseworkers had, but it had always been thick enough to protect her.

Were these visions or some kind of premonitions triggered by her encounter with Henry? She had experienced a brief vision there. That's when they'd started.

Debbie had been first person in all three visions. She was the main act, not an observer, and she had seen her own coppery hair on the fat man's pasty white legs. All three men had called her *Red*.

Were they memories? If so, what triggered them?

Debbie shuddered, lifted the garbage basket, and carried it into the bathroom. She dumped her vomit into the toilet, along with a balled up sheet of paper and a handful of Post-it notes. She flushed, relieved that it didn't clog, rinsed the basket in the shower, dried it with paper towels, and returned it to its place beside her desk.

Returning to the bathroom she hurriedly undressed, shoved her clothes directly into the washing machine, turned on the shower, and climbed in. She scrubbed for nearly half an hour. She tried to make sense of whatever it was she had witnessed in her basement and then her spare room, and tried to wash the memory of it away.

She toweled off, pulled her robe on and tied it tightly. She forced herself to look in the mirror.

"Houston, we have a problem. Mayday! Mayday!" she said to the haunted woman before her and laughed. It was a frightening sound.

Was she losing it? Was everything an illusion, or a delusion? There was so much in her life recently that seemed surreal.

Hey—little Red!

"Fucking shut up!" Debbie screamed at the room . . . at her

mind . . . and at wherever the goddamned voice was coming from.

"I need help," Debbie said. The confession, her first, spilled from her lips like a prayer. "Lost and helpless" was a clear indication that her life was moving out of control. A self-proclaimed control freak, Debbie was not accustomed to being on the other side of help.

FRIDAY
March 14, 2008

CHAPTER 7

Kearney, Nebraska

*T*ravis was getting more and more agitated, pacing back and forth on the far side of Mom's car like a caged lion. "Come on, Marcus!" he fumed. "Just a gram! Today's Friday, right? Listen. I'll have it to you by Sunday night at the latest. I promise!"

Anna was sitting on a large pile of empty burlap bags, upon which the words *NORCO poultry feed, Norfolk, Nebraska* were printed in red and blue ink. She had chosen a corner of the building as far away from the unstable man as possible, wrapped herself in the blanket to protect her from the abrasive bags, and then piled a number of them over her legs and abdomen. They didn't look dirty, just dusty—and they smelled old.

The pain in her arm had become tolerable as long as she moved carefully and didn't jar it, but it remained a dogged reminder of her situation. She was unsure how long they had been inside the metal building—Travis had called it a pole building on the phone— but she felt it must have been a couple of days. She knew it was daytime by the long blades of sunlight that cut across the floor and walls of the building from the gaps around the big door, and that it was noticeably warmer—not warm, but warmer. When that small element of comfort reached them on their first morning, both Travis and Anna had slept for hours . . . until the alarming rumble of a Union Pacific coal hauler roused them. Trains rumbled by her home in Elm Creek numerous times daily, but never had it been so loud. The tracks were clearly right outside the building.

Anna's stomach gurgled with what almost seemed a howl. She had eaten two pieces of cold pizza and some chips, and drunk half a bottle of beer the night before. She had taken them from the front seat while Travis was sleeping, and brought them to her spot at the burlap bags so he wouldn't hear her or catch her eating his food. She thought the beer tasted gross and she knew she shouldn't be drinking it, but she couldn't help it, the pizza and chips had made her thirsty. She had hidden the half-full bottle behind an old wooden nail keg, but it was unnecessary. If Travis noticed the missing food or beer, there was no indication.

Travis met Anna's gaze and quickly looked away. He was sweating and his eyes were desperate and scared. He slapped the roof of the car and ran a hand through his mussed hair. "Marcus!" he begged. "We've been doing business for a long time. I've never screwed you!" He dropped his head onto the car, and then raised it, newly alert.

"What?" he said. "Looking for me? Who? Murdered who?" Even to Anna's ears, Travis's words sounded forced and fake.

Murder.

The word sounded foreign to her. It seemed like something that could not be associated to her, but she couldn't escape the thought that Mom must really be dead. She burrowed deeper into her burlap nest, pulled one over her head, and watched Travis through the narrow gap. The voice on the phone said something and Travis pulled it from his ear and stared at it dispassionately. Looking dazed and defeated, he put the phone in his pocket and sat down on an old chrome kitchen chair. He remained seated, staring at the ground with lifeless eyes—for how long, Anna couldn't be sure. It might have been fifteen minutes or it might have been two hours, but the light around the overhead door had faded by the time Travis vaulted upright and went into a frenzied rage. From the gap in her burlap hideout, Anna watched his meltdown. He grabbed the chair and hurled it the length of the structure, then followed it with just about anything he could lift, from bottles and hubcaps, to lengths of fence rail. He finished his rant by repeatedly kicking the door to her mother's car, leaving a deep dent in the lower panel and causing the glass to fall down off its track, and land inside of the door. Travis stood in one spot, short of breath and scanning the room . . . and then his eyes locked onto where she lay. Dread snared Anna in its clutches, driving a frozen trail from the back of her head to her ankles and numbing her extremities.

Don't move a bit! she warned herself, but Travis raced over, ripped the bags from atop her, and flung them to the floor. He squatted beside her, grabbed a fistful of her shirt and pulled her nose-to-nose with him. Tears flowed freely from Anna's terrified eyes and her body shook so badly she felt on the verge of convulsions. The unexpected urge to pee was nearly uncontrollable.

"I have to go somewhere for a while," he said to her through clenched teeth. "You stay here. If anyone comes while I'm gone . . . you fucking hide."

His breath was vile and Anna could see some yellow ooze coming from the gash on his cheek where Mom cut him with the knife. She fought to hold back her already rising gorge.

"You don't listen to me I'll stick a knife in Hannah. I'll make you watch and then tell the cops you killed your mother and sister. I'll tell them you were jealous because she liked Hannah better. You hear me?"

Anna nodded, spilling tears onto Travis's hand. He had made this threat the previous day, before he crossed the tracks to get food and beer. Anna believed he would kill Hannah if she didn't listen, but the threat gave her some hope that Hannah was okay. He couldn't kill her if she was already dead, could he? Travis dropped her back onto the bags, and turned. She watched him leave through the passage door directly across from the overhead door. The wind slammed the door soundly behind him.

Freed from the burlap bags, Anna was aware of how brutally cold it had become since sunset. She sat for a few moments pondering which necessity to address first, nature's call or warmth. She didn't want what happened in the car to happen again; it was cold and it had taken a long time to dry.

Anna stepped to the floor and the chill of the concrete entered her feet and rushed throughout her body. She ran to the opposite corner of the shed, hurriedly dropped her pants and squatted where she had the day before. She had covered it with a burlap remnant, equally self-conscious and concerned that Travis would discipline her for it. She didn't bother moving the remnant because she only had to pee today. She didn't bother wiping, either. She may get a rash, but it was preferable to using a burlap remnant as she had yesterday. Her girl parts burned for hours. Anna clumsily worked her pants up with her right arm and returned to the pile of bags.

Her feet were aching from the cold, which was becoming as frigid as the first night. Anna wondered how she could best stay warm. The burlap bags helped, but she felt Travis would start the car for heat like on the other nights. *It would still be cold, but not as cold*, she thought, but then she realized she could do both. She could make a nest in the back of the car with the burlap bags!

Her left arm rebelling but tolerable, she grabbed an armful of bags, returned to the car and formed a mattress on the rear floor. Folding Mom's blanket in two, she created an envelope to slide into for insulation from the bags' abrasiveness, and then retrieved another armful of bags. As she lifted, something metallic fell to the floor.

Anna picked up the screwdriver by its wood and metal handle, surprised by its size and weight. It was nearly as long as her arm. The metal was darkened by age and use, but it wasn't rusty. She wondered if she could use it against Travis. Maybe she could bonk him on the head with it when he was sleeping, or jam it into his chest the way he stuck the knife into Mom. *Shhcck . . . Shhcck . . . Shhcck!*

Anna knew she probably wasn't strong enough to do that, and bonking him on the head might just wake him up and make him really mad, but what if she stuck it in his eye? *Or both eyes! He can't catch me if he can't see where I am.*

Anna feigned a stabbing motion with the screwdriver, and pictured it sinking into Travis's closed eyelid and cringed. She doubted her capability to stab anybody with anything, but then she recalled her mother lying on the couch, blood covered and shrieking, "RUN!" Maybe she could.

The wind rattled the overhead door, making Anna nervous. She didn't want Travis catching her with the screwdriver, so she slid it under the car's seat, out of view but easily accessible from where she'd be lying. She spread another thick layer of burlap bags atop the folded blanket for added warmth, and in an act of defiance, took the half-bottle of beer from behind the nail keg and despite the taste, finished it. She threw it against the wall, but it didn't explode like Travis's thrown bottles had, though it did shatter when it hit the floor. That was good enough for her. She returned to the car, and, conscious of her left arm, clumsily slid herself into the folded blanket, between the two thick layers of burlap. She gathered her hair and tucked it into the blanket with her. Normally it was waist-length, and so platinum blonde that it practically glowed. Now it was dirty, dull, and tangled beyond hope.

She tried not to think about Travis, and if she were lucky, Travis wouldn't think about her. Instead, she thought about Hannah and her flying above giant fields of flowers under warm and sunny skies.

SATURDAY
March 15, 2008

CHAPTER 8

The slamming door sounded like an explosion. Anna quickly sat up, reached out reflexively, and then retracted her left arm upon feeling the bite of pain. A shape darted past the car in the darkness, and then the overhead door began rising noisily. The Arctic wind that had howled so plaintively for entry—finally unrestrained—stopped its woeful song. It entered the building and filled the car with swirling dust and a cutting cold. Anna dropped back to the floor of the car and tried to pull the bags back on top of her.

The car's front door opened, waking the dome light, and Travis dropped heavily into the driver's seat. "Fuck . . . fuck . . . fuck . . . fuck . . . fuck!" he cried, a mindlessly chanted litany soaked in blind fear.

The engine roared to life and the car raced backwards, the squeal of the tires ringing on the metal walls as they hurtled out of the building. Not stopping to close the door, Travis slammed it into gear and floored the car off the property, barely maintaining control as he hit the pavement. Wind rushed into the careering car through the opened window with hurricane ferocity, negating any warmth from the burlap bags or the blanket. Anna hunkered against the back of the driver's seat, willing Travis to close the window and turn on the heat. He recklessly negotiated the streets of Kearney, lurching around corners and bucking over railroad tracks. He came to a jarring stop and Anna heard a heavy clack from under the seat. She reached in the narrow gap for the screwdriver, but couldn't feel it.

"What the fuck!" Travis roared, getting out of the car.

Did he find the screwdriver? Anna wondered.

Rounding the car, Travis opened the passenger's side door.

Unable to close the window, he slammed the door shut and kicked it again.

"Fucking piece of shit!" he muttered as he got back into the car.

They started moving again . . . as did the wind, pushing between the burlap layers and cutting into Anna like blades made of ice. Travis merged onto the highway and the wind increased as he accelerated. No matter how she positioned herself, the blankets, or the bags, the wind found her. Her feet, her arms, and her face were on fire from the cold. There was no relief.

"I want to go home!" she cried, unheard in the battering wind.

The pain was blinding by the time Travis pulled the car off the pavement. Anna knew by the distance they had driven since they left the pavement that they were back at Sandy Channel, and the horror she felt was complete.

Were they going to stay all night, again? How long will she have to stay in this cold?

"Jesus!" Travis said from the front seat, rubbing his hands together.

The dome light flared, dipping Anna into transitory blindness. He had left the car running and Anna could feel momentary licks of heat teasing her where she lay, but it was too little to offer a respite. She tried rubbing her feet on the burlap to generate warmth, but the material was too rough for her cold distressed flesh. She lay her head back down and through the gap under the seat she saw the giant screwdriver laying on the floor near Travis's feet . . . well out of her reach.

She heard a lighter flicked and Anna soon smelled smoke, but it wasn't the cat pissy smell of pot, or the unpleasant reek of cigarette. This was worse. It smelled like matches, rotten eggs, and Mom's fingernail polish. Anna knew, somehow, that this was what made Travis a lot uglier than usual. *Hideous ugly* . . . and that terrified her more than the cold, because when Travis was *hideous ugly*, he was dangerous.

She wanted her mother desperately. She wanted to be out of the cold and home with Mom and Hannah. Anna had to tell Travis to take her home. She had to demand it! She lifted herself onto the rear seat, closing her eyes to the pain in her hands, her arm, her feet . . . everywhere, and settled herself into the corner farthest away from Travis, who was holding a lighter to the end of a weird glass tube that he held pinched between his lips. The stink of the drug was worse here than on the floor.

Anna shivered so badly her whole body quaked, but she garnered up her nerve and yelled at Travis, "Bring me home!"

Travis's eyes shifted to the rearview mirror. He was expressionless, but Anna could feel the loathing behind his gaze. "Where's the money?" he said. His voice was as dead and impassive as his eyes and the resounding threat in them, but Anna stared defiantly back at him.

Travis slammed the dashboard with his fist and turned on Anna. He was much scarier face to face. His eyes tiny black beads that vibrated as he tried to focus on her. Drool ran from the corner of his mouth to mingle with the grubby stubble beneath.

"Where's the fucking money!" Travis shrieked and reached for her. Anna raised her right arm in defense and inadvertently knocked the pipe from his hand, sending it spiraling over the front seat, to bounce off the dashboard and fall to the floor. Travis spun to retrieve the pipe and Anna took that moment to slide quickly back to the floor.

Too concerned about the welfare of his pipe, or seduced by the high it promised, Travis ignored Anna and lit up, again filling the car with its acrid haze, despite the open window.

Anna was trying to return to the place inside her where pain, cold, and reality receded, when she heard the low rumble of an approaching engine.

Someone's coming!

Anna tried to lift herself from the floor, but the car bounded forward and sped off in the opposite direction of the approaching vehicle. They bounced back onto the pavement of the highway, the cold wind invading the car, and Anna was once more feeling the pressure in her bladder. The reality of it all happening again was too much. Anna stood up and pushed against the back of Travis's head with all her might.

"I want my mother!" she yelled and pushed again. "I want Hannah!"

The car pitched violently and pulled to the side of the road.

"I want to go home!"

Travis jumped out of the car and yanked open the rear door. Anna pulled away from him, but he leaned in, grabbed a handful of her hair, and yanked her brutally from the car. Still clutching the blanket, Anna fell to the pavement, landing hard on her knees.

"You want to go home?" Still seizing her hair, he tugged her to her feet. "Then GO fucking home, you bitch! Go!" Travis bellowed and kicked Anna brutally in the bottom. The toe of his work boot slammed directly into her coccyx, bringing Anna back to her knees. Shrieking at the pain, Anna tried to crawl away from him, stumbling on the blanket she still held.

"Go! Your home's right across that field!" Travis raged. "Your mother's there waiting for you!"

Right across that field? Was it true? Anna got to her feet, no longer noticing the cold—only the pain. She recognized where they were—near the overpass where the highways crisscrossed—and her house was right across Mr. Benton's field! She could even see the lights from the houses on their street.

Travis slammed her on the back. The pain was so intense and coming from so many directions that Anna's only coherent thoughts were to move *away* from him and towards home. When Anna's bare feet hit the ice-glazed dirt of Benton's farm, she wasn't even aware of Travis driving away.

PART TWO

WEDNESDAY

June 23, 2010

CHAPTER 9

Riverside, Massachusetts

The thirty or so minutes of granular grayness that connected nighttime to dawn were often ominous and sometimes disastrous. Obscured by shadows, objects hid and created false imagery, often forcing bad judgment. Back at the shop, many tales made the rounds about drivers backing their trucks into buildings, taking out plate glass windows, snagging power lines, and even occasionally running down a jogger or pedestrian. These happenings frequently occurred during the blurred moments when night transformed into dawn and darkness gave way to light. Despite all of that, Isaac Rawls found the cold grayness of pre-dawn mystical, sadly beautiful, and even a little spooky.

Recalling the cautionary tales from his workplace, he carefully maneuvered his truck into the dreary alleyway between Madam Curry's Indian restaurant and Riverside Furniture. Taking it slowly, he cleared his outer lift arms by mere inches. It wouldn't be the first time he'd nipped the corner of the furniture shop with his garbage truck, and judging by the building's rounded and chipped red bricks, it had been problematic to many a truck driver before him. He squared his lift arms to the dumpster, engaged the brake, and shook his head in bemused wonder at the garbage bags piled around and in front of it. They made Isaac think of bodies at wartime, unfortunate soldiers around a foxhole.

Isaac actually liked his job. Contrary to what seemed the common assessment, being a waste management worker—or trash jockey, as Isaac bluntly labeled himself—was not a terrible gig. The pay was decent enough, especially for someone lacking a degree. It put plenty of food on the table and played a large role in pushing his two kids through college, an opportunity he'd never had.

Behind the wheel, Isaac dealt with few people. He wasn't anti-social—quite the opposite—but people tended to avoid anyone who wore the uniform it seemed, as if proximity to it might lower their social distinction . . . degradation by association. He felt eyes on him when he went into stores or restaurants, and believed that many classified him as unrefined, or as a subordinate. At those times, he would remind himself that it was the stereotype they shunned, not the person. Isaac appreciated the shelter of the truck's cabin when in uniform. The only inconsiderate types he had to tolerate were the occasional impatient driver with a stick up his ass, vagrants (furred or fleshed), and those who were too lazy or entitled to lift the dumpster cover and threw their garbage on the ground. Sure, dumpsters were dirty and gross, but that's why God invented soap, right? Many jockeys just lifted and dropped the dumpster, leaving the bags and boxes lying around for the patrons to eventually clear, or for scavengers to shred and toss about. Isaac never left a mess—he figured doing it would make him just as bad as those who littered— and he didn't mind picking the messes up if they weren't too bad.

Isaac climbed out of the truck, his knees and hips snapping in protest like old, dry twigs. His jumping-from-the-truck days were far behind him now. Slipping on his work gloves, he pulled a baseball bat from behind the driver's seat. The Louisville Slugger was an asset of his job and a necessity. People disposed of countless treasures daily, a veritable gold mine that he had quarried well over the years. He carried the bat because critters—both the two-legged and four-legged varieties—were often a concern in his business. He frequently came across dogs, cats, rats, and skunks, digging and poking around dumpsters. They typically spooked as soon as the truck made its appearance, but there were the more stubborn ones, like raccoons, opossums, and humans, that would stick around and challenge you. Willingly contending with them was foolish, especially those with babies or rabies.

Employing the bat, Isaac nudged the left side slider open, gave the dumpster a good whack, and readied himself. No cats or rats jumped out, which was reassuring. He jabbed the bat between the rear of the dumpster and the wall of the Indian restaurant and discovered something wedged in there. From his side of the bat, it felt too soft to be metal, wood, or stone. Animals usually escape out the opposite side, or came forward to challenge you. What concerned Isaac was that nothing happened. Whatever was behind there was a mystery. It could be anything from a bag of clothing, a vagabond too drunk to acknowledge him, or the thing all truck drivers dreaded—a lifeless body.

What kind of body? That was the question.

Dead animals weren't uncommon, the majority of them were pets discarded by owners who lived nowhere near the dumpster and didn't want to pony up the cost of proper disposal. Worst of all were dead humans, deposited there by foul play, misfortune, or just sheer stupidity. Fortunately, Isaac had never come across one of those, though some of his coworkers had. He hoped that that wouldn't change today.

Isaac retrieved a flashlight from the truck and returned. He aimed the light beam behind the dumpster and what he saw sent a bolt of dread down his spine clear to his heels.

A little girl!

"Oh, my God, please be alive," Isaac said, but the child did not respond or even acknowledge his presence. "Oh crap, this ain't good."

The girl was hunkered down with her curved back to him. She should have moved when he poked her with the bat, but instead she stayed motionless.

Even through the dirt, her bedraggled hair was a long and knotted chaos that was so strikingly blonde that Isaac thought she might be albino. He wondered if maybe she had died in that position. If she was breathing, it was impossible to tell from her thin, bowed back.

Isaac moved to the other side of the dumpster, bent beside it, and aimed the light beam towards her. She was shoeless, with filthy hands and feet. In her left hand, she clutched a half-eaten candy bar. She wore only a heavily stained, oversized white tee-shirt with a truncated view of *Elmo* peeking over her shirt-draped knees. It wasn't exactly cold out, but it was cool for a June morning, and it had rained for the majority of the night.

She had either green or hazel eyes that stared vacantly ahead as if she were trying to gaze at some distant point beyond the restaurant's wall. He refocused the light beam more directly to her eyes. A shiver and a profound feeling of sadness ran through him. He had often heard of haunted eyes, but had never really understood the expression until now. There was no mistaking them.

"Hi? Can you hear me?" Isaac asked, still getting no response.

What had happened to this child? Any scenario he imagined was not a good one, and a deep anger blossomed within him at whoever had caused this.

Isaac moved the light slightly and saw that her irises had dilated. She's alive!

He wedged his shoulder between the dumpster and the wall and pushed with all his strength, widening the gap. As the child tumbled forward, he reached down and stopped her fall. Amazed and distressed by how light she was, he lifted her. She did not resist, but allowed Isaac to wrap her in his arms and settle her head on his shoulder as he had experienced with his own children so many years before.

"Hang on, honey, we're going to get you some help," Isaac promised.

As he pulled his cell phone out and called 911, he tried to recall the first aid classes he had taken when his children were young. The girl was in shock, which was clear by her stare and shallow breathing. Isaac finished the call and put away his phone.

Moving his face closer to hers, he felt the chill in her skin. Isaac opened his jacket, lifted the child, and wrapped her in it, pressing her snug against his chest, hoping to lend his warmth. It felt as if he were holding a bag of ice.

Holding her firmly, Isaac climbed into the heated cab on the passenger side of his truck and waited for the police. As the child warmed, her body began trembling. He held her even tighter, not concerned that her filthy hair pressed against his face. Her hair, though soiled and smelling of old dirt, also had a vague underlying fragrant scent that was sweet . . . floral.

Whose child is this?

Isaac invoked an endless string of circumstances. Had someone imprisoned her and she escaped? Did someone leave her for dead near the dumpster? Was she the child of an addict who was lying dead somewhere? He thought of his daughter, Diana, who was now thirty-two. What if this had been her? How could people let this happen to their children . . . to anyone's children?

When the Riverside police and ambulance services arrived a few minutes later, Isaac was in tears, distraught by the condition of the child and the depravity of those responsible. He held the dirty, ashen-skinned child protectively, reluctant to release her to the EMTs until they covered her with the warm blanket he'd demanded. He watched them secure her onto a gurney, the straps looking so huge and obscene across her tiny form, he feared they would hurt her.

"Be careful," he said. An EMT turned a considerate eye to him and Isaac could see that the girl was in good hands for now. They lifted her into the ambulance, and when the doors swung shut, Isaac had an almost overpowering urge to follow them and make sure she was safe.

Sitting in a cruiser, Isaac recounted the events of the morning with the police officer. They had little information to offer each other about the girl, there were no recent Amber Alerts, and a quick look in the database had turned up nothing. By the time they were done, Isaac was two hours behind on his rounds, but he couldn't find it in himself to care. All he could think about was the tragic little hazel-eyed girl.

THURSDAY
June 24, 2010

CHAPTER 10

Debbie Gillan had been immediately intrigued by the case of the extraordinary little girl, and was pleased when her boss, Marjorie Faulkner, appointed the case to her. Having a tendency to undermine herself, Debbie wondered if the decision rested more on the child's admission to Riverside Hospital than on her particular merits, since the hospital was convenient to her home. Debbie avoided most hospitals whenever possible, but especially Riverside since the incident with Henry the vagrant during the Ricky Lourdes case two years before. She blamed that evening for triggering the recurring visions she'd been enduring since.

She used the parking lot nearest the front entrance, well away from the emergency room, and stopped in the gift shop to purchase a tin of Altoids and a small stuffed kitten she felt would appeal to a young girl.

Waif, Debbie thought when she first saw the child.

She looked six or seven years old, and so tragically pale and petite sitting on the hospital bed she might have been a ghost. Her snow-blonde hair was pin straight, except that it curled ever so slightly inward at the ends, about five inches below her shoulder blades. The unevenness of her bangs gave evidence that someone, probably a hospital attendant, had recently cut her hair without much concern for style, just convenience and cleanliness. It would be awkward and maybe unflattering on most children, but it was endearing, and only complemented her sweet pixyish face, which was cute and perfectly round. Her hazel doe-eyes stared without focus at some anonymous spot on the floor ten feet in front of her. She remained absolutely silent and, according to the intern's report, had not voiced a single word since the sanitation worker discovered her, filthy and nearly naked, behind a dumpster of all places.

Her expression was vacant, as it had been since the ambulance delivered her to the North Shore Riverside Hospital several hours earlier. She was immediately admitted, evaluated, bathed, and treated. Beneath all the dirt and an insane tangle of hair, the staff had discovered an adorable little girl. Despite her appearance, she was in much better physical shape than expected, save for dehydration and some minor cuts on her hands. Her feet were the exception, with multiple fissures in the tender skin from exposure, and one deep, dirt-caked gash on her left heel that had earned her five stitches and a tetanus shot. She would be wearing bandage slippers for a week or more, the doctors said, but otherwise, she had healthy teeth, lungs, musculature, and although X-rays revealed she had once fractured her right forearm, it had been properly set and had healed well. Fortunately, there was no physical evidence of sexual abuse.

Still, with all of the distressing cases she had seen, Debbie had never encountered such a heartbreaking little child. Although she tried her best to be unbiased, she was human, and some of the children—whether because of their appearance, their situation, or a combination of both—hit the heart harder, as did this little girl. She had an ethereal quality that was compelling. Her startling, milk-white hair and her nearly as pale skin gave the impression she was crystalline, delicate and untouchable as a snowflake, yet still a child. Her button nose, spray of freckles, and full lower lip alone could melt the hardest of hearts.

This was where caseworkers had to be careful. Emotional attachment for a compassionate person in the business was inevitable, but it needed to be closely governed.

Police were checking with the National Center for Missing and Exploited Children, Amber Alerts, and missing person web sites, for the identity of this little stray soul. Meanwhile, the doctors who evaluated her had advised DCF that the child needed to stay in the hospital for monitoring, at least until she regained her health and became responsive.

The ward nurses on the morning shift reported that the little girl had woken up responsive to a marginal degree. She had eaten a startlingly healthy breakfast of sausage, eggs, pancakes, milk, orange juice, and a banana, and then decided to remove her own saline drip when no one was present so she could use the bathroom, which she also did on her own. She had then positioned herself on her hospital bed and stared out the window. It was encouraging progress, though she still hadn't uttered a word.

It was nearly two in the afternoon when Debbie arrived at the hospital despite anxiously rushing through her morning work pile and skipping lunch. The little girl had long since reverted back to the dissociated state of the night before. Debbie tried speaking to her, but to no avail. She gently patted her head, rubbed her back, and even—though not recommended—softly touched her eyelid, hoping to get a response, but the child didn't even flutter.

Pulling a chair beside the bed, Debbie knelt on it, put her elbows on the mattress, her chin on her fists, and stared at the little girl, smiling and hoping to gain her confidence.

Nothing.

She doggedly asked questions, gently trying to evoke any kind of reaction. What's your name? Where do you live? Where are your mom and dad? Do you have any sisters or brothers?

"Well, you won round one," Debbie told her, lightly touching the tip of the child's nose. "But I don't quit." She reached out and rubbed the girl's delicate arm, which was warm and coated with a soft, barely visible down. Lifting the child's arm, she compared it with her own.

"I bet I'd be just as pale as you if I got rid of my freckles," Debbie said. "If only. But that won't be happening."

There was scarcely a patch on Debbie's body without freckles. It was in her DNA and there was no sense in fighting it, though she had spent a better part of her youth hating it. She was as Scottish as haggis and the Highlands. By the time Debbie graduated college, she had learned to accept her freckles and her blazing red hair as part of who she was . . . for the most part.

As it turned out, there was an abundance of people very attracted to freckles, pale skin, and copper-red hair, and Debbie's hair was the first thing most people noticed about her. She thought the same must be true of this girl whose hair made her think of Edgar and Johnny Winter, who were probably as well known for their flowing white hair as their musicianship. While Debbie had never thought of the Winter brothers as particularly attractive, this child was stunning. Even her eyes were fascinating, her irises a concoction of green, gold, and blue flecks, sprinkled over a light brown field; unjustly, yet best categorized as hazel.

Which ethnicities support platinum-blonde hair and hazel eyes?

The thought gave Debbie an idea. Using her iPhone, Debbie opened a web-based translation engine and started asking the child her name in what she thought were the most likely languages: Danish, Swedish, German, Dutch, Russian, and as a last resort, French, Polish, Spanish, and then Greek, before finally giving up . . . at least for the moment.

A phlebotomist entered the room and plunged a needle into a stick-thin outstretched arm . . . not even a reflexive flinch. Debbie started to appreciate just how dire the situation might be. Without outside help or information, getting through to this little girl might prove impossible.

CHAPTER 11

*E*ssie Hiller was a high-spirited dynamo with a fervently positive personality, and exuded more energy than seemed natural for her short, compact structure. She was four-feet-and-eleven-inches of solidly built African-American, piston-legged energy, and normally moved like a super-ball shot from a particle accelerator. She wore a short, black-going-gray hairstyle that fit her personality perfectly. Cut for practicality and ease, all she did was brush it back after showering, whimsically perching it high over her forehead until it resembled a feminine pompadour.

A highly regarded child psychiatrist with extensive experience in treating abused and orphaned children, she was a natural choice for counseling this particular child. Essie desperately wanted—yet dreaded—the case. It was very high profile with little to work with at this point, just a sweet nameless child with no known history. The success rate for cases like this was on the lower end of the curve, which was not where you wanted to be if you were under scrutiny.

Essie's heart instantly went out to the child upon reading her files. In consideration of the circumstances, the little girl had quickly become a ward of the state of Massachusetts, with the Riverside Court assuming responsibility *in loco parentis* until they solved this little mystery.

It was just after three in the afternoon when Essie, sensitive to the young girl's condition, quietly entered room 203, the child's second day at North Shore Riverside Hospital. She recognized Debbie Gillan, who was sitting in a chair on the far side of the bed, gently rubbing the little girl's bandaged foot. Debbie had worked on a few cases with her and Essie liked her a lot. She had a gentle demeanor that blew Essie's assessment of natural redheads being irrefutable feral bitches right out of the water. Debbie was what a caseworker should be: driven, compassionate, forceful when necessary, and focused foremost on the welfare of the child. Essie made a mental note to revise her opinion to *most* natural redheads.

Essie studied the child for a moment. She looked so tiny and forlorn seated on the infinite surface of the bed, staring absently out the window. Her hand lay open at her side, not fisted, which was a positive sign. Whatever the child was experiencing in her present state, she was at ease, not angry or conflicted.

The news had been stirring up quite a fanfare in the days since Isaac Rawls's discovery. A photograph of the child in a hospital Johnny, looking precious and so very vulnerable, had received front-page coverage across the nation. The same photo, coupled with her brief, sad story, had collectively garnered over thirteen million hits on CNN, Google, and YouTube. The world had fallen madly in love with this odd but endearing little vagabond girl, and gifts, money pledges, and adoption offers had started pouring in right away.

The press had labeled her *The Little Trash Bin Girl*, which was certainly a pathetic play on *The Little Matchstick Girl*. Essie despised the moniker and figured the same dolt who came up with crap like *Brangelina* probably thought it up. The implications were negative in every possible aspect, especially on an emotional level. How would the child ever live that kind of designation down?

Why don't people stop and think? Essie wondered sourly. Instead of considering how it would affect the child, they only saw it as newspapers or magazines sold, or possible career advancement. They were blind to the future torment and name-calling the child would most likely have to endure from mean-spirited peers. She had already suffered enough misfortune without some clueless moron laying more on her.

The sad truth about being a victim was that it often became a lifelong label, and was almost inescapable despite the various forms of denial, treatment, relocation, and other often futile means of escape. It was an indelible scarlet letter worn by those guilty only of being too different, too small, or too weak.

Despite the publicity, postings on missing person sites, and tireless police searches, no one knew who this little girl was, and as expected, there were more than a few bogus parental claims. The authorities had followed those to no good end, except for the arrest of a couple of dim-witted but hopeful pedophiles.

Ignorance is everlasting, Essie thought bitterly, but forced it aside, not wanting pessimism to infringe on her work. She pulled a chair to the opposite side of the bed, its leg *rat-a-tatting* across the vinyl tiling and startling Debbie from her thoughts. The woman seemed mildly confused, yet genuinely pleased to see Essie. It took her a few seconds to gather herself.

"Hi, Doctor Hiller," Debbie said, still a little blurry. She searched her lap and then felt between her hips and the side of the seat before extracting her phone.

"Essie's fine, honey," said the psychiatrist.

"I'm glad you won the lottery. It's going to take someone special to get through to this one."

Essie smiled and then positioned herself in the child's line of sight, hoping for a shifting of her eyes or some indication of receptiveness. She fruitlessly waved her hand slowly before the girl's face. "Hi Sweetie, do you remember me?" she asked the child. "I was here earlier."

"She's clearly still detached," she said to Debbie. "Can you tell me anything new about our little lost angel?"

"Did you read the report?"

"Mm-hmm."

"Then you know everything I know," Debbie said and shrugged. "They say she woke about seven this morning, looked around showing signs of mild curiosity, used the toilet without assistance, and ate like a lumberjack. Apparently her appetite is extraordinary for a child her size; she ate all her breakfast and more."

"Where does she put it all? I want her secret," Essie said with a chuckle.

"You and half of America," said Debbie.

"She speak or respond to anyone yet?"

"No. She was back in *the zone* by noon. Zone is my word. It seems the best description for the state she goes into."

"Dissociation." Essie shook her head sorrowfully. "It's a sad story that no one legit has come forward to claim her or reported her missing." She looked at the child's small hands and pressed the fingernails lightly. There was a purple contusion on the top of one hand where an IV drip had breached her skin. It was dark and tender looking, though it probably appeared worse than it was on her pale skin. Essie passed a gentle thumb over the bruise, her mahogany flesh in bold contrast to the child's alabaster complexion. She said, "The report said she took the IV out herself? Amazing she didn't cause herself harm."

"They believe she removed it to go to the bathroom. They said she did it as well as any nurse could and left it neatly coiled on the side table. She refused to let them reinsert it." Debbie said. Reaching into her purse, she pulled out a tin of peppermints.

"She's too young to refuse," said Essie.

"Yes, she is," said a man at the doorway. "She was adamant, curled up in a ball with her arms tucked in, glaring at her nurses, and shaking her head. They had to call me."

He appeared to be in his middle to late thirties, broad shouldered and looked in shape beneath an unbuttoned beige blazer. His straight sandy hair and broad moustache would have screamed nineteen-seventies, but a well-trimmed goatee saved him.

"Are you Doctor Farren?" asked Essie.

"Yes, that would be me," he said. He transferred a small notebook computer from his right to left arm and offered Essie his hand. "And you're Essie Hiller."

"You've heard of me," Essie challenged.

"Only good things," said the doctor. He shook Debbie's hand. "Hi, I'm Doctor Brad Farren. Are you the child's guardian?"

"Debbie Gillan, DCF. I'm her caseworker," Debbie said.

The doctor gave the touch-screen of his computer a few quick taps, lowered the lid, and set it on the bedside table. "I chose not to put the IV back because her dehydration was minimal to begin with and considering the size of her breakfast—the juice, and the pitcher of water she drained—she's out of risk . . . hopefully for good."

Debbie tossed two peppermints into her mouth and offered the pack to the doctor, who declined, and then to Essie, who took a couple.

"I didn't see any mention of medications," said Essie. "I've attempted a mental status exam. I asked if she knew her name, where she was, what day it was, but she was impassive so I didn't continue."

"Yeah. I've requested a neurological consult," Doctor Farren said. "That should tell us if there's any organic basis to her lack of responsiveness. We'll put everything on the table at the case management conference, and we'll tackle the meds issue from there."

"I suggest we wait a couple days before making any decisions about sedatives or antidepressants," Debbie said.

"I'm not totally with you on that," Essie replied. "She's either been abandoned or she's lost. No one legitimate has claimed her and she's clearly traumatized."

"True, but the medical record revealed no malnutrition, no dental deterioration, and no physical signs of abuse, thank God. She's been cared for and fairly recently," Debbie noted. "She's had moments of responsiveness, has a voracious appetite, and she's even removed her IV drip without harming herself."

"She certainly has everyone scratching their heads," Doctor Farren said. "Would you mind giving me a hand? I want to try something and we don't need her to fall off of the bed."

He instructed Debbie and Essie to stand in front of the child in case she reacted, and then he pulled the little girl slowly toward himself until she was lying on her back with her legs still crossed rigidly before her. He lifted the child's right arm, extended it fully, and returned it.

"Instant and intense submergence, mm-hmm," said the doctor. "Some kick out, afraid that they're falling, others resurface from their . . ."

"Zone?" Debbie suggested.

"As good a tag as any," said Doctor Farren. "She's a million miles away. This is a first for me. I think I have some researching to do tonight." He searched for revealing bruises on the child's neck and face. "Would either of you know if they've checked for accidents involving younger folks . . . twenty or thirty-something? I know it's probably a long shot, but she has to have parents somewhere along the line."

"Hard to do without a name," Debbie said.

"I imagine," said the doctor.

Essie handed business cards to both Debbie and Doctor Farren. "I have to return to my office. I have a four o'clock patient scheduled. I'd like to keep in touch if neither of you mind. She certainly has me intrigued. Could you keep me in the loop if anything comes up, and I'll do the same?"

They agreed and Essie bulleted out of the room. Debbie pulled her wallet from her purse, and squeezed the business card into a slot that was already threatening to burst.

"She's twice my age with twice my energy," Debbie said.

"Kind of makes you want to trip her," Doctor Farren said. He smiled and then followed Essie.

Debbie had spent the afternoon tying up loose ends at her office, but the paperwork took longer than estimated. It was well past six-thirty when she returned to the hospital. It appeared the child hadn't moved from her earlier spot.

She set her purse and workbag beside the chair and then lifted the lid from the child's meal revealing a disproportionately large serving of shepherd's pie that made Debbie chuckle. Debbie hadn't seen the dietary host or a meal cart on her way in, but the meal on the over-bed table was still moderately warm.

Hoping to entice her, she raised a forkful and waved it invitingly under the child's nose. The child remained motionless, and was equally unmoved by the Jell-O and cookie. Debbie returned the cover, sat down and contemplated what would happen if the child remained nameless and unresponsive. Would they institutionalize her? There weren't many other options as far as she knew.

Shortly past seven, as Debbie's eyelids started to outweigh her resolve, the child shifted and slowly turned her empty hazel eyes to Debbie.

"Hi, honey," Debbie said. "Can you hear me? Do you understand me?"

The girl turned her sights toward her dinner, then to the doorway, and then towards the bathroom door. Her movements were smooth, yet somehow mechanical, like a slowly panning camera. Debbie gave a single sharp clap of her hands and the girl gradually turned her head back to her. *At least she's not deaf.*

Debbie wondered if she might be autistic or have a dissociative disorder. She could be suffering a severe case of posttraumatic stress or any of a dozen other disorders. It would take time to diagnose her condition.

The child shuffled to the edge of the bed and lowered herself to the floor. She walked into the bathroom and closed the door behind her. It was like watching a slow-motion film. A few moments later the toilet flushed, followed by the sound of running water in the sink. The child's awareness of hygiene was encouraging for Debbie. The girl exited the bathroom, returned to the bed and sat in her usual spot. She pulled the over-bed table with the food tray in front of her, never looking at Debbie. Slowly and methodically, she finished most of the shepherd's pie, a carton of chocolate milk, the cookie, but left the Jell-O.

"Honey, you must have a hollow leg," Debbie said, astonished. "How in the world did you eat all of that?" The hazel eyes shifted ever so slightly in her direction then quickly returned to their aimless stare.

"Do you have a name, sweetie? I'm Debbie. I want to help you."

Debbie gently rubbed her tiny back, testing for a reaction. The little girl betrayed the smallest hint of wariness at her touch, but she did not move away. Her eyes shifted slightly from her plate to her delicate hand.

"My name is Hannah," the child said, her voice monotone and barely present—a flutter of butterfly wings—but her elocution was perfect. She pushed the over-bed table away from her and said, "I have to go."

She spoke! Debbie was buzzing with excitement.

"Where do you have to go, Hannah?" she asked, fighting the urge to barrage her with questions.

"Back," said Hannah, repositioning herself cross-legged. Despite Debbie's efforts to keep her in the present, Hannah's awareness left as fast as it had arrived. She had heard of similar cases, usually formed under extreme duress and generally in the severely abused or traumatized.

Debbie waved a hand before her face. *Can she come and go at will?* Debbie wondered. She rubbed Hannah's upper lip, clearing a chocolate milk moustache, and then lifted the child into her arms, holding the child so her head rested on Debbie's shoulder. She was so light and her legs straightened without resistance, like a loose-jointed mannequin. Debbie lowered the blanket and sheet with one hand, laid Hannah on the bed, and pulled the covers up to her chin.

She finally had a name, Debbie nearly rejoiced. Hannah. Quite befitting, it's a beautiful name.

FRIDAY
June 25, 2010

CHAPTER 12

Debbie entered room 433 of the psych ward, Hannah's new room, at 6:00 am, to find her sound asleep and curled fetally with both hands fisted beneath her chin. This wasn't unexpected, fetal being a common protective position. Her breathing was so slight that Debbie moistened her finger and held it before Hannah's pouted lips to feel for breath . . . just for reassurance.

Essie arrived just minutes later carrying a coffee cup nearly as tall as *she* was. She stood beside Debbie watching Hannah sleep.

"I want to just hold her," Debbie whispered.

Essie answered with a sad, knowing smile. As tempting as it was, holding her could be disastrous and potentially dissolve what little trust the child had for them, if any. Hannah had trusted Debbie with her name, which she felt was a great step in the right direction. A simple touch could catapult abuse and trauma sufferers into a panic. They should always be awake and aware of any attempts to touch them, although Debbie, Essie, and Doctor Farren had all broken that rule to some degree the previous evening. Debbie argued inwardly that picking her up and putting her in bed was different, but she knew it had been a risk. It did prove that Hannah was likely unaware of contact in her dissociative state and she had reacted with mild mistrust to touch in her conscious state, though she did not fully retreat.

The two women sat beside Hannah's bed—Debbie near the window, Essie near the door—each of them content to wait for Hannah to awaken. Debbie opened her folder and started perusing the case file while Essie studied Hannah, looking for informative signs like hitching breaths, a change in breathing patterns, or flexing or balling of the hands. She might as well have been porcelain given how little she moved in the next hour.

"She hasn't made a single attention-grabbing motion," Essie said. "But it's what she *doesn't* do that's so remarkable."

"Like what?" Debbie asked.

"Her eyes haven't moved a bit," Essie quietly said as more of a reflection.

"What do you mean?"

"When she's asleep, her eyes don't move at all. All eyes move at some time during sleep—at least a little bit—even if it's not REM sleep. But not Hannah's . . . at least not observably so."

"She doesn't dream?"

"Not saying that. I'll have to look into it, but as far as I know, eyes still move some even when a person isn't dreaming," Essie said.

Debbie cleared her papers from the over-bed table so the dietary host could set down Hannah's breakfast when it arrived. She moved around the bed, stood near Essie, and watched Hannah's eyes. As if suddenly aware that they were watching her, Hannah's eyes sprung open. She didn't yawn, stretch, blink, or even stir. They were closed, and then they were open and staring blankly but directly into Essie's.

"Good morning, Honey. Are you hungry?" Essie said, shaken but maintaining her composure.

Hannah gave one slow and even blink. When her eyes reopened, they were staring straight into Debbie's. She shifted her focus back to nothing Essie and Debbie could see, sat up, climbed silently to the floor, and headed for the bathroom.

"I have *never* seen anything like that before," Essie whispered.

"That was freaking creepy," said the food attendant. "If she levitates or her head spins, I'm outta here."

They were so intent on Hannah that neither Debbie nor Essie had noticed that the young woman had been standing at the foot of the bed.

"That won't be happening," asserted Essie, eyeing the young woman dismissively.

The attendant quickly spun and left the room. Debbie didn't know if Essie had insulted her, nor did Essie seem to care.

They silently contemplated what had just occurred with Hannah. They both perked up at the sound of the toilet flushing, and Essie chuckled.

Hannah opened the bathroom and shuffled slowly forward. Debbie spotted a hint of movement behind Hannah as the door closed. Looking up, she caught the eyes of a young boy about six standing in the shower stall and staring directly back at her. He looked about six, Hispanic, with straight brown hair and large brown eyes that shifted from fearful to terrified, as the door closed.

What the hell? Debbie wondered, rising from her chair.

Hannah shuffled by her, not acknowledging anything or anyone. She returned to the bed and her meal, as she had on Thursday.

Debbie approached the bathroom door and opened the door slowly, not wanting to scare the child. He must have wandered in before either she or Essie had arrived. She hoped no one was in a panic elsewhere in the hospital. Surely, they would know he was missing by now.

"Hello?" Debbie said quietly.

The boy stood in the shower, motionless, with his back pressed to the wall. He wasn't Hispanic, but of Middle Eastern descent . . . maybe Turkish or Armenian. He watched Debbie and squeezed into the corner of the stall as she cautiously approached.

"What's your name, sweetie?" Debbie asked him. "You're okay. You're safe here," she tried to reassure him.

He shook his head wildly, raised his arms and turned his face away, as if to ward off a blow.

"Bana dokunma!" he shouted in a high, trembling voice, and then disappeared.

Debbie staggered back a step and stared at the spot where the child had just been. There was no way he could have slipped past, yet there was no sign of him.

It's a shower stall for Christ's sake! Was it another damned vision? Had he really been there?

"Is something wrong?" Essie called.

Baffled, Debbie walked out of the bathroom and walked back to the chair, giving the bathroom another quick glance. "I don't know, I thought I saw . . . something."

From where Essie sat, it would have been impossible for her to see into the bathroom.

"What was it you said in there?" Essie asked. "It didn't sound English."

"You heard that?"

"Yeah, they probably heard it on the first floor," said Essie.

Debbie was going to say she hadn't yelled, but decided it was better to look half-crazy for yelling like a banshee than removing any doubt by being delusional. "There was a huge spider on the floor," Debbie lied. "I tried to step on it but it jumped and scared me. I got it the second time, though."

Essie looked at her skeptically and said. "It must have been a tarantula. It had you talking in tongues. It didn't even sound like you."

"Wasn't much," said Debbie. "I just don't like spiders, is all."

"So I gather," Essie said and huffed. She gave Debbie a dubious look and then turned her attention back to Hannah, who was stuffing a large wedge of pancake into her mouth.

"Will you talk to us, Hannah?" Essie asked her soothingly. "We'd like to get to know you."

Hannah responded with a mild shudder, but refocused on eating the small mountain of scrambled eggs.

"Do you know where you are?" Essie asked. Hannah gave a barely perceptible nod.

Essie pointed to a magazine poking out of Debbie's day bag. "May I?" she asked. She scanned the pages of the *Psychology Today* magazine. A small grin touched her lips and then melted into a miniscule smirk. Debbie felt a mild humiliation, unsure if it was the magazine, or Debbie reading the magazine, that Essie found humorous. Essie showed Hannah a picture of a lone strawberry on a large plate.

"Can you show me the strawberry, Hannah?" asked Essie.

No response.

Essie repeated the question and waited. Hannah, probably understanding that Essie would not let up until she responded, slowly pointed to the strawberry.

"Good! Excellent!" Essie patted Hannah's leg and asked her to point to more objects. Hannah complied twice and then stopped responding.

"Try something more difficult," Debbie suggested. "She's shown that she knows common things."

Essie flipped through the pages and stopped at a book club ad with numerous titles. "Can you show me Eduardo Porter's book?" she asked.

Debbie felt the request was impractical, but Hannah surprised them both by pointing to the correct book. Fascination was evident in Essie's eyes, though her voice gave away nothing. Essie searched through the magazine for a while and eventually found what she sought. She showed Hannah a picture of two young, blonde girls sitting on a lawn. One was about five years old, the other about three. A woman with darker, curly hair knelt between them.

"Hannah, where's the mother?" Essie asked. It was a simple question, but Essie was more likely interested in Hannah's reaction than her answer.

Hannah focused, still expressionless, and then slowly reached out to run her finger down the image of the mother. She repeated the gesture on the younger child who probably resembled Hannah when she was a couple years younger. A tiny, yet darker blonde, with long, pin-straight hair.

"Do you remember your mother's name, Hannah?" Essie asked, but received no response.

Essie displayed another ad to Hannah that included numerous snapshots: a boy pushing a lawnmower, a firefighter, a businesswoman, a schoolgirl, a priest, a homeless person, a little girl holding a rabbit, and a father and son wearing matching Miami Dolphins shirts. Hannah stared at it blankly.

"Can you show me the father?" Essie asked.

An indefinable expression formed across Hannah's face. *Was it fear? Anger? Both?* That was how it appeared to Debbie, an intermingling of both emotions. Hannah reached out again, but instead of pointing, she closed the magazine and pushed it gradually but firmly away to her arm's extent, giving it an extra shove at the end. Hannah sat back, expressionless, retreating into her shell.

"Hannah, please stay with us. Can you stay with us?" Debbie asked with a touch of desperation tingeing her voice.

"Can you tell us where you go when you leave us, Hannah?" Essie asked.

Hannah started singing very softly yet clearly. Her voice was a haunting, crystalline monotone, so delicate it could shatter like glass, and so desolate it could evoke tears. Debbie recognized it as *Scarborough Fair*, though the lyrics were different.

> "I am going to Hannahwhere.
> A special place where there is no fear.
> There is love and there is cheer,
> *And there's no pain in Hannahwhere.*"

As the song trailed off Hannah retreated far beyond reach, her moment of detachment so distinct it was palpable.

A rush of goose bumps washed over Debbie, so intense it made her back arch. "Okay, that was a little spooky," she said.

"There's nothing here to fear," Essie said. "Hannah's the one who's frightened and hiding . . . not that there was any doubt."

"The way she pushed the magazine away has me thinking *daddy* isn't or wasn't exactly a standup guy," Debbie said. She ran her hand softly over Hannah's head.

"Maybe . . . maybe not," said Essie. "He could be a standup guy, but too painful to contend with right now. What are you hiding from, sweetie?" she asked Hannah.

There was no reply. She was a statue again.

By nine in the morning, Hannah had not moved and had barely even blinked. Essie had a full day of appointments at her office, but was reluctant to leave. She briefly considered canceling her first appointment, another miserable hour where *phenom-a-mom* and *rad-dad* (both self-assessments) tried to convince her that their rebellious and grossly obese twelve-year-old son needed Adderall or Ritalin. Essie believed in using these drugs in the more severe cases, but not when ADHD is used as a scapegoat diagnosis, as in this case. I don't know what my kid's problem is, so let's call it ADHD. Even with the cause laid out in front of them, subtly and then blatantly, the parents refused to see it. Denial caused severe blindness. Essie saw it often in her practice.

Many children did suffer with ADHD, but even more had what Essie considered *Spoiled Shitless Syndrome*, or *Where Are My Parents disease*. Sadly, many parents tried to blame it on each other—or worse—on the child. *She's so distant. He's so angry. She needs constant attention.* What the kids *did* need was their parents to be present in their lives, not substituted by guilt-gifts like TVs, computers, cell phones, money, and carte blanche access to fully loaded refrigerators. They needed mom and dad there to direct them, hug them, cheer for them, praise them, and when they *did* misbehave, discipline them. Too many children had the impression that there were no repercussions for misbehaving, be it from passive or fearful parents. Essie was often tempted to tell certain parents that there was an earlier form of Ritalin and Adderall back in the Fifties and Sixties when she was growing up. They called it the fear of dad's boot up the ass, and it worked wonders! The beauty was that dad's boots had never once touched Essie's or any of her siblings' posteriors, but there was the awareness that it could, and that there could be unpleasant consequences for bad behavior. It had kept Essie grounded.

CHAPTER 13

Debbie checked in with the office and then made her way to the hospital, determined to stick nearby so Hannah didn't feel alone or abandoned, though *alone* seemed to be her preferred state. She seldom came across a child alone by choice. There were loners and outcasts segregated by fear, race, creed, depression, a means of protection, or myriad other reasons. These children usually longed for love, affection, friendship, and understanding. When they recognized a safe harbor—valid or not—that offered such, they accepted it hungrily. Those were usually the more accepting or less damaged children, and therefore were more open to offered comforts. The others took more time. Debbie understood why a child might be intent on being alone, especially if he or she had been mistreated or abused. She was sure Hannah wanted love and affection, too, but not loneliness.

Debbie did not like loneliness. She preferred people around, yet she lived a lonely life by choice. She appreciated what the experts said, all that psychoanalyzing and psychobabble about *alone time* being essential, but she loathed it. She hated the empty house, the empty bed, and the empty hours, and she damned near dreaded going home at night to no one. She was thirty-three, childless, and—apart from some random dating—four years single. Witnessing far too many bad situations—and some added common sense—made her understand that *not* being in a relationship was healthier than being in an abusive or self-diminishing one, but children Hannah's age didn't operate on common sense . . . hell, *Debbie* barely did. Bad decisions were much easier to make than smart ones, especially if they filled an inner emptiness, felt good, or fooled you into thinking that everything was A-Okay, even when your world was anything but. Debbie wondered when Hannah had last felt safe, if ever.

After sitting for nearly five hours fact-finding and form-filling, on top of far too little sleep the previous night, Debbie started getting woozy. The letters on the laptop screen started swimming and melting together, and she suffered a couple head-jarring nod-offs, once nearly dropping her computer. If she didn't close the cover to her laptop, it would inevitably hit the floor. She needed to stand; to go for a walk and get a coffee, if she could only keep her eyes open. Sleeping on the job was unacceptable, but her eyelids were so heavy and closing them felt so nice . . .

She is standing high on a lush green hillside overlooking endless fields of flowers in vibrant splashes of yellow, orange, white, pink, purple and blue, their little flower faces turned toward the brilliant sun, suspended high in a cloudless sky. Along the distant horizon stand odd-looking ochre hills, alien in their glassy rising surfaces. A light breeze nudges her toward the breathtaking view. She steps forward and she is standing on a precipice easily a thousand feet above the pastel fields, so beautiful, so magnetic, and so high the vertigo sways her. She is nudged from behind and falls forward. She plummets toward the multicolored fields, flailing in terror and grabbing at the passing cliff side. Protruding branches blur past her, and finally she grabs onto . . . nothing.

The cliff is gone, and there is only open air as she free-falls to the earth, now miles beneath her. The wind batters her face, making it impossible to scream, but her panic builds as she flails. In the buffeting tumble, a small, incredibly cold hand grips hers. She looks over and sees Hannah on her left, falling at the same velocity. There is no fear present on her pretty face, just a peaceful expression. Her hair, so perfectly white and so impossibly long and flowing, the streaming strands billow behind her like a single cloud in the perfect blue sky.

Hannah looks at Debbie, her eyes shining and calm, and speaks in a whisper that is clear and crisp despite the roaring wind. "Just fly," she says.

Hannah closes her eyes, her flawless face composed, her arms outstretched, and her body an inverted cross as she plummets downward, leading Debbie toward the miles and miles of flowers that blanket the world below. Just before impact, Hannah levels out above the floral sea, pulling a frantic Debbie alongside her.

They're not falling. They are flying, and flying fast . . . incredibly fast! *Are we going a hundred miles an hour?* Debbie wonders. *Five hundred?*

Hannah reaches her hand down into the vibrant, colorful blur beneath them and withdraws a small fistful of . . . what *are* they, pansies? Jonquils? Debbie can't place them. She has never seen flowers like these before. Hannah brings them to her face and breathes in and she then offers them so Debbie can also inhale. The essence is wonderfully enticing and bold . . . ambrosia.

Hannah yanks Debbie downward into the field, where they catapult into God's garden. They somersault and cartwheel through the endless stretch of flowers with soft and silken petals. Intoxicated and breathless, they come to a rolling stop. Debbie lies on her back as a wealth of sensations wash over and through her. Hummingbirds hover and dart among the flowers, weaving amongst bumblebees, and sipping nectar with long, needle beaks. A large, white rabbit bounds up beside Debbie, sniffs her inquisitively, and then leaps away. A yellow kitten springs playfully beside her, swats mischievously at her hair, and then lunges after the rabbit. A sleek cardinal, vibrant red and tufted, settles on her chest and hops once towards her face. He quickly cocks his head, looking as if he has a question.

"Hey! I know you," says Debbie.

Djou! declares the bird. *Chirby-chirby-chirby-djou-djou!* With a quick beating of wings, he is gone.

Debbie hears the giggles of the child who lies near her. She rolls over to see Hannah, who is also lying on her back, luminous with joy as she drags two great sweeping armfuls of the strange flora over herself. As she pulls the flowers from the ground, more seem to fold up to replace them. Hannah stands, her arms laden with a vibrant bouquet, and throws them into the air. As blossoms flutter down over her, Debbie watches the delighted, transformed child, her snowy hair even longer now, flowing well past her waist . . . so long.

Debbie awoke in an instant, as if reality switched on and she was back in the hospital room. How vivid the dream had been. She could still smell the flowers as if she had carried the scent back with her.

She was irritated with herself for dozing off. It was entirely unlike her, and the unprofessionalism of it distressed her. Even an unintentional catnap, if anyone noticed, could cost her job. She considered running down to the cafeteria for a large cup of coffee when she heard the muted rub of Hannah's bandaged feet on the floor. The bathroom door creaked open and Hannah emerged, heading back for the bed. Debbie had not awakened when Hannah got out of the bed, and the presence of Hannah's meal meant even the food services delivery hadn't wakened her. Usually a very light sleeper, she was upset that someone had seen her sleeping after all.

Wrestling with her better judgment, but unable to resist the beguiling atmosphere left behind by the dream, Debbie extended her arms toward Hannah, offering to embrace the sad whisper of a child. Hannah floated by her without a hint of acknowledgement, leaving Debbie feeling thwarted and somewhat emptier, as if denied something essential. The child climbed onto the bed and settled behind the food tray.

Debbie removed the cover for Hannah, revealing haddock, rice pilaf, and diced carrots that looked too orange to be natural. She set the cover on the nightstand and nearly dropped it when she noticed Essie sitting silently in the subdued light on the opposite side of the bed.

"My God, you startled me!" Debbie said.

"Sorry, just watching behavior patterns, is all," said Essie, offering an apologetic smile. "You were sleeping when I came in. I didn't want to disturb you, but nearly changed my mind. You were having quite the dream."

Debbie smiled meekly but nervously. "I'm so ashamed that I dozed off. I've never done that before in my life. On the job, I mean! It couldn't have been more than a minute or two."

"It happens to the best of us. I won't tell if you don't," Essie said with a friendly smile. "Do you always toss about like that when you sleep? You're so restless. I'm sure I can squeeze you in for an appointment."

Slightly relieved, but still mentally scolding herself, Debbie said, "I seldom remember my dreams, but this one was a doozy. Hannah was in it."

"Yeah, she's been sticking to my conscience, too," Essie admitted. "Have you been here all day? Don't you have kids at home?"

Debbie understood Essie's concern and heard her not-so-subtle request. "I suppose I should go to lunch and then to the office. I could stay a little late to get some work done," she said. She wasn't sure why she was defending herself to Essie. Her status as a parent was of no consequence to the job, nor was her time spent in the hospital. Debbie's insecurity made her feel a little childish.

Essie must have seen the irritation reflected in Debbie's eyes. "I'm sorry, that was rude of me," she said. "Please stay. Without Hannah's history I'm at a bit of a loss as to how to communicate with her, and I need to if there's any hope of finding out who she is."

"I've been thinking about that, too," said Debbie. "I think she does communicate, but in the most prudent sense, like everything else she does." She unplugged her laptop and slid it into her bag. "She wastes no words, movements, or emotions. Think of what she's said to us so far. It's as if she's afraid an excess of anything will upset some balance."

"The unseen child," Essie acknowledged. "They're often from homes where anger and violence reign. They live their lives walking on eggshells and hiding in the shadows, trying to remain unseen and unheard so they don't rouse negative reactions. They become living ghosts. Hannah may be a little lost ghost."

They watched Hannah eat her meal in nearly perfect, metered bites.

How could she not be missed? Debbie wondered, wanting to protect Hannah. *How could anyone mistreat this little kitten?* Embarrassed by her growing attachment to the girl, she averted her face. She shuffled her files so they lined up, slid them into the bag beside her laptop, and started gathering the power cable.

"Debbie. Stay, please," Essie said. "I'd like the company . . . and the help, actually."

Debbie looked at her laptop bag thoughtfully, contemplating the request. She chanced a quick glance at Essie and then returned her attention to the bag on her lap. "The truth is, there's no one at home," Debbie confessed. "There hasn't been for about four years. Kenny and I got married twelve years ago, and like most new loves, it was great. We couldn't get enough of each other."

Ease up, Debbie silently reprimanded herself. She looked at her clasped hands, appalled that she was spilling her guts. She looked at Essie, who said nothing, but held her in a sympathetic gaze.

"He knew . . . he knew I couldn't conceive," Debbie continued, not able to stop the spill of words. "He said it would never change things between us. We could adopt, he said, but when the newness wore off—as it always does—it *did* matter."

But that isn't all of it, is it? a voice within her said. Debbie pushed it away.

"Kenny's remarried. He has a son with . . . her. They live in Pelham, New Hampshire." Her throat tightened as tears built up and Debbie barked a painful laugh. "I had a cat, but I gave her away, too," Debbie continued.

"Too?" Essie asked softly.

"I did say that, didn't I? I felt guilty because she was alone most of the time." She patted the bag of case documents on her lap affectionately. "These are my children. I get to bring them to work with me every day and they come home with me every night . . . we're inseparable. They are all the family I have and probably will ever have. I'm very protective of them." Debbie looked at Hannah and offered a weak smile. "So I do appreciate that you want me to stay. Who knows, I may do something useful."

Essie could have said so many things from a psychiatric angle or about professional separation, but a good psychiatrist knew when words would work in an adverse direction. She remained silent.

Debbie pulled a hair tie from around her wrist, gathered her hair into a ponytail, and tied it. She smirked at Essie. "Damn, you're good. Five minutes and you already have me confessing everything. How do you do that?"

"I just listen, is all," said Essie. "It sounds to me like you've been hauling a lot of pain inside of you. It wants to come out. Maybe you should think about seeing someone."

Debbie shrugged uneasily. "I had for a while . . . didn't work." She watched Hannah lift a spoonful of pudding to her mouth. "I think we're missing our window."

"You're right," Essie said with a self-deprecating chuckle. She turned to Hannah and maneuvered into her line of sight.

Debbie saw the slightest eye shift in Hannah and it dawned on her that despite a convincing display of disconnection, Hannah was paying attention, at least to a degree.

"Hannah, I know you can hear and understand us," Essie said. "We're here to help you. We won't hurt you. That's a promise."

Hannah stopped chewing. Most wouldn't have noticed, but coming from Hannah, this gesture was like a waving red flag.

Careful, Debbie thought. Hannah was like a hummingbird. She could interact, but the slightest wrong move and she'd dart. Wisely, Essie waited until Hannah started chewing again.

"What did I say that bothered you, Hannah?"

No response.

Essie continued. "Did someone promise you something? Did someone break a promise?" Hannah stopped chewing again. "Who broke their promise, Hannah?"

"She . . ." Hannah whispered, and then sighed with resignation as if the thought or effort was futile.

"Who is she?" Essie asked.

"Mom," she said without voice, but it was easy to read on her lips.

Debbie covertly flexed her fingers, trying to get Essie's attention. It threw Essie for a moment, and then she looked at Hannah's hands fisted tightly beneath the over-bed table. Essie's expression made it clear she was aggravated at herself for not noticing. Debbie knew it was part of a psychiatrist's job to notice body language, but in Essie's defense, the rest of Hannah's body looked entirely at ease. Whatever her angst was, be it tension, anger, or grief, it was localized in those hands.

"How old are you, Hannah?" Essie asked, hoping a different approach would relax her.

"I think I'm seven-and-a-half years old," she said. Although she sounded like a child-sized automaton, it was the first thing Hannah had said that held childlike intonations . . . those ever-important half years.

"That's a good answer," said Essie. "You said 'you think'. Are you not sure of your age?"

Hannah gave the slightest shrug. "Maybe eight. I don't know."

"You're a very brave girl being on your own like that. I don't think I could handle it nearly as well, even at my age."

Hannah shrugged again.

"Hannah, what's your full name?" asked Debbie.

"Hannah Joelle Amiel-Janssen."

"Wow, that's a mouthful," Essie said. She eyed Debbie who was already searching her purse for a pen. "What a beautiful name! Did your mother pick your name?"

Hannah's already tenuous attention immediately started to digress at the mention of her mother. Essie quickly changed direction. "Hannah, can you tell me what Hannahwhere is?"

"Where," Hannah corrected.

"But what . . ."

"Safe," Hannah said. "It's . . ."

A loud rap on the door startled the three of them, knocking any sense of the intimacy they had built right out of the atmosphere. Debbie could actually feel the door of Hannah's mental barricade slam shut as her eyes set straightforward and she sat bolt upright. Her sitting up gave evidence that she had allowed herself to settle in a little and be at ease. Translated: she had finally opened up a sliver of trust.

A heavyset man opened the door and stepped into the room. He was of average height—about five-ten—mostly bald with a thick walrus mustache in need of a trim. What hair he had was an unkempt, mouse-brown laurel wreath, three or four days overdue for a good shampooing. Debbie thought he looked like a walrus. She wanted to jump all over this clown.

You don't rap loudly in hospitals! You're supposed to remain quiet, tiptoe into rooms, and murmur greetings.

The man took a hesitant step backwards as if feeling the heat of her thoughts.

"What's all that banging about?" Essie demanded. She wasn't pleased, either.

"Hello? Umm, I'm Detective Phil Davenport, Riverside Police CACU, that's the Crimes Against Children Unit. Is Deborah Gillan here?" His voice was oddly low yet exceedingly nasal and gave Debbie the sudden urge to blow her nose.

"That's me," Debbie said. She wondered if she was just being judgmental because he interrupted them.

"And who are you?" the detective asked Essie.

Nope, his voice sucks, Debbie thought, her stomach doing a little flip.

"I'm Essie Hiller. I'm Hannah's psychiatrist." Essie had composed herself, but the tightness around her mouth remained and she looked ready for a battle.

"Okay. It's probably just as well you're here, and not just for the child's sake," he said, though it sounded more like *Ongay, Int's prombly nyust as well.* "Hell, *I* might just hire you."

Debbie realized that the detective had a cleft palate, which made her feel like a wide-ranging piece of shit.

"How can we help you, Detective?" Essie asked.

"I have some information regarding your little girl, here," he said.

"Why don't you tell us about it, Detective, but down the hall in the visitor's lounge," Essie said. "Hannah's likely incoherent, but let's just play it safe."

In the visitor's lounge, Essie and Debbie sat on a hideous orange sofa that was as uncomfortable as it was unsightly, which was saying a lot. Phil Davenport stood opposite them, rubbing his face warily with both palms. In the amplified lighting, it was clear how exhausted the detective was.

"This little gem of a story has everyone at the station flummoxed, not to mention NCMEC. That's the National Center for Missing and Exploited Children."

Debbie and Essie both nodded, acknowledging that they knew what NCMEC was.

"Having her first name helped. It turns out our little girl here is named Hannah Amiel-Janssen, born September 14, 2000," Davenport said and paused. It was hard to tell if the pause was intentional to be dramatic, or if Phil Davenport was truly feeling the turmoil that showed on his face.

"Two thousand? That can't be right, she's seven," Debbie said.

"And a half," Essie added. "We just found out her middle name is Joelle."

"That's right. It's definitely her," he assured them. He pulled a folded square of paper from the breast pocket of his blazer, unfolded it, and handed it to Debbie. Both women stared at it with creased brows.

"Hannah's a twin?" Debbie asked.

"Hopefully," Davenport said. "The other sister, Anna, has yet to turn up."

Debbie looked at the printout again. She had seen her share of twins, and despite the fuzzy resolution of the copied photograph, it was clear Hannah and Anna Amiel-Janssen were about as identical as two sisters could be. There were no discernible physical differences, and both were dressed in matching ankle-length nighties like a two-pack of *Cindy Lou Whos*. The words *Double Trouble* printed on the front of their nighties, above twin wide-eyed and remorseful puppies. Hannah and Anna stared into the lens, their heads tilted slightly towards each other. They both had sweet but infinitely sad smiles on their angelic faces. If not for the length of their hair, which cascaded in silver-white splendor over their shoulders to past their waists, the photo could have been taken that morning. An NCMEC date stamp clearly showed the date March 19, 2008, more than two years earlier. The present date was June 25, 2010.

"Clearly there's a mistake," Debbie said, her expression troubled.

"Ma'am, I haven't even started yet. Let me tell you the rest, and then we'll see if either of you can make any sense out of it. I sure the hell haven't." He sat in a chair across from them. "Hannah and Anna were the daughters of a single mother named Elizabeth Amiel who was viciously murdered on March 10, 2008, in Elm Creek, Nebraska."

"My God, that's terrible," said Essie.

"I kind of figured the mother was gone," Debbie said. "Did the father . . ."

Davenport held up a finger. "Hear me out," he said. "Elizabeth Amiel came to America as an exchange student from Switzerland in 1997 and stayed with the Janssen family in Lexington, Nebraska. Kyle Janssen and Elizabeth fell in love during her stay, and Elizabeth returned in 1999, hoping to attend college and eventually marry Kyle. Neither of her hopes was realized. Kyle Janssen, Hannah and Anna's biological father, died in a single-car accident on July . . ." He looked thoughtful for a moment and then corrected himself. "January 22, 2000, approximately a month after Hannah and Anna were conceived, and before Elizabeth knew she was pregnant. They figure he fell asleep behind the wheel. No alcohol or drugs in his system and no signs of foul play . . . which makes it even more tragic."

"My God!" said Debbie. "Who killed Elizabeth? Who took the girls?"

"The Kearney Police report states that Elizabeth Amiel, as described by the few that knew her, was a loving and dedicated mother, but a bit of a lost lamb. She was naturally timid and still relatively new in America.

"Her boyfriend, Travis Ulrich, murdered Elizabeth while he was in a methamphetamine rage. You don't want to know how many times he stabbed her. Ulrich was a local bad boy who developed a taste for crystal meth. Elizabeth's body was discovered three days later by a friend named Linda." He paused. "I'd say her last name if I could pronounce it. It has more letters than the post office. She was Hannah and Anna's babysitter on the days Elizabeth worked late and was concerned when the girls hadn't been dropped off after school. Elizabeth had not called to say otherwise.

"The police found Travis three days later in Elizabeth's car, wasted to the point of unconsciousness on meth, alcohol, and a soufflé of other things. He had pulled the car off into some rugged terrain about three miles from Elizabeth's home."

"He was only three miles away and the police couldn't find him?" asked Essie, astounded.

"Addicts aren't known for making wise decisions. He had left and then returned to Elm Creek, which is mostly farmland with few places to hide. He couldn't have been there long before the copter spotted him. There was blood all over the interior of his car . . . well, Elizabeth's car. There wasn't much use denying it. When he came down from his high and realized what a depraved son of a bitch he was, he sang like a bird."

"What about Hannah and Anna?" asked Debbie.

The detective looked from one woman to the other, and shook his head as if he were trying to rattle the details out of it. "No sign of either." He paused again, and then forged ahead. "Now, this is where it gets really . . . fucked up. The forensic team investigated Elizabeth's body and found two sets of handprints on her . . . Travis Ulrich's and Hannah's. The forensics team also noted the blood had congealed quite a bit between the time Ulrich murdered Elizabeth

Amiel and the time Hannah touched her, and that Hannah only touched her on the face. They think Hannah had been there to witness her mother's murder, maybe hid herself, and then checked back approximately two hours later to try to communicate with or rouse her."

"Dear God, the pain she must be feeling," said Essie.

"Oh, the poor, poor baby!" said Debbie. "How do they know they were Hannah's handprints, and not Anna's?"

"Good question," Davenport said. "Elizabeth had Ident-a-Kid kits, photo and fingerprint ID cards, like little licenses . . ."

"I'm familiar with them," Debbie said. "I hope the police took into consideration that the sisters are so identical it's conceivable the Ident-a-Kid crew could also have mixed them up?"

"Don't know. I'll send them a note, but I'm not sure what difference that would make either way," Davenport said. "Neither had been seen or heard from until Hannah popped up two days ago, more than two years later and fifteen hundred miles from home."

Debbie and Essie were both stricken by this information.

"How?" Debbie asked.

"Someone had to have taken them, maybe a relative or neighbor?" Essie said.

Davenport spread his hands in a clueless gesture. "I'm open to suggestions. According to the reports, all relatives and the neighbors were checked, many of whom appeared more distraught about the missing girls than the paternal family. Ulrich was and is a suspect for both Hannah's and Anna's disappearances. He swears up and down that he never touched the girls, yet he's never denied a thing about murdering Elizabeth Amiel." The detective sat back in his seat and massaged at his temples with his thumbs.

"Maybe he was too tweaked to remember," Debbie said.

"Maybe," Davenport said. He shook his head at the wickedness of the whole situation. "The only relatives Hannah and Anna have, outside of Elizabeth Amiel, are an uncle, aunt, two cousins of similar ages, and an incoherent grandfather . . . all on the father's side. The relatives on the mother's side live in Switzerland and supposedly disowned Elizabeth when she returned to America against their wishes. The paternal aunt and uncle, who run a farm twenty miles west of Elm Creek, were reportedly quite upset by

Elizabeth's murder and Hannah and Anna's disappearance, but the farm demanded too much of their time and energy for them to invest in the case. Some speculate that they weren't all that torn up by it, and according to Linda the babysitter, Elizabeth wasn't very fond of Uncle Bobby Janssen. One can only surmise."

"Did they even look for the girls?" Essie asked, astounded.

"Got to milk the cows, you know! Can't let the lives of silly little children get in the way of work," Debbie said with cynical joviality. The single-mindedness of some people never failed to amaze her, but on the other hand, others have dedicated their lives to goodwill. Such was the balance of life.

"I didn't say they didn't look . . . just not as hard or as long as they could or should have. Once the hubbub settled down, so did uncle and auntie's concern."

"What if Hannah escaped from somewhere or someone?" Debbie asked.

"Yes, that is a possibility. There are a lot of *what ifs* and we are mulling them over, but Hannah showed no signs of physical abuse." Davenport said stared at the floor for a moment. "Doctor Hiller, is it possible for a child not to grow, or to grow very little in two years? According to yesterday's measurements she is about the same height and actually six pounds lighter than her NCMEC profile from 2008."

Essie considered the question. "The effects of trauma on a person—especially a child—can be wide-ranging, from minimal to drastic, depending on the susceptibility of the victim," she said. "I've heard trauma can stop the body's growing process, but I've never seen it firsthand. People can start having seizures or their hair may go all gray after suffering shocking life events. I read of a man who allegedly grew ten inches taller within a year after watching his wife tumble over the edge of the Grand Canyon. I'd say Hannah may be solid proof that a severe shock to the system can stunt a child's growth."

Davenport nodded. "Let me add another twist. A number of Elm Creek residents claim to have seen the spirits of the little Janssen girls during the wee hours of the mornings."

"I left my belief in the supernatural about thirty-five years behind me," said Essie. "But it comes with the territory. Hannah already looks like a ghost. Consider what an overactive imagination can make of that milk-white hair and pale skin at three in the morning."

Davenport nodded and looked down the hallway toward room 433. "If we hope to make any sense of this, we need to find out where Hannah's been for the last two years. Hopefully that will lead us to Anna."

CHAPTER 14

Debbie steered her car into the parking lot at Riverside Plaza. It was Friday . . . payday . . . market day. She pulled her Accord into an open space, much to the chagrin of the woman whose car faced hers. Judging by her hand gestures and embellished mouth antics, the task of backing out of her parking spot was an insurmountable feat for this woman, as opposed to pulling forward, which was clearly her divine entitlement—one that Debbie so discourteously thwarted.

Debbie typically went to great lengths to avoid conflict, and for a moment considered moving to another parking spot, which she would have if it had been a man, such being the apprehension most men caused her. Instead, she shifted into park, turned the car off, and got out. She was determined not to let this woman intimidate her.

"I was about to pull out," complained the aggravated woman around a thick wad of gum. She was mid-twentyish and far too severe looking for someone her age, and the pulled-back hair and fiber-thin, penciled-in eyebrows only heightened the effect. Debbie walked dismissively by the little sports car.

"Eat me!" spat the woman.

Just keep walking . . . rise above it, Debbie instructed herself, but her body disobeyed and she turned to face the woman seated below her . . . so close to the ground. Debbie stared defiantly at her and said nothing. She turned for the supermarket, ignoring the onslaught of profanity that spewed from the disgruntled woman's mouth. Onlookers regarded the tirade with disdain, and Debbie strolled through the automatic door feeling a moment of pride at her rare display of defiance. The feeling was to be short-lived.

Her shopping routine usually consisted of a swift excursion through dairy, deli, meats, produce, and bakery—the perimeter aisles of the store—with infrequent diversions through the inner aisles when needed, though the end cap items often covered that. Today was no different. From the bakery, she chose a loaf of sliced artisan bread and for her weekly indulgence, a slice of blueberry ripple cheesecake, both of which white wine would complement nicely . . . if only Massachusetts supermarkets could sell wine. There was a small package in the same plaza, but in the past, the urge had never equaled the effort, and she simply would go home sans wine.

Debbie checked out of Market Basket, pleased to see that her insolent adversary wasn't waiting for her wielding a hatchet, or had flattened her tires or keyed her doors. She loaded the groceries into the trunk, closed it, and glanced at the storefront about halfway along the plaza. Debbie neither knew the name of the store nor if it even had one. Aside from the customary neon signs in the windows, like *Bud, Samuel Adams, Michelob,* and *ATM,* there was nothing defining, except the word LIQUORS in large, lighted, red letters on a weathered, white background above the store.

She stood, indecisive, and finally said aloud, "I'm going to have some wine."

Entering the store, once the door closed, the tinted windows and dim lighting gave one the impression that it was suddenly evening.

The wine section was central at the front of the store, which quelled some of Debbie's anxiety. Coolers with glass-fronted doors lined the majority of the outer walls and the rear of the store. Two college-age men, one wearing a Tom Brady Patriots shirt, the other a Red Sox tee-shirt, stood before a cooler, laughing and debating over which beer to purchase.

Debbie found the white wines and started perusing the selection, picking up bottles, checking dates and replacing them on the shelves. She rounded an end cap where a display announced Kendall Jackson Chardonnay on sale, two bottles for $20. *Bingo . . . good* wine for a great price! She picked up two bottles and turned towards the rear of the store to see the two young men standing before a Miller High Life poster in which Angelica Bridges, wearing red hot pants and a snug white halter, displayed well-toned legs. Brady was sniggering goofily as Red Sox tickled the model's upper thigh on the poster and comically dropped to his knees. "Red-headed Baywatch Babe! Save me!" he cried.

Noticing Debbie, Brady biffed him on the top of the head. "Get off the floor you nub," he said. "You've got an audience."

"Uh . . . hi," said Red Sox, embarrassed and quickly getting to his feet. He smiled awkwardly at Debbie.

"Uhhh. Excuse my friend, please," said Brady. "He has this thing for beautiful redheads . . . it decimates his IQ. Now that you've shown up, he'll soon be a drooling imbecile." He looked at Red Sox, shrugged apologetically and said, "Too late."

"Dude!" said Red Sox. "That was the lamest pick-up spiel ever!"

Debbie smiled bashfully and started to turn away when she saw the St. Pauli Girl poster and it froze her in place. It was similar to so many promotional beer posters—beautiful, scantily clad women luring delusional men with a false promise and a lot of flesh—but this one sent a surge of abject terror coursing through Debbie that started at the base of her spine, and numbed every nerve. The two bottles of Kendell Jackson fell to the floor, one of them shattering.

"Whoa! You okay?" one of the men asked.

Debbie jerked her head towards him, her terrified eyes startling him.

"What the fuck?" said the other.

Want to fuck? The words reverberated inside of Debbie's head in a distant, menacing voice.

Debbie shook her head, backing away.

"Watch your feet on the glass!"

Want your sweet little ass . . .

At the sound of breaking glass, the storekeeper rushed forward to investigate. "What happened? Is everyone okay?" he asked.

Seeing the man approach, Debbie turned his way and then backed from him, her mouth moving, but forming no words. He seemed so large to her, and the smell of his cologne seeped through her nostrils and into her consciousness.

Come here, Little Red. You're going to like what I got for you.

"No!" Debbie cried and started coughing, trying to clear the cologne from her senses.

Just hold still so I can . . .

"Is she okay?" asked Red Sox.

At the sound of his voice, Debbie whimpered and faced him, her arms raised as if warding off blows.

The storekeeper turned on the two men. "What did you do to her? We have cameras here."

"We didn't do anything!" said Brady. "She was just standing there, smiling at us, and then she went all bug shit."

Debbie slid along the shelf, bottles clinking together behind her as she sidled away from them and worked her way towards the door.

"Do you need an ambulance or something, lady?" asked the shopkeeper.

Ambulance? The thought horrified her. "NO!" Debbie shouted, and escaped out the door and into the daylight. The sun surprised her; she had thought it was nighttime. She stood on the sidewalk waiting for the slamming in her chest to subside.

Behind her, the door to the liquor store opened and the two men exited, each carrying a carton of beer. Neither of them acknowledged her, but she felt their eyes on her, making her feel exposed, as if she were standing naked for all to see. She needed to get to her car, separated . . . away from these people.

The storekeeper stepped outside and looked at her. "Are you going to be all right?" he asked.

Debbie unconsciously took a step away from him and nodded. "Yes," she said, feeling confused. She remembered a breaking bottle and said, "I'm sorry. I'll pay you for the wine."

"Don't worry about it. It's a write-off," he said, waving her off.

People milled around her, eyeing her with suspicion or concern, and the ground felt as if it were tipping. She reached out and steadied herself on the storefront.

"You sure you're okay?"

"Yes. Thanks," Debbie assured him as she staggered forward, seeking the sanctuary of her car. She opened the door, dropped into the seat, closed the door after her, and retreated into the hazy surreal comfort of nothingness . . . feeling nothing . . . seeing nothing.

The extended bleat of a car's horn brought Debbie back and chaperoned in her awareness to a cacophony of other sounds: shopping carts rolling across pavement; the slamming of trunks, hatchbacks, and doors; and occasional starting of a car engine. It was now dark outside and Debbie had the sinking feeling in her stomach that usually followed her episodes . . . but deeper this time.

What had happened in there?

She was no stranger to the visions, flashbacks, or whatever the hell they were. They'd been haunting her nights for more than two years, but they had always occurred at home. This was a first, and the truth of it was staggering. If she started having these manifestations in the public and during the day, where would she find asylum? There would be nowhere to hide from them. There would be no sanity.

Looking out her windshield, Debbie saw a familiar form sitting on the hood of her car.

Chirby-chirby-chirby-chirby-djou-djou, said the cardinal. He proudly flapped his wings as if to take flight, and then disappeared from sight.

I'm going thoroughly insane, she thought to herself. It was a common thought for her, but this time she wondered if it were the truth. She dug her phone out from her purse and started calling her therapist, Dolores Kearns, but ended the call. She'd been seeing Dolores for two years and it was only getting worse. *Time for a different point of view,* she figured. She scanned through her contacts and pressed Essie Hiller's name.

SATURDAY
June 26, 2010

CHAPTER 15

*D*ebbie pulled her Accord into a parking spot facing a squat, garish retro-Sixties office building, complete with white La Costa designer concrete blocks supporting porticos at the entryways. The Essex County Counseling Center was two stories of ugly.

Essie shared the lower floor with five other counselors whose names were followed by a salad of abbreviations like Psy.D. LICSW, and CCDC. Debbie depressed a button near Ethel Hiller, M.D. on an intercom box. Within seconds, the door lock emitted an angry, waspish buzz that would probably send neurotics to the deck.

She entered a waiting area tastefully decorated in subtle earth tones, yet as anonymous as paste. Aesthetic regional prints adorned the walls, offering historic aspects of mills that had once housed shoe factories and leather tanneries, the famous turreted bridge looking fresh and sturdy, and other landmarks of a once-thriving Riverside. At the far end of the waiting area there was a hallway with seven doors, all closed.

A girl, fifteen or so and looking utterly bored, sat slouched in one of the eight chairs that lined the foyer. She wore the uniform of so many her age—sneakers, torn jeans, a down vest, and pasty white skin that couldn't be natural, yet Debbie wasn't sure if it was makeup.

Anemic much? Debbie thought to herself.

The girl's face might have been pretty, but it was hard to tell with the piercings in her nostril, the bridge of her nose, eyebrow, and upper and lower lips. She hid the right side of her face behind a swath of hair, dyed as black as a raven's wing. The left side of her head was shaven, exposing an earlobe painfully elongated by a gauge through which Debbie could have poked her thumb. Her mascara, eye shadow, and shaggy hair matched the dark intensity of her eyes, which turned to meet Debbie's, and just as quickly looked away. The look was shielded, yet transparent. It was a secret hidden beneath pain and fear, and wrapped in a thick coating of angry.

Who did this to you? Debbie wanted to ask her, but only offered a gentle "Hi."

The teen raised her hand in an indiscriminate, lackluster wave, as if lifting her arm from her leg was too strenuous. She held Debbie's gaze this time, revealing eyes Debbie had seen so many times before, on so many other faces. They were the eyes of the abused children, the beaten wives, and the neglected elderly . . .

. . . the eyes in the mirror.

The thought startled her. *Where did that come from?* Debbie wondered and immediately pushed it away with a shudder.

"Yeah, it's fucking freezing in here," said the girl.

She was right. Someone must have set the air conditioning to arctic. Debbie looked around the room and spied the little ivory control box halfway down the hallway. The setting lever was bottomed out and the thermometer needle displayed sixty-one degrees. Surprised that the controller wasn't in a tamperproof box, Debbie adjusted it to seventy-two.

"You can do that?" asked the teenager, looking genuinely amazed. "You won't get in trouble?"

"I don't think it'll be an issue," Debbie said. "At least we'll be comfortable until we find out."

The air conditioner dropped out with a subtle *whump* that shifted the ceiling tiles. It became so quiet that even with two white noise machines in the waiting area, the room seemed pathetically hushed.

Debbie looked up at the air diffusers and gave an eager, "Amen!"

The girl's shoulders drooped and she sighed heavily. "You ain't gonna start preaching on me, are you? I've had enough of that shit for five lifetimes."

Debbie smiled and said. "I'm not a fan of religion, and especially not of preaching. I'm just Debbie . . . here to get shrunk." She considered offering her hand but refrained and sat down three seats away from her. They were thick, heavy-duty chairs upholstered in corn silk cloth. *Too heavy to throw,* Debbie thought cynically.

They sat in silence, but Debbie could feel the girl's eyes on her.

The girl's interest was piqued, though she maintained her air of nonchalance. Debbie purposefully avoided eye contact.

"I'm Ab," the girl finally said. It sounded more like a warning than a declaration.

"Hi, Ab. Is that short for Abigail?"

"I fucking hate it," she replied, eyes locked on the carpet.

"Why?" asked Debbie.

"My mother chose it."

"You don't get along with your mother?"

"She got rid of me as soon as she named me. She could have picked a better name," Ab said and laughed sourly. "She must've hated it, too. It supposedly means 'brings joy'."

"You don't think you bring joy?" asked Debbie.

"Oh, I bring joy, all right," Ab said and gave a disgusted snort.

"You could unofficially change it until you turn eighteen, and then permanently," Debbie suggested.

"Nah, I like Ab. It's short for abnormal."

Debbie looked at her and smiled. "I think everyone has some of that in them. Do you live with a foster family?"

"If you want to call it that."

"A family?"

"A life." She sneered, stabbed Debbie with a glance, and looked away.

"They don't treat you right?"

"The parents are okay when they're around, which is almost never, but their son's always home, looking for *joy* . . . otherwise known as a blowjob."

Debbie held Ab's gaze, but Ab just shrugged it off.

Bernard Prioulx liked blowjobs, too, said a voice deep within Debbie's head. His leering face appeared in her memory like a jack in the box, but she pushed the image away.

"Did you report him?" Debbie asked. You know the answer to that, Debbie, old girl. After all, you never reported Bernard, did you? said the voice. It had become so loud lately.

"To who? Mom and dad's precious son would never do that!" Ab said caustically, daring Debbie to doubt her. "Brandon's a pretty hard guy to resist, especially after a few good punches in the gut. That can change a girl's mind."

"Did you tell your therapist?" Debbie sensed an urgency growing inside her. Need to keep busy! Keep talking, move forward and don't look back . . . never look back!

"Never been here before. I don't have an appointment. Just kind of hoping . . ." she trailed off.

With a shaking hand, Debbie pulled one of her business cards from her purse and passed it to Ab. "We're going to get you out of there. Wait here with me a while. There's someone I want you to meet."

Ab looked at the card and barked a bitter laugh. "Ha! No fucking shit! Child and Family? You're the pricks who put me in there!"

Debbie turned in her seat and faced Ab. "I will help you," she said forcefully, half plea, half promise.

Ab searched her eyes a few moments and squinted, as if noticing or deciding something. "Maybe you will. You've been had, too. Who did you, your stepfather? Your brother? Your daddy?"

This sudden change in direction threw Debbie and she suddenly felt angry with this quirky young woman. "No one *did* me," she said, sounding more weak and unsure than she'd hoped.

"Yeah, keep telling yourself that," Ab said. She folded her arms and sunk deeper into the chair. "And *you* fucking want to help *me*?"

From the corner of her eye, Debbie watched the girl brood. Feeling ashamed by her reaction, Debbie asked, "Ab, why do you think I've *been had*, as you put it?"

Ab glanced at Debbie, looking peeved at first, and then she downshifted to just mistrustful. "You have the same look we all have—the *don't look* look," Ab said. "People who've been fucked with don't want to talk about or admit it . . . like you. You look at me, but if I look back at you, you look around me or through me so I can't see you. We all do it."

"What do you mean by . . ." Debbie started to ask, but one of the doors opened and two men stepped into the hallway.

"Keep thinking that way and good things will happen," said the older of the two. The younger man walked by Debbie and Ab and offered them an awkward smile, which they both self-consciously returned.

Two more doors opened almost simultaneously.

"Shift change," murmured Ab.

A couple exited from one, him looking aggravated . . . her, red eyed and exhausted. He wordlessly walked out the main entrance, letting the door close on the woman.

"Jerk," said Ab. Debbie nodded in agreement.

From the other door, a woman and a young boy about five emerged followed closely by Essie. She hugged the boy and watched them as they left, the little boy holding the door for his mother and another woman arriving for an appointment.

"My kind of man," said Ab.

"I'm smitten," Debbie agreed and smiled as Essie approached.

"Hi, Debbie," Essie said. "I'm sorry I couldn't take you earlier." She looked at Ab, offered a questioning smile and said, "You've been waiting here for about three hours. Has anyone been out to see you? Who is your appointment with?"

"You," Debbie cut in. "Essie, this is Ab, whom I've also just met. Could we go into your office? We *really* need to make a few calls."

"Certainly," Essie said, concern knitting her brow. "Please come in."

"This may take a while," Debbie said. "Do you have a three o'clock appointment?"

"I do now."

Forty-five minutes later, Abigail Leverone's caseworker Roana Gutierrez, sat in Essie's office, flanked by Officer Lewis Adler and Sergeant Ned Jens. Ab had displayed the fist-shaped bruises on her ribcage and her abdomen and both police officers looked ready to grind bones.

Roana Gutierrez and the two officers would accompany Ab to the Jaquette home to collect her belongings. Once there, Sergeant Jens and Officer Adler would read Brandon his rights, and if things went well, he would resist arrest. Roana would then drive Ab to the home of Dennis and Rachel Kurzman who had a room waiting for her. The Kurzmans—he a CFO at a Cambridge bio-lab, and she a literary agent who worked mainly out of her home—had had only one child. Gwen, a pediatric nurse, was now married and living in Wellesley. That was the plan at least. Debbie knew these things seldom went as planned . . . but maybe this time.

Debbie and Essie followed Ab, Roana, and the two officers into the waiting area.

"What you did today was very brave," Essie said to Ab and handed her and Roana each a business card. "Would you be willing to come about ten tomorrow morning so we can see how things go tonight?"

"It's a good idea, Ab. You should do it," said Roana.

Ab shrugged and then nodded in agreement.

One of the officers held the door for Ab and Roana. Ab directed a crooked half-smile toward Debbie. "Thanks," she said. She didn't wait for a response.

"You never know where your day will lead," Debbie said.

"True enough," agreed Essie. "Which brings last night's call to mind. You sounded a little shaky."

"I'm sorry about that. I was in a bit of a state. There are so many things I want to talk to you about regarding Hannah . . . and myself."

"Let's go back into the office."

Once inside, Essie shut the door behind them and motioned to the beige leather sofa Ab had occupied just a few minutes earlier.

"You know I can't officially counsel you because of our connection to Hannah, but I can suggest someone," said Essie.

"I know," Debbie said and sat down.

Essie sat at her desk. She caught Debbie looking at her feet, which barely reached the floor from the large leather seat.

"No short jokes," Essie said and chuckled.

"Promise," Debbie said with a smile.

"So, in the immortal words of Chicken Little, what's up?"

"I could use a little guidance and advice, but I wasn't sure where to go, especially considering . . ." Debbie trailed off.

"Considering?" urged Essie.

Debbie started to talk, paused. After two more false starts, she exhaled loudly and said, "This is so convoluted. I don't know where to begin. Hell, I'm afraid to begin."

"What are you afraid of?"

Debbie stared at the floor before her, weighing her answer. She said, "What it all means, what will happen to me."

"Can you explain to me exactly what *it* is?"

"Things have been happening, so many things that I can't explain. Some of them seem random but disturbing, while other things seem almost beyond explanation." *Almost?* Debbie thought, *like the sun is almost hot.* "For about two years I've been seeing some kinds of images—or more like image sequences—and I'm afraid they might be flashbacks. They're very explicit and *grossly* suggestive, and I thought they might be subconscious projections. Maybe I see too much of it in the job."

"Have you been seeing anyone about this," Essie asked. "Two years is a long time to carry something like this ... especially alone."

"I started seeing Dolores Kearns shortly after they started. Do you know her?"

"Yes," Essie said neutrally, disclosing nothing. "Is there a particular reason you didn't call Dolores?"

"Nothing's improved. In fact, last night's occurrence was especially bad because it happened in public and during the day, neither of which has happened before. I feel like they're getting out of control."

Essie nodded. "What do you suspect is bringing this about?"

"I'm not sure. When they happen, I see images from the perspective of a little girl who's being used as some kind of sex toy." Debbie rubbed her arms and shivered uncomfortably.

Essie frowned and said, "Sadly, the scenario is more common than we like to admit, as you well know. Can you describe the little girl?"

"Only that she has red hair—copper-red hair."

"You have copper-red hair," said Essie.

"I know. And she's very young. She has small child's hands and purple sneakers with colorful unicorns on them. These visions are so intense it feels like they're really happening, but I have no memories to connect to them. I can smell their sweat, booze, and cologne." Debbie's voice broke. She wriggled herself into the corner of the couch, wanting to curl inward, to shrink. "I'm sorry," she said to Essie, her eyes burning and red.

Essie moved to the couch and took Debbie's hands in hers. "Debbie, how well do you remember your childhood? Was it a happy one?"

Debbie remembered very little of her childhood or the people in it. She had never known her father, and could vaguely recall her mother as someone more like a distant aunt who made rare and unexpected appearances, always arriving with a different guy on her arm and a backpack slung over her back, as if hoping to hide the enormous monkey. She seldom acknowledged her only child and clearly couldn't care for her. Somewhere along the line, she forgot that she had one, though Debbie had always hoped for her return. Eventually, the monkey grew so large it buried her. Debbie was a teenager when Madeline Prioulx—her hypercritical foster mother whose own addictions, although legal, were just as destructive—told her this.

The Prioulxs were the furthest back she could remember with reasonable lucidity. Madeline's greed, slovenliness, and laziness had been parts of a perpetual vicious circle, each one feeding the other. Mad Mother Prioulx, as Debbie and her foster sisters Terry and Lydia called her, would start her days sprawled across the couch, resembling an enormous baggie stuffed with cottage cheese. If Debbie's memory served right, Madeline weighed at least three hundred pounds. Hers was a ponderous package to lift from the couch, so she did it as seldom as possible. Between regular meals she would inhale profuse amounts of Cheez-Its, ice cream, and Little Debbie snacks, all the while ordering her "children" about. She complained incessantly, bemoaning the stinginess of the government, the unfaithfulness of men, and most of all, the ingratitude of snot-nosed children.

One fateful day, a concerned cashier at a little market on Kinsman Road reported her concerns about a negligent situation. Cleveland Police Department and Ohio Child Services heeded her words, and visited Madeline with warrant in hand. They found the porcine matron prone on the couch, watching *Cops* and feasting on Fiddle Faddle, while fourteen-year-old Terry massaged her fat, filthy feet and thirteen-year-old Debbie cleaned the bathroom. The clincher was the discovery of thirteen-year-old Lydia staring impassively at the ceiling while pinned beneath the thrusting body of Madeline's twenty-four-year-old son Bernard. She had a patina of coke under each nostril, with two more ounces waiting in a bag on Bernard's bureau.

The shit hit the fan full force, achieving maximum coverage. Madeline and Bernard got matching steel bracelets and the three juvenile girls quickly became wards of the state . . . again. Debbie, Terry, and Lydia never reconnected despite the odd little sorority they had formed at the house of Prioulx. Some things were better left behind. In Debbie's case, it seemed everything was left behind.

"I think Bernard Prioulx did things to me."

"Foster home?" asked Essie.

"Yes, when I was thirteen," Debbie confirmed. "I don't remember it happening to me, but when I talked to Ab about what was happening to her, it seemed . . ." She faded into thought for a moment. "I know Bernard made Terry and Lydia have sex with him. Why would it have been different for me? I remember very little of my childhood but it seems like it's coming back. It has me questioning if the red-haired girl is me when I was very young, and it's horrifying to have to question it."

"From my experience, if these images are breaking through it appears you might be ready to confront the source of them."

"Why would it elevate like it did yesterday? Could it be Hannah's case?"

"A word, a voice, a smell, a familiar setting, or a certain slant of light can trigger emotions or repressed memories," said Essie. "Your psyche may have decided it's time to deal and heal. Considering your occupation, I'm surprised it hadn't surfaced earlier. You already know these things, but you may be in denial."

"Whatever happened, I need to know the truth and face it. I don't want this following me around, gaining weight until it crushes me. What would it take to find out?"

Essie closed her hands over Debbie's and said, "You know as well as I that if you do decide to, you must do it carefully and wisely. You would need a support system, some family or close friends you can lean on to help you feel safe if you start to feel flooded by the images."

Support system tally . . . zero. Check! Debbie nodded, but did not disclose this fact. "The first time it happened I was right outside the hospital when a drunken vagrant called me Red. It sent me into a panic . . . so much so I had him arrested. Now the name and occurrences pop up out of the blue. They are depraved and terrifying and I feel sordid and empty afterward."

"Yes, they can be horrifying and even debilitating," said Essie. "But I think the mind, if healthy, is very protective of its owner and doesn't release more than he or she can handle. Yours may be distressed, but I believe yours is a healthy mind."

"Thank you," Debbie said with a meager smile. "Though I can't help but feel there's more to it. I've seen things that I'm afraid to mention that would have people questioning my sanity. It has *me* questioning my sanity much of the time."

"I don't doubt it for a moment," said Essie sincerely.

"Like people and animals appearing and disappearing?" asked Debbie. "Like the little boy in Hannah's bathroom the other night?"

"What little boy?"

"I saw a little Middle Eastern boy standing in the shower stall. He was terrified but when I tried to help him, he screamed and vanished! You thought I yelled in a different language, but I swear that wasn't me."

It was difficult to stop now that the cat was out of the bag, but she feared she might have said too much. Essie looked concerned now, and although she hid it well, Debbie saw uncertainty below the surface. She wondered if Essie now doubted her stability.

"The mind is very powerful. It will do amazing things to protect you," Essie said. "An especially tired and distressed mind can be very tricky. Looking at those purple hammocks under your eyes, I think you need sleep most of all. I'll give you the name of a good psychotherapist. You have a lot of work to do, but you must get some rest before you can even think about confronting it."

SUNDAY
June 27, 2010

CHAPTER 16

Detective Davenport's revelation, her visions, and Essie's session had rocked Debbie emotionally and physically. She had returned home from Essie's office feeling queasy and desperate, took two Tylenol PMs, and crashed into her bed without bothering to change. She had slept for nearly eleven hours, woke at 2 a.m., and tossed and turned until 3:30. She got out of bed, showered, dressed, and made it to Hannah's hospital room by 5:15 a.m. Sunday morning.

Leaning on the bedrail, she studied Hannah's face, perturbed by the unfairness of one so young having to endure such nightmares. She kissed Hannah on the forehead. She knew she was out of line but couldn't help it. Despite DCF protocol, Debbie was becoming very protective towards Hannah and wanted to assure the safety of this little girl whose only defense system was separation from reality.

You kissed a sleeping child. For whose benefit was that kiss, really? The question rose into her conscience like a welt. Despite her denial, she couldn't hide from the underlying truth, buried beneath a thick foundation of professional duty. Hannah was more than another case to her. She was a fantasy in the flesh and the archetype of what Debbie herself could not create. Life. A child. A daughter.

An opportunity.

Hannah and Anna—if found—had no parents or other significant relationships. Of course, the same may hold true with any child in the two-foot-tall stack of case files in her office, but never had a case caused such sentimentality in her and she had handled hundreds. It seemed too coincidental, Hannah arriving in Debbie's life as she had for it not to be serendipitous . . . or maybe it was a wish blown out of proportion by her own desires.

Don't let your emotions get in the way of what is best for Hannah, she reminded herself.

A case review and discharge-planning meeting regarding Hannah's future was scheduled for Thursday night at five, which concerned Debbie deeply. Hannah would need excessive attention, long-term counseling, and love. Because of the high visibility and media involvement, numerous foundations had offered to help, and many people had expressed a desire to adopt Hannah should it come to that, though most of those people were not seriously interested beyond the momentary compassion that surfaced in media-hyped cases like Hannah's. The majority of those who were serious would falter or renege once the reality of such a commitment hit them and they discovered how much time, devotion, patience, and money they would need to care for a child in this situation. Anna turning up would only complicate it more. It would be beneficial that they stay together, and who wanted the burden of two damaged children? Who could afford it?

The sad reality was that these children usually ended up living in foster placement, or worse, institutions because adoption required too much of an obligation. They seldom got the treatment, understanding, and most importantly, the love and dedication required for anything that even remotely resembled a normal life. Regrettably, "normal" was a word that might never be associated with Hannah or Anna in their lifetimes. The kind of trauma children like Hannah and Anna suffered could be an invisible shark that never stops grinding its teeth in.

As demonstrated by the media, Hannah's story was poignant and addictive. It was heroin, and once you had a taste, you needed more. How could anyone resist wanting to be part of her existence? The heart melted upon the first sight of her. The girl made you want to be her savior, her mother, her father, and her protector, even when you knew it was not feasible . . . as with Debbie's thought—okay, dream—of adopting her.

Working for the DCF had taught Debbie a truth she'd seen too many times. Those who were wealthy enough in heart, spirit, conviction, finances—or any combination of the four—often discovered other barriers when contemplating the adoption of foster children. Some wanted infants and felt foster children were too old, while others felt fosters were damaged goods, and adopting one (or more) would be akin to opening Pandora's Box.

Debbie knew her station in life. She woke up to it every morning and went to bed with it every night. It was her invisible mocking spouse. Her two-ton life did not include adoption. She was divorced, single, childless, and broke. *That's four strikes Mr. DiMaggio, with an extra kick in the ass for good measure.* There were so many others better suited to adopt . . . at least in the eyes of those making the decisions.

She was hard on herself, but she understood the system and it wasn't always right or fair. She wouldn't brood over it, and she wouldn't allow herself to bask in disappointment. Any self-pity she had had gone out the window when she had taken the job . . . it wasn't an option. To become a sex toy for some deviant step-parent because bio-mom had a monkey on her back, or to wear a constellation of cigarette burns on your chest because you're a disappointment to daddy or your four-year-old hands couldn't support the milk jug—that was where pity was justified. Compared to what many children went through every day, she knew her pitiable points were insignificant. Self-pity was non-productive.

Debbie sat in the same chair as the previous day and pulled a Jodi Picoult novel from her laptop bag. She closed the book after ten minutes. The subject matter was too heavy at the moment—bullied boy shoots up school. She'd save that one for later. She put the book down and reclined the chair just as the dietary host—a tall, friendly woman in green-blue garb—set Hannah's breakfast on the over-bed table.

"Your daughter is so beautiful," the woman said to Debbie in a strong Southern lilt and flashed a smile that could have lit up Times Square.

"Thank you," Debbie replied, feeling no need to correct her. *She clearly doesn't read the paper or watch the news,* Debbie thought as she watched the woman leave.

When she turned back, Hannah was lying with her head on her pillow, staring directly at her. It startled her and a quick jolt hit the base of her spine. She wondered if Hannah had heard her respond to the woman, essentially claiming she was her mother, and if so, had it offended her?

Hannah sat up drearily, scooted to the edge of the bed, and true to routine, headed into the bathroom. The toilet flushed, the sink ran, and the door creaked open.

"Good morning, honey," Debbie said when Hannah reappeared.

Instead of returning to her bed, Hannah silently climbed onto Debbie's lap, wrapped her arms around Debbie's neck and laid her head on her shoulder. Stunned and touched by the gesture, Debbie lightly rubbed her back as she settled, motionless except for light breaths. Her hands felt huge on her. It was alarming how petite Hannah was, especially for nine years old. Hannah's thin arms gradually tightened, her desire for contact overriding her fear. Debbie closed her eyes and reveled in the sensation . . . how right it felt to hold a child. That this child looked to her for comfort was a revelation. A craving ignited within her heart and burned with raw passion. She had held numerous children in her lifetime, but never had she experienced such a need to protect, to nurture, and to love. The absolute perfectness and the all-encompassing windfall of sentiment in it involved all of the senses and every nerve ending.

This is what being a mother must feel like, Debbie thought. Cradling Hannah, she knew it was true. She settled contentedly into her chair and kissed Hannah's head, smelling the mild floral scent of her hair. Hannah reached up and touched her face, and . . .

High on the same hillside, Debbie overlooks the floral fields and glassine hills. In the distance, several large trees with distinct bonsai shapes trim the field. Fruit and flowering buds of brilliant assorted colors adorn the branches.

Hannah stands beside her. She reaches over, takes Debbie's hand and they leap from the cliff, this time without fear. They fly for miles over mountains, fields, lakes, and streams, the fragrance of flowers on the wind, filling their senses. They cartwheel through God's garden, amid the fluttering and buzzing of hundreds of butterflies, bumblebees, and small birds, laughing and intoxicated by the colors, the smells, and the day.

They tumble through flowers unharmed and walk to a stand of trees where small mango-like fruit with nearly metallic, blue-green skin grow in abundance. Hannah plucks one from the tree, bites into it, and directs Debbie to do the same. The fruit is succulent, the flavor fills and surrounds her, unnamable and exotic, like a merging of all things exotic and delicious.

"These are amazing, what are they?" Debbie asks.

"They just are," Hannah says and shrugs.

Standing in the warm, gentle breeze, Hannah timidly takes her hand as if expecting rejection. Debbie squeezes her acceptance.

"Where are we?" asks Debbie.

"Here," Hannah says. "We are here."

"Hannahwhere?"

"Hannah here," Hannah says and looks up at her.

Debbie sees a telltale glimmer in her eyes and asks, "Hannah, was that a joke?"

For the first time, Hannah smiles. Debbie has never seen anything more beautiful. She squats down level with Hannah and says, "I like it when you smile—it makes you even prettier."

She hugs the child to her, closing her eyes and losing herself to the experience. When she opens her eyes, Hannah is standing about eight feet away, yet she's still hugging her. She pulls back, startled, and sees there are two Hannahs, but there is a difference. The second Hannah has much longer hair, a white waterfall to the back of her upper legs. The one she holds has hair to her middle back.

"Anna?" Debbie asks. The little girl tilts her head and steps hesitantly forward.

"She's shy," says Hannah.

"What long, beautiful hair. I was with you my first time here, right?" The child stands still, a hesitant crease to her brow. "It's okay, honey. Don't be afraid," Debbie says. She reaches out and offers her hand. Anna takes two guarded steps forward and then rushes to embrace Debbie, clinging to her hungrily. Anna's body is so frigid that touching her, even through her clothing, is almost painful. It is illogical, especially considering the warmth of the day. Debbie pulls the child even closer, trying to share her body heat.

"My God, sweetie, why are you so cold?" asks Debbie. "You're freezing!"

"We don't know," Hannah says. "She's stuck."

"Stuck where?"

"Annaplace. She can't go back to where she is."

"Can't go back where?" Debbie asks, but her perception starts to sway, and Hannah and Anna's faces become blurry. Debbie hugs Anna a little tighter . . .

Debbie shook her head and the imagery of Hannahwhere cleared. She was still in the hospital room with Hannah on her lap and her arms wrapped snuggly around her. Debbie felt as if she had carried the coldness over from her dream. She could sense a burning chill rising up her left side to beneath her chin. She blinked, trying to work the dreamlike sensation from her eyes and head.

"That was all kinds of odd."

"What was odd?" asked Debbie. She focused in on Essie seated in the chair on the opposite side of the bed.

"Both of you were sitting there trancelike, staring straight forward, and then both of you lost the glazed looks and refocused at precisely the same moment."

"Someone must have made a noise, or something," Debbie suggested.

"Yeah, I'd buy that," Essie said, "if it wasn't Hannah. A gong wouldn't budge her if it weren't *her time*. Anyhow, I didn't hear a thing. Were you meditating?"

"No," Debbie said. "More like daydreaming."

"I'd say," said Essie. "You didn't even notice me walk in. You keep that up you'll get a room of your own."

"I keep that up, they'll fire me," Debbie said. "I didn't realize I zoned out again. How long?"

"I just got here a few moments ago, so I don't know," Essie admitted. "But it was long enough. It stunned me to see you holding her. How'd you do it?"

"I didn't. She came to me without prompting," Debbie confessed.

Essie nodded, impressed. "It's interesting and very unusual. You've definitely made a connection. You must present some kind of haven to her. Maybe you remind her of someone she knew and trusted."

"I had the most vivid and unusual dream. I dreamt I met Anna."

"Because you have a compassionate heart," Essie replied.

Hannah arched her back in an inward stretch and sat up on Debbie's lap. She put an open palm on either side of Debbie's face, and held her gaze for perhaps five seconds, her eyes seeking with very subtle movement. She released Debbie's face, and with the slightest hint of a smile, pressed her index finger to the tip of Debbie's nose and gave a little thrust . . . the universal nose-beep. Debbie smiled and returned the gesture, which Hannah accepted without reaction, except to briefly study Debbie's eyes. Satisfied by what she saw, Hannah climbed from Debbie onto the bed, and went to work on her recently delivered lunch.

"You poor thing, you didn't eat breakfast!" Debbie said. "You must be so hungry. If you're still hungry after lunch, I can get you an ice cream or a brownie or something."

Essie rooted through her duffle bag sized purse. "I have a bag of Sun Chips, a Dove chocolate bar—make that two—a bag of beef jerky, and a package of strawberry Twizzlers. I've got her back." Essie smiled and patted Hannah's leg, then looked at Debbie. "Are you hungry?"

"All set," Debbie said with a raised hand. "It's no wonder you operate at eighty miles an hour."

"Oh, it isn't for me. It's for the kids who come to my office. There are a lot of them, often hungry, and some spend the better part of their days feeling that way." Essie watched Hannah eat for a moment. "I'm bewildered by the trust she's already given to you, it's almost unheard of considering what she's endured. The poke on the nose was most likely a re-enactment of something done to her by someone she trusted, a comfort act she associates with good memories."

"I hope she has some good memories," Debbie said, "or memories at all."

"Well, let's try to find out. If Hannah will talk to us," Essie said. "Will you, Hannah?"

Hannah's expression became pained as if she were fighting some inner battle. Her little shoulders drooped with resignation and she solemnly said, "'Kay."

Debbie almost protested but held back.

"Hannah," Essie began. "When that man found you, you were hiding behind . . ."

"Isaac Rawls," Hannah interrupted.

"Excuse me?" said Essie.

"Isaac Rawls," Hannah repeated.

Essie looked at Debbie, who shrugged.

"Is that the man who found you? Debbie asked.

Hannah nodded.

"How do you know his name?"

Hannah didn't speak for a while. Essie was about to ask another question when Hannah said, "He said it to the policeman."

"I thought she was unresponsive when they found her," Essie said to Debbie.

"The report said she was incoherent. You've read it, I'd imagine."

"Of course," said Essie.

"Half here, half there," Hannah said.

"What do you mean, honey?" asked Essie.

"When I'm half here and I'm half there, I can listen."

"You mean you can still hear us when you're in your . . . states?" asked Essie.

Hannah looked confused by the question. "What states? Nebraska?" she asked.

"Trances," Essie said with a chuckle. "When your body is here, but part of you goes away."

"Hannahwhere," Debbie said, remembering the eerie little song that Hannah had sung just before she returned to her limbo.

Hannah brightened slightly and said, "I can see and hear in Hannahwhere."

"Is Hannahwhere what you call your trances?" asked Essie.

"Hannahwhere . . . Annaplace . . . Hannahtime," Hannah said whimsically. If she was confused, Essie and Debbie were confounded.

Debbie felt like she had touched a livewire. *She said Annaplace!* She was positive she had heard *that* in the dream from which she had just awoke. *How would Hannah know what she heard in her sleep? Had she even been asleep?* Essie had said they were both staring straight ahead, but miles away.

"Have you heard the name Annaplace before?" Debbie asked Essie.

"Yes. Last night," Essie said. "It's not uncommon for trauma victims to name their mental sanctuary. It gives it credence."

"Not Hannahwhere . . . Annaplace," said Debbie.

Essie contemplated the question. "You're right, I didn't catch that. Maybe she created a mental harbor for her sister to return."

This line of thought was overpowering to Debbie. How could Hannah know about Annaplace? Had Hannah said it in her sleep and Debbie subliminally overheard it? Could she and Hannah have a psychic connection and share dreams?

That's stretching it, Debbie thought. She figured she'd wait for a simple answer that would put logic to it all. If no answer came . . . well, that was an answer in itself. This was a standard progression for Debbie. *When unsure, deny it more.*

"Hannah, can you see and hear us when you're in your . . . in Hannahwhere?" Essie asked.

Hannah nodded. "Half here, half there," she said.

Essie looked at Debbie and said, "Good thing we moved Davenport to the family lounge."

Debbie hadn't thought about it. How horrible it would have been for Hannah to have to go through that, reliving all of it through their words.

"A collective concern with children—and people overall—who have experienced dire trauma and have created an asylum to hide in, is their desire or their ability to stay in the perceived shelter of their asylum," explained Essie. "They build a comfort zone there, and returning to the here-and-now can become more difficult if their dissociative states become longer or more frequent."

"If they decide they want to stay there, can they become unreachable?" asked Debbie.

"They can, and we especially want to avoid that with Hannah. She already spends so much time there."

"Is that what she means by 'half here, half there', that she's not fully inside her harbor?"

"I think so," Essie admitted. "Hannah, what would happen if you went all the way into Hannahwhere?"

Hannah mulled over this for a while and said, "Then all of me is there, not here."

Debbie snorted a quick laugh at Hannah's simple logic, but the significance of it made her nervous. What if Hannah found that comfort zone? She wondered. Would she be trapped there and fall into some trance or a coma? Could it happen to me?

"Why do you go to Hannahwhere?" asked Debbie.

After a long pause, Hannah replied, "It's pretty. It doesn't hurt if we fall."

"It's safe when you go away," Debbie said.

Hannah confirmed it with a small nod.

"Safe from what, Hannah?" asked Essie.

Hannah started shrinking inward.

"Different subject," Debbie said softly. She ran her hand tenderly over Hannah's back and felt a degree of satisfaction when the child leaned slightly in her direction.

Changing course without missing a beat, Essie asked, "Hannah, how did you end up behind the dumpster?"

"I jumped out," Hannah quickly answered. To Debbie it sounded defensive.

"You jumped out of the dumpster?" Essie asked dubiously.

"No!" Hannah said. There was now an underlying element of humor to her tone, as if the suggestion was absurd. "I jumped out of Hannahwhere. I was mad."

Essie glanced warily at Debbie. She asked Hannah, "How do you jump out of Hannahwhere?"

Hannah shrugged. "Me and Anna needed help. I got scared and followed the red bird behind the dumper," she said, as if it made complete sense.

The red bird? thought Debbie. Reality tipped a little bit further.

"What did you get mad at?" asked Essie as Debbie asked, "What red bird?"

Essie again asked, "What did you get mad at?"

"Anna!" Hannah said, frustration tinting her words. "She can't leave with me anymore."

"It's okay, Hannah. You're safe here," Essie said. "Let's go one question at a time so we understand. Anna can't leave Hannahwhere with you?"

"Hannahwhere or Annaplace. We were supposed to go there, to our safe places. I looked for her, but she didn't come for a long time, and then she did come. But she got stuck there, and now she can't come back. She's been there a long time."

Debbie ached to protect her from these questions, but she was also intrigued. "Is Anna there now?" she asked, sounding far too anxious, judging by the curious glance Essie gave her.

Large teardrops ran down Hannah's cheeks, falling to mingle with her breakfast. "A little," she said. "But I think she's sick . . . sick and stuck!"

"Does Anna always go with you to Hannahwhere?" Essie asked.

Hannah wiped absently at her nose. "She always goes to Annaplace, but Hannahwhere and Annaplace are kind of together."

"But she doesn't anymore?" Essie asked.

"She's there, but now she can't leave." Hannah's chin trembled and her lower lip pouted, breaking Debbie's resolve. She couldn't fight the tears either.

"When do you and Anna go to Hannahwhere?" Essie asked.

"When it gets ugly," she said, and looked helplessly to Debbie. Her entire body was shaking. Hannah corrected herself, "When *he* gets ugly." At these words, Debbie felt a shift within herself, and a blaze of anger.

"When you say *he*, do you mean Travis?" Essie asked.

At the mention of the name, Hannah's eyes transformed, displaying her alarm. The child became frantic and started looking around the room, terrified, as if she expected him to leap out from the shadows. Debbie wanted to ask Essie, *who the fuck do you think she means?*

Hannah started singing, "I am going to Hannahwhere . . ."

Debbie took Hannah's hands in hers and squeezed them encouragingly. They were so small they felt like they were dissolving, shrinking within her hands. Debbie looked at Hannah and she literally began fading from Debbie's sight while sitting on her lap. Terror and desperation folded over Debbie and her logical mind revolted.

What's happening? Oh my God, what do I do?

A part of her wanted to flee, to escape from it, and find sanity elsewhere. Another part of her, the moral element, knew she had to remain there for Hannah, even though she was the one causing the madness. She looked to Essie, who was unaware and rapidly writing in her notepad.

Debbie stood, lifting Hannah and holding her firmly to herself. There was no mistaking it. The child was losing substance, dissolving in Debbie's arms.

"Hannah, Travis is gone! He cannot hurt anyone anymore. I won't let anyone hurt you," Debbie said urgently, pressing the child's head to her shoulder. Hannah's arms snaked over Debbie's shoulders and Debbie clung to her greedily, kissing her head repeatedly, trying anxiously to reassure her. Hannah's solidity finally started returning and her weight increased in Debbie's arms.

Am I going insane? Debbie wondered. Her reality warped and buckled, but she knew she wasn't imagining it.

Essie was looking at Debbie curiously. "What's wrong? You sound panicked."

"You saw that, right?" Debbie asked.

"Saw what?" asked Essie.

Thoughts traversed Debbie's mind like bullets from all directions, seeking answers that weren't there. It was horrifying, and Debbie felt a black panic rising in her that she had to keep at bay. She sat down with Hannah still in her arms.

Am I bat-shit crazy?

She had heard that if you could question your own sanity, then you were sane, but how did they verify this with the insane? Too convoluted . . . next question.

Okay . . . What disappears?

Ghosts, aliens, time travelers, money, and delusions. *Brilliant deductions, Einstein.*

Hannah disappearing—if it was indeed real—would draw so much more unneeded attention. It would surely be a celebrated discovery for those of a scientific bent and a giant portent or prophecy among the fervently religious. Who knew what kind of testing and mania Hannah would be exposed to if either community caught wind of it? In their eyes, she would not be a child, a human, or a victim. She would become research or a banner to wave at the non-believers; something they'd tag their name onto for prosperity or recognition, or something even more narcissistic, ominous, or fanatical. That could be as bad as—or worse than—anything Hannah had already survived. Essie had not seen it happen, which, Debbie figured, was for the best.

"Hannah almost blacked out again," Debbie said. "Whatever is happening to her cannot be good. No more questions . . . not right now, okay? She needs a break."

CHAPTER 17

*H*annah calmed down and managed to nap a bit by the time lunch arrived. In spite of the commotion and emotion of the morning session, Hannah stayed in the present and hadn't withdrawn into one of her dissociative states.

Hannah started to disappear! Debbie replayed it repeatedly in her mind. It defied explanation and contradicted her solid foundation of reason. A door had opened, and so much that had been unthinkable a week ago had suddenly become possible. What about time travel, aliens, telepathy, telekinesis, ghosts, God and Satan? She had put these on the shelf with magic, mythology, and all things illogical. The stream of questions that now barraged her seemed endless.

How could the child simply dissolve and reform? How did it happen without pain and without degeneration? It was clearly a defensive reaction, but was it trained into her or genetic? Was Hannah dreaming when she visited Hannahwhere and Annaplace, and did she somehow manipulate Debbie's dreams? Was she connected to Hannah and Anna on some more profound level? Why her?

Where has Hannah been for the last two years? It was especially paradoxical when coupled with the observation that she appeared to have aged little in that time.

How did she end up fifteen-hundred miles from home, and in a place as remote and mundane as Riverside?

If she were to accept this as tangible, then it opened a realm of possibilities. In fact, was anything *not* possible?

Detective Davenport was due to show up at four o'clock that afternoon. He wanted Essie and Debbie present because they—he had the wherewithal to admit—were better versed at dealing directly with children. Debbie figured there was no sense in going home if she needed to be back by four. She lived ten minutes away and it was barely past noon. She knew her logic was twisted, but she would latch onto any motive to stay there with Hannah . . . especially now.

In the face of everything, Hannah still had a hearty appetite. She ate her lunch slowly and methodically, and then sat on Debbie's lap. Debbie brushed and braided her hair into a single whip down her back. When Debbie finished, Hannah scooted down from her lap and walked into the bathroom. Debbie looked at the shower stall behind Hannah, half expecting to see the little boy. Wouldn't Hannah have reacted to a little boy standing in the shower while she went to the bathroom? She wondered if she could ask Hannah in some subtle way if she saw him. Hannah had been standing before the sink for a rather long spell by the time Debbie returned from daydreaming.

"Oh, is it okay?" Debbie finally asked.

Hannah turned to Debbie and said, "Can't see."

Hannah was too short to see herself in the mirror. Either she was the most patient girl Debbie had ever seen or the most disciplined—a disheartening thought. Wondering how long Hannah would have silently waited there, Debbie joined her in the bathroom, encircled her narrow chest and abdomen with her arms, and lifted. Hannah regarded her reflection, checking out the braid from the left, then the right. She looked pleased.

"Mom made braids for me," Hannah said, pointing above her ears. "Two."

"I can give you two if you'd like," Debbie offered.

Hannah met her eyes in the mirror and said, "No, I like just one."

Debbie looked at the small figure in her arms and then back at herself. She considered herself on the prettier side of plain, with her long, straight, copper-red hair, pale skin, and a face loaded with freckles. She and Hannah had very different features, yet she felt they looked right together. *I could pass for her mother,* thought Debbie.

Debbie and Hannah went for a long walk around the hospital. They looked at the courtyard through the fourth-floor windows, browsed the gift shop, had a slice of coconut cream pie in the café, and finally settled down in the main lobby to watch episodes of *SpongeBob SquarePants* and *iCarly* on the widescreen television.

When Essie and Detective Davenport showed up, Hannah was lounging in Debbie's lap reading aloud from a book she had selected from the small mountain of gifts well-wishers had sent to the hospital in her name. She read very well for her age—far better than Debbie expected.

Maybe Debbie was just being mistrustful, but seeing them walk into the room together made her uneasy. She thought about Hannah's terror earlier that day and realized the child wasn't the only one who was frightened . . . she was, too, by what the night might bring and the effect it would have on Hannah. Whatever was in store, she had a gut feeling it was not good. The unknown was something that had never concerned Debbie, but now it was a realm with no boundaries.

They looked at Debbie and she thought she saw disapproval in the psychiatrist's eyes. Debbie held Essie's gaze, refusing to back down or show hesitation. Essie broke the eye contact and moved to the other side of the bed.

"How's our enigmatic little girl doing?" Essie asked, sounding light and conversational.

"We've had a very comfortable day," Debbie said, realizing too late that Essie wanted Hannah to answer her question.

"Can we talk a moment?" Essie said to Debbie, motioning to the doorway.

Debbie looked from her to Phil Davenport. "Let's take our conversation down the hall."

Debbie kissed the top of Hannah's head, silently daring anyone to protest, and had Hannah climb onto the bed. Debbie slowly stood and led them down the hall and into the waiting lounge.

Once inside, Essie closed the door gently and said, "I don't want to overstep boundaries, and I ask this with Hannah's welfare as top priority—and yours, too, of course—but are you sure your involvement with Hannah will not become emotionally damaging for her when it's time to break the connection and part ways?"

Debbie felt the weight of Essie's well-calculated words. The truth that Debbie eventually would have to let go of Hannah was not lost on her, and she dreaded it.

"I do understand your concern," Debbie said amiably but with deliberate emphasis. "Please understand that my role as a DCF caseworker is to assure that the children assigned to me are not harmed, get the best care possible, and feel they are loved and feel wanted. This includes treating them with kindness, respect, and yes, affection. I am doing my job."

"I appreciate your position and sympathize," Essie said. "But don't you feel the excessive amount of time you're spending with Hannah presents the risk of her feeling abandonment once you do have to let her go? You *will* eventually have to say goodbye."

"That's exactly why I'm spending extra time with her," Debbie said with forced aplomb, though a sense of selfishness burned within her and reddened her cheeks. "To waylay the feelings of abandonment I'm sure she is now experiencing. My commitment to her placement in a commendable foster family should shield her from future risks."

"Mm-hmm," said Essie. She raised her eyebrows and deliberately scratched behind her ear, a gesture Debbie found arrogant, though she understood Essie was not being intentionally haughty, but only doing her job.

Phil Davenport looked from one woman to the other as if he were waiting for either a fistfight or a punch line. They had both stated their minds, they both knew where the other stood, but now they were stuck at an impasse.

"Right," he said with some irritation, letting them know they were wasting his time. He straightened his shoulders and plunged his hands into his pants pockets. "Okay. The kid's loved. Meanwhile, I need to get some answers on this case."

"Hannah's safe here," Debbie told the detective. "Elizabeth Amiel cannot be revived and the man who murdered her confessed and is doing life without parole. What do you hope to gain by putting Hannah under the spotlight and drilling her with questions?" Debbie had found some contentment within her little denial bubble, but the reality was never far away—Hannah had started to fade and Debbie wanted to avoid a recurrence.

Was it painful when Hannah started fading? She hadn't fought it. She remained immobile on Debbie's lap while it occurred, as if it were preferable to confronting the memories the questions revived. Debbie understood . . . she'd fade away too, if she were Hannah.

"Hannah and Anna Amiel-Janssen," Davenport said, displaying

a new level of intensity, although his words sounded nasally. *Hannanannanna.* It severely dampened his authority, and Debbie experienced a moment of sympathy for him. "They've been missing for well over two years, and we haven't a clue as to where Hannah has been, where Anna is, or who they've been with. We don't know if anything horrendous happened to them, or if anything is still happening to Anna. This is an open case. It could be a child abduction case, a child abuse case, or, God forbid, a child pornography or sex market situation. Right now our only clue to anything in this seriously screwed-up case—and maybe our only hope of finding Anna—is sitting *in that room*." He accentuated the last three words as if he were talking to a child.

Davenport's reference to sex markets hit Debbie in the gut, its cold fingers clenched and twisted within her. That some sick bastard could use these precious girls like that was beyond atrocious. The only comfort was that Hannah showed no indication of sexual abuse—but Anna wasn't out of the woods.

Davenport's words were far more valid than Debbie's, and arguing them would have been pointless.

"Can we at least have a mutual agreement that if Hannah starts becoming upset, we hold off questioning her until later and give her time to settle down?" Debbie said. "I'm afraid one of these times she may not return from her states, fugues . . . whatever they are." She pointed to Essie. "You, yourself said that people can become imprisoned within their own mental sanctuaries."

Essie nodded her agreement.

"Please!" Debbie said.

Davenport closed his eyes for a few moments and his expression softened a little. "Okay."

Essie and Davenport ate dinner in the hospital cafeteria while Debbie, not wanting Hannah to eat alone, carried hers back to the room. She tried to prepare Hannah for Davenport's return, explaining that the detective needed answers in order to find Anna, but assuring her that Davenport would stop if she got upset. Hannah hesitantly consented, but a gloomy veil settled over her while she finished her meal.

Phil Davenport borrowed a chair from the nurse's station and carried it into the room. He set it beside Essie's seat on the further side of Hannah's hospital bed, sat down, and forced a smile that looked reptilian and a little bit frightening to Debbie. Sometimes it was better not to smile at all.

"Hi, Hannah. I'm Phil Davenport," he said and offered her his hand.

Hannah didn't acknowledge him at all except to gently move from the bed onto Debbie's lap.

Essie was about to protest, but Davenport said, "No, that's good. Let her get comfortable." He shuffled a little closer to the bed, trying to eliminate some of the gap Hannah had created by switching to Debbie's lap. He crossed his legs, trying to exude a sense of easiness, but didn't do so well.

"Hannah, I want to ask you some questions," he said. "This is a very confusing case for us, and it looks like you might be the only person able to answer them. Will you help us figure some things out so we can find Anna?"

Hannah replied with the slightest of nods.

"Thank you, Hannah," Davenport said. "A couple of days ago you were discovered behind a dumpster. Do you remember how you got there or where you were before that man found you?"

"Isaac Rawls found me," Hannah said. Debbie thought she saw the hint of a smile touch the corners of her lips.

"Okay. Before Isaac Rawls found you," Davenport amended. "Did somebody put you behind the dumpster? Why were you there?"

"I was just there. That's where I jumped out," Hannah said indifferently. "I already answered that," she added, sounding irritated. Debbie didn't blame her, considering how the previous session of questions had ended. Hannah clearly did not trust the detective.

Davenport said, "Maybe you did, but not for me. I need to hear the answers, too. What did you jump out of?"

Her eyes shifted towards the ceiling. "Hannahwhere," she said, and then added in a playground rhythm, "Annaplace, Annaday, Hannahtime, Hannahway."

"Hannah refers to her dissociative states as Hannahwhere and Annaplace," Essie said, quickly filling Davenport in with details. "They are emotional havens . . ."

"No, they're places Hannah and Anna . . ." Debbie started to interject, but refrained from saying more. She wasn't sure what had compelled her to correct Essie, and even less sure about why she was so certain it was true.

Hannahwhere and Annaplace are places Hannah and Anna go to when what? she wondered.

"Never mind," she said.

Davenport leaned forward and rubbed at his temples, and then massaged the bridge of his nose.

Someone's getting a headache.

"Hannah, can you tell me how long you were behind the dumpster?" Davenport asked. *Gan you nell me?*

Hannah shrugged again, uncertainty knitting her brow. She wrinkled her nose, and Debbie noticed that she was doing it as well. It dawned on her that it was a reaction to the detective's speech impediment.

"Was it daytime when you . . . jumped out?" he persisted.

After a moment of thought, Hannah's eyes brightened. She nodded and said, "Yes, three daytimes. I saw the red bird the first day when I jumped out."

"Are you saying that you were there three days?" Davenport asked doubtfully, sounding threatening. Another explanation from Essie followed.

Hannah looked warily to the floor. "It was dark four times and daylight three times," she said in a protective tone. "It was cold."

"Three days is unlikely," Essie said. "Hunger alone would have made . . ."

"There was food in the dumper," Hannah interjected. "There was lots at night."

"Dear Jesus," Debbie murmured. Her stomach instantly revolted at the mental image of Hannah sifting through the swill for something worthwhile and edible. The Indian restaurant surely tossed some of its nightly leftovers into the dumpster, and how many half-eaten meals made it there? It had to be dark in that alley at night, even darker in the dumpster. Debbie felt like vomiting, and from the look on both Essie and the detective's faces, they weren't far behind.

"I climbed in by the sliding doors on the sides after the restaurant people would go away," Hannah said. "It was warmer inside, too, especially when it rained."

"Hannah, this is very important," Davenport insisted. "We need to know where you were before you ended up at the dumpster."

"Hannahwhere, I said," Hannah said, showing a hint of frustration.

Davenport's expression dropped. He repositioned, trying to use body language to accentuate his words.

"Was Anna with you before you *jumped* out of Hannahwhere?" he asked.

"A little."

"A little? Great! That's just excellent! A little!" Davenport barked a laugh and said, "Okay, Hannah, can you tell us where Hannahwhere is? Is it a house or a building?"

Hannah faded into thought for a while. She couldn't formulate an answer, so she said only, "No."

"Who else is or was with you in Hannahland?" the detective pressed.

"Hannahwhere," Debbie and Essie said simultaneously. Davenport huffed.

Hannah shifted in Debbie's lap, brightened, and said, "Debbie comes now! My mom wanted to come, but she couldn't."

Both Essie and Davenport looked at Debbie as if expecting some kind of explanation for which Debbie had none. She knew what Hannah was talking about, but how could she explain something that she didn't understand at all?

Best to act clueless, she figured, and said, "We've never left the hospital."

"This is going nowhere fast," Davenport complained.

"She's been beyond cooperative. She's answering your questions in the best way that she knows how," said Essie. "Your frustration won't improve things, but it will distance her from you."

Debbie wanted to high-five Essie, but a thought came to her. The detective had been focusing on Hannah's arrival at the dumpster. Why not try searching in the other direction. Davenport was trying to break the front door down and the back door might be standing open.

"I have an idea, if I may try," said Debbie.

Davenport presented Hannah like a concierge showing the way into a hotel. "Be my guest."

"Sweetie, can you tell us the name of the town you live in?" Debbie asked.

"Elm Creek, Nebraska, six-eight-eight-three-six," Hannah replied with studied concentration.

"Excellent!" said Debbie. "Before the police drove you here to this hospital, do you remember when the last time you drove in a car was? Do you remember who you were with?"

Again she thought. "A long time ago, Mom drove me and Anna home from Linda's house."

"Is that the same Linda who watched you and Anna?" asked Davenport.

"Yup," Hannah agreed.

"What's your mother's name, Hannah?" Davenport asked.

"Elizabeth Doreen Amiel," Hannah said with childlike precision, giving extra attention to pronunciation, as she had with her town and zip code. "Some people call her Liz. She was born in Lucerne, Switzerland."

Someone—in all likelihood probably Elizabeth Amiel—had made the effort to ensure that Hannah, and most likely Anna, knew their address and their mother's full name. Debbie had the impression that Elizabeth Amiel was not a bad mother, but maybe a good person in a horrendously bad situation. She was from Switzerland, perhaps spoke limited English, and was in all probability clueless about life in America. A stranger in a strange land. By the sound of it, she was in dire straits—a single mother of twins with no family or support system. She had had the ill fortune of falling in love with a man who ended up dead shortly after she had abandoned her country to be with him, leaving her in the middle of nowhere with two bambinos in the bread basket.

"When was the last time you saw your mother?" asked Davenport.

Hannah stiffened, put her hands to her mouth, and focused her eyes on her lap.

"Really?" Debbie asked. She shook her head and gave the detective a warning glare.

Davenport released a pent-up breath, his frustration tearing into him. "Why didn't Anna come with you from your home?" he asked.

"Anna's in Annaplace," Hannah said.

"But you said she was with you in Hannahwhere."

"Yup."

Davenport contemplated her over his folded hands for a while. He said, "Then she was in Hannahwhere."

"No," stressed Hannah, as if he was a thickheaded child.

Debbie could see the veins in his temple pulsing. He took a deep breath and released a sigh. He maneuvered his chair again, trying to garner her complete focus.

"Okay, Hannah, why didn't Anna come with you from Annaplace?"

"She wants to, but she can't," Hannah said.

"Then how come you can come here, but Anna can't?"

"We don't know," whispered Hannah. Her feet started moving nervously on Debbie's lap, burrowing between the chair and her leg. "She's stuck."

"Stuck in Annaplace? How is she stuck?" asked the detective.

Hannah shrugged. "She's just stuck."

"Can she move?"

"Yes."

"Is she tied up, or trapped under something?"

"No."

"Did your mother ever go to Hannahwhere, Annaplace, or Whereverwhere with you and Anna?"

"We don't go to Whereverwhere. Is that your place?" Hannah asked.

"I don't have a place," said the indignant detective. "Wherever it is that you and Anna go. Did your mom go?"

"No. She never knew how."

"So you and Anna go alone?"

"Sometimes," Hannah said. "Sometimes we go together."

Davenport's head dropped as if it had just become too heavy to support. "Why do you and Anna go?" he asked, aggravation shaping his words. Hannah shrank back.

"She's getting antsy. We're going to lose her, again," Debbie warned Davenport, thinking *maybe more than you realize.*

"I don't know," breathed Hannah, a barely audible whisper. "It's pretty and no one hurts anyone there. It's where we go when it gets ugly."

"When what gets ugly?" asked Davenport.

"When *he* gets ugly," said Hannah, her anxiety and squirming heightening. Debbie started getting tense, as well.

What if it happens again? What if Hannah starts . . . dissolving again? What if she disappears completely?

Could she?

All hell would break loose. As ludicrous as it sounded, it was now a terrifying notion.

"Must we go there? You clearly know the answer to that. Why put her through this?" Debbie asked, irritated.

"To get the answers we need," Davenport shot back. "I don't see where she's *overly* distressed." He redirected his focus back to Hannah. "How do you get there?"

"I don't know. We just close our eyes and sing loud so we don't hear anything else. We make ourselves tiny. We make ourselves feel nothing and think of nothing but being there, and then we melt and disappear, and we go where we want to go. We just go away. I go and Anna meets me there," Hannah explained, and then added, "Used to."

"In Hannahwhere?" asked the detective.

Hannah nodded. "Hannahwhere is mine . . . Anna's is Annaplace."

"Of course it is!" Davenport threw his hands in the air, but he continued. "So, you would go to these different places together in your minds, but they are not the same place, yet you can be there together except that *now* Anna is only partially there and your mother can't go there at all . . . only *you* can come and go?" Davenport nearly shouted.

Hannah stared at the detective while mulling over the question. "Yeah, I think so," she meekly agreed and pressed tighter against Debbie. Davenport jumped up from the chair, startling everyone.

"Detective," Essie warned him. "Maybe you should take a coffee break or go for a walk?"

"I'm fine," he said in almost a growl. He sat back down, trying to compose himself, but he was clearly tense. "I just wish she'd tell me something useful." *Subsing nooseful.*

"Maybe she did. Maybe you'll see it once you calm down and take some time to consider it," Debbie suggested.

"This is either one of the most severe cases of dissociation I've ever seen, or our little girl here is far too cunning for her years, which is very unlikely," Essie said. She hesitated, and then continued. "We have to understand that in Hannah's reality this all makes sense, even if it's not clear to us. We have to respect her reality, detective, not force it into a shape that you can understand, because then it wouldn't be her reality any longer."

Davenport shot her a derisive glance. "You're making about as much sense as she is," he said. Then he turned his attention back to Hannah. "When you say Travis got ugly, did he get ugly with you, Anna, your mother, or all of you?"

Hannah curled even tighter inward, trying to burrow underneath Debbie's arm.

"Travis got ugly! He got ugly to Mom, ugly to me, ugly to Anna, but always ugly to Mom!" The tension built within Hannah, exuding from her coiled body. Debbie's own breathing increased in response.

"You should stop," Debbie warned Davenport. "What does this have to do with finding Anna?"

"Possibly everything," snapped the detective. "I'll tell you once she starts making sense."

Essie said nothing, but watched Hannah more intently, as if something intrigued her.

Is she fading again? Debbie wondered. Is that what she's seeing?

"What do you mean when you say *ugly*? Did he yell a lot, did he hit you?" asked the detective.

"Yells a lot, and hits. Not me. He hurt Anna. Hit Mom . . . he hurt Mom bad! Really bad!" Hannah squealed. She snaked an arm behind Debbie's back, pulling away from the turmoil, and pressed her face into the crook of Debbie's arm.

"How did he hurt Anna?" Davenport asked.

"That's enough!" Debbie snapped.

"Yes, that's enough," agreed Essie.

"Hannah, you went from your mom driving you and Anna home from your babysitter's to Travis being ugly to your mom, to Hannahwhere, and then to the dumpster? Did you go anywhere else in two years?" Davenport persisted, his voice rising. "You had to be somewhere, Hannah. Nothing else for two years?"

Aggravated, Davenport rubbed his face with open palms.

"Why does she remember everything, *everything*, but where she's been between then and now?" he asked.

"Trauma, most likely," Essie said. "I'm sure she's blocking it."

"Fine," he said. "But where has she been, and why the hell does it seem like she hasn't grown at all?"

"We've been through that. Trauma can do that, too, and there is no need causing her more," Essie insisted, her voice punitive and rigid.

"Trauma can erase two years?"

"Trauma can erase a life!" Essie said, trapping Davenport with a glare.

The detective paused and closed his eyes for a few seconds. When he reopened them, he focused on Hannah, tried softening his voice and asked almost beseechingly, "Hannah, can't you remember anything about where you've been or where Anna is?"

Hannah turned her head and the tears, utter grief, and rage that contorted her face hit Debbie like a punch to the heart.

"Travis got ugly and he hit Mom! He stinks when he's ugly! In the house, Anna yelled at Travis to stop hitting Mom."

"You were outside?" Davenport asked.

"I come in and he's hitting Mom, and Mom is bleeding bad and crying. We have to go to our secret place . . . and I tell Anna . . . and I sang, but I didn't sing loud enough, because . . . because I still can hear him hitting Mom," Hannah sobbed. "Mom is hurt and crying loud. Yelling. Yell-crying! I was scared. Even when I was in the secret place, I still couldn't sing. I couldn't go to Hannahwhere!"

"What is the secret place," Davenport asked.

"Mom says . . . Mom says . . . go to our secret spot under the house, no matter what," Hannah said, hitching and hiccupping badly. Debbie encased her in her arms and rocked, trying to hush her, to comfort her, but Hannah was beyond comfort and the words kept tumbling out.

"Me and Anna tried to go in there—in the secret place—but Travis came in because Anna couldn't hold onto the door. He says he's going to kill Anna and me 'cause we're no good and we don't ever shut up, and we didn't know where Mom's money is so we couldn't tell him." She hiccupped and paused to catch her breath. Tears and mucus soaked her face. "His face was red and he was mad and mean. He dragged Anna outside. He hurt her! He's a mean man! I went to Hannahwhere without singing, but Mom didn't come get me in the secret place, and Anna didn't come to Annaplace! I waited and she didn't come! She didn't come because I didn't sing!"

Hannah was nearly in convulsions. She forced out a sob that was more a shriek than a cry and tried to burrow behind Debbie.

Debbie rubbed Hannah's shoulder, trying unsuccessfully to reassure and console her. She kissed her head, and it started happening again. Hannah's weight lessened on Debbie's lap as her shoulders began dwindling. Debbie shifted Hannah and hugged her urgently, cradling her head to her neck, but Hannah's body became lighter and more insubstantial.

"You stay with us, Hannah," Debbie whispered into her hair. Her heart slammed like it would bust out of her chest. "Don't leave us."

"Well . . ." Davenport started.

Debbie glared at him and her anger swelled dangerously.

"It's done . . . no more questions. I mean it. She's been through enough!" Debbie said. She quelled a sudden urge to strike out at Davenport if he didn't leave. "Why don't you go and talk to Travis, he's clearly lying about not touching Anna. Interrogate him, not Hannah!"

Davenport didn't move, and it was obvious he had no intention of leaving.

"I'm not done," he said.

"Go!" snapped Debbie, much too loudly. She was feral in her need to protect the child. Her lack of control disappointed her, but the regret was quickly dismissed when reality slipped another notch and Hannah fully disappeared from sight.

Davenport lurched backwards as if evading a sword thrust. He jumped up and backpedaled around and behind his chair, his terrified eyes shifting back and forth from Debbie to where Hannah had been.

Reality buckled again, returning and becoming almost too intense for Debbie. She could feel nothing at all where Hannah had just been sitting, beneath her arms or on her lap. Debbie felt like she was coming apart at the seams, as if she was watching everything from outside reality.

Essie's hand flew to her mouth, distorting whatever words tried to escape her. "What . . . was . . . ?" She moved slowly around the bed, looking like she was ready to dart at any moment.

"Shit!" Debbie cried. She started to rise, but Hannah thankfully returned, her full weight pushing Debbie back onto the chair.

"What . . . what was that? What just happened?" asked Essie. She reached out to touch Hannah, rested her hand on Debbie, but immediately pulled back as if touching either of them might burn her. "Did . . . ?"

"I don't know," Debbie admitted, her tears coming against her will. "But if we don't stop, I don't think she'll be here much longer. Please, let's just give it a rest!"

"What the fuck was that?" Davenport asked, moving tentatively from behind the chair as if Debbie was holding a lapful of cobras. "Did she . . . ? No way! Christ!"

He looked uncertain and nearly frantic. Debbie feared he might want to pull his gun.

"Mind your words in front of the child, both of you!" reprimanded Essie, but Davenport was out the door and bolting down the hallway.

"Don't come back!" Debbie said, her words chasing the terrified detective. She settled back in the chair and held the child tightly to her breast. "Damn it," she said, seeing the blank stare on Hannah's face. "She's gone again."

"It did happen, right?" Essie asked, still dumbfounded and not looking very reassured. "How is this possible?" She probed Hannah's arm with her forefinger. An unusual light crept into her eyes, which concerned Debbie.

"Essie, remember . . . everything for the good of the child," Debbie said cautiously.

"My God!" Essie gasped, her eyes electric. She squeezed Debbie's arm firmly and asked, "Could you feel it happening?"

Debbie imagined what Essie must have been thinking and it didn't seem to be Hannah's wellbeing. "Essie, don't you dare make her a specimen!" Debbie said, her words straddling between a command and a plea.

"Don't be absurd," said Essie, gathering herself. She reached out and gently probed Hannah's leg and abdomen with her finger. "I've never seen *anything* like this before, but I've heard about it!"

"What?" Debbie asked warily.

"Dissociation. Not internal dissociation, but external! This is not inversion, but projection, the ultimate response to traumatic experience." Essie was breathless with excitement.

"You mean astral projection?"

"Yes, but so much more! I've read articles about it from the Monroe Institute and attended a couple consciousness seminars at Goddard. I thought most of it was a bunch of bunk or wishful thinking, but this . . . this . . ." She was a woman possessed. She stared at Debbie and took a deep breath. "This might confirm a hypothesis that astral projection is much more than out of body experience. This looks like full-body projection!"

Fumbling, Essie picked up her purse and carryall. She stared at Hannah and Debbie for a moment and said, "My God! What better way to disassociate from adversity than to disappear? You won't be going anywhere, will you?"

"I'm serious!" Debbie warned her.

"I have to do some major research. I'll be back *very* shortly, probably first thing in the morning," she told Debbie.

Debbie watched Essie dash out the doorway and wondered whom she would call first, Harvard, MIT, or *Time Magazine* . . . or *The National Enquirer?*

"God, what a nightmare," she muttered. And the worst of it was just starting!

"What are we going to do, Hannah?" she asked.

She watched the child's vacant stare, reflecting on the lack of control both she and Davenport had just exhibited. If Essie wanted to, she could have them either jobless or at least suspended. The temptation to take Hannah and run away was almost painful, but she wouldn't know where to start, and she knew how far she'd get if she did try. Resting her chin atop Hannah's head, Debbie stared into the dim corner of the room, wondering what her next move would be. If only they could disappear.

If only they could fly away . . .

CHAPTER 18

Hannahwhere

Anna walks towards Debbie through the floral fields. She is wearing an airy white sundress with blue flowery trim. Her long hair, blindingly white in the blazing sun, flows behind her in the breeze. Debbie looks at her more carefully, this time concentrating on her features. She is just as beautiful as Hannah is, and if not for the length of the hair, it would be nearly impossible to distinguish between them. Even the light spray of freckles on the bridge of her nose and high across her cheeks looks the same.

Anna's eyes glisten with happiness. She smiles radiantly and says, "Miss Coppertop! You came back!"

"Why wouldn't I come back?" asks Debbie.

"We were afraid you wouldn't like it here," Hannah says.

She is standing to Debbie's left, and was unseen until that moment. She is dressed in mint-green overall shorts and a yellow-and-white-striped shirt, all topped with a white dress hat with a mint-green ribbon. From her right hand, suspended by the stem, is a large bunch of grapes that are as golden as the summer sun. Hannah bites into one and it emits a snap much like a pinch of Bubble Wrap.

"Who wouldn't love this place?" Debbie asks.

"We were afraid you wouldn't like *us*," Hannah admits sheepishly.

"My God, honey, how could I not? You're sweethearts."

A smile transforms Hannah's face and she rushes forward to hug Debbie, who kneels down to accept her. Anna watches hopefully, but remains hesitant.

"Come here, sweetheart," Debbie says and extends an arm towards Anna. "There's plenty of me for both of you."

Anna steps forward into the shared embrace. From this vantage point, the differences between them are visible, but far from stark. Hannah, as small as she is, is easily two inches taller than Anna, and the bluish shadows around Anna's eyes are unmatched on her sister. Hannah is simply healthier looking than Anna, who is once again distressingly cold to the touch. Debbie rubs her hands briskly over the child's small shoulders and Anna leans into her, shivering.

"Anna, sweetie, why are you so cold?"

Even sandwiched between Hannah and Debbie, Anna inherits no warmth from them. Debbie inspects her hands, cupped behind the child's back. They retain the ache from Anna's cold body. She presses a palm against Anna's icy forehead and then rests it on her cheek. Is the cold she feels genuine, and if so, how can she tolerate it without suffering hypothermia?

Debbie sits down on a cushion of meadow flowers and motions for the two girls to follow suit. "Hannah. Is this all real?" she asks.

"This is Hannahwhere," Hannah says.

"Annaplace," Anna offers with a giggle that floats in the air like the ringing of a wind-chime. A small rabbit emerges from the flowers and settles near Anna. She lifts it, crosses her legs, and sets it into the bowl of her lap, where it rests in nose-wiggling contentment.

"Okay, but I'm not sleeping, am I? Because I can also see the hospital room, and I can see Hannah sitting on my lap, too. I can pull it in and out of focus if I want, like twisting the lens of a camera."

Hannah looks at Debbie, her expression clouded in thought. Brightening suddenly she says, "The zone!" repeating the description both Debbie and Essie have used.

"*Your* zone, but why am *I* here?" Debbie asks. She reaches out and pats the rabbit.

"You're there, just like me, but we're here, too. Just our . . ." Hannah hesitates, at a loss for words. "The *thinking us* is here."

"Spirit!" pipes in Anna, "Like Mom says."

"Yeah, spirit!" echoes Hannah with a nod. "Half here and half there. Just like I told you and Essie."

"How did I get here? Did you bring me?" Debbie shakes her head in bewilderment and wonder. She is flabbergasted by how willing she is to accept it all, but thinks *Isn't that how dreams are?*

"I don't know," says Hannah. "I asked you to come and you came because you wanted to come."

"How could you tell I wanted to?"

"You wouldn't come if you didn't want to, right?" Anna says. "Anyway, you're Miss Coppertop. You're supposed to come."

Debbie chuckles and rolls her eyes. "Of course, that makes total sense to me . . . not! When did you ask me to come?"

"I think-asked you in my head when I thought you were asleep," Hannah says.

"Mom says that people listen most and answer best when they're asleep," says Anna.

"Telepathy?" asks Debbie. Both girls stare at her, uncomprehending. "ESP."

Hannah shrugs.

"Okay," Anna says noncommittally. Neither girl has any clue what Debbie's talking about.

"Never mind," Debbie says. "What have you got there?" She points to the odd, golden grapes Hannah is holding.

"They're yummy. Want some?" Hannah offers.

Debbie pops one of the little orbs into her mouth and is stunned as the delightfully rich flavor stimulates her senses.

"Oh my, these are exquisite! What are they?"

"Alice's Butterscotch Chews," Hannah says.

"I've never tasted butterscotch that delicious. Where'd they come from? "

Hannah holds out her open palms as if cradling a wounded bird and another bunch of golden orbs materialize.

"How did you do that?" Debbie asks.

"I like butterscotch," Hannah explains.

"Of course you do," Debbie says and laughs. It's exactly the type of answer she expects.

"I like Reese's Cups," Anna says, displaying a similar bunch of light brown spheres.

"Those don't look like cups to me," Debbie says playfully.

"Neither do Reese's Cups," Anna says and giggles. The sound floats on the air like the tinkling of a wind chime.

"So you can think what you want into existence?" asks Debbie.

Both girls stare at her, again not comprehending.

"What's existence?" asks Anna.

"You think about what you want and it becomes real?"

"Yeah," says Hannah. She rubs at her nose, leaving a small butterscotch streak that makes Anna laugh.

Anna nods. "Mom said we can do almost anything. We just have to *know* we can do it."

"Believe," adds Hannah.

"I'm thinking your mother was quite a woman. You said she wasn't able to come here."

"She wasn't," says Anna.

"Didn't you ask your mother here, like you asked me?"

"Yup," says Hannah. "Lots. And we tried to bring stuff like these candies back to her, but we never could."

"So why am I able to come here like you?" Debbie asks.

Anna shrugs. "We knew you could. Maybe you're like us in a way Mom wasn't."

"No duh!" says Hannah, mocking Anna.

"Duh, yourself, mutt-face," Anna retorts.

"We have the same face, doofus," Hannah says. They stick their tongues out at each other.

"Has anyone else ever come here with you? Have you ever asked anyone else?"

"We only asked Mom and Linda, our babysitter. Mom couldn't, and Linda thought we were just being silly and making all of it up," says Hannah.

"I didn't want Linda to come here," says Anna.

"Why not?" asks Debbie.

"I didn't trust her," says Anna. "She was Mom's friend, but not that good of a one. This is our place and I was afraid she'd ruin it."

"What about me?" Debbie asks. "Why do you trust me?"

"I didn't, but Anna did," says Hannah.

"Fair enough," says Debbie, understanding, but feeling a mild sting nonetheless.

"But you're different," adds Hannah.

"How?"

"You made it here, like us," she says.

"I always knew Miss Coppertop would come, didn't I Hannah?" Anna says.

Hannah nods and says, "Anna's weird like that. She knew you were coming a long time ago."

"I don't understand," says Debbie.

"Me neither," Anna admits.

They both turn to Hannah, who says, "Don't look at me!"

"If I'm the only one to ever travel with you, this means I'm like you in a way others aren't," Debbie says. "And don't say *duh!*"

"Maybe," Hannah says. "See if you can make some candy, like we do,"

"I bet you can do it, too," Anna says, "If you believe you can."

"Go ahead," Hannah encourages.

"I don't think . . ."

"You can!" Anna insists.

Debbie opens her palms just as the girls did and wishes, but nothing happens. "I don't have the magic."

"You don't believe in yourself," Anna says.

The comment is so mature sounding coming from this pixie-sized girl, Debbie has to remind herself that Anna is only nine . . . or is it seven? Reality is so distorted it seems anything is possible. With that in mind, Debbie figures, *why not me?* She stares at her open hands and wishes again, focused and without thoughts of impossibilities.

"Ewwww!" says Anna.

"Oh, shi-oot. That didn't go so well," says Debbie.

Hannah wrinkles her nose and says, "That looks like dog poop!"

"I know what it looks like! It's supposed to be Godiva chocolate!" Debbie says.

"You should have wished for Godiva chocolate grapes," Anna suggests.

"Anna's Reese's kept melting in her hands, so she made Reese's grapes so she could hold it by the stem. I did it, too. My butterscotch chewies kept sticking to my teeth, so I made them softer. Plus I thought it was a cool idea."

"Very clever," says Debbie, depositing her unsightly creation into the flowers and wiping her hands on them. She figures since she's successfully conjured a convincing Godiva dog turd, then why not grapes? Debbie holds out her hands and concentrates on exactly what she wants. A small cluster of rich, brown globes appear in her hands and Hannah and Anna explode into cheers.

Is it witchcraft? Is it the power of the mind? Even the Bible claims that all things are possible with faith, and isn't that exactly what Hannah and Anna had said? Believe.

If so, how many people have been tormented or put to death as witches and conjurers only because they've discovered a new level of consciousness and have overcome the limitations of doubt?

She holds her opened hand palm up and concentrates on a can of Wilson tennis balls in her garage. A fuzzy yellow ball appears in her hand and falls into the flowers. A frigid can of Diet Sprite appears next.

Generic items, thinks Debbie. There's no guarantee that the tennis ball or soda are from my house. They could be anyone's. Did I create them?

Debbie closes her eyes and focuses. Her favorite Montefiore pen, her name engraved into the marble barrel, appears balanced on the palm of her right hand.

Did I truly conjure this from my desk, or did I create a duplicate, she wondered. Or am I just having a remarkably vivid dream? How deep can this consciousness run? By just believing, can I move mountains, divide a sea, or feed multitudes?

Jesus!

She smirks inwardly at her pun and concentrates on the brilliant green leaves of a tree far across the field. The leaves turn cherry red for an instant, and then change to a soft apricot color.

"Did you change my leaves?" she playfully accuses the girls.

"We don't like red," Hannah says soberly.

The reason hits her and it occurs to her that there isn't a touch of red anywhere in this Technicolor wonderland.

"Okay, no more red," Debbie promises. She looks to the sky and a perfect dove with baby-blue feathers materializes from thin air and perches on her shoulder. "What about the cardinal?" she asks. "It's red."

"We can't change that red," Anna says. "We didn't make it."

"Who did?" Debbie asks and both girls respond with a shrug.

The dove takes flight and Debbie wonders if it is real, or an illusion since it's the cerebral part of her that's present—the thinking her, as Hannah put it—and if this ability extends outside of *the zone,* beyond the boundaries of this arena.

A far more momentous revelation presents itself—one that explains the bold simplicity of Hannahwhere and Annaplace, with their bold primary colors, the vivid pastels, the minimalism of the shapes of the flowers, trees, and the glassy smoothness of the mountains. It also explains the harmless surroundings with its bunnies, kittens, butterflies . . . and the lack of anything red.

"You created this place!" Debbie says. "A place your energy—your spirit—can hide when things are bad. This, Hannahwhere and Annaplace, really exists!"

"I think we made it, but we had help," Hannah explains.

"I think it's your place, too," says Anna.

"No. I didn't create this. You did."

"Yeah, but there's stuff here that wasn't here before you came," Hannah says. "So you must've, too."

"What stuff?" asks Debbie.

"Like the big lake." Anna points to the immense blue body of water in the horizon. "And those tall, green trees. Those have to be yours because they look more real than ours do."

Debbie has to admit that the towering pines, spruces, oaks, and maples interlaced between the surrealistic blue, green, and golden leaved trees is a peculiar assortment.

"If you didn't have your own place, you couldn't be here, could you? It has to be a part of you for you to come here," Hannah says.

"How do you know that?" Debbie asks.

"Mom said so," continues Hannah. "I can be here by myself, but when Anna comes she brings her place and her stuff. We can have our places together in one place, but we need to bring our place with us when we come here so one of us can stay if one of us leaves."

Great, more puzzles, Debbie thinks, utterly confounded. "How did your mom know this if she couldn't travel here?" she asks. Both girls shrug.

There had to be a sound reason for Elizabeth Amiel to tell the girls this, especially since she had been unable to travel here herself. Is it a reference point so they don't get lost, or some kind of port of call?

"It was prettier here when Mom gave us ideas. It was kind of like her place, too," Anna says forlornly. "She'd show us pictures and we'd make them here, but we forgot a lot of it. There used to be better mountains and waterfalls and deers."

"Deer," Hannah corrects her and Anna sticks her tongue out again.

"So all of our places can mix together and become like one world?" asks Debbie.

"Anna likes the bunnies and hummingbirds. I like the butterflies and kitties and bumblebees," Hannah says.

"They don't have stingers," Anna says with a reassuring nod. "They're so cute!"

"So the waterfalls and deer are not here anymore, since you forgot what they look like?" Debbie asks. Both girls nod their agreement.

"Our deer looked dumb," says Anna.

"And the nice mountains," says Hannah. "I tried to make some, but they're yucky. Mom's mountains were from Switzerland, but we forgot most of how everything looked."

Hannah made these mountains? The idea is staggering.

"And when Anna goes back, the bunnies and hummingbirds go away?" Debbie asks.

"They used to . . ." Hannah starts.

"But I can't go back anymore," Anna finishes, troubled.

"Why?"

"Dunno," Anna says and Hannah shrugs.

"Did you forget where your body is?" Debbie asks, realizing how odd the question sounds.

"That's silly. You can't do that!" Hannah says.

"Why not?"

"Because the thinking you and the not-thinking you are both still you," says Hannah.

"Of course! Silly me! It's so clear! Okay, so the spirit and body stay connected is what you're saying?"

"Un-huh," agrees Anna, but she doesn't look all too sure.

"Okay, that would explain why I can still see the hospital room. Bear with me. I'm new at this. So Anna, what does the body or the physical you see?"

"I don't see nothing."

"Anything," corrects Hannah. Anna rolls her eyes.

"Does this have anything to do with why you're so cold?" Debbie asks.

"I don't know. I think so," Anna says.

"Can you remember where you were before you traveled over to Annaplace?" Debbie asks and Anna shakes her head.

"Well, we're just going to have to figure it out," Debbie says and looks into the horizon.

Hannah's mountains—sleek and smooth like gray waves—slope to the extents of their realm, seeming to fade off into oblivion. They are simple and almost cartoonish, as if drawn by a nine-year-old, Debbie thinks and a sudden understanding hits her. *The girls can only create to the limits of their experiences and their knowledge. They can't create what they don't know, and the same would have to be true with me.*

Debbie looks from Anna to Hannah and says, "What the heck, it's worth a try."

Maybe she doesn't know the Swiss Alps, but she's been fascinated by Mount Everest for most of her life. Initially drawn by the tragedy of 1996, she'd become enthralled by the great mountain and the fates of Scott Fischer, Rob Hall, and so many others. She read many of the survivors' accounts, from Jon Krakauer's excellent *Into Thin Air*, to Beck Weather's tragic yet hopeful *Left for Dead*, and mentally climbed Everest numerous times via words and pictures. Debbie had often visited Nepal in her dreams, flying and swooping over the majestic mountains as one can only do in such reveries.

. . . Or in Hannahwhere.

The thought gives her pause. She reflects on the dreams, and a tendril of dread begins slithering its way through her as the memory of her dreams start to solidify. Feeling nervous and uncomfortable, she pushes the images away and redirects her memory to the high-resolution still from Dave Breashear's IMAX movie that hangs in her spare bedroom. In her mind's eye she brings forth her best memory of the great mountain and the surrounding Himalayas, and as with the chocolate, she wills it into existence with her whole being. Far in the horizon, a majestic seam of black and gray granite sluggishly emerges behind the smaller hills, expanding across the skyline in jagged peaks and rising to breathtaking heights. Hannah,

Anna, and Debbie all stare in wonder as the monolithic mountain line forms. Whether cerebral or actual, it's exhilarating and hard to fathom.

"Will that do?" Debbie asks.

Transfixed, Anna and Hannah both nod their approval.

For Debbie, everything switches from surreal to beyond bizarre. *I have just created or recreated a mountain range, and not just any mountain range, but one with the tallest mountains on earth!* Again, she wonders: *is this a different realm or just undeniable proof that I'm as nutty as a PayDay bar? If this is real, shouldn't I be able to carry the ability back with me?*

Back to what? Reality? Isn't this a reality? For the sake of sanity she labels it surreal time. *SST: Surreal Standard Time.* You won't find that option on your computer time settings, kids.

More questions rush over her, pulling her in countless crosscurrent directions. It is a riptide of certainties and uncertainties . . . what-was-truth versus what-is-now-truth. If the ability to create was transferable from surreal time to real time, it could affect so many things.

Wouldn't somebody have done it by now? she wonders.

Surely, Hannah, Anna, and now Debbie, aren't the only ones ever to have this ability. Somewhere along the historic timeline, someone else must have. In modern times, any being having these abilities, whether good or evil, are fictitious or Hollywood creations: angels, demons, witches, genies, superheroes. Two hundred years ago, they would have been burned at the stake.

Does God even exist . . . or Satan? If a seven- or nine-year-old child can be a creator, any human can be a god or a devil. Is that the purpose behind religion, to keep this knowledge at bay through fear and control? *If you can do these things, then you are evil and must be destroyed?* These abilities could improve the world . . . or ruin it.

Hannah, Anna, and Debbie all jump to their feet as the ground starts trembling beneath them. A deep rumbling fills the air, thundering louder and deeper than any of them has ever heard or felt before, echoing and rolling over and through them. Frightened, they search the clear, blue skies.

"What is it?" Hannah yells through the noise.

"I don't know. An earthquake I think, though I've never been in one before," Debbie says and embraces the sisters and prays that a chasm doesn't open beneath them.

It continues for nearly a minute and just as quickly as it started, it is over, the colossal peals rumbling off into the distance in a recurring echo. Both girls look up to Debbie with wide and frightened eyes, yet still intrigued.

"Wow!" says Hannah, "That was cool!"

"I don't like it," says Anna.

"Oh, honey. I'm sure it was nothing," Debbie says, her words much nobler than her hopes. She scans the skyline and the distant mountains for the source of the tremors, and then it clicks.

"Oh my God!" Debbie blurts.

"What?" Anna and Hannah say in nervous unison.

"It was an earthquake," explains Debbie. "But a safe one. The rumbling came from the mountains! It took that long for the sound to reach us."

She smiles encouragingly at Anna and does the math in her head. Sounds travel around 767 mph—give or take on conditions—and it probably took two minutes for the sound to reach them. Therefore, it is approximately twenty-five miles to the mountains, which convinces Debbie of two things. Hannahwhere and Annaplace could be endless and must be real. Mach 1 might factor in Einstein's dreams, but never in her dreams . . . even subconsciously.

Maybe we are in a different universe or an alternate plane.

"If we were on the same plane as the hospital," Debbie says, "there is . . ."

She feels something change in the atmosphere. It's subtle and hard to put her finger on.

"We have to go," Hannah says, grabbing her hand. She's smiling, but there's a thread of urgency to her words.

"How?" asks Debbie.

"Just make yourself look at the hospital, and when you see it more than you see here, jump back there," says Hannah.

"Easy as that, huh?" asks Debbie, but she feels herself being catapulted into darkness.

"Hey!" Hannah says.

MONDAY
June 28, 2010

CHAPTER 19

Riverside, Massachusetts

The nurse nudged Debbie on the shoulder, and then again, more insistently. Debbie woke up, startled. Someone had turned the room lamps off and the nurse was little more than a haloed shadow. The only light in the room was the warm, golden glow from the hallway spilling around a mostly closed door, some hazy moonlight, and a smattering of cold white twinkles from distant city lights stealing in around the blinds.

"You're a sound sleeper," the nurse said good-naturedly. "You've both been there quite a while. I figured you'd want to put her into bed before you both cramp up."

"Too late for that," Debbie stammered, still disoriented. "Okay. I'll put her to bed."

"I can, if you'd like," offered the nurse.

"Nah, I've got her," Debbie said.

The nurse smiled and it looked somewhat ominous in the dark room. "Okay. Just buzz if you need anything," she said cheerily and left to continue her rounds.

She wondered if the nurse tapping her on the shoulder had prompted her return from Hannahwhere, if she had truly been there at all. The nurse called her a sound sleeper, which implied that it took a while to wake her. If that were the case, then maybe it was the light being turned off that had caused a sensory change and gotten her attention. It was a distressing thought, especially if the same were true with Hannah and Anna. Could a subtle change in the environment be more effective than a physical touch, which seemed to her to have gone unnoticed? Wouldn't the ability to block out the physical be the perfect escapism, especially when avoiding something unpleasant? Yet wouldn't it also open an avenue for a tormenter to act out his or her heart's desire without the victim even being aware? The implications had Debbie feeling as if she was in a vortex.

"Hold on, girl," Debbie instructed herself softly.

Regaining her equilibrium, she sighed deeply. Everything was so confusing. She was certain she could still taste the candy. *Real or not, I have to remember what brand Hannah said they were . . . they were succulent.* Debbie was hungry. There was a churning in her stomach, but it was the wee hours of the morning and she would have to wait until breakfast.

She gave the cord for the wall-mounted light over the bed a sound tug and the light flickered on with a barely audible buzz. Her left leg was asleep from Hannah's weight on her lap and numbness traveled from her right buttock to her foot. She shifted and the heat of her blood rushed through her leg. Hannah moved on her lap, sending electrical surges through the awakening nerves in her leg. Debbie looked down to see her staring back with startlingly alert eyes. She was so light-skinned that she nearly glowed. She brushed a few errant strands of hair away from Hannah's face.

"Well, hello there," Debbie said.

"Hi," Hannah replied in a voice as light and sweet as cotton candy. She rose to her knees, wrapped her arms around Debbie's neck, and hugged her cheek-to-cheek with a fervency that nearly relocated vertebrae. A great relief washed over Debbie that Hannah didn't hold her responsible for Davenport's poor behavior. Debbie returned the hug, wanting to bring her somewhere free of all the trauma and madness that only promised to escalate in the near future. Debbie backlit her phone display and was surprised to see it was only 12:22 a.m. It felt like three o'clock in the morning.

Hannah rested her head on Debbie's shoulder for a few moments and then pulled back. She put her palms to Debbie's cheeks as if to hold her head still and looked her eye to eye, as she had earlier.

"When Essie and the detective were here, you said *shit* two times," Hannah told her.

"I did?" Debbie asked and Hannah nodded with such sincere conviction that Debbie had to laugh. "Okay. But now you said it, too." She smiled and affectionately poked the tip of Hannah's nose.

"It's okay. Mom says it's better to spit it out than keep a mouthful of it."

"Sounds like good advice to me." Debbie laughed again and hugged Hannah. "You're delightful. I just want to keep you."

Hannah looked at Debbie again, a sad, hopeful question in her eyes. She put her forehead against Debbie's, looked into her eyes and asked, "Can I keep you, too?"

She pushed Hannah's hair behind her ears, completely taken by how large and stunningly soulful her eyes were. At that moment, Debbie understood that she would probably do anything to protect this little girl . . . this little wonder. Debbie smiled and said, "I think that would be the best thing that could ever happen to me."

The probability was that Hannah and Debbie would never see each other again after the case closed, and the reality of that thought hit Debbie with startling force. The ache and longing that built in her chest wasn't logical—she'd only known Hannah for days—but it was acute, undeniable, and rooted deeply inside her. It was as real as the child before her, and as real as the fact she would never biologically have her own. Despite rationality, Debbie would be willing to do whatever was required to make Hannah legally hers . . . and hopefully Anna. She would mortgage the equity on her home, or even change careers, if that was what it took. The thought of letting Hannah and Anna out of her life, even after such a short period, was unbearable and profane. Especially knowing what she now knew, and what would likely happen to the girls if the wrong people found out.

"So, Sweetie. Was it a dream or were we really in Hannahwhere with Anna?" Debbie asked, still eye-to-eye with Hannah.

She was self-conscious about the question and half-expected Hannah to say, *don't be so silly, you big, dumb adult. Hannahwhere is only in my imagination.* Instead, Hannah offered her a demure smile that seemed too wise for her age. She reached down into the crease of the chair, retrieved something and bopped Debbie lightly on the forehead with it.

A tennis ball!

Hannah reached down again and returned with Debbie's Montefiore pen. Debbie slowly accepted the items from Hannah.

The ball was unspectacular and could be any Wilson #4, but the pen had her name engraved in fine-filled gold along its length. This pen had been a gift from Kenny when she graduated college. She kept it in the top drawer of her desk at home. There was no other pen like it, so that meant transference. She had summoned it. Hannahwhere and Annaplace weren't just cerebral . . . they had to be physical, too.

Un-fucking-believable! Debbie, ol' girl, life as you have known it has just taken a U-turn . . .

Unless . . .

Could she have created an exact duplicate? If the pen was the actual one from her desk drawer, then the climbers on Mount Everest must have had an interesting day. The idea that she could relocate Mount Everest was preposterous, but so wasn't the idea that she could transport or create a duplicate pen from thin air.

Flummoxed, Debbie let her head fall back against the chair and she let out a frustrated groan. She looked at Hannah, who looked back at her with a knowing, smug smile.

"Are you enjoying my confusion?" Debbie asked her. Hannah's smile expanded into a toothy grin that transformed her back into the nine-year-old girl.

Hannah and Anna had proved one concept that would set many in the psychological field on their toes. In situations of severe trauma and abuse, sufferers usually had a tendency to do one of two things. They could withdraw and hide within themselves, making their bodies both a haven *and* a prison, or they could do the opposite and dissociate.

Or, as Debbie had now experienced, *they could do both,* as Hannah and Anna had done.

When trouble arose, Hannah and Anna had trained themselves to 'leave' the questionable sanctuary of their physical consciousness— and the source of their torment—by mentally projecting outward and *going away* to another place in their mind. The difference with Hannah and Anna was that they had found a way to project or create physical items like the pen and the tennis ball, and they had somehow taught the ability to Debbie, or shared it with her.

What if the physical self could project, too?

The notion defied logic, yet there was the tennis ball, the pen, and most of all Hannah twice disappearing from Debbie's lap. What more proof did she need?

"I drank your soda," Hannah admitted.

Debbie looked at her with increased appreciation. "That's okay, you clever little girl. You brought me proof. You knew I'd be a doubting Thomas, didn't you?"

"Who?" Hannah's brow furrowed.

"You knew I'd have a hard time believing everything that happened in Hannahwhere once we got back here."

"You had a hard time believing it when we were there," Hannah said, again impressing Debbie with her unusually mature logic. "Anna made me bring the ball and I thought you'd want your pen back. Mom told us not to bring things out of our places, but we knew we had to or you wouldn't believe it, or think it was a dream."

"Why not bring things out?" asked Debbie. "It seems to me you could bring back such wonderful things." She again thought about the little boy hiding in the shower. *Had Hannah brought a playmate back?*

"Well, we could sometimes bring things out, but only to places where we're safe and where no one can see us. Usually only in our bedroom. Mom said it would mess up people's heads too much."

Debbie thought about blue doves, stingerless bumblebees, and metallic mangoes, and was inclined to agree. "Your mom was right."

"And Mom said we can never-ever-ever bring things in with us," Hannah said. She sat down and folded her legs beneath her.

"Why never-ever-ever bring anything in? I brought things in, like the soda and the pen," Debbie said. "And what about our clothing?"

Hannah shrugged. "Because they might never come back, like Schweizer," she said.

"Wait. Who's Schweizer?"

"He was our cat."

"Was? What happened to Schweizer?"

Discomforted by the question, Hannah started fidgeting. She said, "One time I brought him to Hannahwhere because I thought he'd like to play there, but I didn't bring him back with me. I thought he'd be okay until I came back, but I never could find him. Mom thought that when we come back from our places, they aren't there anymore. They, like, disappear. That's why Mom thought we should have our own places, like Hannahwhere and Annaplace, so if someone leaves, the other person doesn't disappear like Schweizer."

Debbie had a sinking feeling in her stomach and her world stuttered a little. "You never found Schweizer?"

Hannah shook her head.

"But you brought me there with you!"

"No, you followed me," Hannah said with a defensive edge to her voice. "And it was just the thinking you that was there."

This didn't put Debbie at ease. She pictured her spirit floating aimlessly through a giant, empty void, or simply ceasing to exist. Would she have been found dead in this chair, or would she have become a soulless vessel, existing for years on life support in a blank-eyed coma? It was a painful concept.

"My spirit?" asked Debbie. "What if you had forgotten me there?"

Hannah wrinkled her nose at the question.

"Don't make bunny faces at me!" Debbie said, tapering back the dread within her.

Hannah giggled and said, "I wouldn't forget you. I would have brought you back."

"You would have? What do you mean *would have*?" Debbie protested.

"I would have, but you came back before me," Hannah said.

"I did? I came back alone?"

Hannah nodded. "Yeah, I said we had to go, but you were already leaving."

"How'd I go by myself? I had no idea what I was doing there. I've never done this before!"

"We always go back to our . . . body-self. Maybe you do, too. You made your own place, like your own Hannahwhere. You should probably name your place like Mom says, so it's only yours. It's easier to think about when you want to go again. It helps if you have a song to sing, too, so noises and other stuff don't bother you." She nodded with wide-eyed conviction, trying to stress the importance of her words. "Or if you're ascaired."

Debbie let it sink in. It was a lot to process, almost too much, and as terrifying as it was, it was exhilarating. This peanut-sized girl had shown her the gift of magic and had introduced her to the power of the gods. Debbie resisted the urge to retreat, which was her normal reaction when regarding her own issues. She was like a ninja when defending children, but not so when she felt herself at risk. *When things get crazy, go the other way.*

Take it slow and easy and look for the sanity. It worked for the children.

"Hannah?" Debbie said.

"Huh?" She was starting to doze.

"A while ago you said you had to bring me into Hannahwhere to make me believe. Why is it so important I believe?"

"Because we don't know how to make Anna not stuck, and now she's getting sick."

Debbie had seen it and felt it, the intense cold and the darkening around Anna's eyes, but it hadn't hit home until Hannah said it.

"I think Mom would know what to do," she said, looking at Debbie with teary eyes. "But Travis killed Mom."

Debbie pulled her closer, trying to comfort her. "But why me, Hannah? Why not Essie or Detective Davenport? Why do you think I can help you and Anna?"

"Because you're supposed to," Hannah said, sniffing and wiping absently at her eyes and nose. "You're nicer than all the other people, and you let me think-talk to you. They don't."

"What other people?"

"Everyone," Hannah said.

"Do they know when you try to think-talk to them?" Debbie noticed new bandages on Hannah's feet and wondered when they were changed.

"No one ever answers except for you and once a really scary guy, but I ran away from him." Hannah nodded reassuringly. "Mom said we shouldn't trust people who open their ears and their minds unless they open their hearts, too. When someone opens their heart, you can see what's inside. You can trust those people. The scary man didn't open his heart."

"Your mom was a smart lady. I'm glad you decided to trust me," Debbie said. Again, the little boy came to mind. "Hannah, do you and Anna have anyone else to play with there? Do you have any little friends about your age?"

Hannah locked Debbie with a doleful stare. "You're the only person who ever went with us. You're not going to take me and Anna away from each other, are you?"

Overwhelmed by the admission of her biggest fear, Hannah let the floodgates open and her sniffles transformed into heart-wrenching sobs. Debbie could only hold her and try to comfort her. She reprimanded herself for forgetting that Hannah was still a very young and enormously vulnerable child, and for letting Hannah's mature manner slant her view. She held Hannah's head to her shoulder.

"Hannah. Honey. I will do everything I can to help you and Anna. I mean it with all of my heart."

Debbie felt lost. She hadn't recognized the magnitude of Anna's declining health, and significance of her inability to return to her physical self. This meant only Anna's spirit—or the *thinking* her, as Hannah would say—was there, or she would be able to come and go at will. Had Anna's spirit been trapped in Annaplace for two years? If so . . . where was her body? How was she staying alive and why was her health waning now? She would need nutrition. Hannah ate ravenously whenever she returned, so shouldn't Anna's spirit-self be aware of the surroundings around her physical-self, just as Hannah was, being half here and half there? How was Anna receiving sustenance?

Is she on life support somewhere?

The thought rocked Debbie. If Anna's mind was active but her body not, would it inhibit her ability to return? Any hospital would have to report if an adorable little Jane Doe showed up in a stupor or a coma. Hannah became national news immediately and she couldn't imagine it being any different with Anna.

Why was she always so cold to the touch?

"Hannah, do you know why Anna's so cold?" Debbie asked. "Has she said anything to you?"

"I don't know," Hannah said sleepily. "She said it hurts, like being in the snow or in really cold water. We think the body-Anna is somewhere cold and the thinking Anna can feel it, but we don't know where."

"Honey, how long has Anna been there like that?" she asked.

"Since Mom died. She's always there when I go." Hannah settled her head down. She was tired and emotionally exhausted. Feeling guilty, Debbie let her fall asleep.

It hurts, Debbie thought. *Like being in the snow or in really cold water.* Debbie couldn't tolerate standing in the cold water at Hampton Beach for more than five minutes. It was agonizing! *Two years! Dear God! That would feel like an eternity! How could she maintain her sanity?*

The notion that Anna's physical-self was somewhere that cold for that long wasn't feasible. Fatality from hypothermia usually set in after only fifteen minutes in water at freezing temperature, and an hour at fifty degrees. When the core body temperature dropped below ninety-five hypothermia occurred, and Anna was much colder than that—so cold that touching her was uncomfortable.

Could she be in a suspended cryogenic state? It was science fiction, as most aspects of Debbie's life seemed lately, but was it possible?

Of course it was, thought Debbie. The question lately was *what wasn't possible?*

If so, who could? Cryogenics was a financial monstrosity that only the extremely wealthy or funded institutions could afford. Besides, who would do that to a seven-year-old girl? That outlandish train of thought was one Debbie would rather not ride.

If, as Hannah had suggested, the spirit always returned to the body, the most rational reason Anna could not get back to her physical-self would be if . . .

"Oh my God," Debbie gasped. The chill that rushed over her was immense. How horrifying! Nevertheless, it was the only logical concept—logical, as she now knew it.

What would happen if Anna's physical-self died while her spirit-self was in Annaplace?

Doesn't the spirit leave when the vessel dies? That's why it's called the afterlife. Believing the spirit persisted eternally after the body died was the driving force behind most religions. What if her physical self died when her spirit was gone? It surely couldn't return, could it? Why would it? If her ability to transition between the spiritual and physical self were in any way like Hannah's, then her physical body would be spiritless and totally vulnerable.

Even to the cold? Could frigidity be associated with a corpse's transition from body temperature to room temperature? But Anna was seriously sub-room temperature. Once the body died, was the spirit still sympathetic to its physical circumstances? Had Travis, the monstrous bastard, locked her in a freezer after he abducted her? Maybe it was something more obscure. Perhaps the spirit went through some kind of withdrawal or reaction if the body died while the spirit was mobile.

Debbie listened to Hannah's breathing, now deep and even in sleep, but every so often succumbing to an emotional hitch. Who could ever guess the awe-inspiring potential within this little girl? And yet, how defenseless her innocence had made her. Hannah and Anna's world was so tenuous that a single malicious heart could crumble their universe. They did not defend themselves because they did not understand the opposite course. Attack and retaliation were not in their vocabulary. Purity didn't think about manipulation, advantages, or how to convert another person's misfortune into personal gain. It didn't relate with evil. It didn't fit on the same tracks. It didn't know the math.

In a few short days, Hannah and Anna had introduced Debbie to experiences and feelings that she had spent years believing that she could and would never know. They were powerful feelings with sharp barbs that sunk in easily and nested deeply. Once hooked, there was no removing them without a lot of pain and damage. As uncanny, frightening, and frantic as her life had become since Hannah and Anna had stepped into it, Debbie couldn't turn her back on them no matter the cost. Hannah and Anna had suffered so much already in their short lives. They had been victims for too long and Debbie was ashamed, but not too proud to admit that they would fill a very prominent void in her life.

Debbie tried to sleep but after the better part of an hour, the parade of thoughts and scenarios continued their relentless march through her head. Anna's dilemma had her heartsick and nearly desperate. Every minute she sat around doing nothing was another minute longer that poor child had to suffer, which was unacceptable. Of course, all the worrying might be for naught, depending on what Essie and Davenport decided to do with what they had learned that day. Debbie was not overly concerned about Essie. Her professional oath as a clinician, and her compassion as a mother should keep the woman sensible, but she knew very little about Davenport and trusted him even less. Her past had taught her that if she put her faith in the good intentions of the common man, she usually did all right . . . unless they had something to gain, and then she was screwed. Time was priceless.

Debbie wiggled forward to the lip of the seat and rose. She set Hannah onto the bed and pulled the sheet and light blanket up to her shoulders.

She would still have to check in at work and do a lot of catching up. As much as she disliked leaving Hannah, other children needed her.

"You'll come back?" Hannah asked, surprising Debbie.

"A pack of wolves couldn't keep me away," Debbie said. She hugged Hannah tightly, again savoring the smell of her hair. "I have some work I need to do so I have to go for a little while. I will be back in the morning when I'm finished."

Hannah met her gaze, and the look of fear and doubt in her eyes broke Debbie's heart. Debbie pulled a piece of paper from her laptop bag and wrote her phone number in large script.

"You know how to use the phone, right?" she asked.

Hannah gave her an incredulous look and said, "Duh!"

"Okay," Debbie said with a laugh, wanting to cheer the little display of defiance. It felt like a sign that there might be a normal, healthy kid hiding in there. "If you need me for any reason, call me at this number. If someone starts asking you questions that make you uncomfortable, just tell them that you need to call your caseworker and you don't want to answer them until I'm here. Okay?"

Hannah nodded solemnly.

"I'll see you in the morning," Debbie kissed her on the forehead, unable to avoid Hannah's look of mistrust and the profound hopefulness hiding beneath it.

CHAPTER 20

Debbie arrived home at 2 a.m. The frantic pace with which Hannah and Anna's case kept changing and the ever-increasing intensity of this new reality she was learning had her deeply concerned about Hannah's and Anna's well-being . . . and her own. Was her sanity at risk? Debbie was unsure of the answer, but curling up in fear would benefit no one. She needed to learn more about the Amiel twins.

She freed her laptop from its bag and set it on her desk. As it booted up, Dr. Hook crooned the advantages of *Sharing the Night Together* from the radio in her bedroom. Debbie entered her password and her screen switched to a high-resolution background of a bald eagle in noble flight high above mountain peaks of granite and snow. Ranks of icons blossomed on the right side of her screen as if tempting the great bird. Debbie positioned her pointer atop the Outlook icon, hesitated, and then clicked on the Google Earth icon that neighbored it. Email would wait.

Debbie typed in *Elm Creek, Nebraska*, the town where Hannah and Anna had lived. The Google globe rotated, centered, and zoomed in on a small square of a town around two hundred miles west of Omaha. Nestled just east of the intersection of Route 30 and 183, Elm Creek was a small community amidst a sea of green farmland. She zoomed in on the furrowed pastures, dirt access ways, and shining silver grain silos, and moved along the town's streets with no certainty of what she was looking for. She was taken by just how small Elm Creek was amongst all the farmland.

In another browser window, she accessed *www.city-data.com*, typed in *Elm Creek, Nebraska*, and waited for the screen to populate with the facts. Predominantly white with a population of less than nine hundred, but still considered a city, Elm Creek ranked lower in most medians state and countrywide: income, home value, rent rates, and unemployment. Elm Creek High School had had a graduating class of fewer than thirty in 2009.

Their senior proms must be epic, Debbie mused.

Despite all the farmland, manufacturing beat out agriculture twenty-nine percent to twelve percent as the largest industry. Debbie couldn't recall what Elizabeth did for work, if she had ever known. She pulled Hannah's file from her bag and shuffled through the papers. Elizabeth Amiel had been head teller at Firstier Bank . . . respectable enough.

How about our friend Travis? Debbie wondered. At the time of his arrest, Travis had been collecting disability for seven months, allegedly from falling off a loading dock. Prior to that, he had worked for the City of Kearney Public Works Department. He was relieved of his duties for drinking on the job and physically assaulting his supervisor, who had not filed charges.

Debbie returned to the web page and scrolled to the *climate* display. She had always envisioned Nebraska being in a warmer climate than Massachusetts, believing it was southwest, but looking at the USA map showed it was more west than south. It was warmer, but not by much. According to the webpage she was on, it was sixty-nine degrees in Elm Creek, at 1:17 a.m. Central Standard Time. The local weather gadget on the toolbar read currently sixty-four degrees in Riverside, only a five-degree difference.

If Anna's spirit-self *was* sympathetic to her physical-self, as Debbie had earlier surmised, it wasn't cold enough in the Elm Creek area to justify her frigid temperature. Even the bodies of water, if she had fallen in, although cold, would be warmer than the frosty aura Anna gave off.

Then, why is she still so cold? Why hadn't she cast it off? Unless she had in fact died and her spirit-self was sympathetic to the condition of her physical-self *at the time of her death.* Would a freezer go unchecked for two years? She supposed it was possible. Maybe if it was a personal freezer in someone's home . . . maybe somebody who lived alone.

Debbie rubbed her head vigorously, releasing her pent up aggravation and leaving her hair chaotic and snapping with static. She grabbed the case papers, quickly scanning and shuffling them

until she found the photocopied *Lincoln Journal Star* article dated
March 11, 2008.

ELM CREEK WOMAN, 28, BRUTALLY STABBED TO DEATH
IN HOME.

She looked at the climate graph on her laptop. The average daily
temperature for Elm Creek in March was thirty-four degrees, and
probably a lot lower at night. If Anna's physical-self died while her
spirit-self was in Annaplace, she would have died shortly—maybe
days—after her mother was murdered, or she certainly would have
turned up somewhere. The wind blew hard and the cold bit deep
in March. The type of cold that emanated from Anna's spirit-self. It
added up . . . well, it did in her new definition of rationality.

She was wound up and felt she had discovered something vital,
but the excitement dwindled with the awareness that the same two
questions remained. *Where was Anna's physical-self and, what could be
done about her entrapment in Annaplace?* Nothing had been answered.

Had anything like this ever happened before, people appearing
and disappearing, and switching between realms? There were
situations with similar manifestations, like ghost sightings, alien
abductions, and angel visitations. There were stories about people
going into Faerie, of spirit walkers, soul travelers, and astral
projection. What Hannah, Anna—and now Debbie—did, could
fit into explanations for all the above. Of course, anyone claiming
to experience or witness any of it was looked at skeptically or just
deemed crazy.

Yet it went even further. The world Hannah and Anna had
introduced Debbie to had creation, teleportation, and even hints
of telekinesis. Hannah and Anna were adolescents who operated
on what they knew and had learned, but if someone intellectually
advanced learned of or attained these abilities, would there be
limits?

She hoped Essie and Davenport would choose human
compassion over selfishness or the lure of notoriety or power
someone could receive for a breakthrough like this. She drummed
up images of news vans and reporters from every medical research
facility to every tabloid clogging the hallways and parking lots.
She envisioned Davenport intimidating Hannah, trying for a
repeat performance—or even better—Hannah totally blinking out

of existence. Government agencies would want this knowledge. What army could stand against a military force that could spy on the enemy anywhere, and appear and disappear at will? Nothing would be sacred and no place would be safe.

What would they do with Hannah and Anna? This terrified Debbie the most. It would be more shattering for Hannah and Anna than their lives had already been . . . and for Debbie as well. Where would they stop, if they stopped at all?

On the other hand, maybe nobody detrimental would believe it or hold a level of skepticism that would keep them at bay. It was highly implausible—which made it tabloid-worthy—and that was usually where it ended.

It's down to this, Debbie told herself. I have an indefinite amount of time to help a child who may not be alive, entrapped in a place that exists on some bizarre plane that I know next to nothing about. Fucking brilliant!

Depressed, Debbie closed the lid to her laptop and maneuvered her head around, wincing as her neck released an uprising of snaps and cracks. She had been awake for nearly twenty-four hours and her perception was beginning to swim. She picked up the nearest pile of file folders, walked into her bedroom, and dropped them onto her bedside table. She stripped out of her clothes, quickly wrapped in her robe, and headed into the bathroom for a shower. She emerged twenty minutes later with her wet hair in a single braid and wearing pajama bottoms and a spaghetti strap shirt over her bra.

She was exhausted, and knew she wouldn't find answers or be any good to anyone without sleep. She set her clock for 6:30 a.m. as Tina Turner asked *What's Love Got to Do with It?*

She climbed into bed and wearily glanced at the top case file folder. She remembered the case. Jamison Mayo was an eleven-year-old Latino boy from Lawrence, Massachusetts, his father unknown and mother deceased from AIDS. Jamison had lived in three different cities and been removed from five foster homes in seven years. He'd been kicked out of two schools for fighting, and was arrested on four different counts, twice for shoplifting, once for assault with intent (switchblade), and once for sexual assault. Citizen of the Year was not in Jamison's cards.

Have you seen Anna in your travels, Jamie? Debbie wondered. She hoped not. Her thoughts detoured to Anna and she promptly forgot Jamison.

Where do I look for Anna?

Start with the three people present when Anna was taken: Hannah, Anna, and Travis Ulrich. According to Davenport, Ulrich, who was locked up in some Nebraska prison, swore he hadn't harmed Anna, though in Hannah's account he seized Anna and was none too friendly in the process. Hannah had no more of an idea where Anna was than Debbie did, and Anna was unreachable because . . .

Because why?

Death of the physical Anna was the only thing that made sense. This would make the spirit Anna who was stuck in Annaplace her ghost.

This is why ghosts are called spirits, you dumb-shit, Debbie thought scornfully.

Did this mean that the part of her and Hannah that roamed around Hannahwhere and Annaplace was their ghosts? Some describe death as the separation of body from spirit. Was it that simple? The concept was exhilarating yet disturbing.

If Anna was dead, why couldn't she locate her body? Spirits were known to drift around their bodies, or their place of death. If the spirit wasn't with the body when death occurred, could they lose each other? Debbie thought about her consciousness switching between the hospital and Hannahwhere. Wouldn't the spirit remember where the connection was broken? *What if the body was moved after death?*

She needed to talk to Anna. She wondered if she could contact her. She had summoned a pen between realms, created a tennis ball, a blue dove, Mount Everest, and even some Godiva grapes for crying out loud—now *that* was a feat. Couldn't she just *will* herself over to Annaplace, or to where Anna's physical self was, for that matter?

How should she go about it? Could she wiggle her nose *twinkle-twinkle-twink* and fly there?

No.

How about if she crossed her arms, nodded her head, and *sproinggg?*

No go.

That ruled out sitcom magic.

Lying on her back, Debbie centered herself on her bed and closed her eyes. She pictured Hannahwhere in her mind, with its endless flowers, trees, and butterscotch and peanut butter cup grapes. She opened her eyes and stared at her ceiling.

You have to know you can, Anna's voice rang in her memory, but that wasn't the problem. She *knew* she could because she had been there. She had held both Hannah and Anna there, and had rolled in the flowers, flew over the fields and created things.

Created . . . was that it? Hannah had said she should name her place . . . familiarize it so it was only hers. Was that the trick? It sure worked for Hannah.

So what do I call it? Debbieville? Debtropolis? Deblantis? They all sounded so bad she was actually embarrassed. Hannahwhere and Annaplace were simple, smooth, and pretty. *Deborahtopia? Debtopia?* Better, but not great.

She closed her eyes, parked the name *Debtropolis* in the forefront of her mind and thought of falling, but went nowhere. She pictured Godiva chocolate grape vines with *her* Mount Everest in the background, and flocks of blue doves flying . . .

Flying!

Isn't that what she, Hannah, and Anna did . . . and the child in her visions? She imagined soaring over the fields and she could almost feel it; she was so close—just on the edge. What else did Hannah and Anna do?

They sang.

Okay, sing what? Debbie wondered. It was too obvious. So Debbie sang . . .

I want to fly like an eagle
To the sea,
Fly like an eagle
Let my spirit carry me . . .

The bed evaporated from beneath her, and she was hurtled into a deep well of darkness, her senses reeling and quickly shifting into a brutal bout of vertigo. It felt as if she were swinging by her legs in gigantic, sweeping arcs . . . around and around . . . and finally released. She rocketed at light speed out of the darkness into dynamic bursts of color and the roar of wind in her ears. Flashes of brilliant petals blurred by and glimpses of the fields. Her speed increased as she careered out of control toward some unknown limbo, some never-place, unable to stop or control her direction or even focus on returning home. She collapsed into a blind panic, lashing out as her sense of falling into nothingness intensified. She was lost and desperate and knew she would tumble around forever in a vacuum. Flailing frantically she reached out for anything to slow her down.

Something cold touched her hand and everything stopped.

Debbie lies in the floral field, her heart is slamming so fiercely within her chest that she fears it may explode. Anna is kneeling beside her, her arctic hands clenching Debbie's panicked fingers. Debbie's unsure and frightened eyes dart wildly about and then center on Anna.

"Are you okay, Miss Coppertop?" Anna asks, concerned.

"Oh my God! I'm terrified!" Debbie says.

She sits up, the flowers that were beneath her unfolding with a cellophane hiss until they are upright and undamaged. She looks around, doubting the authenticity of her surroundings. It is the same place—or close to the same place—as before, but there are some differences. The vibrant colored Disneyesque flowers and trees and the smooth landscapes of Hannahwhere are still present and forefront to Debbie's monolithic mountain line; however, the peculiar trees of Hannah and Anna's realms are now interspersed by even more towering spruces and pines than before. To their right lies the same huge body of water, over which hawks and other birds of countless species swoop and dart about. The mirror-like surface of the water is wistful and magnetic to Debbie. As she gazes across the lake's surface, a majestic eagle breaks over the trees and issues a shriek as if in greeting. The beauty of the bird draws forth a feeling of contentment within Debbie so powerful that she pulls Anna into an embrace and holds her as if her life depends on it, and she nearly believes it does.

"Am I ever glad to see you, beautiful girl! I've never been so frightened in my life!" Debbie says.

Anna's flesh is downright numbing and Debbie reprimands herself for not wearing something heavier than a spaghetti-strap shirt and bra, and then reprimands herself again for her selfishness.

The poor child exists this way! Is she smaller than the last time I was here? Debbie wonders. Does the skin around her eyes seem darker, like bruises?

Debbie holds Anna tighter, no longer for comfort, but now hoping to draw some of the damned iciness out of her. Anna accepts the hug, curling slightly into Debbie, and then steps away from her. As if in defiance of her condition, Anna is wearing a Hawaiian sundress with an orange, green, and yellow floral pattern on a blue background.

"Why aren't you wearing a coat?" Debbie asks. "You're freezing!"

"Nah, a coat just keeps the cold inside me," Anna says dismissively. There is an odd logic to Anna's comment. Her body is the source of the cold. "Why are you scared?"

"I didn't know where I was. I tried to come here by myself, but everything started moving too fast and got confusing. The more I tried to fight it, the worse it got."

"I wouldn't fight it next time," Anna says.

Debbie stares at her for a few seconds and chuckles. "You are certainly Hannah's sister."

"Ya think?"

"Yes, and I think you saved my life. How did you know I needed help?"

"I didn't. I was sitting in the flowers playing with a rabbit, then you were here and then you started to go away. I didn't want you to go away, so I tried to hold you here. When I did, you grabbed my hand."

"Well, I'm glad you did, I don't know what would have happened," Debbie says. "I don't know if I could have made it here or back."

"But you *were* here all by yourself, before you started to go again," Anna reassures her. "And you're a grown-up, too!"

"Why would that matter?" asks Debbie.

"Mom said that grown-ups probably can't come here. Maybe because when they get old they don't believe in magic anymore, or maybe they never did."

"Well, I'm a believer now," says Debbie.

"And here you are," Anna said with a smile.

Debbie wonders if Elizabeth Amiel's observation is true. Considering the amount of devastation and grief someone could cause with this kind of power, an adult losing their belief in magic would be to humankind's advantage. It's not Debbie's nature to harm people. She naturally thinks of the good this ability might create—curing the sick, feeding the poor, diverting tragedies. The sad truth is that it would not happen. It would birth mania. It would be perverted by fear or greed. Those who fear it would worship it or crucify it, and the greedy would either destroy it with research or employ it in a quest for power. Debbie isn't entirely certain about her own integrity. She knows she would start with good intentions, but would it eventually corrupt her? Everybody loves admiration, but to have the power within one's own grasp to turn admiration into love, and then love into worship? The temptation would be too much for most men and women. Who could resist?

Maybe Mother Nature balances it by installing a mental block at puberty, or maybe it's simply divine intervention. What else can explain how humanity, or the majority of it, grows to doubt the magic? If faith were easy, this would run rampant. Magic, both good and bad, would spread like wildfire, and humanity would likely self-destruct. Maybe it's predestined. Anna had said she always knew Miss Coppertop would show up. How would she know that?

"Come here," she instructs Anna. Anna obliges and Debbie kneels behind her in the soft flowers. She gathers the girl's mane in her hands and lifts it. "Good gracious, your hair is so heavy! Does it hurt your neck or head?"

"No . . . maybe . . . I don't know," says Anna. "But it gets in the way a lot. I wish it was shorter like Hannah's."

"Can't you just wish it shorter?" Debbie asks.

"That doesn't work. Me and Hannah tried. It seems like the only things we can't change here is us. And we can't make sick better, either."

"That seems unfair," says Debbie. "Well, maybe we can change long to short. Let's try."

Debbie holds her hand out palm up and concentrates. After

a few seconds, she is rewarded with the familiar weight of her tortoiseshell hairbrush, followed by her barber scissors.

That is so cool, she thinks. Don't think I'll ever get tired of it.

Anna stands with her eyes closed and an easy and contented smile on her lips, relishing the attention as Debbie brushes long strokes through her hair. Studying the soft perfection of Anna's cheeks and her unusual blonde eyelashes, Debbie understands why some dedicate their lives to the innocent beauty of children, why Anne Geddes has made a career of photographing them, why Bessie Pease Gutmann spent a lifetime painting them, and why parents would sacrifice their life for them. Debbie leans forward and kisses Anna on her soft, icy cheek. Anna gives her a smile so sweet it brings a lump to Debbie's throat.

"You know," Debbie says. "Less than a week ago I believed in very little. I had lost my belief in love, in God, in hope, and I was losing my belief in the kindness of others . . . and then you and Hannah popped up in my life!" Debbie pauses, releases a pent up breath and chuckles. "Well, if you were to tell me penguins were really aliens who pooped marshmallows, I'd believe you."

Anna giggles and looks at Debbie with those hazel eyes so wide and innocent. She says, "I bet you could make one."

"Maybe, but who'd want to be cleaning marshmallow poop all day long?" Debbie works at a final tangle in Anna's hair, points to a spot in the middle of her back and pokes lightly. "Is here okay?"

Anna nods and Debbie lifts the scissors over a small section of hair. Keeping the blades level as possible, she snips. The scissors pass through Anna's hair as if it were made of light, yet the hair stays intact. Debbie tries again to the same effect, and then snips haphazardly at the hair, making Anna giggle.

"Told you," says Anna.

"But I'm using scissors, not magic, or whatever it is."

"But we're here," Anna counters. "We don't change when we're here. Our hair doesn't grow, we don't grow, and we don't get cut."

Debbie presses the point of the scissors into the palm of her hand. There's a sense of pain and pressure, but there is no dimpling where the points touch her hand. She pushes harder. The pain increases as the tip of the scissors sinks into her palm, disappearing into the flesh but still not dimpling or wounding her. She pulls her hand away, shaking it and then rubbing the spot where the scissors breached the flesh without puncturing.

"Why are you doing that?" asks Anna.

"It's weird. Sticking it into my hand gives me pain, but no scarring," Debbie explains.

"If you ask me, just sticking it into your hand is weird," Anna says.

"Point taken, no pun intended," says Debbie. "But it seems strange it would hurt but not scar. You'd think the two would go together."

"I would?" Anna asks, looking unsure.

"Well, I would," says Debbie, flabbergasted. "The fact that we can't be physically harmed when we're here makes me think we'd be capable of eternal life here, don't you think?"

Anna ponders this for a while and then says, "I don't know, but I think we could live forever . . . unless we get sick."

It's not a concept Debbie wants to entertain, but it does lend a good explanation as to why Anna is not frozen solid, even though she is so painfully cold, maybe why Anna hasn't appeared to age much since her mother's murder, though she seems to be getting weaker. Hannah hasn't aged much either, but maybe her time away from Hannahwhere allowed her to grow accordingly. Hannah is taller than Anna, so could it be that when they are here physical growth—or maybe time—is suspended? Also, Anna's physical self is not here. The body can't grow if you're not alive, but then . . . it can deteriorate. That may be what's happening to Anna.

Christ, the whole situation gets more bizarre by the day, thinks Debbie. "Has Hannah been here lately?" she asks.

"She was, but now she's sleeping. She's waiting for you," says Anna

"How do you know she's sleeping?"

Anna shrugs. "We just know."

Debbie notes that Anna has said *we,* not *I,* which makes sense. It's proven that twins communicate on a more intimate level than other siblings do. Perhaps they keep the magic alive through their faith in each other, and maybe it's stronger with identical twins.

If Anna can communicate with Hannah's spiritual and physical self even when she's asleep, then why can't she communicate with her own physical self? *Because her physical self cannot respond if it's neither awake nor asleep,* Debbie thinks.

Debbie turns Anna around to face her. "Anna, I want to help you and Hannah, but to do it we need to know where your physical self was when the thinking you left it."

"I don't know," says Anna. "I tried, but I don't remember."

"Okay, we'll try a different approach. What's the last thing you remember doing before you came here?"

Anna closes her eyes and concentrates. "I don't know."

Debbie reclines to the flower cushioned ground and sits. "Sit here, back to me," she directs Anna, pointing to a spot in front of her. Anna obeys and Debbie shuffles forward a few inches. She pulls Anna's hair onto her lap and separates it into three long and even sections.

"I know you probably don't want to think about this, but it's very important," Debbie insists. "Can you remember if Travis brought you anywhere after he pulled you out from under the house?"

Anna flinches, disquieted by the mention of Travis's name, and Debbie tries to comfort her. She finishes brushing the three sections of Anna's hair, she starts weaving them into a braid. Enjoying the attention, Anna sits up straighter.

"Yeah, I remember he drove to Sandy Channel and said he was going to throw me in the water if I didn't tell him where Mom put her money. I don't know where Mom put it," Anna says, shaking her head as if trying to convince Debbie as well.

"It's alright, sweetie," Debbie assures her. "What is Sandy Channel?"

"Mom used to take us there to swim and play."

"What did Travis do when you were there?" Debbie asks, feeling her anger peak at the scumbag's threat to toss her into the water. In mid-March the water would have been freezing, if not frozen solid.

"It got real cold. I didn't have my coat because it was still at home," Anna says. "Travis fell asleep and we sat there a long time."

"Why didn't you run away when Travis was asleep?"

"Sandy Channel is far away from our house," Anna says. "He said he would kill Hannah just like he killed Mom if I got out of the car."

"How long did he sleep?" Debbie asks.

Anna shrugs. "Dunno. It was nighttime and really cold so I used the blanket Mom kept in the car. It didn't help much. My feet were hurting from the cold, and I couldn't move my arm. When he woke up, he turned the heat on. That was a little better."

"You had no shoes on?"

"No, I didn't get to put some on."

Debbie shakes her head unbelievingly. "You're doing great, honey. What else happened?"

Anna shrugged. "Not a lot. He kept swearing and yelling a lot . . . more than usual and it really scared me. I laid down on the back floor so he couldn't see me and I would fly away."

"To here . . . Hannahwhere?"

"Annaplace. We parked in this big garage for two days. He went out two times, once for food and once for drugs, I think, because that's when we had to leave real fast back to Sandy Channel."

"Why'd he go back there?" Debbie asks.

"He smoked something gross in a glass pipe. It smelled yuckier than cigarettes and farts." Anna wrinkles her nose at the memory.

"Oh God," Debbie mutters, recalling the acrid smell of meth that lingered like ghosts in the homes of some of her cases. She conjures a hair tie and wraps it around the end of the long braid. "Did he get ugly?"

"Yeah. I got mad at Travis and told him I wanted to go home. He jumped and screamed a bunch of bad words, and growled at me like a dog. He started driving and I thought he was going to bring me home because we were near the four corners, but he stopped the car and made me get out. He pulled me by my hair."

"What an ass . . . jerk! What was he thinking?" Debbie says angrily. "Without a coat and shoes? In the middle of the night? In the middle of March? What did you do?"

Anna shrinks back from her and shrugs. "He kept yelling at me and knocked me down. He kicked me in the back. It hurt wicked bad, but I was so scared and I couldn't stop crying, so I got back up and kept running away from him."

Debbie is horrified. She knows Anna's getting worked up, but she feels the answer is there somewhere.

"What are the four corners . . . where are they? Is it an intersection?" Debbie asks.

"It's where the two highway roads crisscross near home," says Anna. "The one-eighty-three overpass?" she adds. It sounds more like a question.

"Did you go back home?"

"I don't know. I can't remember. Mom told us never to walk on the highways, so I think I went through the field, but I don't remember. All I remember is it was so cold that my feet were burning. I was afraid that Travis was still chasing me."

Debbie moves in front of Anna, grasps her gently on her upper arms, and looks into her eyes. "This is important, Anna, try to remember."

Anna's mouth moves as she tries to speak, but instead she bursts into tears. Debbie feels as if they've somehow just broken through and maybe awakened a memory. "I don't remember," sobs Anna. "Don't be mad at me! Please don't be mad at me!"

"Sweetie! No, I'm not mad at all. Never! I'm sorry. No more questions, I mean it."

Debbie pulls her into a tight hug and Anna clings on urgently, starving for her warmth. It's not just physical, but an emotional need for warmth, love, acceptance, and direction. Nearly every component of Anna's support system is gone, her mother, her father, her body, and her sense of being. Her confusion and fear must be all encompassing and nearly crippling. Trust should be a near impossibility for Anna, and yet she trusts Debbie and clings to her.

Debbie lays her cheek on Anna's head, willing heat into her, and the feeling overwhelms her again, the same one she experienced with Hannah; her willingness to do anything and everything in her power to make things, if not right, at least *better* for Anna. It is the feeling of being their only hope, and a vital need to protect Hannah and Anna at all costs. It is the feeling of being a mother.

While Debbie holds Anna, it occurs to her that Anna does not disobey. It's natural to put your own safety first—especially a child—yet Anna stayed in the car and withstood severe physical discomfort for hours. As Travis slept, she nearly froze—trapped by fear and obedience—because he threatened Hannah's life. A moment earlier, Anna was sobbing and nearly frantic that Debbie would be upset with her. As ludicrous as it sounds, Debbie believes a major reason Anna's body hasn't been found is that she obeyed her mother.

Debbie wants to check out her suspicions, but Anna's present state seems too fragile to leave her alone. *Hannah, where are you?* Debbie wonders and calls out mentally. Hannah is standing at her side within seconds.

"Did you hear me call you?" Debbie asks.

"Kind of, I guess. I heard you call in my head, but not in my ears," Hannah explains.

"I guess that answers the telepathy question," Debbie says.

Hannah looks at her as if she's discussing Quantum Physics.

"Never mind," Debbie continues. "I'm glad you heard me. I have an idea where the physical Anna may be, so I have a lot to do, but Anna needs her sister right now. She's upset."

"Come here, silly, chilly Anna," Hannah says and takes her sister's hand. "Nice braid!"

Debbie hugs and kisses both girls. "We're going to make everything better, all three of us. I'll be back for both of you once I make sense of things, okay?"

They nod their understanding.

"I love you," says Anna.

The sentiment is unexpected, and Debbie is speechless for a moment as she swallows the lump in her throat.

"I love both of you," Debbie says and it pleases her that it doesn't feel odd leaving her mouth. Nervously kneading her hands, Debbie says, "I feel like I should be wearing red ruby slippers. Here goes."

She closes her eyes and pictures her body lying on her bed in her apartment. She lets reality go and thinks, *fly home,* envisioning herself skydiving. The ground drops out from beneath her, bringing with it the torrent of flashing colors, lights, and the horrendous sense of vertigo and dread. Debbie careens out of control, flailing her arms and feet.

Debbie slapped the stack of case files to the floor and overturned the lamp on her bedside table. She lay in the darkness trying to gather her senses, her heart hammering so hard that she felt the pulse in her feet. She fumbled in the dark, trying unsuccessfully to find the lamp. She rolled to the other side of the bed and switched on the matching lamp.

On her radio Men at Work were asking if she came from the land *Down Under.* She checked her iPhone. It was 5:44 a.m. and she still had not slept as far as she could tell, but storming through her head were too many questions demanding answers.

She gathered up the case files that had fanned across the floor, carried them into the living room, and set them on the couch atop her ever-increasing backlog pile. No matter how fast she worked, the accursed backlog refused to dwindle, and there would be no headway made today.

She opened Hannah's case file, found the address to the home that Elizabeth Amiel and her daughters had lived in, and released a harsh derisive laugh.

433 North Easy Street.

"You're fucking kidding me," she said aloud.

One thing Elizabeth Amiel surely had not experienced much during her time in the good ol' US of A was "Easy Street". What a sardonic, full-tilt boot in the ass! It didn't escape Debbie that the house also had the same number as Hannah's hospital room.

She opened her laptop, roused it from sleep mode, and punched in her password. Google Earth appeared and centered over Elm Creek, Nebraska. How convenient that she hadn't closed out of her earlier session.

The *four corners* that Anna had referred to were immediately obvious. The tiny city was located on the east side of Route 183, and split by Route 30. There was no need to type the address; the streets were clearly labeled on the map. Why they named it *North* Easy Street was beyond her, since there was no South, East, West, or just plain Easy Street in Elm Creek.

There was no direct route from the four corners to North Easy Street—which ran through most of the little city—on the Northeast quadrant where the two highways intersected. Route 183 ran parallel to North Easy Street, though separated by only an on-ramp and farmland.

Yeah, snow-covered farmland, being traversed by a minimally clothed and barefoot seven-year-old child at the coldest and darkest hour of a freezing March winter night!

The poor child! Her whole body must have been in excruciating pain.

She must still be in excruciating pain, Debbie realized.

There were so many suppositions about what could have happened to Anna. She might have fallen into a well, or perhaps someone driving by had hit her or picked her up . . . possibly some deranged pedophile. Debbie forced her thoughts from that prospect. Wherever Anna ended up, she must have been coherent enough to move her spiritual self to Annaplace.

Debbie started viewing the homes along either side of North Easy Street, pleased that Elm Creek merited *street view*, which was exactly as it sounded, a view of Elm Creek from the perspective of someone standing in the street. As amazing as the program was, the satellite images only provided approximate street numbers, no high-resolution close-ups, and all the images were of indeterminate date. Right in Riverside, which she considered a somewhat current community, some satellite images hadn't been updated in years. Buildings that had burned down or been razed still stood on Google. Long-gone cars still occupied driveways and two-year-old swimming pools had yet to appear in the yards they occupied. Considering these minor setbacks, Debbie would have to rely on simple deduction or—perish the thought—common sense.

The reports verified that Elizabeth Amiel had rented a single-family home, and considering her situation as a relatively new immigrant and a single mother of two, it would likely be a small house on the west side of the street—the odd-numbered side. Most of the properties were adjacent to the farmland and had larger structures that were likely associated with the farms. The house that best fit the bill to be the Amiel home was a beige-roofed modular about a quarter-mile from the four corners. If this was indeed the house, the walk must have been an eternity to Anna. Hypothermia could set in as early as fifteen minutes, depending on how low the outside temperature was. Second-stage hypothermia, which caused violent shivering, stumbling, and confusion, occurred shortly after, especially for such a small being. Frostbite was inevitable.

Where was Hannah during all of this? Debbie wondered. She must have been, as Hannah put it, *all the way in* Hannahwhere. The question raised many others. Hannah had said she "fell out" of

Hannahwhere. If so, why did Hannah stick around the dumpster for as long as she did? Knowing that things were bad, why didn't Anna transfer herself completely to Annaplace . . . assuming that she could? What was keeping her from leaving?

According to Anna, it must have been in the still hours of the morning when she fled from Travis into the frozen night. Somewhere between 1:00 a.m. and 4:00 a.m., Debbie estimated. What would Anna have seen if she made it home that night? It was maybe three days later. Everybody would surely have been gone by then: the police, the ambulance, Hannah, her mother's body . . .

Her mother's body!

Had Anna returned home expecting Hannah and her mother to be there? The intense cold likely had Anna confused and in pain, and the last time Anna had seen her mother, she was alive. Travis had been attacking her, but Mom was crying and telling them to hide, so maybe in Anna's seven-year-old mind she must still be alive.

Sadly, Hannah had seen her mother's body, had touched her and ineffectively tried to awaken her. Anna didn't have that kind of confirmation. What would a seven-year-old child do if she came home to an empty house or, even worse, locked doors? Would she have gone to a neighbor's house? Maybe not, considering Anna's need for approval, and desire to please. Debbie believed Anna would have obeyed her mother without exception.

While 6:39 a.m. might be a little earlier than Phil Davenport preferred to rise, with so much in the balance, Debbie couldn't find it within herself to care what time the detective did anything. She fished through the pockets of her laptop case, pulled out Davenport's card, and dialed his number.

Call forwarding.

"Shit," Debbie muttered. She left a message with a callback request and disconnected the call.

With a head full of questions and a heart full of purpose, she selected some clothes from her closet, a bra and panties from her dresser, and tossed it all on her bed. In the bathroom, she stripped naked, loaded her toothbrush with too much Tom's toothpaste, and brushed her teeth. She rinsed, and righted herself to regard the naked woman staring at her from the mirror. Nakedness was a condition Debbie avoided. She was a stranger to herself in this context, having convinced herself that she was marred and ghastly.

Look! Debbie demanded of herself. *Don't hide.*

She stared into her vivid blue eyes and at the shocking copper tone of her hair and saw nothing vile or hideous. She ran her hand across the constellation of freckles coating her face, arms, and shoulders and felt no gruesome scars or deformities. She looked at her chest and the creamy white flesh of her breasts.

Hey Red!

Debbie started, grabbed a towel, and quickly wrapped herself in it.

CHAPTER 21

Debbie tiptoed into Hannah's hospital room at around one in the afternoon. It was a pointless act being that it would take something in the range of a landmine to rouse Hannah when she was in Hannahwhere.

She wasn't. She was sitting up in the bed, facing the large windows that overlooked the parking lot two stories below. Hannah spun on the bed and pinned Debbie with gleaming eyes and a beaming smile.

"Hello, Sunshine," greeted Debbie. She set her purse on the chair and placed a Kohl's shopping bag on the bed. "How'd you know I was here?"

"I heard you thinking about me," Hannah said.

"Really?" Debbie asked, concerned that she might have to start monitoring her thoughts.

"No," Hannah admitted with a toothy grin. "I saw you get out of your car."

"You're a little prankster," Debbie said, still a little uneasy. It's amazing, she thought, how quickly I'm now willing to accept that which was implausible just a week ago.

Then again, why wouldn't it be possible? All you had to do was think outside the reality box, as Anna and Hannah had demonstrated repeatedly. The ability to read minds; what a terrifying thought. It could turn the most passionate lovers into enemies. Everybody would be pre-guessing everyone. It could put the world into disarray. Debbie figured it'd be better to leave well enough alone, though the apprehension stuck with her, hovering just beneath the surface.

Hannah crawled to the edge of the bed and threw her arms around Debbie.

"Wow! What a greeting!" said Debbie. "Someone must have slept well. Why so chipper?"

Hannah lined up eye-to-eye and nose-to-nose with her, a position Debbie had seen so many children take with their parents; a show of cohesion and conviction she never thought she would experience in her lifetime. Debbie again felt that maternal rush and the ache of longing that accompanied it.

"You went to see Anna last night . . . by yourself!" said Hannah conspiratorially.

"That's right, I did. Are you proud of me?"

"You so totally rock, Squirt!" Hannah said, adopting a decent "surfer-dude" accent. "So give me some fin."

She offered her hand for a high-five, which Debbie dutifully slapped.

"Noggin . . ." Hannah said and bumped her forehead none-too-gently into Debbie's forehead. Debbie rubbed her head, stunned but delighted by Hannah's good mood.

"Dude!" Hannah drawled, swaying her head and body to one side. "Come on, you're supposed to say it, too!"

"Dude!" they said in unison.

"No! Like Crush and Squirt, like this!" Hannah said, stressing the surfer dude accent, "Duuuude! Okay, on three. One . . . two . . . three!"

"Duuuuude!" they repeated.

"You need practice," Hannah said and gave her the international so-so sign.

"You like Little Nemo?"

Hannah rolled her eyes. *"Finding Nemo!"* she corrected. "Who doesn't like it? *Little Nemo* is a stupid movie about a boy who flies around on his bed."

"Good point, flying beds are as absurd as bedknobs and broomsticks," agreed Debbie.

"Huh?" said Hannah.

"Never mind. Bad joke. I like Dory."

"Me too!" said Hannah. She looked at the buttons on Debbie's blouse and then reconnected her gaze with her. "Anna said you were really scared when you got there."

"Well, Anna's right. I thought I was a goner until she pulled me out."

"Why?"

"I felt like I was completely out of control. Like falling, but more like . . . being whipped around."

"I like that feeling, it's cool!" said Hannah. She settled back on the bed.

Debbie said, "Well, maybe if I go back and forth a few times like you and Anna, I'll get used to it, but . . ."

"Shhhh!" Hannah interrupted, directing a warning glance over Debbie's shoulder. Changing to a demeanor of exaggerated juvenile innocence, she said, "Can we watch SpongeBob later?"

"I don't see why not," Debbie said, playing along.

Doctor Farren knocked lightly on the door and entered the room carrying a coffee and an alluring scent of cologne.

"Good morning, Hannah," he said from within his flawlessly groomed moustache and goatee. "Hello, again, Ms. Gillan."

"Hello, doctor. Debbie is fine," she said.

"As is Brad," he countered. "I hear you're with Hannah often. Very admirable." He flashed a million watt smile and turned to Hannah. "How is our little celebrity doing this morning?"

"Okay," Hannah said cagily.

"No worries, Sweetheart. I'm just here to check on you like yesterday. No shots today. Scout's honor. Do you mind if I take a look at your feet?"

Hannah smiled timidly and moved to the edge of the bed, taking extra precautions to keep her Johnny tight around her legs. Doctor Farren smiled and removed the bandages. Standing behind the doctor, Debbie waggled her eyebrows at Hannah and mouthed *he's cute*. Hannah smiled and restrained a giggle.

"You're sure looking a lot better than the first time I saw you. I never expected to find such a pretty girl under all that dirt," Doctor Farren said. He looked questioningly at the soiled dressings, shook his head, and dropped them in a bio-barrel near the bed. "Have you been outside, perhaps climbing a volcano or trudging through the Everglades?"

Hannah and Debbie exchanged a quick glance. Hannah shook her head while Debbie smiled reassuringly and said, "Not yet, but we have done a surprising amount of walking."

"It concerns me that so much dirt can be lifted from a hospital floor," Doctor Farren said.

"I like to walk," Hannah added.

Debbie tried to place the cologne. It was very pleasant. Was it Armani? From behind the doctor, she mimed hugging him. Hannah covered her smile with her hand and Doctor Farren quickly looked at Debbie, who now stood wide-eyed and innocent behind him. She shrugged.

Returning his attention to Hannah, Doctor Farren poked and prodded her feet for a few moments and squeezed the area around the sutures. Hannah flinched mildly, which seemed monumental to Debbie. It was the first time she had witnessed Hannah react to any form of physical pain.

"This is very good, you are healing splendidly. Your doctor did a stellar job stitching up your foot, if I can be so humble as to pat my own back."

Doctor Farren winked at Hannah and smiled at Debbie, which she returned in spades. Debbie made little kissy motions towards him when he turned back to Hannah, and this time Hannah failed to restrain her giggle.

"I get the feeling I'm missing something here," Doctor Farren said. He raised an eyebrow, rubbed at his goatee in animated contemplation, and asked with jocular suspicion, "Do I sense a conspiracy here?"

"She's flirting with you," Hannah said, and then furtively whispered with enough volume for Debbie to hear her clearly, "I think she likes you."

Debbie felt as if the heat in her face might blister her. She glared at Hannah who shrugged and smirked defiantly.

"Do you think so?" Doctor Farren asked.

"Uh-huh. She said you're cute."

"Really?" he leaned close to Hannah and stage whispered, "Well, I think she's very pretty. Do you think she'd let me buy her a cup of coffee or a drink some night after work?"

"Maybe you should ask her, not me," Hannah advised.

"Oh, okay," said Doctor Farren. "Make me do all the work." He met Debbie's eyes and offered an endearingly crooked smile. "Well?"

Thoroughly self-conscious, Debbie smiled and squeaked out a mousy, "Um . . . okay."

"Great!" He slipped a business card from his blazer's inner pocket. "Give me a call when you get your voice back." He turned back to Hannah, winked and said, "Maybe she should have that checked."

"You're the doctor," Hannah reminded him.

He laughed and said, "Okay, Cupid. I think we can leave the bandages off so the sutures can breathe, but only if you're in bed. If you're walking about, you'll need the stitches bandaged because there's still a little seepage where cooties can get in. Wear sterile booties and white socks . . . only white."

"Doctor?" said Debbie. "Seeing it's so beautiful outside, I would like to take Hannah for a walk. She's been cooped up for days and I believe the media pressure is mostly over. Do you feel she's ready physically?"

"Probably more than you or me, but I'd say give it until tomorrow. After that, have a blast. It'll be good for her as long as she doesn't overdo it. Regarding the stitches, cover her foot as I suggested," he said. "Does she have appropriate clothing?"

"Taken care of," Debbie said, patting the Kohl's bag.

"Has Child Services come up with a plan?" Doctor Farren asked. "She's physically fine and she seems to be responding quite nicely, in my unqualified opinion. Will she be staying under your jurisdiction, or will she become a ward of Nebraska?"

"Not Nebraska!" Hannah nearly yelled. Her eyes narrowed. "I want to stay with Debbie!"

Debbie moved protectively near Hannah, put a consoling hand on her back, and cryptically said to Doctor Farren, "Hannah has superb hearing."

Patting Hannah's pale leg, the doctor said, "Understood. Well, I hope you get your every wish."

He finished with his checkup and made a few notations with a stylus on his Palm Pilot. He offered a farewell wink to both ladies, pointed to Debbie, made the universal "call me" phone sign, and then left the room.

"Right now I don't know whether to growl at you or hug you," Debbie said. With her arms folded and foot tapping she stared down at Hannah.

"I'll take the hug," Hannah said, and Debbie obliged.

"We're going to get to be with you, right?" Hannah asked. Her concern was a thick presence in the room.

Debbie reminded herself, *no promises you can't keep.* She sat near Hannah on the bed and nudged the girl's chin so she was looking directly at her.

"There is *nothing* I want more than to have you and Anna with me, but it is a long and hard process that requires a lot of work, money, and time. This is what I can and can't promise you. I can promise that I will do everything and anything possible for as long as necessary to help you and Anna, and to get you to be with me, but I cannot promise that in the end they will see me as the most suitable caregiver. I need you to understand this, and I know you can because you've already proved you are very, very smart. Okay?"

Hannah nodded and her eyes moved to her knitted hands resting on her lap. Large teardrops ran their quick course to her chin.

"But," Debbie said, and again turned the child's face to her and wiped the tears away. "If there's one thing you and Anna have taught me it's that anything is possible, and I'm counting on this to get us through. So, are you with me?"

Hannah nodded lightly.

"Nope, need more of a confirmation than that," Debbie said, tickling Hannah gently on the ribs. Hannah emitted a high-pitched squeak.

"A mouse!" said Debbie, tickling a little harder. "Are you with me?"

"Yeah," Hannah agreed, squirming through a bout of hearty giggles.

"Good! Noggin!" Debbie said, and shared another hearty head-bump.

"Duuude," they said in unison.

"I bought you some clothes," Debbie said while opening the Kohl's bag. "You like Dora the Explorer, right?"

Hannah gave her a horrified look.

"Kidding!" Debbie said. "*Big Time Rush* for you. Try them on. If they fit properly, then tomorrow we can go for a nice long walk outside."

"Really?" Hannah perked up.

Debbie agreed and tucked Doctor Farren's card into the front pocket of her purse.

TUESDAY
June 29, 2010

CHAPTER 22

Worried and frustrated, Debbie tossed and turned for half an hour. She was trying to squeeze in a few more moments of much needed shut-eye, but it wasn't in the cards. It was 6 a.m. and she had managed only five hours of solid sleep since she had returned from the hospital the evening before, so exhausted that she was dozing on her feet. She was still restless despite the severe sleep deficiency, and what sleep she did get had been infused with grizzly nightmares of Hannah and Anna, skeletal and mummified, being chased endlessly around Hannahwhere by red-eyed wolves.

Debbie sat up and scratched her head. Glancing down at her feet, she had an abrupt sense of being very young, maybe nine or ten. The floor beneath her faded and transformed into unfinished pine planks, worn and stained by years of dirt, spilled oil, and splattered paint.

"Oh, Christ, not again," she whined.

The light across the floor altered with the creaking of old door hinges, followed by the defeating *clack* of a padlock, sounding as deadly as a shotgun blast. She sensed a presence there with her. A waft of expensive cologne hung in the air. It was tantalizing and fresh and it only made it more disturbing that *this* man could smell so appealing. It was like the ultimate insult, and that knowledge turned the cologne into something cloying and menacing. It flooded her sinuses.

Hey, little Red on the bed, said an astonishingly deep voice from somewhere inside of her mind. A large black shoe appeared near her feet. It was highly polished and looked completely out of place on the worn wooden floorboards. Dread flowed over her from her head downward, like hot oil. She wanted to run but knew she couldn't or she'd get the strap. Besides, he always locked her in the shed, imprisoned until this man—this beast—finished with her.

He . . .

This was the man who hurt her so badly . . . who made her feel as if hot knives were stabbing and twisting into her *down there*. But there was nothing she could do except obey. Terrified, she silently lay back, avoiding any eye contact with the nasty man as he undressed. Instead, she focused on what was tacked on the shed wall. A pretty blonde woman wearing a blue-and-white dress and presenting a generous display of cleavage stared down at her from a *St. Pauli Girl* poster. As the hideous man repeatedly stabbed her with white-hot agony, the poster girl's beatific smile offered her a bold lie, promising her that life was great. To the right of the poster a green-and-gold banner boasted St. Edward High School Eagles. She preferred that one and centered her gaze on it until her vision blurred and spun. She latched on and soon she was spinning and soared with the eagle. She was the noble bird, flying miles above the world. She could see the floral fields far below and she was safe to fly out of the reach of all, for who could touch an eagle?

A tear escaped from the corner of her eye and trickled to her ear, which only excited the sweaty, depraved fiend more . . . and then her world erupted. She was launched into an agony so torturous and searing that—despite the anguish she had already known in her short life—she couldn't fathom its magnitude. It tore into her as if a barbed wire were being dragged through her abdomen. Her scream was more of a shriek—an eagle's shriek—that escalated higher and higher. The man attempted to cover her mouth, at first with his hand, and then with the pillow.

The pain was unbearable. She knew she was dying, yet dying was okay. Death would be a relief. It would free her from pain and she'd be free to fly forever . . . if the pain would only go away.

"NO!" Debbie screamed.

She jumped up, slapped her hands over her ears, and bolted into the bathroom. She slammed the door and locked it, then spun, closed, and locked the dining room entry as well. She turned the knob for the hot water and—still wearing her pajamas—lay down in the bathtub. She could still feel him on her and in her and she needed to wash him away. She had to remove his sweat, his spit, his . . . his . . . burning inside her. And her blood . . . there had been so much blood!

"No . . . no . . . no . . . no . . ." she moaned aloud in a litany of denial. She rocked back and forth in the scorching water, trying to push the images from her head.

Why is this happening to me? What is wrong with me?

Debbie stopped rocking and allowed the slow rise of the water to cover her. She did not move while an arm and leg, then her face, and then her other leg were immersed. Her eyes remained open as her head submerged and the steaming water cauterized her thoughts and insulated her pain. She stayed immersed until her vision wavered and her lungs grieved. When she could no longer hold her breath, she surfaced, pulling a long, ragged breath into her burning lungs. She waited until the water rose above the overflow drain to shut the faucet off with her foot. Rolling onto her back, she lay with only her face above the surface, listening to the muffled hum of the house through the water. She soaked, nearly catatonic, until long after the water turned from hot to cold, and then to frigid, which finally brought her back.

Dripping, shivering, and bewildered, Debbie rose from the tub and stepped onto the shower mat. She removed her drenched pajamas and tossed them into the sink, then pulled a bath towel from the rack to dry off her shivering body. Returning the towel to the rack, she grabbed her robe from a hook on the bathroom door, and wrapped herself in it. She closed the toilet lid and sat down.

"God! I need help as much as Hannah and Anna do," she thought aloud, but unheard. There was no one to confide in. She had no spouse, lover, parents, siblings, or even a best friend. She was profoundly alone, and although she had always known it—and even preferred it that way since Kenny had left—it was the first time that she had truly felt it. It was the first time it had truly mattered.

She had workmates with whom she coexisted in a cordial enough setting, but the other caseworkers had long ago given up on inviting her out for Friday night drinks or dinners. She had rejected all date requests, and Doctor Farren's business card would likely go ignored. That she had no one to confide in or to seek comfort from didn't disturb Debbie as much as the truth that she had no one, period.

It's better alone. Alone is safe. When you're alone no one can leave you and no one can harm you or steal your innocence.

She had fared just fine in her self-isolation . . . until now. She refused to trust anyone. Trust lets you down and leaves you exposed and vulnerable. Yet there was Hannah and Anna, and she trusted them. But they were children and looking to her for help.

Oh, those poor girls, Debbie thought and sighed heavily. Talk about seeking help from the helpless!

Debbie rose and moved to the sink to brush her teeth. She risked looking at herself in the mirror again. This time she didn't look at her physical reflection as a whole but concentrated on her eyes, and into her eyes. For the first time in years, Debbie allowed herself to confront and experience her loneliness and her fear, and most frightening of all, her desire to be needed, accepted, and not abandoned. It was a profound disclosure, a gargantuan weight that she'd been carrying, and a staggering revelation of how much larger than her it was. She felt miniscule in the reality of it. She had never felt this weak or helpless, even after Kenny left, or if she had, she hadn't allowed herself to acknowledge it. As huge as Kenny's departure was, she had put it behind her and walked on, not stopping to look back and not seeing that it had joined forces with all her previous fears and weaknesses. It was still following her, and my, how it had grown!

Debbie concentrated on her pupils, looking deep and trying to focus on the woman inside. All she could see was a little girl . . . a terrified little red-haired girl trapped in a prison of darkness. Bound by the chains of fear, she was too traumatized to move, feel, or grow . . . and too weak to escape. Debbie had known the little girl, but now she was a forgotten stranger. She had abandoned her years ago and left her chained in the damp darkness of her past, alone in her cell and ignored until now. Her little redheaded prisoner was finally breaking free.

At the onset of her day, Debbie's energy had been below sublevel, but after an hour at the gym, a shower, and an energy bar with enough protein in it to cast a cinderblock, she actually felt good.

"Thank you for agreeing to see me, again." Debbie offered Essie a meager smile.

Essie patted her on the back, led her into her office, and motioned her to the loveseat. Essie was uncharacteristically quiet and Debbie couldn't tell whether she was put out, introspective, or simply tired. Debbie also had a natural inclination to be a bit paranoid.

"So, you feel you had a breakthrough?" asked Essie. "You said you had another vision?"

"Yes, but now I'm pretty sure they're flashbacks."

"Me too," Essie said with a soft smile.

"I also want to talk about what happened the night before last. Before you talk to anyone, and I hope you haven't. I think we . . ."

"I haven't spoken to anyone," Essie said.

"Well, you were very excited by what happened. I was afraid you'd want to report it."

"Of course I was excited."

"Still . . . I'm afraid it could put Hannah and Anna in so much danger . . . not to mention, me," Debbie pleaded.

"I understand," said Essie. "But you need to understand the sensitivity of my position. In addition to our fears for Hannah and Anna, we need to consider what happened from a professional angle as well. Not reporting something of this magnitude would unquestionably put our licenses at risk. On the other hand, people aren't as open to extraordinary experience as some would think, especially in professional or clinical circles. You could present indisputable evidence, and most of them will find reasons not to believe, and question your stability to boot. Either way could potentially put my career at risk. There is also the matter of a certain detective who reacted rather intensely."

"I know," Debbie agreed, forlornly.

"Right now my job is to protect Hannah and her sister, not exploit them," Essie said. "I won't report anything until I have more of a grip on what's happening."

Debbie still wasn't sure if she should trust Essie, but considering what she already knew, it was moot. "I feel there's more to it regarding Hannah and Anna," Debbie said.

"Oh, I don't doubt it for a moment," Essie said sincerely. "Remember, I was there Sunday night. I saw."

"Yes, but it goes even deeper than Hannah disappearing. I think there's a commonality between Hannah, Anna, and me."

"Clearly between you and Hannah," said Essie. "No question.

Was it you or Hannah who initiated it?"

"Initiated what?" Debbie asked. "Disappearing? That had to be Hannah. How could I make her disappear?"

Essie gave Debbie a questioning look, and then said, "Debbie, you do realize that you disappeared, too?"

She looked at Essie as a river of thoughts and fears raged through her. "I disappeared, too?" Debbie asked.

"My God, you didn't know that? You both faded. How could you not know?" Essie asked, animated in her excitement. "Couldn't you feel it? What did you feel?"

"I'm not sure. I only felt Hannah disappearing," said Debbie. "It was surreal, like everything else lately. I was panicking. I was afraid that if Hannah disappeared, she would never return. I just wanted to keep her there."

"So Hannah triggered it?"

"I don't know. I guess," Debbie said. "That wasn't the first time Hannah started disappearing, and it makes me wonder if it wasn't my first. I thought I was just traveling with them in my mind."

"Traveling? With *them*?" asked Essie. "Wait. What do you mean by *travel*?"

Debbie was afraid she had already said too much. Would Essie have her committed to the booby hatch?

"Are you talking about Hannahwhere?" Essie went on. "Are you saying that you project with Hannah?"

Debbie shrugged sheepishly and nodded. "I think so."

"I've never heard of such a thing," Essie said, sounding truly intrigued, not condemning. "Two people dissociating together. Is that possible?"

"And Anna," Debbie said.

Essie gave her a disbelieving look.

"I mean it," Debbie insisted. "I was with Anna. We—Hannah and I—were with Anna. We spoke with her. I braided her hair. It's exactly like Hannah's, but quite a bit longer."

"Okay. Wait a moment. Are you sure your hopes aren't skewing your perception, here?" Essie asked. "What you are suggesting is beyond telepathy. I don't think that's possible."

"And disappearing is?" Debbie said emphatically.

"True," Essie agreed. "But if you were actually interacting with

Anna as you say, then you would know where Anna is."

"No. That's one of the problems. It's a long, confusing story. Anna doesn't even know where she is physically." Debbie knew it sounded weak, but she knew no other way of explaining it.

"This is too much," Essie said. She still looked dubious, but an edge of confusion tinted her suspicion.

Debbie leaned forward on the couch, intense in her conviction. "You're being like the people you just talked about, who are not open to the extraordinary and find reasons not to believe. You saw it! My God! And there's so much more. Part of me wants to say everything . . . to spill my guts. Another part of me wants to climb into bed and sleep forever, and a third part of me knows I have to protect Hannah and Anna with every fiber of my being."

Essie looked distraught and Debbie understood what she was feeling. Debbie had been feeling it for days herself . . . ontological shock. Essie and Debbie were both questioning their view of what reality is.

"I'm listening," Essie finally said, though hesitantly.

Debbie told her everything . . . almost.

It was well past 4:00 p.m. when Debbie left Essie's office. As she drove away her usual thread of doubt weaved into her comfort zone, and the further away she got the thicker the thread became. Was Essie trustworthy, or was she gathering proof for the DCF that Debbie was going bug-shit in the head and should be locked away? Was Essie collecting information so she could present it for research somewhere, like Harvard, The Monroe Institute, or some sleazy tabloid?

Debbie intended to visit Hannah and play a game or go for a stroll through the hallways, but realized she hadn't eaten anything but a protein bar earlier that morning. She detoured into the hospital cafeteria, built a rather respectable salad, and grabbed a bottle of iced tea. For Hannah, she selected a Frisbee-sized chocolate chip cookie that could have come with a deed.

As she was cashing out at the register, her iPhone came to life. She fumbled nervously in her pocketbook. By the time she found her phone, Alanis had sung a stanza for her.

You live, you learn
You love, you learn
You cry, you learn

She always felt a sense of embarrassment when her phone rang in public, for reasons she'd never understood. Debbie answered with a hushed, "Hello?"

Other people's cell phones chimed just about everywhere.

"Davenport," the voice on the other end of the connection grumbled. He sounded pissed off, exactly as Debbie expected.

"Good evening, Detective," Debbie said. "I apologize for calling so early this morning. I hope I didn't disturb anyone."

Davenport gave a huff, but said, "It's all right. It's not like I've been getting much sleep since your little performance the other night. Excuse my French, but what the fuck happened there?"

"I wish I had a decent explanation for you," Debbie said.

"Essie Hiller saw it, too, right? It wasn't just me?"

"Essie saw it too."

"So, what's going on with you and the girl? It's like something from *Star Trek*. I haven't touched the bottle in twenty-five years, but I could have used a couple of shots after *that* let me tell you. Christ!"

Debbie quickly moved to a table in the emptiest corner of the cafeteria. "Phil," she said, "I hope you're not thinking of making a media circus of this. Do you know what that would do to Hannah?"

"Miss Gillan," he said. "I know I often come across as a soulless prick. It's one of the hazards of this trade, but I do have some compassion and some common sense. I haven't called anyone . . . yet."

"Yet?" Debbie asked.

"My superiors wouldn't believe me for a second. They might think the pressure's gotten to me and I've gone over the deep end. Shit, what I saw sincerely has *me* questioning my sanity, or you and that little girl's reality. I've thought of little else since." He paused, taking a deep breath and releasing it. "However, if I don't report it, then I'm guilty of withholding vital information. Either way, both Hannah and my career are potentially at risk."

The same as Essie, Debbie thought. She was foolish to hope it'd be different.

Debbie said. "Well, if you're nuts, then you'd better save two more seats on that bus for Essie and me."

She resisted the slightest urge to hint about all the inexplicable things she'd seen, but didn't know Davenport well enough to trust him, and especially to that degree. Such talk could ruin her career as well. Right now, the safest route was to take a conservative approach, go bare bones, and not mention anything regarding Hannah and Anna that seemed any further beyond the real.

"I've been talking with Anna quite a bit, and doing a lot of research," Debbie said.

"Anna?" asked Davenport.

"I mean Hannah," Debbie amended, aggravated at her unconscious gaffe. She had to be more careful. "I think we're close to uncovering some information that may help with the case. Is it possible to hold off on any definitive actions that would affect Hannah and Anna until we, or you, check some potentially vital information out with the FBI, the Elm Creek Police Department, or whoever is handling this?"

"The Kearney Police Department," said Davenport.

"I thought you had said that the other day. Why Kearney?"

"It's Kearney, Nebraska jurisdiction. Elm Creek is too small to support a police force. Might be why they don't seem too particularly interested in this case."

"Dear God."

"Indeed," said Phil. "And regardless of the indifference of their police department, what you're asking is a mighty big request."

"I'm aware of that, Phil, but can you hear me out first, and then decide?" Debbie took a sip of iced tea and grimaced, checked the sell by date, checked the label, and sighed. *Organic, it figures.*

"Will whatever this theory is make things easier for our little girl over there in Riverside Hospital?" asked the detective.

"I think so," Debbie said.

Was he being sincere? she wondered. Was he really concerned for Hannah? Maybe seeing us disappear the other night changed him. It certainly changed me. She took a hearty gulp of iced tea, shuddered, and set it back down.

Davenport hesitated and Debbie was sure he was going to deny her after all, but he released a long breath and said, "You do understand that I'm putting my job at risk, here. In three years, I'll be sixty. My goal is to retire then with full pension, not a premature relief of duty. Understand that I will listen, but I cannot promise anything."

"Thank you," Debbie said gratefully. It was a start in the right direction. If the odd, greasy detective had been there at that moment, Debbie would have hugged him. "My first concern is with Travis Ulrich. Has anyone spoken with him since Hannah verified he took Anna?"

"I relay all relevant information to the Kearney Police Department and the NCMEC, who work closely with the FBI. I can, and will suggest it. Beyond that, I have no power. As for Kearney, they closed the case. With Hannah turning up, they'll probably reopen it, but I doubt they'll make it a priority . . . not without irrefutable proof of Travis Ulrich's guilt concerning Anna. The fact that Hannah has been found alive actually puts Travis in a better light and strengthens his plea of innocence. They may not do anything."

Debbie huffed in disgust. "But it's a missing child case with the child still missing! How can they not at least look into it?" she asked, her voice rising.

"The case is still alive with NCMEC. It's their baby now, if you'll pardon the pun. Ulrich already has life in prison without parole. Any added penalty would be inconsequential."

"They could hang the bastard," Debbie mumbled.

"Nebraska uses lethal injection," Davenport said. Debbie released a dramatic sigh. The detective continued. "This is a 'he said, she said' situation with no solid evidence and the testimony of an impressionable nine-year-old child. Juries will already be skeptical about her dependability as a witness due to her age. For what it's worth, I agree with you. They should hang the bastard and save the taxpayers a boatload of dough."

"God! Did they at least perform a DNA test on the car's interior?"

"Of course they did. It was Elizabeth's car and it was soaked with DNA from her, Hannah, Anna, and Travis, but only Elizabeth's blood."

Debbie wanted to pursue the Travis connection, but wasn't sure how. She wanted to shake Davenport and make him understand what she already knew. Even if Travis didn't outright kill Anna, he may as well have. He was just as guilty—even more so, considering how much she was still suffering—but there was no good way to reveal this without hard evidence or a confession, both of which were near impossible.

"I think Travis took Anna," Debbie said, "just as Hannah told us. She told us Elizabeth came into some money. Probably not much, but enough to make Travis hopeful for a couple fixes, which was what he wanted most . . . enough to kill for. I think he holed up in the car with Anna, hunted for those fixes, and spending a good amount of time sleeping off his high, and essentially forgetting Anna was there. This would be especially easy if Anna had lapsed into dissociative states similar to Hannah, which I have little doubt she could since they are twins. I think that when Travis came back to earth, after he murdered Elizabeth, he realized what he did and figured the best way to hide from it was with another high. I'm sure he was Jonesing and all he craved was another fix. He surely had no desire for the responsibility of looking after, or in his case putting up with, a seven-year-old child, so he booted her out of the car somewhere."

"We would need more than that. *Thinking* Travis took Anna is too weak. I think he took her, too, but it's just a mountain of speculation," Davenport said. "And anyone else at NCMEC, that's only one of countless scenarios and I'm sure they already heard them all. No money was found at the house, on Travis, or in Elizabeth's bank account. Travis didn't have a bank account. This, of course, doesn't mean Travis didn't take money and stash it, squander it, or that there was any money in the first place. In fact, chances are all of this might have zero impact on Anna's situation."

"Maybe," said Debbie. "But why was Travis found five days later only a few miles away? Why would he risk returning to Elm Creek? Surely he knew they were looking for him and Elizabeth's car. I don't think even the smallest part of him wanted to bring Anna home. I don't think he gave a shit about her or them. Something else lured him back."

"Or after he came down from his high, maybe he felt remorse for what he did and wanted to be caught. There's no tangible proof that he took either girl. You're still running on assumptions," Davenport pointed out.

"Why haven't they found her body?" she asked.

"We don't know if she's even dead. Remember, Hannah turned up alive," Davenport said.

She ached to tell him Anna's story of how Travis dumped her at the juncture of Route 183 and the Route 30 connector road. But how? Seeing her and Hannah disappear had rattled Davenport's reality. Would he believe she'd communicated with Anna? The detective scratched his stubbly cheek and it sounded like distant maracas to Debbie.

"They are twins, Phil, and twins are usually inseparable. They would have stuck together if it were humanly possible," Debbie said. *Like they have even when it's beyond humanly possible.*

"Maybe, but this is all conjecture," Phil said. "There's nothing concrete enough here to change their direction. Travis knew what he had done. He was undoubtedly trying to hide when they found him, and if there was money at the root of it, that adds weight to his reason for returning to town. Drug addicts aren't known for being rational. Still, it adds nothing solid to Anna's situation."

Debbie was silent. The frustration of knowing what she knew and not being able to express it had her feeling tense and powerless.

"Another thing, and correct me if I'm wrong," Davenport went on. "Why would Hannah being Anna's twin have any bearing on whether Anna suffers dissociation, too? Isn't dissociation psychological, not genetic?"

"According to most studies," explained Debbie. "But there are different views leaning towards genetic connections, especially regarding twins. By studying the way Hannah acts and what she says, I feel I have a good idea as to where Anna is."

"And where would *that* be?" Davenport asked.

Debbie hated his patronizing tone. She felt like hanging up on him, but instead she said, "Phil, you're coming across as a soulless prick."

To her surprise, Phil erupted into a hearty bout of laughter that even sounded sincere. He said, "I warned you, charm isn't one of my stock features. I was trying to answer as the other agencies would, but now that you've called me on it, I owe you a listen. Where do you think Anna Amiel-Janssen is?"

"Phil, do you know who lives in the house where Elizabeth, Hannah, and Anna lived?"

"No one," answered the detective.

"I figured that. Nothing comes up on the web in real estate, and according to Zillow.com, the last time the house sold was in 1997. Nor does anything come up searching the reverse listings. On Google Earth, the house looks small, possibly a modular. Despite the poor resolution of close-ups, the yard looks somewhat unkempt . . . not horrifically so, but a few years abandoned. It's also somewhat remote from the surrounding properties and homes. Elm Creek is a small town, so I'm sure the news traveled fast to all corners. People aren't quick to forget when tragedies as grisly as this happen, so I'm betting that house is considered cursed land, and that no one has resided there since. I sure as hell wouldn't live there."

"Granted, but if you're implying Anna's inside the house, I can assure you they have combed the house extensively and repeatedly. If it is abandoned, regardless of how small the town is, I'm sure local kids have entered there on dares, to party, to make out, and God knows what else."

"Not *in* the house, Phil . . . under. Do you remember Hannah telling us that Elizabeth told them to meet in the crawlspace under the house if things got *ugly*?"

"Yeah, but they would have checked under the house as well . . . the police, the forensic team, search dogs. I'm sure of it," Phil said.

"Yes, I'm sure they checked it, too, right after the murder, but what if Anna somehow ended up back home about five days later?"

"Why would she go back there?"

"Where else would she go, Phil? She was seven years old, her thought process wasn't as logical as ours, and she was freezing and irrational from the cold. Remember, it was March. She goes home looking for her mom and Hannah, and they aren't there. Maybe the door is locked or boarded over. Maybe there's a hidden key, but either way, no one is home. Hannah and her mom were alive the last Anna knew. Travis was hurting her mom, but she was alive."

"Why wouldn't she just go to a neighbor for help?" Phil asked. He no longer sounded completely confident, and this uncertainty was the element of doubt for which Debbie had been hoping.

"I can think of a few reasons. If Anna is at all like Hannah, and I'd wager she is, she wouldn't have disobeyed. It's in Hannah's nature.

It's very important to her to stay in favor. Hannah has verified that Elizabeth Amiel told her to hide way under the house if things got ugly. She's alone, horrifically traumatized, freezing, and scared shitless . . . things don't get much uglier, especially to a seven-year-old. Next, *way under the house* is instilled into her subconscious as a safe place, and even disoriented she would probably recognize it. Finally, from everything we've seen, people, outside of her mother and possibly her babysitter, haven't exactly been a source of comfort for her. I can't blame her for not running to her neighbors, even though they might be wonderful people who could have saved her life."

"If she's even dead," Phil reiterated. "Okay, it sounds possible, but we could staple a million probabilities to this. I don't think you're presenting anything here that will widen eyes or make them stop and backtrack."

"Is there any way you can convince them to check under the house one more time?" Debbie asked. "Tell them Hannah thinks she's there. Say anything that will convince them to take one quick look. If I were there, I'd do it . . ." Debbie's voice trailed off as her own words registered.

"I'll give it a shot, but don't get your hopes up. Maybe they will, but I'm guessing they won't. I can't see them jumping through hoops for some overzealous crackpot detective who's two thousand miles away and can't even speak right," Davenport said.

However, Debbie wasn't listening. Her thoughts had shifted to other possibilities.

"Okay, please do whatever you can," Debbie said. "I have to go, Phil. Something just came up."

Debbie disconnected the call and put the phone and Hannah's cookie in her purse. Standing, she gathered her barely-nibbled-at salad and the nasty iced tea and headed for the trash. She refrained from tossing out the salad, figuring Hannah might like it, but took great pleasure in dumping the tea.

It was nearly 6 p.m. and there was still plenty of daylight to go for a little walk. She was positive Hannah would be up for it.

CHAPTER 23

*H*annah smiled radiantly as she raced—only slightly favoring her sutured foot—from the hospital's back-street entrance towards the Lincoln Avenue crosswalk, directly across the street from the brick-walled perimeter of Riverside Stadium. She stopped and glanced back at Debbie who luckily wore flat-soled shoes and was therefore able to keep up . . . nearly.

What is it that makes Hannah so effervescent in spite of the tragedies she's seen and the hardships she's suffered? Debbie wondered. Whatever the source, it only made her more endearing.

"There," Debbie said, pointing left, to the east end of the Park.

Riverside Park had five baseball diamonds, five softball diamonds, four tennis courts, three basketball courts, two horseshoe pits, a street hockey field, and a volleyball court, all arcing around the east and south sides of Riverside Stadium. It was the sports arena for many Riverside Schools and leagues, and with its beautiful, tree-populated grounds, a skating area, two child play-lots, a handicapped swing set, a boat ramp, numerous walking paths, and plenty of parking, it was also a favorite visiting spot for Riverside residents.

The park was alive when they entered, as it always was on days like these, when the warm caress of a gentle breeze drifted off the Merrimack River. Amidst fading hints of contrails from passing aircraft, slow-moving cotton-ball clouds scattered across a brilliant sky, dragging shadows across the lush green lawns.

The air vibrated with life as parents and siblings cheered the clink of bats against balls, and laughing children and barking dogs defied the loud and tinny strains of music forced through the speakers of portable radios. The savory aroma of Italian sausage drifted over them and Hannah unconsciously let out a hum of approval.

"I agree," Debbie said. "And there's the culprit." She pointed to a street vendor at a silver-and-red hawker's cart. A delicious cloud enveloped him while he pushed onions and peppers atop the cooking surface. "Let's lighten his inventory a little."

Hannah smiled her agreement with a sparkle of delight in her eyes. Debbie purchased two subs, with chips and two bottles of lemonade, which they ate while sitting on the lawn near the basketball courts, watching four young men in a vigorous and sweaty battle of two-on-two. Hannah finished her sandwich before Debbie had taken three bites.

Impressed, Debbie asked, "Hungry much?"

"Snarfed it," Hannah said, followed by a startling belch. "Sorry," she giggled, embarrassed.

"Nothing to be sorry about," Debbie said. "I'm just mesmerized by how fast you ate it, and surprised that burp didn't pop you inside out."

Hannah surrendered to a bout of giggles, amused by the mental imagery of Debbie's statement.

Unable to finish the remainder of her sandwich, Debbie balled it up in her napkin and tucked it into the chip bag. "Hannah, I want you to help me," she said.

"Okay," Hannah replied.

"I know we can make things appear and disappear when we're in *our places*, like my pen and the tennis ball, and what you said about your cat makes me pretty certain you can jump back and forth totally, as well . . . not just the *thinking* you, but all of you. Is this true?"

"Unh-huh," Hannah agreed without the slightest hesitation.

"Okay. Well, today I learned something I did not know. Do you remember the two times you started fading away while you were sitting on my lap?" asked Debbie. "I just found out that I started fading away with you the second time."

"I know," said Hannah.

"You know? How come I didn't?"

Hannah shrugged and they remained quiet for a moment.

"Why here?" Debbie asked. It wasn't what she intended on asking, but the question popped out of nowhere and she realized how much she wanted to know. "Did you choose Riverside? You said you jumped out of Hannahwhere. Did you end up behind the dumpster by chance? If I were able to choose where I ended up, it wouldn't be behind a dumpster of all places."

Hannah said nothing. Debbie couldn't tell whether Hannah knew the answer and couldn't formulate the words, simply didn't know, or didn't want to answer.

"Is it like a lottery?" Debbie pressed. "Do you, like, think *jump now,* and poof!" She threw her hands up. "Where you end up is where you end up?"

Hannah stared at the ground looking guilty and uncomfortable. "I didn't come here from Hannahwhere," she confessed.

Debbie didn't expect *that* answer, but wondered what answer she was expecting. "How'd you get here, then?" she asked.

Again, Hannah hesitated to answer. Debbie moved closer to her, rubbed her back.

"Honey, whatever it is, you can tell me. There is no way I'll ever be upset with you."

Hannah's nose and cheeks blossomed deep red with withheld tears. She said, "Mom would be *so* mad at me if she knew I snuck a ride in a trailer."

"You stowed away in a trailer?" Debbie asked, astonished. She pictured Hannah squeezed between large shipping crates and assorted cargo in the back of a tractor-trailer. It was a disconcerting image. "Why?"

Hannah shrugged. "I was afraid Travis was looking for me. He took Anna. I kept thinking he was following me. I wanted to go somewhere he couldn't find me."

"How'd you open the trailer door? Did you sneak in while they were loading or unloading?"

Hannah stared at her uncertainly for a long moment and finally said, "It's like a house door . . . just littler."

It was Debbie's turn to look confused, and then she said, "Ohhh, it was a camper! Like a Winnebago?"

"Yeah, one of those, like a little house that a pickup truck pulls," Hannah said and sniffed.

"How'd you know it was safe to go inside the camper?"

"Because the old man and lady who went into Stuck's for dinner looked friendly, and they were nice to Mrs. Cullen's daughter Jillian," Hannah said and shrugged again. "But mostly because the red bird sat on the roof of the camper and kept chirping at me. I know I'm supposed to listen to the red bird."

"The cardinal?"

"Un-huh."

"How do you know you're supposed to listen to the cardinal?" asked Debbie.

"It's what Mom wanted."

Although it kept popping up, the bird confounded Debbie, but she was going to stick with the concrete facts. She'd address the bird later.

"What's Stuck's? A diner?" Debbie asked.

"It's a place to eat in Elm Creek. Mom used to take us there sometimes. Stuck's Lasco."

Stuck's Lasco? *Odd name,* thought Debbie, *though it did sound like an oil company, like Sunoco or Arco . . . why not Lasco?* She had seen plenty of strange small town businesses with strange names. The web was full of them, like Bung Hole Liquors and Boring Business Systems.

"Wait! Do you mean Stuck's Last Call?" asked Debbie.

"Unh-huh," Hannah agreed. "That's what I said."

"Got it," Debbie said. "Mrs. Cullen runs it?"

"Yup." Hannah nodded, and then excitedly added, "Oh! Plus the camper had a Massachusetts license plate." She had a little difficulty spitting out the state name.

"Why did Massachusetts plates make it okay?"

"Because the New England Patriots are from Massachusetts, and it means Tom Brady is from here," Hannah said. "Mom loves Tom Brady. He's her hero, and that's what Anna and me need to help us . . . a hero."

Seeing the conviction in Hannah's face, Debbie couldn't restrain her laughter.

"What?" asked Hannah, confused, but with a defensive edge to her voice.

"You are such a doll!" Debbie assured her and gave her a quick hug. "It's funny because Tom Brady is my hero, too."

"Really?"

"Absolutely! Who can resist him? He's soooo cute! Do you know who else is my hero?"

"Brad Pitt?"

"Hardly," Debbie said, rolling her eyes. "You are!"

"Me?" Hannah asked, crinkling her nose.

"Absolutely! What you've been through and how you've stayed alive through it all is more than anyone I know could handle . . . including me." Debbie rubbed the top of her head playfully. "What I have seen and learned since I met you, I never thought was possible, and I'm not talking about just the magical stuff. I'm talking about you surviving this long without adult help. You are amazing!"

Hannah held Debbie's gaze for a few moments and then gave her an embarrassed, toothy smile.

After another pause, Debbie asked, "Hannah, if you can just wish yourself to be wherever you want to be, then why didn't you just wish yourself to Massachusetts, or even into Tom Brady's house? Why'd you take the camper instead?"

"Because Mom made me and Anna promise to never-ever-ever try to go someplace unless we already been there before," Hannah explained.

Processing this, Debbie asked, "What would happen?"

Hannah shrugged. "It's like going someplace that isn't real because you don't know anything about it, or where it is. Mom was afraid we would go where someone or something bad is, or in the same place where something or someone else is."

Debbie thought a while and then the understanding settled in. She imagined appearing exactly where someone was standing, or within a cement wall, or where a giant turbine or propeller was spinning. The thought made her queasy.

"Oh my God, I'm glad you obey your mother!" she gasped.

"Mom wouldn't like me going in the camper," Hannah said.

"But they didn't catch you, did they?" Debbie reassured her.

"Almost. They stopped one time when I was peeing in their bathroom. I had to hurry. I hid under the seat cushions at the table where they eat. It was like a box with a cover that lifts. It only had two pillows and an orange, swimmy-so-you-don't-drown-thing in it, so I fit in, too," Hannah said. "I got the old man in trouble because I was hungry and I took the Fig Newtons that were on the counter into the box with me. I felt bad because she called him a pig face and wouldn't believe he didn't eat them."

"I'm sure he's fine," Debbie chuckled. "This is quite the adventure you had. That's a long ride."

"Yeah, but I think I slept a lot. It was real hot in there," Hannah said.

"Why'd you get out in Riverside?"

"Whenever the truck turned off, I'd look out the window at other cars and trucks to see if they had Massachusetts license plates. There were none for a really long time and I was afraid they weren't going to Massachusetts, but the last time they stopped, Massachusetts license plates were on almost every car, so I knew that's where I had to get out."

Debbie imagined being nine years old and alone in an unknown city, with no one to turn to and no idea what to do or where to go. She was thirty and dreaded going into Boston. Everything seemed so large, the buildings so imposing, the streets an indecipherable spaghetti plate, and any strange face a potential threat. Boston never failed to put her into a near panic, and New York City made her a complete wreck.

"You must have been so frightened," Debbie said.

"I was more tired of being alone," Hannah said. "Can we go for a walk?"

Debbie arose and tossed the wrappers and bottles into a green trash receptacle. She offered Hannah her hand, squeezed it reassuringly, and then they followed a paved path bordering the Merrimack River along the rear of the park.

"Does it bother you to talk about all these things?" Debbie asked.

Hannah looked up at Debbie. "No. I like to."

"Really?"

"With you," Hannah said. "I like Essie, too, but I'm scared to talk to her because she can't think-hear me like you do."

"I think Essie's okay to talk to if you're comfortable with her. She's just not like us with the traveling."

They wandered silently until Debbie said, "So, my little pioneer, how did you get from the trailer to the trash bin?"

"The red bird," said Hannah. "He has a really weird but neat chirp. It goes like, *burpy-burpy-peep-peep*. When I snuck out of the camper, the red bird was on top, looking at me and chirping like crazy. We were in a parking lot, but he flew across the street and down the little road. I knew I was supposed to follow him."

The cardinal again. Debbie remembered the one that landed on her during her first visit to Hannahwhere, and on the hood of her car after the liquor store fiasco.

"I've seen one around, too. Do you think it's the same one?" Debbie asked.

Hannah shrugged. "I don't know, but he's always around. Even at the hospital, I see him in the tree outside my window. It's like he was trying to say something, like when he landed on the dumpster and kept tweeting and flapping his wings. I knew he wanted me to stay there, so I hid behind the dumpster." Hannah looked around for a few seconds and then pointed to a thick-breasted cardinal high in a silver birch. "There," she said.

Debbie put two fingers to her lips and gave a high, sharp whistle. The bird jerked its head, looked directly at them, and responded with the characteristic *chirby-chirby-chirby-chirby-djou-djou*. He swooped to a closer tree and watched them.

"I'll be damned," said Debbie. Even if it wasn't the same bird, it was too odd not to be significant. Debbie returned her attention to Hannah and said, "You stayed at the dumpster for three nights?"

Hannah shrugged.

"You shrug a lot," Debbie said and poked Hannah's nose playfully.

"You ask a lot of questions," Hannah countered.

"Touché," said Debbie. "And don't you dare say coulé."

"Huh?"

"Never mind. So, did the cardinal stay at the dumpster with you?"

Hannah shrugged again, smiled, and said, "Coulé?"

"Smart aleck," Debbie said. There were so many questions, but Debbie decided she'd broach the subject of the cardinal later. To keep the conversation on track, she asked, "What happened to your pants, underpants, and shoes? All you had on was an oversized shirt when Isaac found you."

Hannah's cheeks flushed and Debbie understood.

"Had an accident?"

Hannah nodded. "A bad one," she said. "I threw everything in the dumpster, even my shoes and socks."

"Happens to the best of us sooner or later," Debbie said. "But you could have gone back to Hannahwhere at any time to get new clothes. Why didn't you?"

"The thinking me went back," Hannah said rationally. "But I have to get help for Anna, and I can't do it in Hannahwhere. When I go there, I want to stay there, so I promised Anna and me that I won't go back until I find someone to help her. The cold really hurts her, but every time I tried to ask people for help, I got afraid and didn't. I almost went all the way into Hannahwhere when Isaac Rawls found me, but I somehow knew I had to stay there and let him. When he picked me up he was warm, and it made me think how cold Anna is. If I went back, I wouldn't get help for her and she would stay cold and stuck forever. Mom says we have to watch out for each other, and I didn't watch out for Anna good enough."

Debbie crouched before Hannah. "Honey, none of this is your fault, not even the smallest bit. You've done *nothing* wrong. In fact, everything you've done has been astonishing. You should get a medal. Do you hear me? Look at me."

Debbie lifted Hannah's chin. The stark terror she saw when she met Hannah's eyes stole her words and the breath to propel them.

"If I don't get Anna help," Hannah said, her chin trembling. "If anything happens to Anna and she dies like Mom, then I'll be all alone!"

Alone.

Abandoned.

The weight of this fear staggered Debbie as an adult, how enormous it must be for a nine-year-old child. Debbie embraced her tightly.

"Hannah, you'll never be alone again. We'll figure this out. No matter what, you will not be alone. But, like I said earlier, I need your help, okay?"

Hannah dolefully scuffed at the ground with her sneaker and nodded again.

"You know how you make *all of you*, not just the thinking you, go back and forth to places?" Debbie asked. "I want you to show me how to do that. I know, I know . . . I just need to *know* I can do it—and I do because I faded with you—but I need help with how to do it myself."

Hannah stood thoughtfully for a while and then met Debbie's eyes. "But you did it last night," she said.

"I went to Debtopia . . . my place," Debbie said, feeling slightly embarrassed verbally hearing the name she had chosen. Hannah shot her a quick questioning glance but made no comment. "Why would you think all of me went last night?"

"Anna told me all of you was there. You were scared," Hannah said.

"How could she tell?" asked Debbie.

"She said your eyes were popping out of your head."

"No. Anyone could have seen I was scared," Debbie said. "How did she know all of me—my body—was there?"

Hannah hesitated then said, "The flowers were squished."

Debbie eyed her doubtfully. "Are you telling me our bodies don't crush the flowers when just the thinking us is there?"

"Un-huh," Hannah said compellingly. "Our thinking selves don't weigh nothing."

"Are you messing with me? You just used a double negative. I don't remember crushing the flowers last night," Debbie said.

"Do you remember *not* crushing them?" Hannah asked. Debbie stared at her and Hannah held her gaze, a smile hiding just beneath the surface.

"You're messing with me!"

"Okay," said Hannah.

"And you're patronizing me?" Debbie said.

"What does patronizing mean?"

"It means belittling. Are you making fun of me?"

Hannah said, "Touché?"

"What do you mean *touché*?" Debbie asked, feigning outrage. "Remember, smarty pants, the queen of tickle-torture is bigger than you." She playfully poked Hannah in the ribs eliciting a giggling shriek. Debbie cocked an eyebrow. Hannah returned the gesture and started walking.

Debbie watched her walk a few yards along the path and followed her. After a short silence she said, "The second thing I need you to do is take me to Elm Creek."

Hannah stopped with her gaze anchored to the ground before her.

"Yeah, I knew you weren't going to like it any more than I do, but you know where it is and I've never been there." Debbie rested a hand on her shoulder. "I think I have to go there if we hope to help Anna."

Hannah didn't respond. Debbie felt an edge of panic and wondered if she'd pushed Hannah back into a dissociative state.

"It's okay, Honey. You don't have to," Debbie said. "I got a good view of Elm Creek from satellite pictures. I can do it by myself."

Hannah shook her head emphatically and glared at Debbie. "Never, ever, ever go anyplace you never went before," she reminded her. "You're being dumb."

Debbie felt as if there were a shift in roles and she wondered *who's protecting whom?* "I'm sorry," she said, stooping before Hannah and trying to give her a reassuring hug. Hannah resisted at first, and then finally conceded with brimming eyes.

How could I be so thoughtless and so . . . so stupid? Debbie admonished herself. Hasn't Hannah been through enough?

"You're right. That was dumb of me," she said. "We probably should head back soon."

Hannah extracted herself from the embrace. "I'll take you to Elm Creek."

"No, it's all right, honey. I'll figure out a way. I could take a plane."

"No. We have to help Anna. The cold hurts her . . . and it hurts me, too."

"You can feel Anna's pain?"

"I'm not cold, but I know she is, and I feel it in my tummy and head. I think it hurts her more than she says. She doesn't want us to be sad, but I am."

Telepathy, magic, witchcraft, miracles, and teleportation, so many things could be explained by this incredible truth Hannah had introduced and given to her; the gift of believing in the inexplicable. Maybe *anything* was possible if your conviction was strong enough. The ability to exist in such a realm could be wondrous in one person's control, yet terrifying in the hands of another.

"I'm sad too, honey. It's why I also want to help her," Debbie assured her. "Are you sure you want to do this?"

Hannah nodded and took Debbie's hand. "When should we go?" she asked.

"Well, I have to confess that this is part of the reason I took you out for a walk. I was hoping that while we were away from the hospital we could try something quickly so we can familiarize ourselves with traveling together, and then we could come right back unnoticed." Debbie looked at Hannah, trying to appear as contrite as a puppy. "We can start out simple like traveling a few feet, and then we can try something further like my house. It's close enough that if we can't travel back, we can walk back easily enough. If that works, we can quickly go to Elm Creek and back, so I know where it is. Then I can go back later without ending up part of a porta-potty or something."

Debbie watched Hannah's expression, but could read nothing.

"We'd have to do it here," Debbie added. "It would be impossible to do back at the hospital with all the staff."

"Okay," said Hannah.

Debbie led the way through a thick stand of trees to a narrow boat ramp that sloped down to the Merrimack River. They were at the head of a hairpin bend in the river, which curved out of sight to the east and west. It gave them the impression of being isolated in this pretty location, surrounded by trees. The distant sound of people in the park was mostly drowned out by the rush of the river.

"We didn't have any rivers like this in Elm Creek," Hannah said. She stepped toward the water, and something small skittered into the underbrush on the riverbank.

"Well, be careful," warned Debbie. "It looks mild on the surface, but the undercurrent here will grab you and whisk you away like a leaf."

"How about here?" Hannah said, bouncing on the balls of her feet.

"Yeah, you're okay there," said Debbie.

"No, I mean, what if we go from here?"

"Travel from here?" Debbie asked uncertainly.

"No one's around."

"Yeah, but what if I don't do it right? Someone will come by and find a zombified me standing here, and no you. To make it worse, we're near the river. They'll think you're somewhere out in the Atlantic Ocean looking for Nemo."

"Nemo's in the Pacific," Hannah corrected.

"It has a Maine lobstah with a Boston accent," countered Debbie.

"In Australia," Hannah replied and stuck out her tongue.

"Nemo's a cartoon," Debbie mocked in return.

"I'll hold your hand and make sure you do it right," Hannah reassured her, again giving Debbie the sense of being the subordinate in their odd little team. "It won't take long."

Debbie was a little hesitant, yet excited by the prospect of traveling again. "We'll be coming right back once I learn where it is," Debbie said, and then hesitantly asked, "We will be able to come back right here, and not in the middle of the river, or up in a tree . . . or in the center of a tree, right?"

"On a dime," Hannah said.

"On a dime," Debbie repeated. "Dimes are pretty small."

"Yup," Hannah agreed.

Debbie rubbed her hands together anxiously. "Okay, you're going to have to lead."

"You go to your place and I'll go to Hannahwhere, but we'll go together, I think," Hannah said, unsure.

"This continues to be very confusing for me, you realize, but I thought about that last night," said Debbie. "It didn't make sense that Anna would be in my place, so I figured I somehow went to Annaplace because it was Anna I wanted to see. But I really think all our places are the same place. I bet your mom was afraid when your cat never came back that it could happen to her daughters, so to protect you she said you needed your own places. I would have said the same thing to keep you safe . . . well, as safe as possible."

Hannah looked confused and doubtful.

"Well, I'm determined to get to the bottom of it and figure all of this travel stuff out." Debbie huffed.

"It's common sense," said Hannah, rolling her eyes.

"Are you kidding me? There's nothing common or sensible about any of this!" Debbie blurted. "How long will this take?"

"Not long. When we go, I still want to go to our own places.

We'll still be together, but I'll be in Hannahwhere and you'll be in . . . Deb . . ."

"Debtopia," Debbie said and Hannah unconsciously scrunched her nose. "What, you don't like the name of my place?"

"No, Debstupia is fine," Hannah said and giggled.

"Fine, wisenheimer, let's hear you come up with something better!"

"I would have called it Abracadeborah."

"I refuse to believe you just thought that up," Debbie said with mock aloofness.

"Okay," Hannah said, unperturbed.

"Well, I'm stealing it," Debbie said.

Hannah made a la-de-da expression, fortifying just how much Debbie loved the girl's personality.

"Okay, we have to sit," Hannah instructed, looking for a suitable spot.

"Why?"

"Why not?" Hannah replied, and then with conviction said, "Trust me, you want to sit." As if in example, she sat cross-legged facing the river and motioned for Debbie to join her. She did.

"So, how do we do this together?" Debbie asked. "Have you traveled with Anna at the same time?"

"Sometimes. We tried with Mom, but she never could."

"Did you ever have problems when you and Anna traveled?"

"No," Hannah said. "We always knew we could do it."

"Mind sharing some of that childlike faith?" said Debbie.

Hannah took her hand. "Don't let go. You have to think about going to your place, but don't just think the thinking you going, think about *all of you* going."

"That's a lot of thinking," said Debbie.

"Try not to hurt yourself," said Hannah.

"I beg your pardon!" Debbie barked, stunned, but humored.

"That's what Travis used to say to Mom when she'd say *I'm thinking,* or *let me think.* I don't get it, but Mom used to tell us Travis was just teasing her."

The barb suddenly wasn't funny now that Debbie pictured the cruel words thinly disguised as a joke spilling from the sneering, spiteful mouth of Travis Ulrich. His image from file photos floated in her memory. His dark malevolent eyes glared from a face that would have been handsome if not transformed by the demons inside the man.

"Did I say something bad?" Hannah asked, wide-eyed with alarm.

"Why would you think that?" asked Debbie.

"You look mad or something."

"No, baby. Not at all. What you said isn't bad, it was funny, but when I thought of Travis saying that to your mom, that turned it ugly," Debbie explained. "Words, no matter how pretty or ugly, don't just tell you what a person is saying, they tell you who the person saying them is. You know what I mean?"

"Yeaa . . . no," said Hannah.

"If you took the world's most beautiful rose and flushed it down a toilet, what kind of shape would it be in after?"

"Shitty."

"I supposed I asked for that, but that's right," Debbie said. "Travis is like a toilet, but enough of that. What were you telling me about how you travel?"

"Okay," Hannah said. "I start thinking about my feet going where I want to go, and my legs, my butt, my back, until I get to my head. Let's go to our places first, okay?"

Debbie closed her eyes and envisioned herself flying. She instantly felt the familiar centrifugal spin, and they were soon sitting in the fields, the flowers around them as brilliant as ever.

"Wow, that was easy," Debbie said, starting to rise.

"Don't get up!" said Hannah. "Let's go to your house. This time you go first and I'll follow. Think about landing somewhere safe, like a couch or a bed, but don't get scared." She grabbed Debbie's hand again, not giving her time to rebel. "Go!"

Debbie went without allowing herself the chance to doubt. She envisioned her home and willed her thoughts toward flying safely to her bed. Again, they catapulted through buffeting winds with swooping gyrations, though it was different from last time. Her whole body felt as if it was latching onto the pummeling winds and gliding. The swooping feeling was still present, but there was an added sense of weight as the gyrations increased, intensely magnifying the vertigo until it was so dense Debbie started to black out.

They had arrived, sitting cross-legged on Debbie's queen-sized bed. She was dazed and floaters swarmed her vision as she fought to keep her gorge down.

"Yay! You did it," Hannah cheered, raising her arms in the air. She paused and critically asked, "This *is* your bedroom, right?"

"Yes," Debbie said, gasping. "Oh my God, that was terrible, far worse than last time!"

"Yeah, the first time was really bad for me, too," said Hannah. "You gonna hurl?" She moved cautiously away.

"You told me . . ." Debbie started to say, trying the settle her nausea. "Wait a minute! You lied!"

"Yup," Hannah said, just as perky as ever.

"Why?"

"That's how I got Anna to go the first time, too, but she chucked all over," Hannah said. "See, you did it without chucking!"

Debbie held Hannah's gaze, feeling a combination of irritation and gratitude. She had been duped, yet, if she hadn't, she and Hannah would still have been sitting at the river's edge while she procrastinated.

Hannah jumped from the bed and headed into the connected room. "Wow! You have your own bathroom!"

"Yes," Debbie said, still shaking off the last of the butterflies.

"It's cool and it connects to the dining room!" Hannah's voice faded, and then she reappeared full circle at the bedroom door that connected directly to the living room. "Neat!"

Debbie laughed at her expression. This little girl could perform feats that would make her appear a deity in the eyes of most, yet she found a common bathroom a thing of wonder.

"You didn't make your bed," Hannah informed her.

"Neither did you," Debbie countered.

Hannah sent her a smile and dashed back into the living room and onward to farther reaches of the house. Debbie followed, amused by Hannah's enthusiasm.

"Do you have a cat?"

"No."

"Dog?"

"No."

"Why is your sink in the middle of your kitchen?" Hannah asked.

"It's called an island," Debbie explained.

"We had one, too, but the sink was still in the right place," said Hannah.

"Maybe *your* sink was in the wrong place," Debbie offered.

Hannah formed a slightly pained expression as she mulled over the question. Choosing to dismiss it, she was off again. She traipsed through the living room and stopped before the closed door. She looked back to Debbie.

Debbie halted as uneasiness built. *It's just a room*, she reminded herself. *The visions are mine, not Hannah's.* It still didn't keep her from picturing the grossly porcine man stepping through the doorway, putting a hand on Hannah's back, and directing her inside.

Hey, Blondie.

Debbie closed her eyes, trying to drive the disturbing visualization away. *It's just a room . . . It's just a room . . . It's just a room.*

"Can I look?"

Debbie nodded and moved forward. Hannah twisted the doorknob and slowly pushed the door open.

"I can't see," she said.

"The light switch is on the wall inside."

Hannah searched around and seemed to be struggling.

"Push the button," Debbie said.

With a *click*, the room illuminated.

"Cool!" Hannah said, brightening again. "We don't have switches like that."

"It's an old-fashioned switch. This house is *very* old."

Hannah stepped into the lighted room and sized it up. There were two file cabinets, a rolled Oriental rug, numerous boxes of books, kitchen supplies, clothing, and countless other items stacked haphazardly throughout. It was unlikely that Debbie would use most of it, but she didn't have the heart to dispose of it. She would let it linger under a stratum of dust in *The Realm of All Things Abandoned* . . . like the wedding photo album set alone atop a pile of boxes. *Much like me*, Debbie thought, and then pushed it away. This was not the time for a pity party.

"Hey, if we cleaned this room up and put beds in here, me and Anna could stay here!" Hannah said enthusiastically.

"Anna and I," said Debbie.

"Okay. I'll take your room."

"Nice try, Cupcake," Debbie said.

Hannah watched her, waiting for a confirmation, but Debbie said, "We have to get back soon. You lead."

"Okay," Hannah said, trying to mask her disappointment.

Debbie hadn't said no, which left enough promise for Hannah to hang her hopes on, but there was a glimpse of anger visible behind Hannah's eyes since Debbie hadn't said yes, either. Debbie saw her anger as a potentially good sign. Hannah needed to express herself so resentments wouldn't build between them. They returned to Debbie's bedroom and sat cross-legged on the bed.

"Okay, on three," Hannah said soberly, taking hold of Debbie's hand.

They jaunted to Hannahwhere and relayed back to the boat ramp. Debbie experienced the vertigo and a very mild nausea, but this time was easier, except there was a different sensation. Debbie felt a cold wetness on her legs and below her waist. She gasped and opened her eyes. They were back on the boat ramp, but Debbie was at the low end of the ramp, submerged to her waist in the Merrimack River. Hannah was sitting just to her right . . . on dry cement. She was smirking and there was a devilish glint in her eyes.

Debbie jumped up and dashed away from the frigid water. "You did that on purpose, you little shi . . . shenanigan!" Debbie accused her.

"Nun . . . unh," Hannah said, shaking her head.

"You're not getting away with this one, missy! I asked if we would be able to come back without ending up in the middle of the river, and you said, 'On a dime'!" Debbie sat her soaked bottom on the ramp and pulled off her sneakers and sopping socks.

"You weren't in the middle," Hannah said. She was clearly trying to maintain her anger and disappointment, but couldn't control the giggles.

Debbie glared at her.

"Someone moved the dime," she added, and then burst out laughing.

Debbie tried to hold a stern posture, but Hannah's laughter was contagious. Despite her irritation she let a smile slip and was soon laughing as well, thinking to herself, *hey, you wanted her to express her anger.* She scooted beside Hannah and draped an arm over her shoulders.

"I know you're angry with me, but would you want me to say something that may not be true or right just because it's what you want to hear?"

"Yes," Hannah said, pouting stubbornly,

"I don't believe that," Debbie said. She wrung out her socks and pulled them back on.

Hannah said, "I'm sorry I got you wet. We can go back to your house so you can change."

Debbie stood and offered Hannah her hand. "No time. The sun's starting to set and we have to get you back to your room. Besides, I need to get home. I'm so far behind on my work that my cases are older than their foster parents."

"Huh?"

"Never mind. Let's go," Debbie said. "I want to do this again tomorrow . . . without the dunk in the river."

Hannah shrugged. Debbie pulled her to her feet and holding hands they began walking, Debbie's sneakers squeaking and sloshing as they walked.

"Uh-oh," said Hannah, stopping abruptly.

"What?"

"Someone saw us," Hannah stage whispered and nodded towards the top of the access ramp.

Slightly off the ramp and hidden amongst the trees stood a boy of about eleven. He stared at them, open-mouthed and daft looking.

"Just play it cool," Debbie whispered. "No one will believe him anyway."

Hannah walked by the boy, mimicking his expression.

Debbie said, "Close your mouth, kid. You'll eat a bug."

WEDNESDAY
June 30, 2010

CHAPTER 24

Hannahwhere

"I want my hair as short as yours," Anna says. "Debbie tried to cut it but couldn't."

She is sitting at a table of intricate white ironwork, bordering the field of flowers. A large brown-and-caramel-colored rabbit rests motionless on her lap except for the perpetual pulsation of its nose. Three more rabbits hop around Anna's feet, weaving through the legs of the table and chairs, nibbling at the bounty of greens growing there.

Hannah is standing beneath a lush, fruit-laden tree with large green-and-gold foil-like leaves. She grips the lowest branch, swings her legs up, hooks them over the limb, and suspends upside-down. Above her, a flash of brilliant red heralds the cardinal. It perches in the branch near her legs and offers a greeting, *chirby-chirby-chirby-chirby-djou-djou.*

"Hello," Hannah says and returns the salutation to the bird. She turns her attention back to Anna and says, "You know nothing on us changes when we're here."

"Yeah, but I was hoping it'd be different with Debbie, since she's Miss Coppertop. Besides, if we can't change, why am I getting colder and feeling poopier all the time? Those are changes, right?"

At a loss for a proper answer, Hannah shrugs. "Mom liked our hair long."

"Yeah, but I want it shorter. It's a pain without Mom to help with it."

"It is better short," Hannah admits.

The cardinal hops to a slightly higher branch. This time his call is a rapid and shrill *djou-djou-djou-djou-djou*. Anna shoots it a wary look.

"That's weird. I never heard him do that before," she says. "He sounds like an alarm clock."

"Uh-oh," Hannah says. She drops to the ground with her eyes locked on the horizon and takes a few hesitant steps in the direction she is looking.

"What?" Anna asks, rising from the table. She sets the rabbit on the ground amongst the others, which are now stirring nervously.

From all points on the blue horizon, black and grey clouds boil up, gathering, expanding, and connecting. Lightning pulses behind the swollen, billowing sky, painting it blood red and stabbing the landscape with blinding spears. A heated breeze rushes over the land and the flowers bow, thrash, and rustle in its wake. The branches of the trees protest with strained creaks and the clicking of the foil-like leaves.

Anna moves nearer to Hannah as the sky surrenders totally to bruised, black and red clouds. A hiss rises around them, low, like a light rain, barely discernible through the rush of the wind, yet gaining volume until it sounds like applause. Matching and then surpassing the rushing wind, it becomes thunderous, bringing the floral meadow to life. In the distance, flowers fade and turn to black, spilling an ebon path that spreads and encroaches on the sisters. A pool of death washes over the field, extinguishing each flower with a hiss, each hiss adding to the thunderous din.

The girls back away from the field as scores of rabbits scatter in a frenzy to escape the floral overgrowth. Lightning slams the tree Hannah has just vacated, hewing it in two . . . the concussion deafening. Ozone and sulfur fill the air with a stench so thick they cover their noses and mouths and retch.

A black, doglike creature with a sloping back and crouching hind legs bounds from deep flowers, landing with a fierce snarl. It clamps a rabbit in lethal jaws and turns on the girls, pinning them with its feral yellow eyes. A horde follows, leaping forward from the field in a drove of baleful glares and snapping jaws. Some claim rabbits while others are only intent on the sisters.

Hyenas, Hannah realizes. Too terrified to look at her sister, she slowly reaches for Anna's icy hand. She feels as if electricity is traveling from her legs, holding her to the ground.

The first hyena approaches. Its malignant gaze dares them to run, and it looks excited in anticipation of such a game. The rabbit kicks feebly, its fur matted by the hyena's fetid drool as it hangs helplessly from the beast's maw. With a brutal shake of its head, the hyena kills the rabbit and discards its limp body with another shake.

As if on command, the hyenas encircle the girls in unison, removing any means of retreat. Another deafening peal rings out as lightning strikes nearby. A rustling ensues beyond the circle of hyenas as cornstalks sprout violently from the ground, row upon row, shooting up ten feet tall towards the ferocious, bloodied skies, trapping Hannah, Anna, and the hyenas within a cornstalk prison.

Hannah slowly looks at Anna who is shaking wildly and staring through red-rimmed eyes at the horror before her. With hands pressed to her mouth, Anna backs away from the carcass of the rabbit. Gusts of wind force the corn to sway and lean, dispersing a searing acrid reek of chemicals, anger, and addiction over them and they know Travis is there even before his dreaded brown work boots breach the wall of corn.

"Where are you, my little girls?" Travis calls in his hateful, mocking voice. "My little snow angels. My little . . . shits?" He puts his hand above his eyes as if blocking out the sun, making a dramatic show of searching for them. Lightning flashes over his tall form as he bends slightly at the waist. He feigns surprise as if he's just noticed them.

"Ah . . . there you are. You hide so well in my darkness."

"Go away! You don't belong here!" Anna yells at the detestable man. She grips Hannah's hand tighter.

Travis regards Anna as if she's a curious, but brazen oddity . . . a three-headed puppy.

"But of course I do," he says. "Your momma shared all your little secrets with me . . . the man she adored. The man she lived for . . . and died for." He steps in front of the sisters and leans forward, his face level with theirs. "Of course, I did have to convince her a little," he says, his putrid breath washing over them.

Hannah wants to vomit. She wants to leave, but she knows Anna can't, and she can't leave her alone with him.

"Go away," says Anna. Hannah hears the acid in her voice and wants to tell her to stop and be quiet.

"I had to practically *cut* it out of her," Travis says, slashing his hands before their faces. "Which reminds me . . . we have unfinished business."

His hand shoots out as fast as a rattlesnake strike, grabbing Anna's braid and yanking her brutally to him. Anna squeals in pain and reaches out defensively, but blindly.

"What a frigid little girl," Travis says with a terrible grin. He winks at Hannah. "This is good—really good—because I *love* cold cuts."

Travis reaches behind his back and retrieves a large knife—*the knife*—from his beltline and waves it hypnotically before them. Splashes of their mother's blood dapple the blade and congeal near the handle. He tucks the knife under Anna's chin.

"Leave her alone!" Hannah shrieks.

"Don't be jealous, sweetheart. You're next."

He leads Anna by the hair to the white iron table. The hyenas obediently part as he moves to a chair and makes her sit. He looks at Hannah and says, "Now you. Come here."

Hannah doesn't move. She can't move.

Travis's eyes widen as the anger grows within him.

"Come here!" he says louder, pushing the blade against Anna's throat, but Hannah still can't persuade herself to walk. Her legs are as rigid as iron and refuse to obey. Insanity sinks its teeth into Travis, and his eyes bulge hideously, looking ready to spring from their sockets. The lightning seems to intensify as bolts flare and strike in a relentless display around them.

"COME HERE!" Travis bellows.

Something heavy and growling pushes Hannah from behind, trying to propel her toward him. She resists, preferring the touch of the hyenas to the alternative. Travis, now more intent on Hannah than her sister, steps toward her, wildly waving the knife.

"When I say come here, you—fucking—come—here!" Travis roars and lunges.

Hannah knows she shouldn't. It's the ultimate betrayal, but she can't help it. She looks at Anna, who meets her with tear-stained eyes, and then, with the memory of Travis lunging at her, she thinks herself away.

CHAPTER 25

Riverside, Massachusetts

Something was different. Debbie felt it from behind the wall of sleep. Something changed.

She had worked for nearly five hours after she arrived home earlier that evening. She started scanning profiles, planning visits, and making recommendations, hoping to put a decent dent into her DCF backlog, but thoughts of Hannah and Anna soon pushed everything else away. Exhaustion took over far sooner than she had hoped, leaving her short of her objective and just coherent enough to save her work before shutting down her laptop. Her head barely hit the pillow before she was asleep.

Now, despite her fatigue, something was working at her consciousness. She had heard a noise in her hypnopompic mind and it drew her upward, away from sleep, even though she still balanced on the threshold between slumber and wakefulness. Steve Perry's alto croon swelled and ebbed with his admiration of "Oh Sherrie". It sounded surreal and miles away, but coming closer.

Debbie felt a weight on her legs that she knew didn't belong there. She opened her eyes marginally and saw a luminescent figure sitting on her bed, looking like a ghost in the nominal light of the bedroom. Debbie couldn't move her hand, or even a finger. The paralysis of semi-sleep had her trapped as if she were lying under a mountain of sand.

No one should be in her house. She was certain that she had locked the doors, and that knowledge gave her enough resolve finally to break free from the clutches of sleep that held her. She scrambled away from the visage and pressed herself against the headboard as if awaiting an attack or the cold touch of death. It took a second to comprehend what she was seeing, but recognition set in . . . first the face, and then the expression of Hannah sitting at the foot of the bed, broken with stark terror and anguish. Whatever had put her in such a state was severe and maybe devastating. Panic sank into Debbie's shoulder blades like shark's teeth, triggering her into full wakefulness. She slid forward and pulled Hannah to her.

"Hannah! My God, what is it?" Debbie asked.

Hannah clutched to her urgently, digging her fingers into her back and burying her face in her neck. A hard knot of dread formed in Debbie's stomach when the full magnitude of the situation hit her. It all seemed too familiar, the bizarreness, the utter fear, and the sudden helplessness. She felt as if she had stepped too close to the edge and the momentum was bringing her over. In the weak resolve of midnight, and for the first time since she had taken on this case, Debbie wasn't certain if she could go through with it any longer, or if she even wanted to.

Hannah hugged her tighter as if sensing these thoughts. Her desperation was palpable and her trembling limbs and body so small and fragile in Debbie's embrace that she knew she could never give up on Hannah or Anna, despite her fears and reservations.

"What happened, Hannah?" Debbie asked. "Did something happen at the hospital?"

Hannah's mouth moved against her as she tried to form words, but she was too frantic to speak. Debbie placed a hand on Hannah's head and rocked her gently, giving her time to settle down, but she couldn't help asking, "Are you hurt?"

Hannah gave a sharp shake of her head and choked out, "Anna!"

The knot in Debbie's gut clenched tighter. She pulled Hannah back so she could see her face. "Honey, what's wrong with Anna?"

Hannah was unable to force the words out at first, and then with a keening sob she said, "I left her there! He had the knife and he . . . he's going to kill her! I got scared and I left her there with him!"

"Wait," Debbie said, trying to decipher the words, though she was sure about whom Hannah was speaking. "You left her where with who?"

What Hannah was saying couldn't be. How could Travis be

there? Was it a dream or a memory?

"I left her with Travis 'cause she can't leave and I was too scared to stay. Now he has her and he'll kill her like he killed Mom!" Hannah wailed.

Debbie had a hard time wrapping her mind around the frantic flow of Hannah's words. *If Travis was truly there, why now and not two years ago?*

"Hannah. Hold on, honey," Debbie said. "Even if Travis was there, he couldn't hurt Anna. Remember, I couldn't cut Anna's hair. We can't change people when we're there. I think it's because we are there in our thinking or spiritual form, not physical."

"Not always," argued Hannah sullenly, yet hopefully. "But we can still feel pain there. He can hurt her!"

"Maybe not. We know for sure that Anna's there only in her spirit form and she's disconnected from her body. He can't hurt her! It'd be like trying to hurt a ghost." Debbie insisted. She cringed inwardly at her hopeful lie, wishing she hadn't used the word *ghost*, and wishing she felt the conviction that her voice carried. "Are you sure it wasn't a nightmare? It's not logical that Travis didn't show up before. Nightmares can seem very real."

"He said he made Mom tell him where we were. He made a giant storm and turned Hannahwhere dark and ugly." She sniffed and wiped an arm across her eyes. "He killed all the flowers and his hyenas killed Anna's bunnies!"

Debbie saw an opportunity and leapt on it.

"See, it can't be real. You can't ruin what's in Hannahwhere or Annaplace, like the flowers. We fall on them, we jump on them, and we sit on them and squish them, but they always pop right back into shape afterwards, even when we are in our non-physical form . . . " Debbie's words tapered off as she hesitated for a thought. "Yeah, I checked after you tricked me . . . they may recover, but they do squish." She handed Hannah a few tissues from a box on her nightstand.

"Even if it was a dream, why's Anna still changing and getting more sick?" Hannah pointed out and Debbie could not deny the truth in it.

"I don't understand, either," Debbie admitted. "But I bet it's not something that someone else is doing to her. I think you had a bad nightmare and that you . . ." She paused again, and then gingerly squeezed Hannah's shoulders and upper arms as if checking for freshness. "Sweetie, this is the real you here, right?"

"Uh-huh, both," Hannah said. "This isn't Hannahwhere."

"Exactly!" Debbie said. "I think you only go to Hannahwhere in spirit when you're at the hospital."

After a moment of reflection, it all seemed to come together and an intermingling of excitement and anxiousness ran through her. Questions and considerations somersaulted in Debbie's head, each one opening another trove of possibilities.

"Oh shit . . . uh, I mean crap! I just realized something. First, we have to get you back to the hospital before they notice you're missing and all heck breaks loose, if it hasn't already, but more importantly, second . . ."

Hannah started to respond but Debbie held up a finger, stopping her.

"I know. It can't be more important if it's second, but logic has no place here—especially the way things have been lately. So secondly, I think you did something extraordinary . . . well, even more extraordinary than usual."

Debbie jumped off the bed, rooted through a laundry basket of folded clothing, and quickly dressed. She dragged a brush through her hair ignoring the static halo she had created.

"I want you to bring yourself back to your room at the hospital and I'll take the car."

"I want to go with you, please . . . please!" Hannah begged, terrified at the prospect of being alone if even for a moment. "I don't want to go back there even if it was a dream." She got onto her knees, with her hands clenched in supplication. She looked despondent, and Debbie felt terrible about it, but it was the only sensible option.

"Honey, if you came with me, we'd have to go past the outpatient desk or through the emergency room. Everything in there is locked up, and we'd have to be buzzed in, which would be impossible. I'll be there just a few minutes after you." She paused a few seconds and then said, "Shoot. That won't work either if people are already looking for you. We can't have you just popping up where nurses and orderlies might be crawling all about."

Debbie could imagine the hullabaloo that would ensue if Hannah unexpectedly materialized. It made for an amusing scenario, but it'd be devastating. There had to be an alternate place to play it safe. *The cafeteria? The visitor's lounge?*

Debbie glanced at her clock, which displayed 3:17 a.m. Hannah's room was the best option, but even as late as it was, it was still too risky . . . or was it?

There's another way, Debbie told herself. It's nuts, but it could work.

Debbie cinched her belt and tucked the remaining flap into a loop. She sat on the bed near Hannah, who was forlorn, but no longer hysterical.

"Listen, Hannah, this is important. We need to get you back fast." Hannah started rejecting it, but Debbie said. "Hannah! I said listen, so please hear me out, okay?" The intensity of her voice startled Hannah and she immediately conceded, as Debbie knew she would.

"Thank you. As I was saying," Debbie continued. "I don't think you have to go through Hannahwhere to get back to the hospital. I believe that when you're in your hospital room and you go to Hannahwhere, it's only your essence—the spirit you—that goes. I've seen it . . . your body stays at the hospital. It's when your spirit goes from Hannahwhere to somewhere real, or maybe in this physical realm, then your body follows. Both times that you started to disappear in the hospital you were panicking. I believe you just wanted to get away. Not just your mind, but all of you—just like this time."

Hannah mulled this over but looked confused and doubtful. "You disappeared, too," she said.

"I know . . . which is really odd. Maybe you were bringing me along, like you did with your cat. I bet that's why you can't be changed in Hannahwhere or Annaplace. There is no physical there," said Debbie. "It may also be why you dissociate in the hospital, why I can't cut Anna's hair, and why we can't warm her up. You know what I mean?"

"I think so," Hannah said. "In Hannahwhere we are like 3-D movies of our real selves?"

"Excellent! Yes, smart girl! And if the physical—the body—isn't in Hannahwhere, you can't be hurt." *Although you can feel pain*, she mentally added.

"Then, how come we can feel when we're in our places, like Anna's cold or hugs?" asked Hannah.

Damn!

"My God, you're a thinker, but so am I. I think we feel our energy and share it. If we want to feel a hug, or if we want to convey something, our desires let us feel things as if we are really experiencing it. Get it?" asked Debbie.

"No," Hannah said blankly.

Debbie said, "I know it's confusing, but this is why I'm so sure you had a nightmare. The other reason is you said you were so scared you wished yourself out of there. Where did you wish to go?"

"Here," said Hannah. "But the body me is here and it can't go anywhere without going to Hannahwhere first."

"That's my point. It can and it did!" Debbie took Hannah's face gently in her hands. "I don't think you would have willingly gone through Hannahwhere after a nightmare like the one you had. I'd bet you were so frightened you panicked and came straight here. I know your mom told you to go to Hannahwhere first, but I think that was for your safety. She figured Hannahwhere was a safe place between two uncertain places. You can always jump quickly back to the safety of Hannahwhere if there was anything dangerous or unexpected at either end, I think." A line of doubt etched Debbie's face. "Holy cow, this is confusing. Come here."

Hannah hesitantly got off the bed and moved beside Debbie, who gripped her hands. "I want you to try going straight to the hospital from here. Don't worry, I'm going with you, but I want you to think yourself into your hospital room's shower on three," Debbie said.

As Hannah had done to her earlier that day, Debbie counted to three before Hannah could hesitate. The jaunt was nearly effortless, with no nausea and just a hint of vertigo. They stood inside the shower stall in a nearly pitch-black bathroom, save for a barely visible strip of less-darkness at the base of the door.

Debbie reached out for Hannah and found her shoulder. *Shhhh*, she hissed quietly, and slowly stepped from the shower. Feeling blindly before her, Debbie found the light switch, flicked it on, and then twisted the deadbolt lock above the handle. They squinted at each other in the dispassionate glare of the bathroom light. The gray pallor of sleep deprivation and the darkened crescents beneath Hannah's eyes made her look ill and depleted.

She is ill, Debbie realized, and in a concerned whisper said, "Honey, you need to get some sleep. You're completely wiped out." She ran a hand over Hannah's head, pushing her hair back. "You're safe here in the hospital."

"What about Anna? What if *he's* with her?"

"He's not," Debbie assured her, still whispering. "Have you tried communicating with her? The way we did when I called you?"

"She can't hear me, but I know she's still there. I can feel her, but I think he has her."

"Come on, let's go see Anna." Debbie said and grabbed Hannah's hand. It seemed the only way to win Hannah a little piece of mind and much-needed sleep.

"We're supposed to sit!" said Hannah. "Or our bodies fall when our spirits leave them."

"Makes sense," Debbie agreed. As soon as Hannah's bottom hit the cool tile floor, Debbie pulled them to the flowery fields. It stunned her how quickly she had caught on to traveling, as if it were a hidden talent. She was also aware that she had dragged Hannah along before she could protest.

"You pulled me!" says Hannah, looking around, a hint of panic forming on her pretty but tired face.

"That's right. You're in Abracadeborah . . . my place," Debbie says. "But you're in Hannahwhere and Annaplace, too. They're all the same place."

Hannah looks around warily. "Really?"

"Positive."

"Okay, but don't leave without me."

"Promise," says Debbie.

The day is clear, as it always is here, but Anna is nowhere in sight. There's a new sound, like the muffled *Thoom—Thoom—Thoom—Thoom* of a bass drum, reverberating all around them as they wade through the flowers, looking for Anna's signature sundress or long white braid.

"There," Debbie says, pointing to a large tree with metallic blue-green leaves. "You see? I told you. No one has her."

They walk towards Anna, who is cradled in the crook of a sturdy branch. As they get closer, it becomes clear she is not entirely right. The changes that were once subtle have become severe and more accelerated, and she looks so achingly frail that Debbie can't quite retain her gasp. *Something* surely has Anna. Hannah pauses to collect herself before resuming her steps.

"Hi," Anna says weakly, yet still good-naturedly from dry and puckered lips. "I don't feel that good."

Glazed and sunken eyes stare at them from hooded lids. She is draped along the length of a branch with her arms dangling to either side, her pasty cheek pressing the smooth bark surface.

Thoom! Thoom! Thoom! Thoom!

Debbie puts her cheek to Anna's forehead expecting the blazing fever of influenza, but finds the same freezing flesh beneath the coat of sweat. Hannah's chin quivers and she blinks rapidly, trying to hold back tears. She reaches out to take Anna's hand.

"You look like shit," Anna says to Hannah. Her voice is tired and rattles with her words.

Debbie barks a pained laugh. Hannah also looks bad, and now that it's brought to her attention, it seems Hannah is mirroring Anna's decline, be it delayed. The state of both girls terrifies Debbie.

Thoom! Thoom! Thoom! Thoom!

"We have to go back," Hannah says.

"Yes, Hannah, we're wasting time." Debbie brushes her fingers along Anna's cheek, and then leans down to kiss her. "Anna, you stay strong, honey. Please. If there's any way I can figure this out, I will, but I have to get on it right away."

Hannah again says, "We have to get back *now!*"

"Okay. Let's go," says Debbie.

They returned to the hospital bathroom where the sound was magnified tenfold.

Thoom! Thoom! Thoom! Thoom!

"Hannah, are you in there, sweetie? Are you okay?" a woman's concerned voice called from beyond the door.

Hannah looked nervously at Debbie, who pointed to her lips and mouthed, *say something!*

"I'm here. I was trying to take a poop but fell asleep," Hannah replied. Debbie rolled her eyes and Hannah shrugged.

"Oh! Okay, honey," the nurse said with a chuckle. "You had me worried. Are you sure you're okay?"

"I'm okay. My legs are asleep, but I'll be out in a minute when the tingles go away." Hannah flushed the toilet for effect.

"You're surprisingly good at this fibbing thing," Debbie said, using the flush to cover her voice. She hugged Hannah and kissed her on top of the head. "I'll be back in a little while."

Debbie was gone before Hannah could protest.

CHAPTER 26

*L*ying on her side, Debbie hugged her pillow like a long-lost lover. There were eight pillows surrounding her . . . a fortress of comfort. She opened her eyes and looked at her alarm clock. *8:55 a.m.* Five hours sleep, a veritable slumberfest by recent standards. She rubbed her eyes, plucked sharp pebbles of sleep from the corners, and then settled her head down on another pillow.

Her attention was drawn by the lyrics spilling from her old radio . . . Owner of a lonely heart (much better than an) owner of a broken heart.

"Screw you, YES," Debbie groaned. She rolled over and depressed the alarm plunger, which was set to launch its cranky salutation in three minutes at 9:00 a.m. She never liked the song much, anyway.

Her mind was a thoroughfare of thoughts, barraging her as she tried to prioritize her schedule. Dozens of chores needed doing that day . . . dozens of chores that wouldn't be done. She needed to swing by the DCF office for an update before four o'clock that evening. That wouldn't be happening either. For Debbie, all that mattered was Hannah and Anna. All else could, and would, wait.

The next day, Thursday, she had the important meeting with the doctors, Essie, and DCF at 1:30 in the afternoon. She needed to prepare for that. They would be discussing Hannah's condition and plan for her future placement. Debbie knew how that would most likely go; Hannah would remain a ward of state, be placed with hopefully nice foster parents in a hopefully nice foster home with hopefully nice foster siblings, and have a fifty-fifty chance of coming out of it in better shape than she went in. It was the second fifty percent that concerned Debbie. She had to have multiple recommendations and alternative placement plans handy that would agree with Essie's and the specialist's evaluations of Hannah. Debbie had only one plan in mind, and it was a self-serving request. It was anyone's guess if it would float or fall onto deaf ears, but Debbie would slay dragons to make sure they heard her. If any of those involved knew of her recent experiences, or if Essie, God forbid, spilled the beans, Debbie knew she could punt that dream right out the window. She was determined not to let that happen.

She knew exactly what they sought when screening potential foster parents, and for Debbie fostering was the only place to start, and the safest for Hannah and Anna. Adoption was out of the question at this point, and would be for quite a while . . . maybe a year, three years . . . maybe never. She'd climb that mountain once it loomed closer.

Fighting the need to get up, Debbie rolled onto her belly and bunched a pillow beneath her head.

You know how doggies do it, Little Red?

The words were whispered directly behind her ear. A warm breath washed over the back of her neck, carrying with it the stink of hard liquor that mingled with the reek of sex and filth emanating from the grossly stained pillow beneath her cheek.

"No . . . no . . . no fucking way!" Debbie sneered. She shoved herself upwards, tossing the covers from her and scattering pillows to the floor. She jumped to her feet and spun to confront her tormentor.

"Get out of here! Stay out of my fucking head!" she screamed, her body tense beneath her nightclothes.

The rage boiled within her, drowning out the fear. Breathing heavily, she coiled with clenched fists, ready to spring. Debbie stomped into the living room and screamed towards the ceiling, "I won't live like this! I'm done with this shit! Come back, you bastard! You degenerate! You repulsive pig! You . . . fuck! Try to get me!"

Get you? We've already had you . . . over and over and over again, said a raspy voice from the spare room.

"Well, no more!" Debbie grabbed the stapler from the top of her desk and hurled it toward the voice. It struck the door, leaving a formidable dent, and ricocheted into the room.

We'll always be here, a deeper voice promised from her bedroom. *You're ours whenever we want.*

"Then come and get me, you bastard!" Debbie took a large pair of scissors from the top drawer of her desk and ran to her bedroom door, arm lifted and ready to attack. "Come on, you cowards!"

She stood in the doorway, panting and scanning the room. No one was there.

Whenever we want, someone whispered behind her.

Debbie spun and lashed out with the scissors, impaling only air.

"You're only in my head," Debbie said breathlessly.

Not in your head . . . but I have something that can be.

"Prove it!" Debbie challenged, walking to the spare room.

She grabbed the bottom edge of her pajama top with one hand, pulled it over her head, and threw it to the floor. She stood naked from the waist up, staring into the shadows.

"I'm here, you pussies! Are none of you man enough to take on a woman?" Debbie taunted. "You're afraid! You cowards only want children?"

Debbie caught her breath, and as she settled down and gathered her senses, a realization came to her. Regardless of all the voices and flashbacks she'd had, none had physically harmed her. How could they? They had no substance. They're . . .

. . . only in my head, she thought. Let's exorcise some childhood demons. Let's find out what it's all about.

For Debbie to be considered a suitable foster mother she would have to be unequivocally present and emotionally collected. Flashbacks or visions in the middle of the meeting would not go over well.

Leaving her shirt off, Debbie walked through her home and she could feel her fear dwindling. In her bedroom, bathroom, and kitchen, she encountered only silence. She reached for the basement doorknob and halted. *That can wait,* she decided. *Start with baby steps.*

She returned the scissors to her desk, retrieved her nightshirt from where it lay near the spare room door and pulled it back on. She sat down at her desk and yanked open the bottom drawer of her oak, two-drawer file cabinet. Shuffling through the folders, she scanned the tabs and removed one labeled *Vital Docs.* She fished through its contents until she came across her birth certificate. It was dog-eared, but otherwise looked new and formal with its stamped seal, scrolled blue border, and indistinct watermark. At the top, two lines of bold, block letters read *State of Ohio—Office of Vital Statistics*. Beneath that in a slightly smaller font was printed *Certificate of Birth*. This was not the original. Where that was, even the gods probably had no clue. She was fourteen when she had ordered the copy she held in her hands. She had needed it to work at the local donut shop.

Debbie knew all the standard information: Deborah Rose Gillan, six-pound-fourteen-ounce Caucasian female with blue eyes and red hair. Born 8:59 p.m., August 28, 1979, at Lakewood Hospital, Lakewood, Ohio, to Patricia Jean Gillan—father unknown.

What she hoped to find was any clue linking her youth to the flashbacks or visions that she had been having. Whatever had happened with Bernard Prioulx she had blocked from her memory, yet she knew it happened and she remembered Bernard's face too well. There was the difference. Regardless of how vivid her flashbacks were, they were of places and men whose faces she could not remember.

But weren't flashbacks memories?

Another detail Debbie could not deny, although every iota of her wanted to, were the sneakers. She was thirteen when she resided in Mad Mother Prioulx's home, but the sneakers in her flashbacks were those of a child of maybe six or seven. The implications were beyond nightmarish, and her not remembering was probably for the best, but it also scared the shit out of her and didn't bode well on the psychological front. Misplaced childhoods were usually blocked out childhoods, which frequently meant there was a lot of crap in the cupboards that you didn't want anyone to see . . . even yourself. If these evocations were any forecast as to what was in her cupboards, then Debbie had a mighty big pantry.

As for Lakewood, Ohio, Debbie knew near to nothing about the town, and this had always been fine with her. She opened her laptop, waited for it to return from sleep mode, and searched Google Earth. Lakewood was a small city on the southern shore of Lake Erie, about five miles west of Cleveland . . . trivial facts that were of no help to Debbie. If her intent were to discover anything personal, she would have to make the search more personal, which she was avoiding. Relenting, Debbie released a stifled breath and toggled to a standard search window. Searching *child molestation* and *Cleveland*, Google turned up three million hits, the most prevalent and relevant ones linked to a prominent case in Cleveland, England in 1987. Adding *Ohio* whittled the hits down to just fewer than 1.9 million. *Well, that simplifies things*, Debbie thought, feeling dwarfed by the colossal task ahead, assuming any wrongdoing even occurred.

You know it happened, a voice within her said. Denial is futile.

Even if it happened, it might have not been discovered or reported.

Was that possible? Not likely, she ended up in foster care for a reason.

"Where to start, where to start?" she mumbled. She changed *Cleveland* to *Lakewood*, turning up three-hundred-thirty-five-thousand hits, most of those seemingly linked to abuse prevention organizations, lawyers, and counselors, or sex offender registration. Adding her surname brought 3,200 hits, but nothing relevant— not without hours of deciphering. *"Deborah Gillan" Lakewood Ohio* brought back a mere six hits, though none were exact—not a hint that anything had ever happened to her in the proximity of Lakewood, Ohio. Christ! She might as well have never existed. It may well have happened in Phoenix, for all she knew. Frustrated, she added her mother's name *Patricia* in the search bar, which returned a hit-count of slightly less than sixteen hundred. Again, nothing exact or pertinent turned up.

Debbie had always been impressed and intimidated by the bewildering amount of information available on the Web. It had information dating back decades, well before the computer was inaugurated, never mind PCs. If anything was to be found, she figured it would be conspicuous like the Cleveland case in England.

She switched back to Google Earth and was dismayed by the numerous pop-ups born from other windows . . . there must have been fifteen. Right-clicking on the tabs, she halted when a prominently green thumbnail caught her eye. Expanding the window, she clicked on the link and a page from Cleveland.com opened, displaying a large photograph of a football team in action. Their uniforms were not far removed from the Green Bay Packers' uniform, except where the Packers had their trademark *G* within an oval; this team sported an *E* that looked more like an inverted three. Debbie knew that logo, but she couldn't place how or from where.

The headline read *Lakewood-St. Edward High School Eagles—The Big Green Machine!*

The name ricocheted through Debbie's mind like a distant echo.

St. Edward Eagles.

Green Eagles.

Fly like an eagle . . . to the sea . . .

She could see it above his sweaty, fat shoulder, and amidst the cloying reek of alcohol, cologne, piss, and sex. She stared at it where it hung on the wall near the smiling, lying St. Pauli Girl . . . the green flyer for St. Edward High School Eagles.

Good Girl, the fat man panted.

The faces revealed themselves . . . those filthy, leering men who used her and hurt her. Debbie slammed her palm on the pointed corner of her desktop. The jolt of pain drove the flashback from her head and brought her back to the present.

"No-no-no-no-no-no-no-no!" she sobbed, her tears falling to her keyboard and she started to lose grip. "I was just a baby, you bastards!"

Her biggest fear was realized, the evidence was irrefutable, and it hit her like a knife to the gut. In her heart, she had known it was true, but she had clung onto that shred of doubt.

With a soul-rending shriek, Debbie fell to the floor and curled into a shivering fetal ball.

How could they do it? They were monsters! Their faces taunted her and Debbie whispered to herself, "Fly away. Fly away from here."

And Debbie flew . . .

She soars from her tormentors, to a place where she can be free of the pain and all the ugliness. She gains speed as the hill- and tree-populated world far below her gives way to a huge body of water, its mirror-like surface reflecting the skies. She sees herself from a hundred feet above, spinning and swooping in the company of the dazzling sun. She plunges downward, faster and faster, nearer to the water, and then levels out to speed missile-like mere inches above the crystalline lake. She is impervious when she flies. She leaves everything behind, returning only when the defiling act is complete and the corrupting demons have fled for the time being, leaving her to soak in her pit of agony and shame, blameless, yet feeling worthless and hideous.

Debbie rises upward, climbing above the trees towards the cleansing heat of the sun. She realizes that this is not Hannahwhere or Annaplace; there are no towering mountains and no foil trees bearing alien fruit. This place has no name, yet she knows it is hers. It has been hers all along and she has carried some of it to this day, apparent in the landscapes of Hannahwhere and Annaplace. This realm may be old and elapsed, but is her place. This is her escape. She traveled here long before Hannah and Anna were born. This is an old talent reborn. It is why traveling came so easy to her. She just put it on the shelf at the back of the closet, only to take it out for a spin years later, like an old forgotten bike. She had needed Hannah and Anna to remind her that it is still hers.

Debbie came to on the living room floor. Her body felt disconnected as she pushed herself into a sitting position, as if some unfamiliar force was moving her. She rose and went into the kitchen and ran a glass of water from the refrigerator tap. She returned to the living room and sat at her desk, hazy, yet intent on finishing what she started.

She wanted the whole story. She wanted to confront the truth and not fear it . . . to laugh mockingly in its face like Renfield and say *I beat you! You don't scare me anymore! You can no longer hurt me!*

She was the red-haired child, and she knew now that it all happened in Lakewood, or damned near it. Debbie closed all the browser windows on her computer except for one, which she homed to Google. In the search bar, she again typed *Lakewood, Ohio,* and *Gillan.* Debbie figured it was not a very common name, unlike its ancestral predecessor Gillian, which she thought must have been her family name before it fell victim to the Ellis Island name butchery. The search turned up 8.9 million hits.

"Holy shit! So much for that," Debbie muttered.

She used quotation marks to streamline her search, enclosing "Lakewood, Ohio" in one set, and "Gillan" in another. Eighteen-hundred-seventy hits, that's better. Adding *sexual abuse* narrowed it down to a mere three-hundred-fifty-six hits. She slowly scanned the links one at a time, looking for hope hiding in bleak improbability. Her surname popped up often. Joshua Gillan, a star tackle at Lakewood High School, looking proud and grass stained. Lakewood's own Denise Gillan had obtained her undergraduate business degree from Syracuse. Lakewood youth, Jaime Gillan had received minor injuries in an auto/bike collision.

There were plenty of possibilities for her to follow, but three of the links stood out for Debbie. One linked to Melanie Gillan, a fourth grade teacher at Grant Elementary who received a college grant two years earlier in order to pursue her master's degree. Using Melanie Gillan's e-mail link at the school's webpage, she sent her a quick note explaining that she was interested in Lakewood's history—primarily the nineteen-eighties—and that perhaps they were related and she'd love a reply or a phone call.

Another linked to a Facebook profile photo for Stephanie Gillan, a pretty teenager with ivory skin, blazing red hair, and wide blue, owl-like eyes trimmed by bold black eyeliner. She stared coquettishly upward at a camera held at arm's length in an Oliver Stone worthy angle, displaying a deceitful wealth of adolescent cleavage, tactically forced upward and inward by a snug fitting top.

Debbie found it disconcerting the amount of personal information people were willing to divulge. Stephanie was seventeen years old and soon to be a senior at Lakewood High School. She liked Adele, Pink, The Black Eyed Peas, Johnny Depp, Hugh Jackman, and laser tag. Her latest post read, "OMG my mother is OTR again!" Stephanie Gillan looked like the alter ego of the seventeen-year-old Debbie who, half a lifetime ago, hid similar assets beneath unflattering jeans and loose-fitting sweatshirts. Debbie bookmarked her page, but was hesitant to communicate with her considering her age.

The third link pointed to a profile on LinkedIn for Brandon Gillan, a prosecuting attorney with the Cuyahoga Department of Children and Family Services in Cleveland. His LinkedIn photo depicted a rugged man with compassionate eyes and, as it seemed with most Gillans, a rebellious crop of lively copper-red hair. Between the historically botched surname and the red hair, it seemed too unlikely that these were happenstance. If nothing else, it was a starting point. Debbie jotted down the number, picked up the phone and dialed.

A secretary answered and informed her that Attorney Gillan was with a client and that she'd let him know she called. Debbie thanked her, left her number, and returned the phone to its cradle.

Debbie was freshly showered, dressed, and finishing up with the blow dryer when her iPhone rang. She answered.

"Miss Gillan?" a man asked.

"Yes, this is she."

"Brandon Gillan, returning your call?"

His voice was as common as milk yet sounded shaky, giving Debbie the impression that he might be elderly. This surprised her. The photo of Brandon Gillan depicted a man just about the same age as her. Maybe this was Brandon Gillan, Sr. She also found it remarkable that he returned the call not even an hour later. The divorce lawyer she hired after Kenny left did well if she called within three days.

"Oh, hello. Thank you for calling back so promptly."

"My pleasure. How are you?" he asked.

How are you? She found the question odd. She was expecting *what can I do for you?* or some remark about having the same surname.

"I'm fine, thank you," Debbie said after a short pause. "Well, I'm actually not fine. I'm sure you're very busy, but could I trouble you for a few minutes?"

"Certainly," said the attorney.

"Thank you. You see, I'm originally from Lakewood," Debbie said, unsure of how to begin. "I spent the first few years of my childhood there. The problem is that I remember very little of it. When I was around nine or ten, I was put in foster care. This started a cycle that eventually landed me here in Riverside, Massachusetts. I'm sure you're aware we have the same last name. Quite candidly, I'm calling because I saw your name and photo on LinkedIn and I think we may be related. We have very similar red hair . . . and facial features, for that matter. I know I'm rambling, but I'm looking for answers about my life in Lakewood and I'm hoping you'll be able to help me."

"I'm glad you called, Debbie," said Brandon. "Though I never imagined I'd ever actually speak with you again."

"You know who I am? Are we related?"

"Yes, we're cousins, Debbie. I was only fourteen when you . . . when you were put into foster care, but I always remembered you," Brandon said.

"Why's that?"

"Just how much of your life in Lakewood do you remember?"

"Very little, as I said, but I know major events—devastating events—happened during my time in Lakewood. I'm positive of this, and I have a good idea the nature of it, but I'm not clear on what exactly happened. It sounds as if you might know. Can you help me, Brandon?"

She heard a heavy, quavering sigh over the receiver, and then Brandon said, "I do know what happened, Debbie, but over the phone is no place to talk about it."

Debbie digested this for a while, and then said, "Brandon, I'd come to your office, but I'm in Riverside, Massachusetts, and I can neither afford the time from work nor the money. I'm aware that horrendous things happened to me and I had repressed it for years, but a series of recent events have triggered some gruesome flashbacks. I don't want to go into detail except to say they are about unspeakable men—many men—who did hideous things. They're crippling me to the extent that lately I can't function properly. What happened back then, Brandon?"

"Memories are surfacing? That was bound to happen eventually. Are they that vivid?"

"Too vivid," Debbie acknowledged.

"My God," Brandon said, and Debbie heard sorrow in his voice. "When I found out what happened I wanted to kill them, I swear it, but, like I said, I was only fourteen."

"I see them clearly, as if they are right beside me. Who are they, Brandon?"

"I shouldn't say any more. You don't need . . ."

"Brandon, please . . . I know what I need, and that's answers and closure. You've been very kind, but I need to know why this happened to me."

Brandon paused for so long that Debbie thought he had broken the connection. "Are you sure you want to hear it, Debbie?" he finally asked.

"Hear it? I've been living it. I need to face it if I want to survive."

"Do you have a support system there? A counselor, or someone to confide in?" he asked.

"Yes," Debbie lied. The day Kenny had left, so had Debbie's

support system, and she had flown solo ever since. As for now, Essie Hiller was the closest thing she could consider a support system, and she couldn't even act as her counselor legally. Calling this a support system was like calling a silk thread a lifeline.

"Okay," Brandon said. "I'm bringing my daughter to check out UConn in Storrs, Connecticut, this weekend. I can redirect to Logan instead of Hartford, and if you meet me somewhere in Riverside on Thursday, we can talk more on this."

"I can't have you do that!" Debbie said. "That's at least a hundred miles out of your way and you'd be missing work. Can't you tell me over the phone?"

"These are things you do not talk about over the phone," Brandon said. "You may find them easy to handle or you may be devastated, depending on your frame of mind. I have made a career of trying to protect people, and that will not change. I cannot and will not take that kind of risk."

Debbie felt like she'd been reprimanded, but she understood . . . her job had similar ethics.

"Why are you willing to do this?" Debbie asked. "You don't even know me."

"You are family, and *yes*, I do know you. I remember the little girl you were back then and I cared very much for you, so please."

After some deliberation, Debbie conceded. "Okay, but please let me cover the expenses."

"Debbie, I'm a wealthy man and I don't just mean monetarily. I'm called brutal, ruthless, and a hard-ass, and I know defense attorneys fear me. As an attorney who specializes in child advocacy, I take pride in that. I feel I owe you and my brother a lot. I do my best to prevent what happened to the two of you from happening to others, or if it does, that the perpetrators are punished to the fullest possible degree."

"I still feel wrong about taking you and your daughter's time."

"We're already heading that way. Besides, the UConn meeting is on Saturday. My daughter loves the cities and I personally think Boston is a lot more fun than Hartford. I'll take her there Friday."

"I'm guessing your daughter's name is Stephanie?"

"Yes! How do you know that?" Brandon asked, genuinely surprised.

"Her Facebook profile came up when I did a Google search for Gillan and Lakewood. She's beautiful."

"Oh, jeesh!" He gave an exasperated huff. "Well, thank you. Yes, she is beautiful and she is well aware of it. I get nervous about the pictures she posts. I hope she's at least not public."

"Don't know very much about Facebook, but . . . . well, according to Stephanie, your wife's not in a good mood," Debbie said, not able to keep the smile out of her voice.

"Yeah, I'll bet," he chuckled. "Okay, so Thursday can you have someone with you when I come there? Maybe a close friend, or if you have a therapist, even better, we can meet with him or her."

"Yes, I think so," Debbie said.

"Good! Call me with a time and an address."

Debbie hung up feeling wrung out but appeased by finally knowing the truth . . . or more of the truth. She looked at the kitchen clock and did a double take. It was not yet 11:00 a.m. and she felt like she'd already had a full day. It felt like ten at night.

She pondered her conversation with Brandon. Knowing she had a blood relative—especially one willing to offer so much while not knowing her or if he'd ever meet her again—felt odd. Not bad, but awkward, like wearing a shirt backwards.

Debbie called Essie and left a message. She said, "Hello, Essie, it's Debbie. Could you call me? I'd like to meet in Hannah's room at one this afternoon. I have something I'd like you to see. I think it just may change your life."

Essie returned the call within minutes.

CHAPTER 27

*H*annah was dressed and sitting on the edge of the hospital bed when Debbie and Essie walked in. She wore the second set of clothes that Debbie had bought her: her skinny jeans and a white-and-aqua-blue blouse that brilliantly emphasized Hannah's eyes. The rings under her eyes had nearly faded and she looked healthier and more rested today. Debbie latched onto this as an omen of good things to come.

"Hello, Sunshine! It looks like you were expecting us," Essie said.

"I was," said Hannah. "Debbie said we're going back to the park today."

"Yes, we are," said Debbie.

On the television, an NBC News reporter moved to one side as the camera panned across the front of a white clapboard tenement building with yellow crime scene tape strung across the front porch. Across the lower quarter of the screen, bold red letters on a bright yellow background declared *Murder in Brockton!* The volume was at a barely discernible level, but Debbie quickly changed the channel to Disney. Hannah already had too much trauma and violence in her life.

"Who turned that on?" Debbie asked, planning to have a word or two with the tactless dolt. She switched the channel with the remote pendulum.

"Me," said Hannah.

"Why in the world are you watching that?" Debbie asked.

Hannah shrugged and said, "I don't feel like watching cartoons."

Then why turn the TV on at all, Debbie wondered, but said nothing. It wasn't worth getting upset over. A cartoon now played.

Its characters were frantic and spastic with oddly shaped geometric heads, pointed, angular, and eccentric. Debbie found many of the modern cartoons disconcerting and the characters seemed poorly drawn by artists lacking effort or imagination, as if they were content with scalene triangles with a sprout of hair, or misshapen orbs for heads.

"What is this?" Essie asked, motioning to the television with a suspect glance.

"*Phineas and Ferb,*" said Hannah.

"They sound like lab cultures," Debbie said and chuckled.

"You look very pretty this afternoon," said Essie. "I love the new clothes. Hey, I hear they're letting you out of here!"

"The doctor said I should be ready to leave on Friday," Hannah said. She looked hopefully at Debbie.

"That's wonderful!" Debbie said, trying to appear perfectly positive. "You look fresh as a daisy. You must have slept well last night."

Hannah shrugged. Her spirit seemed a little dampened.

"Did you eat?" Essie asked.

"A little bit. They had chicken nuggets with some kind of sauce that tasted gross." Hannah grimaced.

"Really, what flavor was the sauce?" asked Debbie.

"Crap," Hannah said impassively. She was unclear as to why Debbie and Essie found this so humorous, yet she couldn't refrain from smiling.

"If you're up for another sausage sub or maybe pizza, we could stop before we walk in the park," Debbie suggested.

Hannah shot a quick glance to Essie and said a cautious, "Okay, but I'd rather have a BLT with extra bacon?"

"BLT it is," said Essie. "After that, if you still have room, there's a bakery in the plaza that makes the world's best whoopie pies."

"Whoopie piiiieeesss," Debbie said, as if experiencing a divine touch.

"What's a whoopie pie?" asked Hannah.

"You don't know what a whoopie pie is?" asked Essie, feigning shock.

"How tragic. This is unacceptable," said Debbie.

"We must rectify this immediately—sooner than immediately!" said Essie.

They ate in a little sub shop in Riverside Plaza, just east of the park. Hannah devoured a large BLT sub with the requested extra bacon and finished the last three slices of Debbie and Essie's spinach pizza. The amused women watched her as she took a sip from a second glass of lemonade.

"God bless your appetite," said Essie.

"Are you going to eat the table, too?" teased Debbie.

Hannah smiled and quietly said, "No, but I want to try a whoopie pie."

"That girl's powerful hungry!" said Essie.

At the little bakery two doors down, Essie bought six whoopie pies; one for Hannah, one for herself, three for her grandchildren, and one for her husband . . . Debbie demurred. They walked across the plaza parking lot and took a little footpath into Riverside Park.

"Why do they call it a whoopie pie?" Hannah asked, thoroughly involved with the sweet pastry.

"Because you want to scream *WHOOPIE* when you taste one," Debbie said.

"But it's not a pie," Hannah pointed out.

"She's got you there," Essie said.

"True enough," agreed Debbie.

They continued walking along the tarred pathway until Hannah finished her pastry.

"Are you full yet?" Essie asked.

"Yup." Hannah nodded, wide-eyed and a little more animated.

Debbie put an arm over Hannah's shoulder. "Hannah," Debbie said. "Remember what we did here yesterday? Remember the little boy who saw us?"

"Yeah."

"I was thinking if we were to do it again, we should have someone with us to be a lookout. What do you think if we had Essie do that?"

"Okay," said Hannah. "Are we going from the boat ramp again?"

"Oh! Yes," Debbie said, surprised, yet pleased by her easy acceptance. "No dips in the river this time."

"You are both being very cryptic," Essie said, baffled by their curious exchange. "I know there are some curious things involving the two of you, but why are we going to the boat ramp?"

"We're going to travel," Hannah said as if she was telling Essie she was going to chew gum.

They veered onto the ramp.

"Travel?" Essie asked.

"Not entirely," said Debbie. "Though I think that is how it originated for Hannah."

"We're going to help Anna," Hannah said.

"Anna? How will you help Anna? Does this have to do with how you both faded the other night?" asked Essie. She was becoming very animated. "Does this go beyond fading? Is that what Hannah means by 'travel'? Do you really travel, or just disappear . . . like dissociation?"

Debbie laughed and rested a hand on Essie's shoulder.

"Maybe not dissociation in the clinical sense," Debbie said. "Maybe not at all . . . I'm just learning about this, too. The closest definition I can give is teleportation."

"Teleportation!" barked Essie. "Teleportation is just a bunch of hype. It's unsubstantiated quantum theory."

"Okay, then call it astral travel or translocation. You were there the other night," Debbie said. "You saw. Why the denial?"

"I don't know what I saw the other night. It was bizarre and inexplicable, but it wasn't teleportation. You're calling a flickering light a blackout."

"No, it's more astounding and something Hannah—we—can control."

"Control it . . . like shamanism?" Essie asked. "It's not involuntary or something triggered under duress?"

"Stay tuned," Debbie said and smiled.

"Whatever you two are playing with, I'm not sure it's good," said Essie, nervously wringing her hands. "Triggering it might present a serious risk for Hannah and maybe for a prolonged time . . . possibly permanently."

"We've done this a number of times now, Essie. We've gotten pretty good at it," Debbie assured her.

"I've done it a lot," added Hannah. She sat on the ramp about five feet from the river's edge and Debbie sat beside her.

"What do I need to know about where we're going?" Debbie asked Hannah.

"Bulls," said Hannah.

"Bulls?" Debbie and Essie repeated simultaneously.

Hannah nodded her head and said, "Yeah, but if you run real fast the second we get there, the bulls shouldn't catch you. I think . . . maybe."

"What?" Debbie repeated with a heavy edge of concern in her voice. "You're messing with me again, aren't you?"

Hannah just offered her a smart-ass smile.

"Wait! What are you talking about?" asked Essie, her frustration showing. "Why here? This can't be safe!"

Debbie gave Hannah's back a quick reassuring rub. "Okay, Hannah. On three, take us somewhere outside the house where we won't be seen, but *not* inside the house. Understand?"

"Yup."

"We need you to stand guard," Debbie said to Essie. "Just enjoy the show. If we're not back within two hours, we'll be in Elm Creek, Nebraska."

"Elm Creek? Wha . . ."

Debbie counted, thoroughly amused by Essie's confounded expression as they left her and tumbled into the ever-more-familiar vortex. As the dizziness expanded, Debbie felt something solid and unyielding behind her head force her forward. A panic started growing in her lower abdomen, twisting eel-like and then burrowing throughout her body and burying its claws into her shoulder blades.

They had made a fatal error, Debbie was positive. They stopped in absolute darkness and she could still feel Hannah's hand clutching hers. She tried to rise, but her world kept spinning, and the roar of traveling still echoed in her ears. Hannah said something that wasn't clear and Debbie wondered if the girl was hurt or maybe crying for help. She tried to rise and her head connected painfully with something above her.

"Ow! Shit!" Debbie cried. She sat down again.

"I told you not to stand," Hannah said.

"When did you tell me that?" she asked.

Debbie vigorously rubbed the tender spot on the top of her head, but the pain was stubborn and set up camp. Whatever was above her would not allow her to sit upright.

"Just before I heard you bonk your head on the boards," Hannah said.

"Boards?" Debbie asked. Well that answers that.

There were boards above her head, but not impaled through her or in a cellular mesh with her flesh. She wasn't a physicist but this made sense to her. How could something materialize where something solid already existed? The solid object would be unforgiving and meshing, melding, or interjecting would be impossible unless both objects were atomically loose, like a bag of marbles. The body could not arrive where something else existed, so the body regulated. That would be why she felt the pressure. If something big was in the way, like Hoover Dam, would the body reject arrival and return to where it came from, or would it relocate to the nearest available space like her head had just done?

Debbie heard a mild hissing coming from Hannah's direction. She recognized the sound.

"You're laughing at me!" Debbie said, and despite herself, she joined in. "I'm starting to be a little concerned by your sense of humor."

Their eyes had conditioned to the darkness and random spots of light became visible around the far edges of the obscure confines. Debbie patted the floor to verify if it was soil as she expected, which meant the boards over her head were rafters.

"We're under the house?" Debbie asked.

"Yeah," said Hannah.

My God! What if my suspicions are true and Anna is under here? Debbie wondered. What if Hannah sees her?

"Shit," Debbie muttered, but Hannah overheard her.

"You said not in the house, but where no one can see us," Hannah said defensively, misreading Debbie's dismay. The mirth was gone from her voice. "No one can see us here."

"You did wonderfully," Debbie assured her.

For Debbie, being there brought to mind Hannah's account of her and Anna's last time there. She envisioned Travis in a meth-charged rage, yanking Anna out through the access. Her stomach knotted as she thought about the terror the poor girls must have felt, and the dread Hannah probably felt right now.

"I was wrong having you bring us here," she said to Hannah.

"This is too emotional for you. We should go back."

"No, I don't want to. I want to help Anna."

Debbie considered it for a moment and said, "You are one amazing little lady. In that case, let's get out from under this house, it creeps me out. Where's the door?"

Hannah shuffled past her on the right and Debbie followed, ducking to avoid the rafters and trying to leave her fear behind her in the dark. Hannah scuttled along the wall, searching until she found the access door. She pushed against it, but it didn't give.

"I think it's latched outside," Hannah said.

"Okay, show me where the door is."

"Right here," Hannah said. She directed Debbie's hand over the outer frame.

"Can you hear anyone in the house?" asked Debbie. "It looked vacant online, but you never know."

They could hear the distant barking of a dog and the sound of farm machinery, but nothing from inside the house.

Satisfied, Debbie said, "Move back a little, and be ready to go back to the ramp if anyone's out there."

Debbie faced the access and slammed the bottom of her feet against plywood with all her strength. It held, but a sliver of daylight lit the edge of the door and ignited the space where they sat. Her second kick splintered wood and left the door and its frame hanging in shattered strips. She made light work of the rest.

"They didn't want visitors," Debbie said, nudging the shattered door with her toe. Two unpainted and weatherworn one-by-fours had been nailed across the access, holding it closed. Debbie looked across the crawlspace, which was slightly better illuminated by daylight. The outlines of an assortment of wood, a small stack of patio blocks, two dented gallon-cans of paint were visible, and in the distance, the chimney.

"Wait here," Debbie said to Hannah.

She crawled across the dirt floor, visibility decreasing dramatically as she neared the far end of the building, everything becoming lines and shadows. She glanced back at Hannah, small and angelic in the outlining brightness of the opening. The sunlight illuminated her hair so radiantly it looked like flames.

Debbie turned back and it seemed even darker. She waited for her eyes to readjust, but the improvement was minimal. She forged onward and then remembered her iPhone had a flashlight app that supplied decent light, though it voraciously ate the battery's charge. The phone-light illuminated the cinderblock facing of the chimney, which was about four feet wide and ran up into the rafters. She moved hesitantly around the side and then into the two-foot gap between it and the rear wall of the house.

Nothing.

She dowsed the light and freed a huge sigh that sent a quake through her body. She'd been sure Anna would be there and had even prepared herself to deal with it, but now she had to prepare herself for the even *more* disheartening probability that they would not find her. Considering the condition Anna had been in when they last saw her, it didn't bode well, though the deeper truth was Debbie had no notion as to what Anna's circumstance meant. Was Anna's deterioration a positive or negative sign? Was she preparing to crossover to a better place? Was her destination conditional on whether they found her alive and well, or not? If they didn't find her, would she be trapped in some form of limbo? The million-dollar question was, is she dead or alive? It seemed death was the obvious answer, but Hannah was written off as dead and she popped up alive and mostly well.

Debbie took a settling breath and returned to Hannah who wore an expression that was somewhere between indecision and expectation. Debbie considered the tidal wave of emotions that were probably washing over Hannah. It had to be terribly upsetting to return here.

"Are you alright, honey?" Debbie asked.

Hannah hesitated, looking more uneasy. "Yeah, I'm okay."

"If it gets too much for you, just tell me and we'll return to Riverside."

"I'm okay," Hannah insisted.

"Okay," Debbie said as she led her into daylight. "Watch out for nails."

They emerged from the crawlspace and stood up side by side on the gravel driveway, taking in the property Hannah used to call home.

"Yuck," Hannah said. Her voice was emotionless and her

expression forlorn and bewildered as she looked over the yard her mother had tended so well.

What had once been a twenty-by-thirty-foot patch of flourishing flowers and vegetables was now a litter-strewn blotch of weedy clumps and leaves. The two-foot-tall white border fence that had once surrounded it now lay trampled and faded, the brightly colored plywood animal cutouts of bunnies, lambs, and geese, now bleached and dirty. Debbie gauged Hannah's reaction as she approached the ghost of her mother's garden. Hannah rubbed the toe of her sneaker over the cutouts, outlining a lamb and then a blue-eyed skunk.

"Mom made these for us," she told Debbie. "She said they made the garden happy so it would grow better. She had the prettiest flowers. People used to stop their cars to look at them. Some people would ask if they could have some and other people just took them." She pushed her foot down on the goose cutout until its neck snapped. "Now everything's dead."

"Did it upset her when people took her flowers?" Debbie asked.

"No. Mom said if we share what we have, God makes sure we always have enough."

The sad irony of this statement caught Debbie. How often it seemed the more compassionate a person, the more they suffered at the hands of others. It was just another of life's cold, hard injustices.

Something in the back yard grabbed Hannah's attention. Debbie followed her as she made the corner of the house. A rusted and ivy-choked swing set stood waiting like a forgotten friend. Its bars, once striped white and cherry red with hand-painted scrolls and lettering, were now faded, and sagged with age and the longing of two snowy-haired children. The swings were long gone or stolen, and the chains hung at varied lengths like broken promises.

"Anna and I used to sit there, facing each other with our lunches on our laps," Hannah said.

She nudged one of the four L-shaped bars that hung arbitrarily, swinging with silent, insolent ease. It was all that remained of the glider. She looked at Debbie, gave a solemn shrug, and headed for the dilapidated rear deck of her former home.

"We should go," Debbie said. "I'll come back later, now that I know how to get here."

Hannah gave a mild shake of her head. "We're already here,"

she said. "If we go now, you might not get the chance to come back, or it might be too late to help Anna."

Debbie wanted to dispute this, but Hannah seemed to be holding it together amazingly well, considering the magnitude of what she was facing. She also saw the truth in her words; a logic so advanced in a child who should have been thinking about Barbie dolls and the Disney Channel, not about odds and emotions. She followed Hannah to the rear deck, still monitoring her from a few steps back.

Debbie had earlier told Hannah that the house looked vacant, which was a huge understatement. The place more than reeked of abandonment, it gave the sensation that it had been dropped and forgotten . . . aborted. The atmosphere that surrounded it—in the yard, the garden, and the swing set—told that life here didn't taper off or fade away, but was guillotined and cut off mid-breath.

Waist-high weeds had conquered the lawn and the garden and forced their way through the cracks in the driveway and along the base of the house. The vinyl siding looked in decent condition, but some creative sorts had spray-painted colorful and swishy logos and jargon across a lot of its surface. "Pimp", "The Dead House", "Badass", "Pham"—whatever *that* was—and several more adorned the rear of the house in various tones from black to fluorescent. The rear door was shoddily boarded over with plywood and a sign—*No Trespassing— Police Take Notice*—was stapled to the face of it. Someone had covered *Police* with black spray paint. Clearly they were not taking notice. A fist-sized hole was punched clear through the double-paned glass of what Debbie assumed was the kitchen window.

Debbie quietly followed Hannah onto the deck and watched as she ran her hand along the edge of the plywood. Hannah grabbed the board and tried to wrench it away from the doorframe, her face reddening and her fingers turning white with the effort.

"Hannah! Hannah!" Debbie said, afraid she might tear off her fingernails. "There are at least twenty screws holding that in place. You'll never pull that off."

Hannah dodged by her, leapt onto the railing, and tried unsuccessfully to push the window open. She jammed her arm through the hole in the pane and started pulling at the glass.

"Hannah!" Debbie demanded like a drill sergeant. "You stop right now!"

Hannah froze. Breathing heavily, she stared into the window.

"Pull your arm out of the window slowly. Be careful that you don't cut yourself," Debbie instructed.

Hannah obeyed, her face contorted into a combination of desperation, shock, and humiliation. "Are you mad at me?" she asked in a barely audible whimper.

"Yes!" Debbie said. She checked Hannah's arm. Amazed to find her unscathed, she grabbed her by the shoulders and then hugged her tightly. "What were you thinking? We didn't come all this way so you could slice yourself to shreds, or so I can lose you! What were you doing?"

"I feel Anna inside," she explained and wiped at her nose.

"I feel something, too," Debbie said and released her. "But you won't be helping anyone by severing an artery and bleeding to death."

Debbie assessed the window. It was a white, plastic-framed horizontal slider, a style common with most economically priced modular homes and condominiums. The fist-sized hole near the base of the glass was dirty, jagged, and too small for Debbie to be comfortable sticking her arm through. She pushed on the frame, but it wouldn't budge. Kneeling on the railing, Debbie first saw the low-profile lock latch, and then the screw in the slide track, drilled in at an angle to hold the window closed.

"You were lucky, pretty girl. That could have been disastrous," Debbie said. "It's screwed closed. I'll have to break out the window."

Looking around quickly, Debbie saw nothing useful to break the glass. Seeing no other option, and feeling they were safely out of view from the street and other houses, Debbie removed her T-shirt leaving only an aquamarine bra.

"A week ago, I wouldn't have done this if my life depended on it," she said, wrapping her shirt around her fist the way she had seen on so many crime dramas. Feeling Hannah's evaluating gaze on her, Debbie paused.

"What?" she asked.

"You have humongous boobs!" Hannah said with a giggle.

Debbie hesitated again, suddenly feeling very vulnerable, but she forced herself to push it aside for Hannah and Anna's benefit. With forced bravado, she said. "In time you will too."

"You have a ton of freckles, too," Hannah informed her.

Debbie sighed. "Believe it or not, I'm aware of this."

"I wish I had freckles like you."

"You do have freckles."

"Not like yours."

"Why on Earth would you want freckles like mine?" asked Debbie.

"Then we could look like each other," said Hannah.

"I'd like that," Debbie said. "But I'd rather have your amazing head of hair."

"Your freckles are cool."

"Your hair is dazzling."

Figuring they were at a complimentary standoff, Debbie said, "Now, how about *us* getting into this house? Stand on the far side of the deck."

Hannah moved, as suggested and Debbie swung at the window, landing a pathetic, limp-wristed tap. Hannah smirked.

"God, I'm such a girlie-girl," Debbie complained.

Hannah looked over the back yard as if she'd just found something very enthralling. Debbie unwound the shirt from her left hand and rewound it on her right. Standing with her back to the wall, she closed her eyes and using her arm as a lever, she hammered the window dead center. With a high-pitched snap, the outer pane of glass fragmented into a starburst, leaving large and lethal-looking spikes jutting from the frame. Debbie removed each shard from the channel, dropped them down into the long grass against the side of the house, and repeated the process on the inner pane. When the glass was clear, she shook out her shirt and pulled it back on.

Debbie hoisted herself onto the deck railing, knelt before the window, and then leaned through to look around. She was above the kitchen sink, which was empty except for ashes from a fair number of cigarettes. From her vantage point, she could see the entire kitchen and most of what was the living room or den. It was dusty and stale with an underlying scent of mildew, but it looked better than she had imagined. She had expected a vandalized shell. A refrigerator was to her right, the doors removed and set atop the far counters. To her left, dust coated and lonely, was the oven. It surprised her that these appliances remained, and appeared to be in respectable condition.

"Hello! Is anybody here?" Debbie called, feeling absurd yet wary. She was fairly certain no one would be inside, but taking the last week into account, she wouldn't have been surprised if John Lennon and E.T. rounded the corner riding tandem on a Day-Glo unicorn. As she expected, no one answered.

She maneuvered herself through the opening, twisting a little to allow her hips through, and nearly tumbled off the sink. Searching for a handhold, she gripped the lip of a cupboard to right herself until she was squatting in the sink. She leaned back through the window and offered a hand to Hannah, who skittered quickly up the railing and slipped easily through the window. Debbie climbed down from the sink using the island for balance, and then helped Hannah.

"We could have traveled into here," Hannah said. "And not broke the window."

Debbie laughed and said, "You're right! Why didn't you, instead of taking a chance of cutting yourself?"

"I didn't think of it," said Hannah. "Why didn't *you*?"

"I didn't think of it, either. This is going to take some getting used to."

Hannah walked around the kitchen, solemnly taking in the cabinets, but saying nothing. The cupboards were painted white and trimmed with fine, hand painted sandalwood designs. Each cabinet was adorned with small, intricate Tole paintings of fruits, berries, birds, and leaves. One drawer was missing, as was a cupboard door on the island.

"Did your mom paint all of this?" Debbie asked.

Hannah nodded and brushed her hand gently along the top shelf of the refrigerator. "No more SunnyD for me," she said in a whispered croak.

Hannah moved around the island, through a vacant area where a table once surely stood, and into the living room. A dazzling display of sunlight poured through four large windows, igniting the crystalline tears that coursed down her delicate cheeks. Debbie ached for her. She wanted to take her from this place, to hold her and help her pain go away, but she resisted. Healing was happening before her, within this house and through acknowledgement and acceptance.

In the far corner of the room, a small circle of discarded beer cans and candy wrappers littered the lauan plywood underlayment. The carpeting had been removed from the floor, but it was about the only confirmation of the horrors that had occurred in the room, or the abandonment that came afterward. There were no markings on the walls and no graffiti, which seemed odd to Debbie. There were no huge colorful swirling letters and illustrations like the ones covering the outer walls of the house. Even the circle of cans and papers seemed to be reserved as if any outward displays of negligence would have been a further act of desecration.

Hannah walked to the small circle of detritus, averting her eyes from the large span of wall on the right side of the room. It was the obvious place for a couch, where the ravaged body of Elizabeth Amiel was found . . . where Hannah had found her. Hannah tapped a beer can dispassionately with the toe of her sneaker and returned across the room, still not looking at the area where the couch had been.

On the left side of the living room stood three doors . . . all of them closed. The one nearest to the kitchen led to the bathroom, evident by the double fan/light switch outside the room. On the wall, about five feet up from the floor, was a small wooden plaque with the rendering of a doghouse painted on it. Five brads on which to hang five dog figures were evenly spaced across the plaque, one inside the doghouse and four outside. One lonely dog hung inside the doghouse, while two more waited patiently outside. Two of the brads were unused. The words *Family Doghouse* were painted across the top in red letters. Debbie hadn't seen one of these tacky doghouse setups since she herself was a child.

The farthest of the three doors led to Hannah and Anna's bedroom, in front of which Hannah now stood. On the door, two painstakingly painted faeries hovered beneath a large rainbow. They were excellent caricatures of the sisters, from the long, snowy hair to their sweet, freckled pixyish faces. Wings aflutter, they held a sign aloft between them with *HANNAH* painted across it in a bold, playful font. The H's were pink, and the A's and N's were black with white polka dots, so *ANNA* stood out boldly from within the name HANNAH.

"That's excellent! What a neat idea! Did your mother paint it?" Debbie asked.

"Uh-huh," Hannah said. "She said identical twins are extra special because they are part of each other before they are born, and will be forever after that. She picked our names because they are part of each other just like Anna and me. "

"It's beautiful. It sends shivers down my spine," Debbie said.

Hannah gave a hint of a smile, closed her eyes, and released a deep breath. She turned the knob and pushed the door open, revealing an empty room. The sun shone through the window so brilliantly that Debbie had to raise an arm to shield her eyes as they entered. The room was standard and nondescript—four walls, a window, and a closet—until Debbie saw the two walls to the left.

"Oh my," she said with a hint of wonder in her voice.

"Anna and me had bunk beds over there. I mean, Anna and I." Hannah pointed to the opposite corner of the room.

Debbie stepped closer to observe an amazing mural that fully covered the two walls. It was so intricately painted with so much detail it would probably take days just to discern everything.

"It's Hannahwhere," Debbie whispered, lost in the elaborate panorama.

"It's Annaplace, too. Mom drew it so we could see it and learn it, and remember it in our heads, so we could make it when we were there," Hannah explained. "I started to forget what it looked like."

It was all there . . . from the countless extraordinary flowers to the colorful odd shaped trees with blue fruit or chocolate hanging from their sturdy branches. Along the top of the mural on both walls, a vast array of what appeared to be large, elongated stars populated the skies even though the sun was also dazzlingly displayed. Dense along the top, the stars then tapered down into a scattering among the trees and flowers. Each one was a painstakingly formed point of light spraying out from the center into five points . . . clearly star-shaped, yet without any definitive lines.

"Are there stars like that in Hannahwhere?" Debbie asked.

"Yeah," Hannah said.

"When?"

"All the time," said Hannah.

"Really? I didn't see any," Debbie said.

"They're all over the place," said Hannah. "They're hard to see when it's sunny." She seemed sincere.

Debbie dismissed it and returned her attention to the painting. On the top left edge of the mural, a series of images flowed in clockwise fashion, starting with Elizabeth Amiel standing amid the flowers with her abdomen distended in pregnancy. Next, newly born Anna and Hannah, their eyes closed and content in sleep, are swaddled in thick blankets and rest upon Elizabeth Amiel's lap in the shade of a blue-leafed tree. Over the trio, a dazzling red cardinal is perched on the lowest branch of the tree and appears to be watching them. The next in series, pudgy-cheeked Hannah and Anna sit delighted amidst the flowery field, their hands raised to the hovering cardinal. The succession continued year by year until the last image climbed the left edge of the mural to meet the first. Hannah and Anna, at seven, are draped over and clutching the lower branch of a tree. The toddler plumpness is leaving them in their transformation into girlhood, and their smiles are genuine and all-encompassing. The cardinal is again perched on the branch, as if waiting to greet them.

"The cardinal," Debbie said. "If I hadn't seen him myself, I wouldn't believe it."

"He's always around," Hannah said and smiled.

Debbie followed the story of the mural, stopping at the figure of a woman standing in the field near a river's edge, silhouetted by a distant gray and ragged mountain line. She is in profile and dressed in an emerald-green Victorian gown with a laced, form-fitting bodice that accentuates an already bountiful bosom. The green of the gown contrasts perfectly her pin-straight hair, which is slightly wind tossed, and so very red it seems closer to orange. Her hands are raised and her palms cupped, ready to catch a floating red heart that hovers before her. A rush of disbelief ignited Debbie's nerve endings so intensely that her legs nearly buckled.

"Is that . . . me?" Debbie asked. She knew the answer.

"Well, duh!" said Hannah. "Look at the hair and the boobs!"

"But . . . how did . . ."

"Me and Anna already told you that. You're Ms. Coppertop. Mom painted the picture, but Anna made the name up. I liked it, too. Mom said that we had to remember what you look like because someday you were going to help Anna and me. Mom used to dream things and paint them, like the bird. She said it is a rep-er-en-sation of our real father. She dreamed a lot and she dreamed about you, too. She said you knew our real dad when you were both small like us, and that we would find you near the river." Hannah pointed to the river on the mural. "Mom said you're a good person because you follow your heart, and that good people who follow their hearts shine, and that makes them easier to find. You shine like a penny," Hannah said with a determined nod.

"And you shine like the snow," Debbie said. *Kyle Janssen knew me as a child? How is that possible?* Debbie wondered. Case documentation showed that he was born and raised in this part of Nebraska. Had Debbie lived in Nebraska during some point of her life? How would Elizabeth Amiel know this?

Debbie moved to the wall and held a swatch of her hair to Elizabeth's rendition of her. It was nearly a perfect match, even to the copper dusting.

Remarkable!

"Your mother was a very talented artist," she said to Hannah.

Hannah nodded in agreement. She reached out and ran a finger over the image of her mother.

"She was very beautiful. You and Anna look just like her. It's very easy to tell that she loved you girls very much."

There had once been love here, evident in the paintings on the door and walls, in the fine stenciling on the cupboards, and in the shadows in Hannah's eyes.

"I thought she'd be here. I can still feel her here," Hannah said.

"Of course you do," Debbie said, and realized Hannah was speaking of Elizabeth. "Can you feel Anna, too?"

Hannah nodded.

"Can you pinpoint it—the feeling—where it's coming from?"

Hannah closed her eyes in concentration, and then shook her head. She leaned over and picked up something small, a pullover shirt for a Barbie doll, and slipped it into the pocket of her shorts. She opened the closet door and stared into the darkness for a while before slowly closing it.

"Where'd they put everything, like our pictures of mom and us,

Anna's and my You & Me dolls?" asked Hannah.

These words wracked Debbie, driving home the fact that fate had seldom smiled on Hannah. The poor child had lost nearly *everything* in her lifetime: her mother, father, home, every personal possession . . . and maybe even her sister. Even the shirt she wore when they found her wasn't hers, yet Hannah still had the constitution within her to be perpetually sweet, to smile, and even joke at times, regardless of the perverse weight life had forced her to carry.

"I'll try to find out what happened to everything. I'll get them back if I can," Debbie promised. Hannah flashed a quick look and nodded.

They left Hannah and Anna's bedroom and entered Elizabeth's, which was empty except for two bed rails leaning in the corner, either forgotten or abandoned. An intricate, hand-painted border crested the walls with pairs of conjoined hearts and cardinals, backed by a sweeping slate-blue ribbon. Debbie did not miss the significance of the twin hearts or the cardinal.

"I don't think Mom put herself in the border," Hannah said. "She should have."

It did seem unusual to Debbie. Was Elizabeth being prophetic? Maybe she knew her time here was limited. Her eyes traveled along the border and it hit her.

"Your mom's the ribbon keeping Anna, you, and your dad connected," Debbie said.

"Really," asked Hannah, giving her a quizzical and guarded look.

"No question. Do you see how the ribbon always wraps around the cardinal and the hearts?" Debbie explained.

She smiled tenderly at Debbie, shrugged, and then walked to the closet door, which was open a quarter of the way. She opened it the rest of the way with her sneaker and peered into the dim depths of the closet for what seemed like minutes.

"Is there something in there?" Debbie asked, but Hannah didn't answer. Dread swelled within Debbie's numbed limbs. She was torn between running like hell or dragging Hannah away from there.

Hannah lifted something from inside and backed out carrying a trophy topped with the figure of a baseball player in full swing.

Hannah stared impassively at it, and then swung it at the closet door with a savage shriek. Debbie jumped back as Hannah lashed out again, repeatedly slamming the trophy against the door. She waited as Hannah ranted on, hoping that she didn't injure herself, yet knowing the show of anger was due—maybe far past due—and an essential part of Hannah's healing process.

Hannah whirled and launched the trophy with every ounce of her being, following it with a bellow of rage and anguish so total that Debbie literally felt the energy project from her. An impressive heave, it left the trophy embedded halfway through the drywall and Debbie grateful she wasn't in line with the toss. Hannah stood rigid, moving her hands reflexively, still vibrating from the outburst.

"That was *his*. He loved it more than *anything*. If anyone touched it, he'd flip out." The acid in her words was almost visible. "Fuck head!" she screamed at the embedded prize.

She stared at it for a while and then her whole body sagged with the departure of her anger. She looked at Debbie and wiped a tear from her cheek. "Am I in trouble for what I just said?" she asked.

"No. Those are pretty much the same words that come to my mind when I think of him," Debbie assured her. She pushed some tousled strands of Hannah's hair back into place and smiled. "I bet that felt good."

"Yeah," Hannah said and offered her own awkward smile.

Again, Debbie wondered how a woman who loved her children as much as Elizabeth apparently did let someone like Travis Ulrich into her life.

"C'mon," Debbie said.

Hannah took her hand and they returned to the living room. The day had shifted slightly and exaggerated slants of sunlight exposed empires of newly disturbed dust motes as they traversed the room.

Debbie moved to another door. "What's this, a closet?"

She opened the door to a little utility room, tightly populated by a heating unit, a water heater, an electrical panel. A network of copper and PVC pipes rose upward, penetrating the ceiling and upper wall at various points.

"Boring guy stuff," Debbie said and closed the door. "Is there an attic here?"

Hannah shook her head and pointed to the cathedral-style ceilings. "They go all the way up." Hannah's eyes shifted upward along the wall near the bathroom door. "The Travis dog is gone," she said.

"What?"

"The Travis dog." Hannah nodded up to the doghouse plaque.

"Good! It doesn't deserve to be there," Debbie said. "It's on the floor near your foot."

Debbie lifted the Hannah dog from the pin inside the doghouse, and moved it between the Anna and Mom dog. "Why are you in the doghouse? I can't imagine you being bad."

"Not really bad. Mom said I was rambunctious and not careful enough. She caught me running across the roof and put me in the doghouse."

Debbie blinked and said, "The roof? How'd you get up there?"

Hannah just stared at Debbie.

"Oh, right. Well, your mom was right!"

"Yeah, I was always in the doghouse," Hannah said.

"Not Anna?"

Hannah let out a good-natured scoff and said, "Ha! Anna? She'd have a heart attack if her dog ever ended up in the doghouse. She used to burst into tears and think Mom was mad at her if Mom forgot to kiss her goodnight. Anna wouldn't disobey if her life depended on it!"

Ironically, Debbie thought. Hannah took the Anna, Hannah, and Mom dogs from their pins and put them in her pocket. She picked up the Travis dog and stared spitefully at it.

Something danced on the edge of Debbie's mind, but she couldn't call it forward.

"What's wrong?" Hannah asked.

Hannah's words kept replaying; *Anna wouldn't disobey even if her life depended on it.* Debbie rubbed her forehead as if she were trying to erase thoughts or massage new ones into existence. "Hannah, honey, I'm sorry," Debbie said. "I thought Anna would be here, but clearly I'm wrong. You said you felt it, too. Is there any place nearby you think Anna might have gone?"

Hannah paused, looking thoughtful yet uncertain. Her eyes diverted almost imperceptibly as Debbie watched the curious inner battle. An ugly feeling of ineptitude blossomed within Debbie like a virus, expanding slowly and weaving its blackness around her thoughts.

Any place.

Annaplace.

No place . . .

Debbie peered into the bathroom . . . not large, but larger than Debbie had expected. It was a common bathroom turned quaint by Elizabeth's talented hands. Four paintings with an ocean motif added atmosphere to the little room's walls: a shoreline with a lighthouse over the towel rack, two seagulls silhouetted by the summer sun over the toilet, a leaning buoy near the sink, and a beached lobster trap on the narrow closet door to the right of the bathtub. She stepped into the room and noticed something protruding over the lip of the bathtub. She told Hannah to stay back and inched toward the tub.

Could Anna be there? Undiscovered?

It wasn't logical, but an anxiety bloomed through her nonetheless. The shower curtain had either fallen or been pulled down inside the tub, covering something beneath it. Gingerly reaching forward she pinched a small section of the curtain and started lifting it, exposing a pile of maybe eight bath towels. Soaked and sodden, someone had tossed them into the tub to dry like papier-mâché cow patties. Debbie released a pent-up breath and shook her head at Hannah.

Hannah copied Debbie's sigh from the doorway.

"Maybe we should head back," Debbie suggested.

Hannah gave a disheartened nod of agreement and another peculiar flick of her eyes. Debbie ran her hand appreciatively over the painting on the closet. They were exceptional, and it seemed a shame the art was painted directly onto the walls and doors. Debbie knew little about art, but she felt that Elizabeth Amiel's was worthy of framing.

"How long did it take your mother to paint this?" she asked.

Hannah shrugged. "I don't know. She was always painting and making things, like that closet and those shelves."

Debbie pulled on the handle to open the closet, but it held fast. "Does it have a lock?" she asked Hannah.

"Pull hard. It's a magnet," Hannah instructed.

Debbie yanked harder, surprised by how strong the magnet was, but the door finally obliged. She looked in the closet and saw the two-foot-long magnetic strip on the jamb, which explained why it took a Herculean grip to open the door. She also saw the back of the door and started laughing. Despite her difficult life, Elizabeth Amiel had had a good sense of humor. Centered on the backside of the door was another one of Elizabeth's paintings. It was a very good portrait of Tom Brady, looking as if he were leaning against the companion steel strip to the magnet. He had his thumb and index finger at his chin as if he was observing a masterpiece, one eyebrow raised in an expression of shameless appreciation. Debbie understood the humor. With the closet door fully open, Tom would have a direct, front-row view of whoever was exiting the bathtub.

"Your mom was funny," Debbie said.

"Whenever we'd take a bath she'd say, *say hi to Tom for me*," Hannah said.

"What a hoot," Debbie said.

She pushed the door closed, which slammed with a loud *CLACK* as the magnet strip took hold.

Hannah froze.

"What's wrong, honey, did you hear something?" Debbie asked.

Hannah said nothing, but moved to the closet. She tugged open the door and let it slam shut again.

CLACK!

Hannah started to say something and balked.

"What is it, honey?" Debbie asked, squatting to meet her gaze, but Hannah's eyes were locked on the closet door as she opened and closed it again.

CLACK!

Hannah's eyes darted quickly to her right, as if something only she could hear had moved outside the room.

"What is it, Hannah? Why are you doing that?"

A huge tear ran down Hannah's cheek as a look of profound grief and confusion contorted her face. She rushed from the room.

"Hannah!" Debbie called. She rushed after her through the living room and into the kitchen. "Hannah, what?"

Debbie caught up to her, pulled her into an embrace, and held her tightly.

"Honey, what's going on?" Debbie asked. "Something's eating at you. Why won't you talk about it?"

Hannah said, "I can't."

"You can't talk about it? Why?"

"Mom made us promise to never, ever tell anyone."

"Tell anyone what?" Debbie released Hannah and then held her at arm's length. "Look at me, Hannah. Is there something you're not telling me about Anna? If your mom could, I'm sure she'd want you to talk for Anna's sake."

"No one is supposed to know where it is," said Hannah quietly.

"Where what is?" pressed Debbie.

"Our secret place . . . where we hide."

"Under the house? I checked."

Hannah stared at Debbie with terrified eyes.

"Is there another secret place, Hannah?" Debbie asked.

"I'm not supposed to . . ."

"Do you think Anna's there?"

The horror on Hannah's face amplified, showing she had not considered that possibility. She yanked herself free and darted into her and Anna's bedroom with Debbie stumbling behind her. Hannah yanked open the closet door and rushed in, crashing hard into the rear wall. She slammed into the wall again and then dropped to the floor. Sitting with her legs in the closet and her bottom in the bedroom, she hammered against the baseboard with both feet.

"What are you doing, Hannah? It's just a closet!" Debbie shouted, afraid that Hannah would hurt herself.

"She's in there!" Hannah cried, still kicking at the wall.

"Where, Hannah?" Debbie asked, reaching for her.

"The chimney! Where Mom told us to be!" Her voice cracked with desperation and a nuance of defeat.

"I checked. She wasn't there."

"It isn't real," explained Hannah. "We're supposed to hide inside!"

Hannah jumped up and ran for the door, but Debbie grabbed her arm. Hannah yanked, and unable to free herself, started to fade. Debbie felt the change in her wrist. Fighting panic, Debbie hollered, "HANNAH, STOP!"

Hannah stopped, distraught and shaking so badly Debbie feared she might start convulsing. Debbie pulled her into a tight embrace and said, "Honey, please calm down and breathe."

Once Hannah seemed calmer, Debbie said, "Please tell me what you're talking about."

"The chimney isn't real," Hannah said.

"I don't understand. I saw it under the house."

"Mom made it with real blocks and cement. It's for when things get ugly, so we can travel and come back and no one can see us. Mom made us promise never to tell anyone about it, and I told you! I'm stupid! I'm stupid!" Hannah drove her fists into the side of her head and her control started slipping again.

"Hannah, stop it!" Debbie demanded, grabbing her arms. "You are not stupid and you are not in trouble. Please settle down and I'll help you. I'm positive that your mother would not be upset with you. I know she'd be proud."

She held Hannah in an embrace and watched her as she tried to process Debbie's words. She finally felt some of the tension leave Hannah's body.

"Why were you banging on the closet wall like that?" she asked.

"It's a door," Hannah said. "The closet used to be a lot bigger, like Mom's walking closet."

Debbie didn't correct her, but thought about the closet in Elizabeth's room. It wasn't quite a walk-in closet, but it was much larger than the one in Hannah and Anna's room. Debbie released Hannah and looked into the closet. It was ordinary looking, with an upper shelf with a hanger rail attached, and carpeting up to the baseboards.

"I don't see a door," Debbie said.

"It's a flap, you know, like the back of a dump truck. It has really strong magnets like the ones on the bathroom closet, so we can kick it open and go in fast if we have to."

It took Debbie a few moments to see how well designed it was. The only giveaway was that there was corner molding at the rear wall junctures beneath the shelf. *Who puts molding on the real wall of a closet?*

Looking closer, Debbie could see an ever-so-slightly exaggerated gap behind the molding. Again, it was not obvious to those not looking for it. Debbie pushed against the rear wall and felt the slightest give. This enlightened Debbie to an oversight on her part. When standing at the access to the crawlspace, the chimney was at the far right corner of the house, directly below the girls' room. The house had no chimney protruding from the roof, only the PVC pipe standard with modular homes. The average manufactured home did not have brick or cinderblock chimneys unless they were owner installed for woodstoves or fireplaces, of which this home had neither.

The things you don't notice if you're not looking for them, thought Debbie. "How do you open it?" she asked.

"There are two ways . . . well, three ways in," Hannah said. "You have to push really hard at the bottom where the magnet is, or the other way is the metal door on the chimney under the house."

Debbie pushed against the wall, harder than the first time, but it held fast. "Either those are insanely strong magnets or it's jammed," she said.

"It locks, but only from inside," Hannah explained. "Mom made it that way so . . ." Her words trailed off when she saw Debbie understood. "If Anna is there, it's really bad, isn't it? If she's still there, it means she isn't alive anymore, right?" She started sobbing.

A chill rushed through Debbie as the guarantee of what lay behind the wall became valid. She wished she could hide from Hannah's anguish, yet abandoning her was not an option and never would be. The desperation that radiated from her eyes was painful for Debbie to see, and must have been a living hell for Hannah. For a nine-year-old child to face the possibility that she was all that was left of her family was unimaginable, yet here it was. She pulled Hannah to her, hoping that the simple gesture would not only convey a sliver of comfort, but that it would hide her own tears.

Hannah had been through enough, Debbie decided. The rest could prove too difficult for her to handle. Debbie would have to come back and do it herself.

"You are a very brave and special young lady," she assured Hannah. "I am so proud just to know you, and you should be very proud of yourself, too. We have to go back, now. We're going back on three."

She didn't give Hannah time to argue.

CHAPTER 28

When Hannah and Debbie returned, Essie was standing near the water's edge at the base of the ramp looking worried and a little lost. Hannah was entwined in Debbie's arms, grief and defiance wrestling for precedence on her face.

"Oh my God! Oh my God! Where'd you go?" Essie blurted. Her words gushed forth in a frantic outpouring, seeking explanation. "I . . . this is unbelievable! Did you really go to Elm Creek? This is really screwing with my worldview!" Essie then noticed Hannah's tears. "My goodness, you're crying! Did something happen? Are you all right? Is she all right?"

"She's had a shock," Debbie said. "I think we may have found the answers we are looking for, but I need to go back to verify something. I need you to take care of her. It's been a very emotional experience for her."

"I want to know!" Hannah said through gritted teeth. Tears flew as she angrily tried to pull away from Debbie.

"I'll tell you as soon as I know, but it'll be better if you stay here," Debbie explained. "Please stay with Essie. *Please!* It's getting late and they'll be expecting us back soon."

This was not likely true since she had told Doctor Farren and the ward nurses they'd be back at the hospital by five-thirty for dinner, and they hadn't been gone much more than two hours.

"What do you want to know, Hannah?" Essie asked.

Hannah scrutinized Debbie's eyes and set her jaw. "We know where Anna is."

"It's just speculation so far. It's just a guess, honey. But if it's true, I don't think you should . . ."

"I'm not stupid and I'm not a baby! Whatever we find, I can

handle it!" Hannah said with blazing eyes. "Remember, I made it two years without your help!"

Debbie could not deny the truth of that. Hannah had witnessed the grisly death of her mother and had somehow made it through on her own, sanity intact.

"Okay. I'm sorry I insulted you, but I'm only acting as I would with any nine-year-old girl or boy, regardless of how crazy this whole mess is. If you were any other kid, I'd insist you go back to the hospital," Debbie said. "What am I saying? If you were any other kid, nothing like this would be happening. My God! If anyone knew what we're doing, I'd be out of a job . . . if they could believe any of it."

"I won't tell anyone if you let me go," Hannah said.

"I think Essie may have an inkling of an idea that something is not exactly normal here," Debbie said. She looked at Essie and raised a questioning eyebrow to accentuate her point and their good fortune. "She hasn't blown the whistle, which means she cares about your well-being. I think she'd agree that it would be best for you to stay here this time."

"Why did you bring her there in the first place? You are too good at your job to not know the risks," Essie said, not completely able to control the accusation in her words.

"Essentially, *Hannah* brought *me* there. It's a long story, but trust me . . . they were necessary steps," Debbie said. "You have to agree that this is a unique situation. The rules and laws we operate by don't necessarily apply here. I'll tell you everything later, but you'll have to believe us and be prepared to open your mind to the truly extraordinary, okay?"

Essie stared at Debbie as if she'd just sprouted horns. "Sweet baby Jesus! Sister, you'll have to be shooting rainbows out your backend for this to get any more extraordinary. Open-minded? I think empty-headed is a better description for me for getting involved in this." Essie shook her head in wonder.

Debbie knelt before Hannah and held her gaze. She said, "Hannah, I need you to stay with Essie until I get back. No argument. You understand?"

"Yes," Hannah answered. She was clearly not pleased, but Debbie knew she would obey.

Debbie sat in approximately the same place on the ramp and watched Hannah and Essie as the world around her faded to black. In seconds, she was sitting on her bed in her house.

She rummaged through her night table drawer until she found her chrome and red plastic flashlight that looked circa 1960. She tested it and a strong circle of light appeared on the ceiling, reinforcing her faith in Duracell . . . more expensive, but worth it. Debbie repositioned herself on her bed and prepared to travel back to the crawlspace in Elm Creek.

Hey, Little Red on the bed.

"Fuck you," Debbie said indifferently and left for Nebraska.

Daylight still flooded through the access, so it was not as dark as the first time she and Hannah had traveled there, but the light had shifted away from the concrete enclosure, leaving the crawlspace deep in shadows. She couldn't dismiss how cold and alien it felt without Hannah by her side. She was a foreigner in a bizarre land where Hannah was her connection.

She clicked on the flashlight and ran the beam along the extent of the crawlspace, hesitating in the corners, at the woodpile, on the paint cans, and on the brick pile, dreading the appearance of anything with any combination of four legs, fur, and teeth. Relieved, she settled the beam on the cinderblock enclosure Elizabeth Amiel had built for her daughters. It looked authentic. The cinderblocks were evenly placed, and the cement mortar was groomed, giving it a professionally done appearance. The common soul would have never stopped to think about the placement of the chimney in relation to the rooms in the house, or that a base this size would normally foot a fireplace and a large chimney. It seemed Travis hadn't figured it out either, though he was about as bright as an eggplant in Debbie's opinion.

She crawled towards the enclosure, struggling to keep the light trained on her target, when a sudden thrashing of wings sent her sprawling to the dirt floor in a panic. Bats terrified her and the thought of one of those flying rats becoming tangled in her hair sent spikes of terror coursing through her. When the fluttering stopped, she lay flat on her belly, sweeping the light's beam throughout the crawlspace in search of the little bastard. She heard rustling ahead of her and to the left, and when she aimed the light she saw it perched on a black iron pipe just to the left of the enclosure.

"Are you fucking kidding me?" she said, holding the light on the familiar red-feathered bird. "I don't need a kick in the ass to convince me you're not just your average Yogi. You have a message for me?"

Chirby-chirby-chirby-chirby-djou-djou!

"And what is that supposed to mean?" Debbie asked.

The bird shifted a little, watching her with undisguised interest. *Djou-djou-chirby-djou*, it proclaimed, as if they were truly conversing.

"Whatever you say," Debbie said. She rose onto her hands and knees and resumed on course. "Love it if you could hold the flashlight."

She rounded the left side of the enclosure and peered into the gap between it and the rear wall. There was less than two feet between the cinderblocks and the wooden apron of the house, enough for a child or small woman to fit. It would be tough for someone Debbie's size, and damned near impossible for most men. She steadied the light on the cast-iron clean-out door. It had a plain, unadorned cover and its base was about two feet up from the earth. The look of it disturbed Debbie and she found herself thinking of the oven doors of World War II concentration camps.

Djou-djou!

"I know I know . . . I'm moving," Debbie said.

She wedged herself between the walls, trying to clear her mind of thoughts of spiders and rodents and failing miserably. When the iron access was within reach, she lifted the small nub of a handle and swung the door open. Two small L-shaped brackets were fused to the inside of the small door as a makeshift hold so it could be internally secured. From within the enclosure came a waft of dust and abandonment, carrying beneath it a mild but unmistakable hint of decay. *Mice or a squirrel*, Debbie hoped, but her gut said different.

Debbie shined her light into the portal illuminating the cinderblock wall inside, which was more painstakingly mortared than the outside, and then painted. *So as not to injure the occupants*, Debbie realized. She took a couple of deep, calming breaths, wriggled closer to the opening, and looked at the floor of the enclosure. A large pile of blankets covered most of the bottom of the enclosure, though the outer edges faded off into obscurity. Maneuvering her arm through the small opening, she shined the flashlight on the material and saw a navy-blue sleeping bag that was wrapped around something.

Something about the size of a seven-year-old child.

Beneath it was another sleeping bag, or maybe a quilt, maroon in color, atop a small cot mattress. It seemed Elizabeth Amiel had tried to make the concrete box comfortable.

With a shaking hand, Debbie reached for the top edge of the sleeping bag and pulled gently back, just enough to expose the silver-white head of hair, and to let her know that she had found her.

Anna.

The sob escaped her like an arrow. She had known Anna would be here—there was little reason to doubt—but seeing the snowy hair brought it all rushing home. Debbie reached out and lightly ran her hand over Anna's head.

"I'm so sorry, baby. I'm so sorry this had to happen to you. It's all so unfair to you and Hannah," she cried. If only someone had been here for her. If only she could have flown her body from here, she could have been safe and warm.

Djou-djou!

Safe and warm, Debbie thought. If Anna had made it all the way here and wrapped herself in the blankets, shouldn't they have kept her warm enough to stay alive? How unfair, to have the drive and stamina, even if running on autopilot from dissociation, to make it through the bitter cold and into this enclosure, only to die once she had reached her destination. Was it just too much for her young body, or did something else keep her from persevering?

Debbie tugged at the top sleeping bag, releasing it from Anna's body, and drew it back to expose Anna's desiccated shoulders and baggy, light blue shirt, stained brown by a patch of blood. Protruding from between her shoulder blade and spine, the wood and chrome handle of a large screwdriver stuck out from her tiny back like a mammoth and obscene accusation.

"You son of a bitch!" Debbie said, quietly at first and then louder. "You murderous, hateful son of a bitch, she probably would have lived!"

Don't touch it! Debbie thought. *His fingerprints will be on it.*

What good would that do? Nothing would change for him. Maybe he'd get the death penalty, but what would that accomplish? To give him a tiny puncture, a nearly painless death by injection, would be the vilest of insults to these poor children!

The cardinal, to Debbie's amazement, fluttered off its perch on the gas pipe and dropped down onto Debbie's shoulder.

Chirby-djou-djou!

It looked into the enclosure, and with a series of jerky head movements, cocked its head as if it was staring directly at Debbie. It bobbed its head a couple of times, gave one final *djou*, and took flight, leaving through the access at the far end of the crawlspace. Debbie squeezed ahead to watch its departure. She whispered a goodbye, somehow feeling that it had thanked her.

Debbie looked at the two slide bolt locks that were holding the rear closet wall in place and wondered if Anna had locked them. She kissed Anna's withered hand and touched the top of her head, saying a silent prayer and asking whichever god, goddess, or divine influence oversaw the spirits of the young and innocent to guide Anna. Debbie quietly closed the metal door and wiped her tears on her forearm. She returned to the spot where she and Hannah had traveled to and from the house and returned to the boat ramp in Riverside.

She had a lot to do, but the appearance of the cardinal in a nearby tree made the reality and unreality of everything so suddenly overwhelming that she was compelled to sit riverside to think it over. She stared over the water and into the trees on the opposite bank for nearly an hour, contemplating what she had discovered in that little home in Nebraska. Denial or disbelief would benefit no one. She felt as if she was in the center of a huge blizzard, stranded and unsure of which way to move, but she knew that moving was the best way to handle it. She pulled her iPhone from her pants pocket, called Essie and asked to meet her at the hospital cafeteria at twenty past five, which worked out well since dinner normally arrived in Hannah's room around five-thirty.

Debbie led Essie to a far corner of the cafeteria, well away from the other patrons. She knew she was taking a huge risk, but she told Essie everything about Elm Creek, the enclosure, the amazing mural in Hannah and Anna's room, and about Anna's body. She told Essie all that she had refrained from telling her in her office and asked her not to be swayed by the potential offered by what she now knew, but to be an ally for Hannah's benefit. To Debbie's great relief a very dazed Essie agreed.

"Honey, after hearing the story you just told me and seeing what I saw today, I'm not so sure I'm steering straight," Essie said. "But I know I didn't choose this profession for fame or fortune. I chose it to help those who need help, and Hannah, Anna, and you clearly need help."

"Thank you," Debbie gushed.

"Now, don't hear me wrong," Essie cautioned her. "If we come to a place where I think Hannah and Anna—and you—are safer with this in the open, I'm morally bound to do just that. For now, and this could be my professional demise, I won't say a word to anyone. What do you intend on doing?"

"I have to let the authorities know where Anna is," Debbie said. "And then I have to tell Hannah . . . which I dread."

"How will we do that?"

"Fucked if I know," said Debbie. "But I'm glad you said *we*."

Debbie pressed her cheek to Hannah's head and shared a sad smile with Essie. Hannah had cried bitterly when they told a softened version of what Debbie found in Elm Creek. It was a grief-saturated cry of revelation, the kind that usually came on when dreadful long-standing questions were answered. Hannah said she had known Anna was there since she had felt her presence so strongly. There had to be a connection on the subconscious level . . . a psychic link. Debbie didn't even hesitate at the possibility of it. She had traveled fifteen hundred miles in less than a minute. A psychic link? Why the hell not?

Hannah slept sporadically, twisting and repositioning on Debbie's lap. She absorbed the reality of Hannah, her warmth, weight, and her sadness. Tomorrow she might have to let her go and that possibility was a huge callused hand that clenched her heart. Hannah's life was fraught with sorrow and loss, and the idea of throwing her into an unfamiliar environment with absolute strangers—regardless of how nice and sympathetic they might be—seemed unusually cruel, especially when she had someone who would protect her with her life, and would give up anything to have that chance. The DCF could make curious decisions and go in unexpected directions, away from what seemed like the best and most obvious decision. *Of course, I'm biased,* Debbie thought.

Hannah desperately wanted to travel to Hannahwhere and check on Anna, but Debbie had convinced her to wait until she was rested and less upset. It would be too emotionally risky to take a trip yet, and when they did go, they would go together. Debbie had no idea if the discovery in Elm Creek was a form of closure, or just another piece of a greater puzzle for Anna. Anna had looked so diminished the last time they had been there, lying draped over that branch like an ill cat. Was she still in Annaplace, or had she moved on? If so, Debbie hoped she was in a less lonely place. Every time Hannah twitched, Debbie wondered if not knowing would be too much temptation for Hannah to resist traveling.

The whole state of affairs had Essie straddling a fence between exuberance and utter confoundedness. She had more questions than a month of *Jeopardy* and she'd been peppering Debbie with them since they returned to the room. *What does it feel like? Can you change mid-route? Why do clothes and jewelry travel as well? Can you bring someone else with you? Are Hannahwhere and Annaplace physical realms, and if so, where?* Debbie and Hannah could not answer most of the questions, which frustrated Essie.

"You said you could physically feel Anna when you're there . . . not just a feeling of intense cold, but her actual body?" asked Essie.

"Yes," Debbie said.

Hannah shifted, scratched her head, and looked up at Debbie who gratefully welcomed the distraction. Hannah sat up and rubbed her red-rimmed eyes and a troubled expression crossed her face.

"What's wrong, honey?" Debbie asked and immediately wanted to kick herself. Her father, whom she never knew, is dead, her mother was murdered by an abusive, drug-addled lunatic . . . the same one that later murdered her twin sister, she has no home, she has no family, and her caseworker was an insensitive dolt . . . other than that, life is fucking grand!"

"What's going to happen to Anna's body?" Hannah asked, knitting her brow. "We're not going to leave it there, are we? I don't even know where my mom or dad is buried. They should all be together."

Essie quietly clucked her tongue, an audible companion to Debbie's thoughts. A nine-year-old child should never have to concern herself with such thoughts or utter such words.

"Essie and I already called Detective Davenport," Debbie said. "Anna will be treated respectfully."

"Did you tell him you went there and found Anna?" Hannah asked.

"No," said Debbie. "We can't exactly tell them we traveled to Elm Creek by astral projection or teleportation, can we?"

"What's that?" asked Hannah.

Debbie looked at Essie and smiled. It was yet another contradiction in this paradox named Hannah . . . being so adept at something and not even knowing what it was called.

"That's what you do," Debbie said. "Astral projection is when your spirit leaves your body, and teleportation is when your body instantly goes from one place to another."

Hannah's expression was slightly pained. "That's confusing. Mom just called it traveling. I like that better."

"Then traveling we shall call it," Debbie said. "You're not the first person to do it, but you and Anna may have taken it to a whole new level."

"You did it before me," said Hannah.

"I'm not so sure I did it physically. Maybe I did, but I think we should be careful where we do it. If anyone saw us it'd be big news and every lab, college, and medical research facility on Earth would be anxious to know how we did it."

"I don't want to lie," said Hannah.

"And we won't lie, but we won't tell them everything," said Debbie.

"I don't think we have to worry about it," Essie said. "They wouldn't believe it. Even you both appearing in Harvard's Director's office while he was sitting at his desk enjoying his mocha latte, others would be naturally skeptical."

"I'm not so sure about that," said Debbie.

"I am," countered Essie. "It doesn't fit into their current worldview. It doesn't agree with their wideworld perception, so they would reject it. There are amazing things happening all around us. There are shamans who have been doing these things for years, like spirit walking, telekinesis, telepathy, precognition, clairvoyance, psychokinetic phenomenon, reincarnation . . . the list goes on. All this mind-power and the greatest minds on Earth can't or won't relate with it. If you told them that you and Hannah teleported to Elm Creek, they'd probably laugh at you. If you showed them, many would reject it."

"Wow," said Debbie. "That struck a nerve."

"Don't get me going, honey," Essie said, laughing. "We'll talk about it later. Back to Anna."

"Uh, okay," said Debbie, feeling a little derailed. She turned to Hannah. "Well, we told Detective Davenport about the cinderblock enclosure your mom built under the house, and that you hadn't told us because you promised your mother. Every bit of that is the truth."

Hannah contemplated this for a moment, nodded in agreement, and then settled back against Debbie. "Was he mad?"

"Not at all. He understands, and he respects your loyalty to your mother. He'll want to ask a few questions tomorrow, once they verify everything," Debbie stifled a yawn. She looked at Essie, and then shifted her gaze out the window. "I can't believe there's still daylight. It feels like three in the morning."

"It's eight-ten," Essie said. "It's been a day like no other for me. I need to get myself home before my husband sends out an APB, but I'll be here tomorrow . . . nine a.m. at the latest."

"Davenport said he wouldn't come any earlier than that," Debbie said.

"You should both get decent sleep tonight," Essie said. "Tomorrow's going to be another busy one. Davenport in the morning, lunch with your cousin at noon, back to my office by one to meet with him, and then our DFC meeting at five p.m."

Debbie could sense Hannah's eyes alternating from her to Essie, probably concerned and a little hesitant about being alone after a day like today. "Are you going to be here when the detective gets here?" she asked. Debbie could see the fear building in her eyes, betraying a new level of insecurity and causing Debbie to feel pangs of guilt.

"Absolutely," Debbie said.

"We both will," Essie assured her. She kissed Hannah on the cheek and hugged her, repeated the process with Debbie, and left them with the sound of her flats chuffing like a train down the hallway.

"Are you staying tonight?" Hannah asked.

"I'm not going right yet, but I will need to go home to take a shower," Debbie said.

"There's a shower here," Hannah said hopefully.

"Yeah, but I need clean clothes. I feel like potatoes are starting to grow all over me."

"Ewww!" said Hannah, literal as always.

"I know . . . not pretty," Debbie agreed.

Hannah showered and pulled on the *Wizards of Waverly Place* pajamas that Debbie had bought. She brushed her teeth and then Debbie brushed and braided her hair. Hannah climbed into bed, lay on her side, and granted her a weak smile. Debbie pulled the blanket over Hannah and tucked it in.

"Want TV?" Debbie asked.

"Nah."

Debbie dragged the chair to the bedside and sat down. She leaned over and crossed her arms on the mattress.

"Tomorrow is when they decide what to do with me, right?" Hannah asked.

"You make it sound like you're a leaky roof when you say it that way," Debbie said.

"Are you going to try to get it so I can live with you?" Hannah asked.

"I promise you that I will try my best."

Hannah blinked, trying to ward off her drowsiness. "Debbie?"

"Yeah, sweetie?"

"I'm scared."

"Of what, honey?"

"That I might not get to live with you," said Hannah. She thought for a while. "Would it make you sad, too . . . if I can't live with you?"

"Very much so, but I'm your caseworker so I would still come and see you. I mean that with all of my heart."

"I wish I was a leaky roof. That way I could stay at your house, and you could keep me if you want."

"I want," Debbie said, and kissed Hannah on the tip of the nose to disguise her loss of words.

"Why are you crying?" Hannah asked.

"Because," Debbie said, "sometimes you see something so amazingly beautiful it steals your breath and brings tears to your eyes."

"Really? What did you see?"

"You," said Debbie.

THURSDAY
July 1, 2010

CHAPTER 29

Debbie stood at the doorway watching Hannah sleep, taken by her peacefulness and innocence. She was lying on her back, her head turned slightly toward Debbie. Her pouted bottom lip was dark and glistening with moisture, looking as if she'd nervously chewed it swollen.

Essie appeared beside Debbie carrying a Tupperware container. "I woke early so I baked Blueberry Surprise muffins." She lifted the corner of the container, exposing muffin heads the size of grapefruits.

"Aye, those are freakin' huge!" Debbie said, astounded.

"I heard the Scottish in you just then," Essie laughed.

"Yeah, it happens when I'm near good food," Debbie said.

Essie opened the shades. The brilliant sunrise transformed the white walls to a cheery tangerine.

"You look fantastic!" Essie said.

"Thank you," Debbie replied. "Meeting attire."

Debbie's dress was forest green, chic, and form fitting. It went mid-calf, stylishly revealing pale yet shapely legs. Kenny had bought it for her, paying what Debbie thought was an exorbitant amount. It wasn't Erdem or Michael Kors, but it was in the upper four-hundred-dollar window and far more than Debbie would have ever paid. She hadn't worn it since "The Kenny Years", mostly because it—though classily so—accentuated her figure . . . something she avoided.

"Honey, with that body, you should make dresses your standard," Essie said. "Those legs should be in magazines. You're a goddess."

"Thanks," Debbie said, blushing and wanting to hide herself. Compliments made her uncomfortable and she received them clumsily. They seemed to refer to someone she didn't know, like the woman Debbie had seen in the mirror at home. The woman on the far side of the mirror looked stunning and confident, while the woman on Debbie's side felt awkward and constricted by the dress. The light makeup and glaze of the lipstick she had chosen felt alien. It was a battle not to remove it before leaving the house.

Essie pulled a few plastic plates from her carry bag and set them on the over-bed table. She set one of the colossal muffins on it and handed it to Debbie.

"Bon appétit."

"I'll have to diet for a week," Debbie said. "How many grams of fat are in one of these babies?"

"You call them fat grams, I call them flavor crystals. Anyhow, if they're made with love, they aren't fattening."

"Is that so?" Debbie asked.

"Well, if it is, no one told my husband," said Essie. She placed the largest of the muffins on the over-bed table and maneuvered it before Hannah.

"Wait!" Debbie whispered. She found the proper button on the touchpad, and pressed it. Hannah's bed started rising to a sitting position. Halfway up, Hannah wearily opened her eyes, which became huge upon seeing the muffin. Wordlessly, she leaned forward and sank her teeth into the regal-sized pastry.

"Thought we'd help you with breakfast," Debbie said, and bit into her muffin.

"Yemf I Wanmff mnnk," Hannah responded. She swallowed and wiped her mouth on her pajama sleeve. "It's a monster muffin. Got milk?"

Intent on scoring some milk from the ward kitchenette, Debbie nearly plowed into Phil Davenport. "Nmiilnk," she explained, spraying him with muffin crumbs. She slapped a hand over her mouth to contain her laughter.

Phil watched her shuffle down the hallway, a rare smirk on his face. Debbie returned with four eight-ounce cartons and handed them out. Phil was sitting in a metal folding chair, tearing into his own muffin with boyish glee.

"YUM!" Hannah suddenly blurted.

"Ahhh! The surprise center," said Essie. "Blueberry crisp crumble."

Hannah continued eating, stopping only when her plate was

empty. She thumbed the few remaining crumbs into her mouth and then realized she had an audience. "What?" she asked of the three bemused faces watching her.

"You're a gastric wonder," said Debbie.

"I don't fart," Hannah said defensively. "Not that much!"

"Your appetite," Debbie said.

Phil put his remaining muffin on the windowsill, got up and closed the door, and then sat back down. Debbie, Hannah, and Essie watched him pensively as he leaned forward and rubbed his forehead. He shook his head and sat straight up. Debbie drummed her hand apprehensively on her lap.

"Alright. I put this off long enough," he said. "As you can imagine, I—and the Kearney Police Department—have questions. I suppose others will too in time." He looked at Debbie and Hannah, gave a flustered huff, and again shook his head. "I don't know how sensitive the subject matter is." He motioned towards Hannah with a slight nod.

"I know they found Anna in our secret space," Hannah said.

"Use discretion," Essie said.

He mentally contemplated his words and then said, "Okay, Hannah . . . about this secret place. I heard that your mother made the cinderblock room. I also heard that she built it to protect you and Anna. Can you tell me what or who she was protecting you from?"

"Bad people," Hannah said. "But mostly Travis, I think. Mom knew there would be dangerous things."

Phil turned to Debbie and sputtered, "Why would she . . . if she knew that danger was eminent, why the heck . . . ?"

Essie cleared her throat and Phil composed himself and started again. "The secret place was very well made—professional quality. It was built on a concrete foundation and it fit perfectly between the floor struts, which she cut and reinforced to support the hole in the floor. Your mom was very talented and very concerned about your and Anna's safety. That closet fooled everyone."

Hannah gave him an appeasing smile.

"What I don't get," Phil continued. "Is how did she do all that work with the cement mixing, bricklaying, and woodcutting, without Travis knowing?"

"She built it before she knew Travis," Hannah said.

"Why? Was there someone else she needed to protect you and Anna from?"

Hannah shrugged. "She made it so we always had a safe place to go when we . . ." Hannah paused, unsure how to explain it. "Mom said we needed the secret place because we are special."

"How do you mean *special*?" Phil asked.

Hannah looked at her table and then flashed a quick, uneasy glance Debbie's way, which Phil surely caught. She suddenly perked up and said with a charming tilt of her head. "Well, just look at us!"

Phil smiled as Debbie and Essie shared a laugh.

"I knew I wasn't going to get far here," Phil said without animosity. "Let's change tracks. When I spoke with Kearney Police about the house in Elm Creek, they were a little mystified by something. There were signs of movement in the dirt under the house . . . very recent movement." He pointedly gazed at Debbie.

"Animals?" Debbie offered.

"Yeah, two animals that wear sneakers and have elbows, hands, and knees," the detective said. "The marks appear to be made by an eight- or nine-year-old child and a woman or small man. They also found a nearly perfect shoeprint, so perfect they said they could figure the size and make if necessary."

"What's odd about that?" Debbie asked.

"Where they found the footprint. It was on the inside of the door for the crawlspace under the house," Phil said with a shrewd smile. "They're trying to figure out how the door had been kicked outward when it was boarded shut from the outside, yet there was no evidence of entry through the cinderblock enclosure, which is the only other way someone could have entered."

That hadn't even crossed Debbie's mind. *Some thief I'd make*, she thought scathingly. "That's weird," she said.

"Indeed it is," Phil agreed. "Whoever was crawling around under the house also opened the cast-iron door to the cinderblock enclosure, because her prints were in the soil there as well. Fortunately they don't feel it's pertinent to Anna's . . ." he paused, choosing his words, "circumstances . . . especially considering her state. It's a very curious series of events. Whoever this *possible* woman and child are, you'd think they just appeared under the house like magic."

Debbie felt the heat of his words and she felt that he was toying with her. What point was he trying to make? Hannah and Essie remained silent, and it seemed she and Phil had come to an impasse, but Phil said, "Your feet look to be about a size eight. You wouldn't have a pair of tennis shoes, would you?"

"I do," Debbie said. "Why would that matter?"

"It doesn't. Just ironic that the shoe prints under the house happen to be tennis shoes, about size eight," Phil said.

Debbie held the detective's gaze as steadily as possible. "Well, it's a good thing Hannah and I were here yesterday."

"True enough. I know you were here yesterday," Phil said. "In fact, I saw all three of you in Riverside Park, but I must have been tired, because I swear I saw things happen down on that boat ramp that I never would have dreamed possible."

Wary yet intrigued, Essie studied the detective. Debbie, in a near panic, started trying to convince Phil of Hannah's need for protection. Phil held up both hands to stem the barrage of Debbie's words.

"Ba-ba-ba-ba-ba! Don't say another thing. I don't understand it, nor do I want to," Phil said. "I *really, really* don't want to know. In fact, it'd be best if you never said another word about it . . . to anyone. I'll do my part, but if you want to protect this amazing little lady, you should, as Essie says, use *a lot* of discretion and be more conscientious. I don't know what would ensue if this came to light, but I'd rather have no part of it."

Essie repeated her belief that Hannah would be safe due to implausible deniability.

"Don't depend on plausible deniability or implausible deniability, that's poop philosophy. It's not corrupt government or clandestine Orwellian research labs I'm talking about, that's big-screen hyperbole . . . for the most part. It's the unbalanced ones like the uber-fundamentalists and the crackpots who might see this as divine and prophetic or the corrupt and greedy who might see this as a windfall. Don't underestimate the wickedness of your fellow man . . . he's always stooping to new lows."

The relief Debbie felt could have deflated a dirigible, but the importance and validity of Phil's words were just as significant. She nodded her agreement.

"Yesterday could have been devastating," Phil said. "Hopefully I was the only witness other than Doctor Hiller." He looked at Hannah again. Changing the subject, Davenport asked, "DFC make a decision?"

"The meeting's today at five," Debbie said. "I've applied to be Hannah's foster mother."

"Good . . . good. That would be best," said Phil. "If I can help that to happen, I will." He rose, walked to Hannah's bed, and knelt beside it. He took her hand in his and said, "I'm very, very sorry about your sister and your mother, and that you had to live through such tragedy. You are a beautiful, brave, and vibrant young lady, and you deserve a good and normal life from now on. Do you understand?"

Hannah nodded.

"When I leave this room," Phil said. "All that we've talked about disappears. Hannah once again becomes a magnificent little girl with an amazing survival story . . . nothing more." He looked at Hannah. "Next time you see me, I'm just Phil or Mr. D. Deal?"

Hannah nodded and to everyone's surprise—especially Phil's—Hannah gave the detective a long, earnest hug.

"I promise," she said, and Debbie knew that a promise coming from Hannah's mouth was ironclad.

"You too," Phil said to Debbie. He took his half-finished muffin from the windowsill and said to Essie, "You should open a muffin shop. These are too good not to be therapeutic." Detective Phil Davenport opened the door, winked, and left the room.

The room nearly inflated from the collective release of breath that ensued, followed by a long silence.

"Do you think he's sincere?" Debbie asked.

"I think so," said Essie. "Hannah seems to think so."

"He's right," said Debbie.

"Yes," agreed Essie.

"One meeting down . . . two to go," said Debbie.

"Today's going to be a long day," Essie said.

"All days are twenty-four hours," said Hannah.

"I stand corrected," said Essie.

"How are you feeling about the next meeting?" Essie asked.

Debbie turned from Hannah's line of sight and mouthed, "Terrified."

CHAPTER 30

Debbie and Brandon agreed to meet at The Grill Next Door, a friendly and well-received pub that offered a decent food selection, but was renowned for its thirty-six varieties of beer on tap. Debbie felt nauseous with anxiety when she and Essie arrived. She ordered a spinach salad and a cranberry spritzer, not her usual fare of bleu cheese-stuffed Angus burger, fries, and a Sierra pale ale.

Brandon and his daughter seemed to ignite the room upon entering, first with their smiles and hair, and then with their kindliness. Both greeted Debbie and Essie with hugs.

Debbie was astounded by their similarities, not just to each other, but Brandon's to Conan O'Brien and Stephanie's to Debbie herself.

"You look more like me when I was young than I did," Debbie said to Stephanie.

Stephanie recognized the wordplay and replied, "Awesome! That means I'll be hot, too!"

"Told you," Essie said to Debbie.

On the rare occasions when she would *dress up* to appease Kenny by wearing a pretty dress and applying some makeup, she would morph into something elegant and even sensual, but to be described as gorgeous, hot, or sexy made her feel extremely vulnerable and exposed, and it scared the shit out of her. Kenny had tried doggedly to change her perspective, tactlessly mistaking insensitivity for encouragement by describing Debbie's clothing style as *frumpy* or *unbecoming,* and saying her aversion to makeup made her dowdy and colorless. To be regarded as pretty always brought her to a place of shame. She tugged at the hem of her dress and sat down.

Brandon and Stephanie quickly defused Debbie and Essie with their wit and easy manner, telling lighthearted tales of their life in

Lakewood and surprisingly sparking a few memories for Debbie. Brandon spoke of many of his cases that were heartbreaking, yet ultimately had positive outcomes.

They left for Essie's office in good spirits, but a blanket of circumspection slowly embraced Debbie.

"I'm scared," she said, the words slipping out before she could bite them back.

Essie gave Debbie's leg a comforting pat. "Of course you are. It's a natural and healthy reaction when facing the unknown."

"It has to be bad if Brandon insisted on coming here all the way from Cleveland."

"He had already planned to travel this way," said Essie.

"Not really. It's a two-hundred-mile diversion. It's going to be bad," Debbie repeated gravely.

"Maybe," Essie said. "But you're a lovely, smart, and compassionate woman whose wonderful essence has not been compromised by whatever happened all those years ago and all those miles away. No matter what you hear, you can handle it because you've already defeated it and risen above it."

They drove in silence until they reached the office. Before they got out of the car, Essie hugged Debbie and said, "Chin up and stay strong, beautiful girl."

Essie's words were similar to those Debbie had used with Hannah and Anna. That she had become fond of Essie was no surprise, but the desire to latch onto the maternal figure Essie represented was. *Mother* was a void never filled, and even at thirty, Debbie was in a place not unlike Hannah. Comforted by Essie's compassion, Debbie got out of the car.

Inside the office, Essie led Stephanie to a small break room and showed her a cabinet with a nice offering of *healthy* snacks and a small refrigerator with a variety of juices. Stephanie pointed to a Keurig coffee machine and raised a questioning eyebrow.

"K-cups are in the top left cupboard," Essie said.

Stephanie raised the same eyebrow to a computer station in the corner. Essie gave her thumbs up and said, "Username, Freud. Password, Jung with a jay."

"I feel terrible having you come all the way to Boston and further, and now you have to sit by yourself while I . . ." Debbie said, and at a loss for words dropped her hands to her sides.

"Are you serious?" asked Stephanie. "I've got internet, an endless supply of caffeine, and NuGo bars. *Plus,* I've seen genetic evidence that I could have a rocking bod once mine decides it needs a shape."

"You have a lovely shape," said Essie.

"For a twelve-year-old boy!" Stephanie argued.

"I saw your Facebook page," said Debbie. "No twelve-year-old boys look like that!" Stephanie blushed and chanced a glance at her father.

"Yeah, I saw it. Wish I hadn't. You have more lift than a Harrier in that photo," Brandon said.

"What's a Harrier?" Stephanie asked.

"Google it," said Brandon with a wink.

Brandon followed Debbie and Essie into the private office and set his briefcase down near one of the seats. Debbie sat on the beige leather sofa that she and Ab had shared two days prior and Essie sat beside her and crossed her legs. Debbie had a sudden jab of paranoia. Had Brandon and Essie spoken about her life in Lakewood without her knowledge? It was unfounded and improbable, but the notion made her feel at a disadvantage, as if they knew all her secrets. Essie patted her reassuringly on the leg as if she were aware of her thoughts. Brandon sat down and offered a supportive smile that fell a little short.

"I feel as nervous as you look," Brandon said to Debbie.

"This has been hanging over me for a few days," Debbie replied. "I'm sure what you have to tell me won't make it to a Walt Disney film."

"No, it won't," Brandon said. "I'm not entirely sure how and where to start. Maybe I should start by asking you what you remember of Lakewood?" He looked to Essie for an affirmation. She nodded and shared a comforting smile.

"You asked me that the other day," Debbie said. "I remember more lately but . . . still just little snippets. I feel the most important things are those I don't remember, like my mother. Why would I block her out? I envision her as a faceless, long-haired absence and me as a little girl, saying goodbye. I can't even conjure an image of my father. I have fond and faded memories of Nan. They feel like safe memories. I think she was my mother's mother, but I'm not sure."

"She was," Brandon affirmed.

"I remember Nan's funeral, or at least the memory of her lying in her casket. I also remember running in the woods and playing . . . tag . . . or hide-and-seek. Those were the good memories. The bad memories were hidden from me until shortly after my ex and I split. Something dredged them up, and they kicked into hyper-drive when Hannah appeared. That's about it."

Brandon repositioned on the seat and scratched his head nervously. "Now, I can tell you some of what you don't remember if you're sure you're ready."

"You drove hours out of your way, I'm not about to waste your time like that," Debbie said.

"That's not the response I need. You have to tell me you are ready or that you are not ready to hear about Lakewood. If it's too much to deal with right now, I can't and won't blame you. This has not been a waste of time for me. I have thought about you often over the years. If I were to leave right this moment, I would leave content that I did see you and talk with you, and knowing that you are doing well."

Debbie looked at Essie and then closed her eyes to calm herself. "Okay," she says. "Let's have it."

After another deep breath Brandon said, "Everything was good until 1987 when grandmother died. She was your self-appointed caretaker since your mother was seldom present and not too *with it* when she was. I don't remember her that well, but my father, your mother's brother, said she was always chasing romantic dreams, pursuing promises, and coming back a little emptier each time. She was exceptionally beautiful and he said that her beauty was her biggest folly. She thrived on attention and would take off for long spells to places like Vegas, Cancun, Rio, or wherever her latest suitors took her. There were many men. They would use her then lose her, but she always found her way back to Lakewood, broken-hearted, penniless, and quite often addicted to one thing or another."

"Which finally killed her," Debbie said.

After an extended pause Brandon said, "Debbie, your mother's not dead."

"But Mad Mother Prioulx told me she overdosed," Debbie said. "She said she died like a whore, in an abandoned building with a needle in her arm."

"Madeline Prioulx. Not exactly the honorable type," said Brandon.

"How do you know her?" Debbie asked, her agitation rising with the timbre of her voice. It was daunting talking with someone who knew her history better than she did.

"Don't know her, but I know quite a bit about her," Brandon said. "Madeline wasn't in Lakewood, but she was in the Cleveland area. The Prioulx case is one of notoriety in Cuyahoga County. Your mother overdosed on a number of occasions, but it was never fatal. Nan and my father were usually there to catch her. In retrospect, it was probably for the best that you thought she had died. She was sentenced to ten to twelve years in the Ohio Reformatory for Women, and was released after seven on good behavior."

"Sentenced for what?" Debbie asked.

"You," answered Brandon.

"She was involved?" blurted Debbie. A strap around her gut tightened and pushed it up against her heart.

"Not directly, but she may as well have been. She was found guilty on several accounts of gross negligence and failure to protect. My God, she was your mother for crying out loud. Parents are supposed to protect their children." Brandon complained. "Could I have some water?"

Essie quickly got up and left the room.

"Where is she now?" asked Debbie.

"In Lakewood. She changed her name to protect herself. How's that for a kick in the teeth? Ten or so years ago she married a fellow named Grafton. That's what she goes by now, Patricia Grafton. She has a court-ordered, non-expiring restraining order, which means she cannot attempt to contact you in any way . . . for life. Jail sobered her, dried her out, and gave her plenty of time to acknowledge how she failed her only child. She's forty-eight but looks seventy. I imagine the guilt is eating her alive. I know she's my aunt, but I say *good!* She deserves it."

Essie returned with three bottles of spring water.

"Who did she fail to protect me from?"

After another pause Brandon said, "Our grandfather. We called him Grumps."

"Grumps?" Debbie repeated. The word felt odd as she spoke it and it tasted wrong on her tongue.

"Not a good man," Brandon said.

Debbie hissed introspectively as fragmented images of the man speckled her memories like mud on a windshield. "I vaguely remember him, but I thought he was nice to me."

"So it seemed. So much so, it made us jealous. He showered you with gifts, gave you the best room in the house, and always took you places. Little did we know that the whole time he was *paying* you for *being good* and for keeping silent," Brandon said. He paused, not sure how to go on.

"Fuck," Debbie muttered. It kept getting more and more bizarre. She felt miles away from the conversation, yet confined, as if she were in a soundproof box and hearing his words shouted through the tiniest of pinholes.

"He wasn't our biological grandfather," Brandon said. "He was Nan's second husband. Harold Gillan, our real grandfather, died in an industrial accident long before either of us was born. The bastard's name was Stafford Dunne. As I mentioned, we called him Grumps, but most people just called him Dunne."

"Stafford Dunne," Debbie whispered more to herself. The name claimed no hold in her memory.

"He was a tenant in Nan and Harold Gillan's marriage home on Atkins Avenue, off Hilliard Road. Dunne ended up marrying Nan, and when she died, he got the house.

"My father said he was neutral about Dunne before the truth was discovered, but my mother despised him from the get go. She thought he was obnoxious—one of those over-friendly face-talkers. She suspected he was dirtier than a hog's heel and tried convincing your mother to get you out of that house once Nan died. Your mother told her that she worried too much. Of course, the situation was ideal for your mother. She lived there rent free and Stafford, being retired, was a built-in babysitter."

Debbie let this sink in for a moment. "I remember the woods. I think there were two boys who played with me," Debbie said, recalling the vision of the same boys trying to hide her beneath the basement stairs. "I've even dreamt about it."

"There was a wooded area behind the house where we used to run around as kids," Brandon said.

"One of them had a different name, like Scooby or Scooter or something. I have the feeling that was you," Debbie said.

"Yeah, Skipper or Skippy. I haven't been called that in years. This is not a complaint."

"Who was the other boy?" Debbie asked.

"My brother Glen," Brandon said. "He was eleven then. He was also *used* by Stafford Dunne, although we hadn't known it at first. I was older, which I think dampened their interest in me."

Brandon seemed lost in thought for a while, his eyes brimming. After a prolonged blink, he spoke. "Once Dunne was discovered and convicted, Glen became increasingly troubled. We started seeing a psychiatrist who discovered that Glen had a horror story hiding within him. Turned out that one of our neighbors, a scumbag named Beebo Grant was also involved. Beebo often articulated to Glen in Technicolor detail what he would do to him if he exposed them. Glen was plagued by what had happened to him and was unable to get past it. The psychiatrist was good, but ultimately not good enough. Glen hanged himself in 2002 when he was twenty-four. By the time he died, he was surviving primarily on whiskey and peppermint Life Savers. We tried everything to help him, but it was too late."

"My God," Debbie said. "If I remember right, he was animated and seemed so happy."

"So did you. But you were—and are—stronger than Glen was," Brandon said. "We practically lived in those woods, you, Glen, and me, but Dunne also had his shed there. It wasn't much more than a tool shed, but it was always locked and he kept the windows covered."

Debbie raised her hands to her temples and stiffened. "The shed is where it all happened. That's where the flashbacks bring me," she said.

Her thoughts traveled there, though it was more than twenty years ago, flashing quick, fleeting images of Atkins Avenue in her mind. She saw a house with a small front porch. She saw a tree-lined driveway that narrowed down into a pathway leading to the distant outline of the shed. She felt as if she were there. Fear numbed her extremities and charged the nerves throughout her body, wracking her with a severe shudder.

"Guest of honor," she said. The words spilled unconsciously from her lips.

"Guest of honor?" repeated Essie.

Debbie's head jerked to face her, her eyes wide and dilated with fear. She felt small, like the seven-year-old girl in that godforsaken Lakewood, Ohio, shed all those years ago. "I have to treat the guests of honor right," she said, her voice tiny and childish. "I have to give them whatever they want."

She could see the little unicorns on her sneakers, as one foot stepped in front of the other, marking her obedient walks from the house and through the trees to meet up with whoever the next *guest of honor* was.

"Foul bastard," Brandon muttered.

"Why'd he do it? Why'd he let them do that to me?" asked Debbie, trying to push away the memories of that damned life, on that damned street, in that damned city. The images blurred as her tears welled.

"Money," said Brandon. Essie let out a small moan.

And there it is, Debbie thought. "He sold me," she said. It wasn't a question, but a murmur of acknowledgement. "My grandfather sold me like an old record. No . . . no, not sold, he rented me out as if I were real estate. Not once, but repeatedly. I was his little whore."

"Oh my God! No Debbie!" said Brandon. "He was . . . he . . ."

"He was sick, demented, and evil," Essie completed.

"No . . . it's okay. I get it now," Debbie said. The trancelike feeling within her deepened, obvious in the slowness of her words, yet she sat up straighter. "How did he find people to . . . you know . . ."

"There are bad people out there, Debbie," Brandon said. "For every depravity, there are multiple markets."

"Real estate markets," Debbie said. "Child sex for sale or rent."

She had seen it fairly often in her job. She had come upon people who had *lent* their own children out for favors, fixes, and once, by Christ, for tickets to a basketball game, but she had never expected it to hit home. It hit so much harder this way. She was at the center of the blast—ground zero—and it slammed the structure and fractured the foundation. There was nowhere safe to hide from it.

"He must be in his seventies by now. Where is he?" Debbie asked.

"Dead," said Brandon, hoping it would bring her at least a small victory. "He was found guilty on profuse charges of molestation and aggravated rape of two juveniles, and a laundry list of charges that would have assured prison without bail for three lifetimes. He was sentenced to the Lorain Correctional Institute, but barely lasted three months before someone twisted his neck. They're not too tolerant with his kind in most prisons."

"Dunne gone," Debbie said, and chuckled bitterly. "He served only three months?" she clenched her fists on her shaking legs. "That's not long enough . . . not for what he did to two children. He should have lived through his death—through a hundred deaths—like Glen did and like I did. Like I'm still doing! He should have been hanged a hundred times for what he did to your brother."

"This is one of those examples where the expression, 'Death isn't good enough' works," Essie said and squeezed her hand.

Brandon said, "I'm an Atheist, but I truly hope there is a hell for people like him."

"Who else was there? Who else was involved?" asked Debbie, not wanting, yet needing to know.

"There were three other men the police were aware of besides Stafford Dunne and Beebo Grant," Brandon said.

Aware of, thought Debbie. Her stomach clenched even harder. *That means there were five and maybe more.* She felt like she needed to shower, to cleanse off the grime that covered her, the filth that was seeping into her pores, her ears, and mouth, polluting her and infecting her. "Who are they?"

"Their names were Darrell Shipman, Albert Polevik, and Roberto Juarez," Brandon said. "Roberto Juarez disappeared but surfaced a couple of years later in Miami where he was arrested for killing a cop in a drug sting. He's doing life on countless charges. Shipman was found in his cell at Lorain with a handmade knife in his throat. He was seven years into his sentence. Albert Polevik was a wealthy executive and considered a pillar of the community. He owned AKP Manufacturing, was a devout elder at his church, and gave generously to charities. Albert's dirty little secret instantly became enormous and his dignitary status was instantly crashed. To save face, Albert put a .45 in his mouth just as the police broke his door in."

"There was a fat man with shiny black shoes in my flashbacks.

He reeked of cologne that was nauseating and made it hard to breathe," Debbie said. She shuddered, leaned over, grabbed a thick throw pillow from the foot of the sofa and hugged it to herself. "He hurt me. At least in my flashback he did. I don't know what he did, but I think he really hurt me."

"He did," Brandon said in a voice heavy with emotion. "It was horrendous. I've tried for years to get your screams out of my head, but I can't. They still haunt me."

"You were there?" asked Debbie.

"No, not when it happened, but before and after. Glen and I tried to hide you that night, but Dunne found us."

"Under the stairs," Debbie mumbled, hazy with the memory.

"Yes. In the basement. We lived three houses down on the same street. We heard you . . . everybody did. They echoed through the neighborhood, those screams." Brandon's voice broke under the weight of his memories.

"He tried to run from it—Polevik did—but he didn't have time to dress and run. The neighborhood men and women caught him. He was covered in blood, but no one knew whose blood until they found you." Brandon sniffed. "Should I be telling you this? Is it too much?"

"Maybe we should take a moment to check in," said Essie. "How are you doing, Debbie?"

"I'm not sure yet, it's the most hideous thing I could have imagined, but it feels as if we're talking about someone else," Debbie said. "I think that's the only way I'll get through this is to handle it that way."

"It could become overwhelming," said Essie. "If you feel like it's too much, we can stop at any time, but the floodgates may already be opened."

Debbie considered her options and decided it would be better to get everything on the table. Sometimes it works better that way . . . it's less painful to jab the needle in than to slowly push it in by increments.

"Okay, Brandon, what did the *honorable* Mr. Polevik do?" Debbie asked.

"Oh God," Brandon said, his voice guttural and shaking. He paused to collect himself. "He ruptured you. He punctured you inside and nearly killed you. The doctors said that he nearly ripped your cervix off." Debbie felt the sharp stabbing sensation in her abdomen as the phantom pains returned to torment her.

"After that, Glen started acting odd. He became jittery and reclusive. He didn't want to go to the hospital to see you and would disappear whenever it came up in conversation. My mother made the connection, but when my parents asked him about it, he denied it. He finally told our psychiatrist that he, too, was abused. As I mentioned, they had threatened him, saying they would kill my parents and me. Without Glen, Darrell Shipman, Beebo Grant, and Roberto Juarez would have gone free. Up to that point it was believed that only Polevik and Dunne were involved."

"Were there other children?" asked Debbie.

"None were ever discovered. Every poor child in our neighborhood was put through physical examinations and counseling," Brandon said. "You were in the hospital for weeks suffering multiple surgeries and a lifetime of agony, battling infections and fighting for your life. It haunts my memories and it never slackens." Brandon's distress was apparent in his eyes and the wringing of his hands.

"I used to sneak into the hospital to visit you. They'd let me in some evenings, but Glen was never able to cope. The more we tried to help him, the deeper his desperation got. He was an addict by fourteen, begging, borrowing, stealing, and selling himself to feed his pain. The police tried to be understanding, but they could only look away for so long. He did six months for breaking and entering when he was seventeen. At nineteen, he held up a market, and when a patron tried to restrain him, Glen panicked and stabbed him. The injuries were superficial, but Glen was deemed dangerous. He earned a five-year stay at Ohio State Pen, but was released in three. His demons wouldn't let him go, or maybe he wouldn't let them go, but he had a bottle in his hand by the time his feet hit the pavement. He hanged himself three months later."

Debbie felt an enormous sense of compassion for Glen. Her emotions jostled and volleyed within her, and what was most prominent and so huge and weighted that it felt like it would crush her was, oddly, the emptiness she felt. It wasn't an entirely bad feeling. There was an element of relief in the nothingness, in not knowing what would happen, how she'd react, and not knowing what her next step would be if she survived it. Now that the monster had a name, she found it wasn't that scary after all. It was vile and diseased, and it left many scars, but like a tornado, it had raged and left a disaster in its wake, only she had survived. All that was left to do was clean up the mess and forge ahead.

"Debbie? Are you okay?" Essie asked.

The words reverberated within her. *Are you okay? Not "all right"*, Debbie was certain things would never be "all right", but "okay" was within reason. It had been more than twenty years since the events Brandon disclosed had transpired, and as horrific as they were, Debbie realized that she *was* okay—damaged . . . but okay.

"Yeah," Debbie said. "You know, they didn't just steal a little boy's future . . . they shattered it . . . and a huge part of a little girl's."

Debbie wiped away a tear that had settled on her upper lip. Essie retrieved a box of tissues and handed them to her. "Stolen things can be recovered and returned, but shattered things cannot," she continued. "I can't remember those men, but I can still hear them and smell them." She put a hand on her lower abdomen. "I can feel them ripping and tearing at me and inside of me, and sometimes I swear I can even taste them.

"I cannot have a wholesome relationship. I cannot make love to a man properly because it is excruciating for me both physically and emotionally. The only man I've ever loved left me because I couldn't give him those things that were stolen from me. I can never have my own children. Internal scarring won't allow it. At first, my gynecologist thought I had Asherman's syndrome. She tried doing a diagnostic hysteroscopy and I nearly went through the roof. She knew what really caused it, but I wasn't about to listen to her. I knew about the scarring. I just pretended it wasn't real. Ignorance is a great defense system. Looking back, Kenny wouldn't have been able to handle the truth . . . not that it mattered in the end."

"They've made great strides with surgery," Essie said.

Debbie smiled softly and shook her head. "No. My reproductive system is too incompetent to carry a child, and if I could, I'm not so sure I would. I'd have to live with the fear of what he or she might have to endure in life."

"So, will this affect your ability regarding Hannah?" Essie asked. "You want to be a mother to her."

"Hannah's different. I didn't bring her into this. She existed before I got involved, so I'm not accountable for what has already happened to her, only what will. I'm prepared to protect her by any means to assure that she never experiences what I have."

"You could call it karma, but most of these men died ugly, dishonorable deaths, exposed as the monsters they were," Essie said. "Even though they did those horrendous things, they weren't able to destroy you. Before you learned of your past, you consciously—and I'm sure unconsciously—chose to become a social worker who specializes in child advocacy. What you've become is the greatest testament to you, and it shows that the strongest part of you knew how to survive. Can you accept that?"

Debbie gave a quick, gentle nod.

"I'm impressed by your strength, by who you are, and by what you've accomplished," said Brandon. "I was thrilled to hear you got your degree in social work from Boston College . . . not too shabby."

"You seem to know quite a lot about me, Cousin Brandon," Debbie said.

"Yes . . . guilty. Glen and you motivated and inspired me. You did before we even knew Glen was a victim."

"How's that?" asked Debbie.

"So many reasons." He took a sip of water and continued. "I think the enormity of it all hit me when I saw you on the stretcher. I knew you were dreadfully hurt—even life threatening—but I didn't know *how* you'd been hurt until I saw Polevik being led away. Right then I understood how horrendousness it was, and the absolute wickedness of the demon that did it, but what came clear to me was how powerless I was to do anything about it."

"You were just a kid, yourself," Debbie said.

"Maybe. But I was old enough to recognize my weakness. You looked so tiny lying on that stretcher, covered in so much blood. It was so vivid and immediate that something within me died, yet something else was born. I wanted so badly to help you, to compensate for not being able to hide you and protect you. I would have done anything to take your pain away, but the truth was like a brick wall between us, exposing just how amazingly insignificant I was . . . how powerless I was."

"Which is exactly what the depraved feed on," said Essie. "They target children, and even more so, children from broken homes or with disabilities."

"That night, I witnessed firsthand how unfair our world is and how those we trust most can be our greatest tormentors," Brandon said. "When Glen died, I knew—regardless of how others perceived him—none of it was his fault. I wonder what he would have accomplished if these things had never happened. He might have still ended up a train-wreck, or he might have discovered the cure for cancer, but thanks to those bastards we will never know.

"I'm now driven by the need to set things right. I want to do whatever necessary to prevent abominations like what happened to you and Glen from happening to others, and if they do, to make sure the perpetrators pay to the fullest degree possible. You and Glen became many things to me. You could call it an obsession, but I think of it as an inspiration."

After a moment of retrospection he said, "You know what else I remember from that night?"

"What?" asked Debbie, not entirely sure she wanted to know. Essie gave her a reassuring smile.

"Although you were in unimaginable pain and quite literally dying, you fought like hell not to go into that ambulance. You were sure a ride in the back of the ambulance was the same as a ride in the back of a hearse." Brandon chuckled lightly at the memory.

"That explains my fear of ambulances," said Debbie.

"And who could blame you?" added Essie.

"You latched onto the door, howling, biting, and kicking as they tried to roll the stretcher in. You even hooked the door with your leg. It took four people to hold your arms and legs still and push the stretcher in. I found it reassuring that you had fight left in you, despite enormous odds. You're a survivor, and you kept on proving it through the years. I know your story, but I can't start to imagine what it must be like standing on your end of the looking glass, or on Glen's."

Brandon's depiction of Debbie's valiant struggle at the ambulance brought Hannah's and Anna's spirit to mind. "I appreciate that more than you know," Debbie said. "I'm not through healing yet, far from it, but I'm determined to get there."

Fighter and Survivor were tags Debbie had never pinned on

herself, they were always overshadowed by her self-assessments of being odd, unworthy, and unlovable. She now realized she was looking at it the wrong way. She had fought for independence, for Hannah and Anna and countless other abused children, against the demons of her past, and so far hadn't lost. *You have plenty of scars, Mr. Marciano, but you're still undefeated.*

"It's going to take time to process all of this and maybe I never will," Debbie said. "Right now, I feel like I'm totally encased in gauze. When it wears off, I have a feeling it'll hit me like a bomb."

Brandon reached down and patted the side of his briefcase. "I have a folder with copies of newspaper articles and court documentation regarding your case, and Glen's, too. It's an account with follow-ups, an extended case history of sorts. I figured if you ever showed up and wanted . . . well, like now, it's in here. It's yours to keep. You can open them or you can toss them in the fireplace. It's your call. I also have Patricia Graft's information, should you ever . . ."

"Thank you. I'm not sure if I'm ready for any of that yet, especially confronting Patricia Graft. Possibly someday," Debbie said. She sat silently for a few moments and then asked, "Is the shed still there?"

"The police cordoned it for a while, but then my father and some of the neighborhood men burned it."

"Good," said Debbie. She wiped her eyes, looked at Essie, and smiled sadly. "As bad as it was, this wasn't as hard as I thought it would be."

"Take time to process it," Essie said. "You have a lot going on, so you haven't come to a full understanding of it. It may become a lot larger when you're by yourself or in the middle of the night."

Debbie stared ahead, unfocused, but thoughtful. She suddenly looked up and smiled. "I think I'll be okay once I get past the anger."

Brandon looked at his cousin, shook his head, and said, "So what's next? Climb Everest?"

"Close," said Debbie. "I need to request a new caseworker for Hannah."

"Why?" Brandon asked. "I thought you were her caseworker."

"I am, but I can't be her caseworker and have any hope of being her foster mother," Debbie said.

"You have a license?" Brandon asked.

"I do," Debbie said. "Up to this point I've only done short-term stays during transitions, but I hope to foster and then adopt Hannah."

"Wow! That could be a challenge, considering Hannah's history. Are you certain it's something you're up for, considering . . . ?" Brandon hesitated.

"Considering my history?" said Debbie. "Absolutely! For that reason all the more and I'll be damned good at it."

"Amen," said Essie.

"I don't have an ounce of doubt about that," Brandon said, granting them his crooked smile. "And I know a damned good lawyer who can help you with the legalities. It's out of my jurisdiction, but I know the dance steps, and I have a few colleagues in the Boston area. Interested?"

"Things are starting to look good," Essie said, and again she patted Debbie's leg enthusiastically. Debbie wished she felt the same way.

CHAPTER 31

The DCF office occupied a unit in a small plaza in the befittingly small township of Fielding, a community of Riverside, Massachusetts. An exercise club took up the majority of the building, but there was also a dry cleaner, a Laundromat, a pizza shop, and an assortment of smaller businesses. Within two hundred yards of where Debbie stood, there were three restaurants, two fast food joints, two donut shops, a super-pharmacy, a post office, a computer repair shop, a gas station/quick-mart, a self-defense studio, a hair salon, a bank, and the ever-important liquor store, solidifying it as the center—and ugliest part—of town.

Marjorie Faulkner was ordinarily in her office between two and four o'clock in the afternoon. Her door was open and the light was on, but it was her remarkably loud voice that betrayed her presence.

"No, no, Ms. Bale," she said. "We cannot act on assumption . . . that's libel. If we assumed that every child with a thumb-sized bruise was being abused by their father, we'd have to remove nearly every kid in town. I know, Ms. Bale, but this is the fourth accusation you've made this year, the second about your ex-husband, and it's only June. No, it's June, Ms. Bale. July doesn't happen for two more days. Yes, we've checked him out twice, and there is no evidence of abuse. Your daughter's doctor said there's no sign of abuse, and even your daughter said no one is touching or hitting her. I understand you feel you're certain, but there has to be evidence, and a bruise on the arm could come from a table corner, a friend, or even from you, Ms. Bale. Ms. Bale, I would appreciate you not swearing at me, or I will end this call. Ms. Bale . . . Ms. Bale, please calm down." Debbie heard the phone hit the cradle and Marjorie mutter, "Fucking nut-case."

Debbie stepped into the doorway and said, "Business as usual, I see."

Marjorie was leaning forward and massaging her temples, only her blonde, coiffed hair was visible. Adjusting her tortoise shell glasses, she looked up and said, "Oh, hi, Debbie. I tell you, these phones should come with a terminate button, and I'm not referring to the call. Lucy Bale, again."

"It's odd that they were married for all those years with all those kids, and it never became a concern until he left her," Debbie said.

"Poor bastard. I've known him forever. He's a great guy. Coaches my daughter's soccer team." She shook her head and grinned. "So what can I help you with? You have the case review and discharge planning meeting for the little Amiel-Janssen girl today, right? How's that going?"

Marjorie was sixty-eight and as thin as a wire. She would have been attractive if she'd let her hair go gray instead of dyeing it what Debbie could only describe as ochre, and if she hadn't spent so much time in the sun.

"That's why I'm here," Debbie said. Her body was quivering with apprehension. "I would like to discuss something with you." She self-consciously scratched her upper arm.

"Certainly. Come in and have a seat. Shut the door first," Marjorie directed. "And for Christ's sake calm down. I'm not going to bite you."

Debbie nodded, took the offered chair, and said, "I'd like someone else to take Hannah's case."

She pinned Debbie with intelligent, no-nonsense eyes that were so vividly blue she could feel them searching her soul.

"She's being placed tonight. Isn't it a little late in the game for that?" she asked.

"I'd like the opportunity to foster Hannah. I've thought it out, and I know I can handle it financially. I feel it'd be a good atmosphere for her."

"You've bonded with her?"

"Yes. Hannah and I have bonded, but it goes so much deeper than that. She looks to me in a maternal way."

"Which is highly frowned upon, of which you're well aware," Marjorie said with enough accusation in her words to make Debbie's heart sink. Despite what she knew would be the worst reaction, Debbie started to feel a panic growing inside her.

"I'd be a great foster mother to her," Debbie said defensively.

"And what of the next child who comes along? And the next one? You are a compassionate person, Debbie. It radiates from you, and it's evident in your work and your commitment to the children, but I feel you have let your emotions get ahead of you."

"But those are the qualities needed with any child. Hannah's psychiatrist, Essie Hiller, will give me a recommendation." Debbie felt as if she was whining, but couldn't help it.

"Essie is a great psychiatrist, but if this is true, then I feel she is wrong." Marjorie put a finger to her desk to accentuate her point. "One, you have only known Hannah for slightly over a week. Two, yes, her story is heartbreaking, but so are so many others. Three, just look at her. She's heartbreakingly beautiful, and I stress the *heart*. Who wouldn't fall head over heels for her?"

"Please understand it's more than you think. It has to do with Hannah's condition and her dissociation," Debbie said, feeling fear trump good sense. She desperately fought tears.

"I'm going to be brutally blunt, Debbie. Are you letting your inability to conceive children get in the way of logic?"

Debbie was stunned. Had she ever told Marjorie she was infertile? How could she know that?

"No! She's not an infant. She's nine, and she needs me."

"Debbie, you've overplayed your importance here."

"So you just tear her life apart again?" Debbie asked.

"Hannah has proved to be a very strong and resilient girl. She will survive. I am questioning your intent. I believe your attachment to her has become dangerous to her and to you."

"Love and compassion are dangerous?" Debbie asked.

"Yes. In this situation, it's the miscomprehension of love and compassion. Let me ask you this. Would you give up your job to have Hannah?"

"Yes," Debbie immediately answered, and at once realized her error.

"And that seals it, Debbie. You have overstepped your boundaries and lost your scope of responsibilities. You have put your emotions ahead of rationality." Marjorie folded her hands, preparing to dismiss her. "I cannot rightfully let that happen, nor will I transfer Hannah's case to anyone else. This is in your best interest, and even more so, Hannah's. You are right that she needs you, but as her caseworker. She does need that stability. Believe me . . . you'll thank me for it later."

The words were bullets, each one killing her a little more than the last. Debbie knew a denial was possible, but she wasn't expecting it. Feeling totally hollowed out, Debbie rose from her chair.

"Have you decided on a suitable foster home or parents? I do hope you did that," said Marjorie. "I would like a copy of the file and your selection on my desk before you leave for the meeting tonight."

She *had* made a decision. It would have been negligent of her not to, but she hadn't expected to use it. The family Debbie had selected was the Pielechs: a husband, wife, and a seventeen-year-old daughter. They seemed an ideal, well-respected upper-middle-class family in a sturdy household. Katie, their daughter, was a consistent honor-roll student and the second foster child Debbie had ever placed. The Pielechs eventually adopted her and now felt it was time for another child.

"I went with the Pielechs," said Debbie. She opened the door and started down the hallway.

"Good! You're damned good at your job, Debbie, probably the best on the North Shore," Marjorie called after her as she left the office. "Go to that meeting and do what is right for Hannah."

Debbie retrieved her files and exited the building. It was another gorgeous day. The sun and the light breeze carrying the smell of freshly cut grass seemed to mock her as she climbed into her car. She sat and pondered the depressing twist her hopes had taken.

How will Hannah handle it? Will she be devastated, or was Marjorie right that she'd overestimated her importance? Will Hannah simply move on with the Pielechs, and ride off into the sunset, leaving Debbie behind and soon forgotten?

What if her foster home turns out to be like the Prioulx house?

What if there's another Bernard Prioulx or another Stafford Dunne?

Debbie knew she'd survive, but what of Hannah? There were no guarantees that she wouldn't end up like Glen Gillan. The Pielechs had proved themselves ideal foster parents, but at the moment, it felt like the greatest of tragedies. She could have given Hannah a wonderful home life. They would have both needed a lot of time to heal from their pasts, but that commonality would have been something that could work for them. Debbie could have supported Hannah through her trials because she understood the terror, the fear, and the need to hide from the world and its demons.

Debbie actually entertained the thought of disappearing with Hannah and taking her to some location where they could start a new life together—mother and daughter, but it would never work. It would cause Hannah a life of abnormality. They would still live in fear, always looking over their shoulders, living on the lam with no hope of normalcy, and that would create the exact life from which Debbie was trying to save Hannah.

What a fool to let the lure of motherhood deceive me like this! Debbie chastised herself. Falling apart wouldn't help Hannah, either. She had to, in the words of Mad Mother Prioulx, *Suck it up, and deal with it.* Debbie shifted the car into gear and left the parking lot. She had a meeting to attend.

CHAPTER 32

*H*annah was stir-crazy. She moved from the window to the corridor and then back, looking for Debbie or Essie. She tried lying on the bed, reading, and watching television, but she couldn't stop the anxiety building within her. On the television was an oldie cartoon with the ultra-polite Goofy Gophers. Her mother had said their names were Mac and Tosh (like the apple) and that Warner Brothers Merrie Melodies were made long before Hannah's mother's mother had been born. Hannah usually liked cartoons, but today was the day she would find out if she would live with Debbie, or with another family in another home, which she had already decided would not happen. Hannah figured she'd just disappear to somewhere else if they didn't let her live with Debbie. Where, she wasn't sure, but she had survived this long using her smarts, and now she was older and smarter. She had spent two years traveling between Hannahwhere and Elm Creek, jumping between Stuck's Last Call, Foster's Market, Elm Creek Elementary and High School, and countless homes, raiding kitchens and sleeping wherever she felt moderately safe and warm—or cool, depending on the season. Hannah hadn't told anyone, even Debbie, this bit of information. It was her insurance policy. Elm Creek was all she knew, but most people thought she had been anywhere *but* there. She had managed to fool everyone except maybe Debbie. She had an inkling that Debbie knew better.

Debbie was convinced Hannahwhere was not a physical place like Riverside, Elm Creek, or Disney World, but a conscious place in their minds. Hannah thought it sounded plausible, though most of her life she had thought differently, and according to her mother's beliefs. It made sense that her physical body had always been somewhere in Elm Creek, and only her spirit traveled to Hannahwhere, but a part of her still felt Debbie wasn't right. She'd have to test it someday.

She had had some great hiding places in Elm Creek … even during the daytime. She had enjoyed exploring abandoned buildings and barns the most, but she'd sometimes pop into businesses after hours or people's houses while they were at work or on vacation. Locked doors were never a problem, only people, alarms, and animals.

There had been a few narrow escapes with people showing up unexpectedly or too early, or if she overslept or traveled too long. Once, after a long spell without incident, she had become a little careless. It was about three in the morning, the wee hours when she felt safest, few things stirred and sounds seemed amplified. She had been showering in the girls' locker room at the high school when the banks of lights flared to life. Hannah barely had enough time to turn off the water and grab a towel. She had trekked to the stockroom at Foster's Market, where she had squatted for more than an hour, soaked, freezing, and naked but for the towel . . . a most miserable experience. From then on, she kept her clothes nearby when she showered. The narrow escapes mostly happened at the school. She slept on the cot in the nurse's office, which was far preferable to a booth at Stuck's . . . or the interior of a dumpster.

After her first return to her home on North Easy Street, Hannah was never able to go back. Not until Debbie went with her. The memories of her mother's body on the couch, and of Travis swinging the knife, were far too vivid. She had feared he would be there if she returned, despite the newspapers' promise of a life sentence for Travis. She had read a lot about the case in the newspapers, most articles focusing on her and Anna's whereabouts. There were speculations on whether they'd been abducted or secreted away by a concerned relative, but most ventured that Travis had killed them and hid their bodies. Much of what she read, she didn't fully understand, but a lot of it she did and it usually sounded sad or bad.

She had first started popping into Foster's Market during the nighttime, usually setting off the motion alarms, but eventually learning the safe spots where she could "shop" undetected. She usually ate a sandwich and a bag of chips with a bottle of juice, topping it off with cookies or maybe Pop Tarts. She'd then go somewhere safe and remote to visit Anna. It was during one of these jaunts to Foster's that she had seen a large picture of herself and Anna on the front page of a local newspaper. It was one of the "bigger" papers, who printed new issues every day, unlike the *Beacon Observer*, which stayed on the rack for days and sometimes weeks before they released a new issue.

Each night Hannah would read any newspapers with articles about them and then return them the following night. The papers always seemed to have the same picture of her and Anna—the one of them in their matching pajamas—with bold-lettered headlines like *The Amiel-Janssen twins—Where are they?* It seemed to Hannah that there were no other pictures of them, although her mother had taken quite a few.

She had found one story especially disturbing. The headline teased, *Madman Travis Ulrich Cavorted with Satan . . . We Have Proof!* Travis was on the cover wearing orange prison garb. His face was half in shadow and bright orange flames surrounded him. After reading the tabloid article, Hannah had suffered horrendous nightmares and slept with a flashlight at her side for days. She never liked reading about Travis, yet she had forced herself to read everything, no matter who was the subject of the stories. The articles had been plentiful at first, but eventually tapered off and then stopped altogether, which wasn't a bad thing . . . especially concerning Travis. She figured the newspaper and magazine people had forgotten about them. If only *she* could forget.

Hannah didn't like living that way, hiding in one place or another and having to steal to eat, but she got into a routine. She had Anna to spend the lonely hours with, but that had also been the problem. With Anna trapped in Annaplace, Hannah had not confronted anyone about it for fear they would somehow have kept them apart. Now, since they had found Anna's body, Hannah was unsure if Anna existed any longer. She would be completely alone if she returned to that way of living, but it seemed better than living with strangers.

The temptation to check on Anna was nearly excruciating, but she had promised Debbie she would wait so they could go together. She wished she hadn't.

Hannah returned to the corridor and peered down its length.

Nurses crossed here and there, entering rooms and answering calls and an old man shuffled away from her, wheeling an IV rack and flashing glimpses of his pale, sagging back end to those unfortunate enough to notice. He stopped to endure an onslaught of rattling coughs and then resumed his stroll. A young girl in a bright red jumpsuit walked toward Hannah, past the coughing man, her long, snowy hair swinging back and forth with her steps. Hannah's heart paused for a moment. There was no mistaking that hair or the way the girl walked, but as she neared, their eyes met and Hannah saw that it was not Anna, just wishful thinking. This girl had dirty blonde hair and was too tall to be Anna. The girl timidly smiled and waved as Hannah watched her pass.

Disappointment darkened Hannah's mood and she returned to her room. The Disney Channel was airing *Good Luck Charlie*. Hannah wasn't very fond of it, but the background noise usually helped her feel less lonely . . . it wasn't doing its job today. It sounded tinny, and the cold dishonesty of the laugh track added a chill to the air.

The room had no clock and the television had no time display, but Hannah felt like time had slowed to a crawl. There was some kind of meeting at 5:00 p.m., but she hadn't heard a thing. The feeling in the pit of her stomach was not just nervousness . . . it was dread. It was not knowing that was getting to her; not knowing if Anna's spirit was okay, not knowing the outcome of the meeting, not knowing where she would live tomorrow, or with whom. She felt like she was at the end of a dark, abandoned hallway full of locked doors with no way out . . . *except Hannahwhere.*

What could possibly happen if she went?

Nothing bad had ever happened there. Sure, she had dreamed about Travis, but Essie said that was just her acknowledging her fears. Hannahwhere was and had always been a safe harbor, but the thought of disobeying Debbie ignited fears within her.

Will Debbie still love me if I disobey, or will she think I'm bad and not want to live with me?

Dinner came shortly after five, but Hannah left it untouched even after a fair amount of coaxing by the nurse named Jaime. Jaime was a nice nurse, very pretty with long, wavy black hair, but Hannah thought she smiled too much and that her voice was too sweet, like maple frosted cotton candy. Could anyone be that friendly?

Hannah changed the channel to The Cartoon Network but paid no attention to it. When six o'clock rolled around, she was scared and irritable. A series of worst-case scenarios had played through her mind, from the reviewers—whom she pictured as an evil empire—not granting Debbie the right to parent Hannah, to Debbie abandoning her altogether.

Unable to sit still any longer, Hannah locked herself in the bathroom and sat on a folded towel in the shower stall. Despite her fears and guilty feelings, she traveled to Hannahwhere in search of Anna.

CHAPTER 33

The trip to Hannah's room was solemn and torturous, and Debbie was having a hard time keeping her emotions at bay. Essie squeezed Debbie's hand sympathetically, but Debbie barely noticed. Doctor Farren walked behind her and slightly to her right. He had noticed Debbie's torment in the meeting and asked if she was all right, which she dismissed with a nod.

Debbie was livid. She had given six years of unwavering dedication to the office and to Marjorie. She had the most successful placement rate in the office and the highest positive feedback from the families involved, and Marjorie had the audacity to say she was wrong for the job?

She had to read the fucking reports to get an idea of what was going on with Hannah's case, Debbie thought. Yet she deemed herself knowledgeable enough to decide who was or who was not best for Hannah . . . in spite of Essie and Doctor Farren's recommendations!

It was all politics, Debbie figured. Because of the high-profile status of this case, they felt they had to flex their muscles for their public. *As if life wasn't hard enough for Hannah, they dragged her out of a comfort zone and threw her out into the unknown. The thoughtless fucking apes!* She felt like raking her nails down Marjorie's sun-parched face.

"You're hurting my hand," Essie whispered.

Debbie apologized, released her grip, and paused a moment to settle her anger.

"Take a breath and let it go," Essie softly suggested, rubbing circulation back into her hand.

Debbie knew Essie was right. Operating in a rage would only make things worse for everyone involved, be it justified or not. The practical part of her understood that Marjorie's decision was one of sound reasoning. If Debbie were watching another caseworker handling Hannah's case, unaware of all the bizarre details, she'd most likely have agreed with Marjorie. But that didn't make it any easier.

Doctor Farren pressed the elevator call button, and the door immediately opened. The five of them stepped in and rode in silence, like hangmen destined for the gallows. The doors opened facing the nurse's station, where a few nurses stood huddled, speaking among themselves in hushed tones. At the desk, a doctor and the charge nurse murmured to each other. All conversing stopped when they noticed Debbie, Essie, and Doctor Farren. Debbie found it all a bit ominous.

"How's Hannah?" Debbie asked.

"I imagine she's fine," said the charge nurse.

Debbie looked at her doubtfully. "You imagine?"

"Yeah. It appears she's locked herself in the bathroom again, but she's not answering us."

As petty as the situation sounded, Debbie felt herself slipping closer to the edge. Working at maintaining control, Debbie headed for Hannah's room, Essie and the nurse following closely behind her.

"What happened?" Essie asked. "Did someone or something upset her?"

"Not that we know of," said the nurse. "Dana was doing her rounds and she noticed Hannah wasn't in her bed and that the bathroom door was closed. She knocked and called for Hannah, but there was no answer."

"How do you know she's inside?" Doctor Farren asked.

"The door locks from inside," Debbie said, not able to hide her frustration.

She knocked soundly on the bathroom door and called Hannah's name, but there was no response. She had a good idea as to why, but she had hoped Hannah would wait for her. Had she somehow discovered what had gone on in Marjorie's office? "Fuck!" Debbie muttered under her breath and apologized. "Sorry. There must be a key?"

"It's not a key," said the nurse. "It's a . . ."

"Could you get it, please?" asked Essie.

"We keep it in a toolbox drawer at the nurses' station, but it's not there. We called maintenance," said the nurse.

"Call them back and tell them it's an emergency," demanded Doctor Farren.

"We did."

"Call them again and *convince* them it's an emergency," Doctor Farren instructed.

Flustered, but looking relieved to have an out, the nurse returned to the nurses' station. Debbie rapped on the door again as a petite brunette nurse with tired but pretty eyes entered the room and approached them.

"Hannah is my charge today," the woman said, and everybody watched her expectantly.

"What's your name, hon?" Essie asked.

"Dana Tessier," she said nervously. She turned to Debbie and asked, "You're Debbie, right?"

Debbie nodded.

"Well, I'm not sure how pertinent this is, but Hannah has asked for you repeatedly throughout my shift, which started at 3 p.m. She seemed to get more and more upset each time," Dana Tessier explained. "When I checked on her to see if she had eaten her dinner, she was sitting on the chair, acting kind of antsy. I was afraid she was about to go into one of her zone-out thingies. I nearly forgot she did that, it had been so long since she's had one."

Debbie's heart clenched, feeling whatever anxiety Hannah was experiencing was her fault. She looked around for something she could use to pry the door open. The flowers and the gifts from all the well-wishers were still all about the room, but their vibrancy seemed to have faded.

The magic is gone.

The thought popped into Debbie's mind unexpectedly. She could feel the emptiness within her arms and legs . . . in her eyes. The magic that was Hannah had left. She knocked on the door again.

"Hannah . . . honey . . . please open the door," she pleaded.

"Where in the hell are the maintenance people?" asked Dr. Farren.

"I'll check on them," Dana Tessier said and left the room.

Debbie sat on the chair that she and Hannah had shared for

hours on end and slumped under the weight of the guilt that saddled her shoulders.

"They'll have her out in a few minutes," Essie said and rested a comforting hand on Debbie's shoulder.

Debbie's eyes were fiercely red and miserable. Her professionalism had crumbled, but she couldn't bring herself to care what others were thinking. "She's not in there. I can't feel her. I feel a change in the atmosphere, like the gravity in the room is reversing."

Essie looked at her, understanding. There was no reproach in her eyes. She sat down on the arm of Debbie's chair. A sudden hiss like an air leak filled the room, followed by a pop, like the sound of a vacuum-sealed jar being opened.

"What is that?" asked Doctor Farren. He moved closer to the bathroom door. "It sounded like of a flock of pigeons taking flight."

Debbie looked at Essie and said nothing, but she jumped up and rushed to the bathroom door beside Doctor Farren. She started pounding on it with the flat of her palm and calling Hannah's name. The lock disengaged with a sturdy *clack* and the door swung outward. There was a collective breath of relief as Hannah was revealed, standing just inside the room with a radiant smile plastered across her face. Debbie grabbed her and pulled her into an embrace.

"My God, are you trying to scare us to death?" asked Debbie. "What on earth were you doing in there?"

Hannah returned the hug for a moment and then pulled herself free. She looked at Debbie and saw the truth in her eyes. Hannah's smile faded and she backed away from Debbie. Breathing heavily and nearing hyperventilation, she looked from Essie to Doctor Farren and back to Debbie, shaking her head in denial.

"Sweetie, wait!" pleaded Debbie.

"Hannah. It'll be all right," Doctor Farren assured her, though he had little clue as to why she was acting this way or of what he was assuring her.

Hannah faced him, eyes glaring and body shaking with fear and rage. "No it won't!" she screamed, and then she disappeared from sight.

"Jesus Christ!" Doctor Farren bellowed. He leapt backwards as if the bathroom had just burst into flames. "Where'd she go?"

Debbie and Essie looked at each other, unsure of what to do. Frustrated, Debbie looked at Doctor Farren with an imploring expression that seemed to say *Please understand,* and then Debbie, too, disappeared.

Nearly frantic, Doctor Farren looked at Essie and asked, "What the fuck is going on here?"

Essie wished she could disappear, too.

CHAPTER 34

Debbie's decision to follow Hannah was purely impulse. She had had a couple of precious seconds to consider the consequences but Hannah had already spilled the beans, so the decision was made for her. She had no idea which direction Hannah had gone, but the choices were few since Hannah knew of so few places—the hospital, the dumpster, Debbie's house, Riverside Park, and Elm Creek. Strike the hospital and she'd most assuredly not be at the dumpster. That left Debbie's house, Riverside Park, and Elm Creek. She made a hasty decision and figured that her house was where Hannah most wanted to be. A two-minute search around her house made it clear that it was the wrong decision. She didn't think Hannah would go to Riverside due to the number of people who would be wandering around, and its proximity to the hospital. This left Elm Creek.

Debbie was soon standing in Hannah and Anna's bedroom within the house on North Easy Street. Nothing had notably changed since they had last been here. She opened the closet door and looked inside. It appeared the same inside, but this time when she pushed at the back wall with the toe of her shoe, the magnets briefly resisted, but then the door swung smoothly inward.

"Hannah. If you're in there, honey, I need to talk with you," Debbie called, peering down into the dark chamber. She received only silence in response.

Debbie turned from the closet and was soon enthralled by the level of detail in Elizabeth Amiel's painting, the alien strangeness of the leaves and fruit that Elizabeth had created using metallic paint, the odd stars that seemed aflame, and the flower petals with their near coloring book simplicity. Hannah and Anna had taken Elizabeth's imagination and replicated all of this in bold 3-D grandeur, and then somehow shared it with Debbie. Another uncanny aspect of the mural was how Elizabeth had painted a precise timeline that started with her meeting Kyle Janssen, to the appearance of Debbie. It was disquietingly accurate, even after Elizabeth's death.

Debbie moved closer to the picture to inspect Elizabeth's rendition of her. Elizabeth got Debbie's characteristics spot on, from her long red hair and pale, freckled flesh, to her body, which seemed far more flattering from Elizabeth's perspective than Debbie's. She couldn't remember ever looking that good in the mirror, but then, no one saw Debbie in the same light that she saw herself. It was astounding that Elizabeth and Debbie—or Ms. Coppertop—had never met.

From the immediacy of her new vantage point, Debbie noticed something she hadn't the first time she'd been there. The frilled lacy edges of her dress were script, a string of words written along the wrists and beltline in delicate print. Though it was still daylight, Debbie had to get within inches of the wall to read the exquisite handwriting.

"Memory is the mother of all wisdom"—Aeschylus.

Similar script was present throughout the mural. There were hundreds of words—maybe thousands—that had not been noticeable when she was standing away from the wall. The most visible script ran along the border where the walls met. It was written, *"Yeah we all shine on, like the moon, and the stars, and the sun."—John Lennon.*

Written along the inner perimeter of the heart that hovered above and in front of the painted Debbie, it read, "The ears of men are lesser agents of belief than their eyes."—*Herodotus.* Debbie pondered the words for a couple of seconds. It was the ancient Greek philosopher's way of saying *"seeing is believing".* Debbie understood the truth in this . . . especially after the last week. *Seeing is also remembering,* amended Debbie.

She moved to the image of a pregnant Elizabeth Amiel. Along the outline of her swollen belly were the words, "And it came to pass in the time of her travail, that, behold, twins were in her womb"—Genesis 38:27.

The words were compelling and Debbie wanted to read more, but she forced herself to step away from the wall to look around the house.

Someone had cleaned up the small pile of debris that had been in the far corner of the living room, to the right of which lay the large expanse of wall where the sofa had most likely been. She envisioned Elizabeth Amiel fighting off the drug-crazed Travis Ulrich while Anna watched, probably standing where Debbie now stood. How devastating for a child to see her own mother butchered. Debbie tried to shake the vision from her mind.

The kitchen window she had busted out was boarded over with plywood; otherwise, it looked the same in there. Moving further into the room, she glimpsed motion through the window near where the table had once been. Outside, all looked still in the yard. The swing set stood at an awkward angle like a hobbled recluse, looking forlorn beyond the abandoned, weed-choked garden, then something on the roof of the dilapidated shed caught her eye. There was a flash of red as the cardinal spread its wings and flapped once.

"Well, hello, Mr. Janssen," Debbie said.

The bird bobbed its head with staccato jerks and centered its gaze on her. *Chirby-chirby.*

Soon nothing will shock me, Debbie thought. She headed for the front door, turned the knob and pulled, but the door had been boarded over from the outside. She hated the thought of breaking another window, then remembered and laughed at her foolishness. Within a blink, Debbie was beside the shed upon which the cardinal was perched. He looked down at her expectantly.

"Not even a flinch?" Debbie asked. "Aren't birds supposed to be timid?"

Djou-chirby-chirby, said the bird.

"Why don't you make this easy on both of us and start talking English?" said Debbie. "Disney's birds do it all the time."

The bird said nothing, only stared at her.

"I figured as much. But that's okay, it would surely earn me a course in basket weaving. Are you friendly at least?" She raised her hand towards him. The bird calmly regarded her hand as if contemplating a taste sampling, then suddenly took flight and swooped across the street to alight upon a telephone pole.

"Oh, I see how it is," Debbie said, dismissing the peculiar cardinal.

She turned her attention to the house and noted that the access to the crawlspace was again boarded over with plywood. Posted on the face of it was a new white paperboard sign with bold red lettering, *PRIVATE PROPERTY*—TRESPASSERS WILL BE PROSECUTED TO THE FULL EXTENT OF THE LAW. Another one was stapled to the plywood covering the rear door. Debbie couldn't remember any postings on the house during her last visit and wondered why it mattered now and not before.

Djou-djou-chirby-chirby-chirby.

"You still here?" Debbie asked her chatty companion.

Djou! The bird swooped to the right and landed atop the next phone pole. It faced Debbie, ruffled its feathers, and released another *djou-djou!*

"You want me to follow you?" Debbie said to the cardinal, feeling as if the eyes of the neighborhood were on her. No one was within eyeshot on the streets as far as she could tell, but if anyone were watching from behind their windows, they'd surely think she'd skipped a cog on her mental sprocket. The bird did nothing.

Debbie walked to the end of the driveway and said, "Okay, Lassie, where next?"

Sure enough, he took flight. This time he headed south, stopping to perch four poles away—about the length of a football field. An early-model Ford pickup truck approached, bouncing and clattering and sounding more like an approaching train. Debbie worried that her being a stranger would make her conspicuous and raise some suspicions . . . not that a pale redheaded woman was very intimidating. Fortunately, her presence only inspired the driver to lean out of his window to daftly gawk at her. He looked as if doubling his IQ still wouldn't scrape one hundred, and his *"hey honey"* greeting only reinforced that notion. Debbie did her best to ignore him, but she couldn't help feeling as if she had "USDA Choice" stamped on her ass in blurred blue ink.

As Debbie walked toward the pole on which the bird rested, a street sign became visible. *West Boyd Ave.*

"Okay, Cardinal Kyle. Where next?" she asked. He promptly took off eastward on West Boyd Avenue.

They continued in this fashion for about half a mile until they came upon a large structure of red brick and beige cement. Behind a four-foot chain-link fence, half-a-dozen children reveled in a playground while their parents looked on from a small field, smiling amiably at Debbie as she passed. The cardinal landed atop a basketball backboard in the courtyard behind Elm Creek Elementary School. Debbie walked onto the schoolyard, concerned that local eyes might be on her. If they were, no one complained. The bird flew again and landing on a windowsill. Debbie moved beside it and it stayed facing the glass.

"Now what?" Debbie asked.

The bird ruffled its feathers again but remained silent. Debbie looked into the classroom through cupped hands. It was clearly abandoned for the summer. She walked to the school door and tried to open it, but it was locked as expected. Returning to the window near Cardinal Kyle, Debbie studied the classroom arrangement. She then walked around the south end of the school where she came upon a white modular unit not unlike Hannah's home, presumably used as offices or maybe an extra classroom or two. Debbie moved between the school and the mod unit, again praying that no one was within eyeshot. She closed her eyes, envisioned the classroom, and was soon standing among the empty desks, looking out at Cardinal Kyle. Debbie opened the window enough to allow the bird entry, but it merely looked at Debbie and cocked its head as if to say *"I got you this far, so the rest is up to you"*.

Debbie understood the gesture. Birds were known for not handling indoor spaces very well, especially ones with windows. She watched as the bird took wing and disappeared over the school's roof.

For the better part of an hour, Debbie silently combed the school for Hannah. She searched the cafeteria, the gymnasium, the girls' and boys' locker rooms, the bathrooms, and the principal's office. She cursed the cardinal and her own foolishness for believing he was anything more than a bird . . . a peculiar bird maybe, but just a bird. She left the principal's office and stopped outside the nurse's office.

She approached the door but hesitated before opening it, knowing if Hannah was in there and the door were to suddenly open, she'd spook like a fawn and be gone in a second. She also suspected the nurse's office would be locked. Standing inches from the door, Debbie willed herself ahead by two feet, figuring it unlikely that anything was directly behind the door. She reappeared on the other side of the door, in a suite of two rooms and a large closet. It was larger than she had expected. The first room housed a desk, three horizontal file cabinets, and a bank of oak cabinets—four upper and four lower—topped with dark blue Corian countertops for work surfaces. The top cabinets had lockable glass-front doors displaying a wide array of first-aid items. Debbie moved to the doorway of the second room, which appeared to be a small sickbay with three cots. On the nearest cot, Hannah lay with her back to Debbie.

"How'd you know I was here?" Hannah asked, startling Debbie. She hadn't moved at all.

"A little bird told me. How'd you know I was here?" Debbie echoed the question.

"You popped the air when you came. It's loud," Hannah said.

Debbie recalled the sound of air displacement Hannah had made when she arrived in the hospital bathroom. *Why would it be any different for me?* she wondered. *And why is there no sound when we leave?* She figured it should be the opposite.

Debbie sat on a folding chair set against the wall across from the cot on which Hannah lay. A small stainless-steel cart, empty but for a box of tissues, was set to Debbie's left. She rested her arm on it.

"Can we talk about what's going on?" asked Debbie.

"I'm not going to anyone else's place. I'd rather stay here," Hannah said stubbornly.

"You're telling me you'd rather spend all of your time alone, hiding from everyone, with no friends, no nice bed to sleep in, and no nice warm meals?" asked Debbie. "That doesn't sound like a nice life to me."

"I did it before. I know how to take care of myself," Hannah said defiantly.

"I have no doubt. I'm pretty convinced you can do just about anything, but *can do* and *want to do* are two very different things," Debbie said. She decided to go the nonchalant route. "You're nine years old, which means you'd only have to hide for another, oh, let's say nine or so years until you can legally be on your own. Of course, you wouldn't have any schooling, so you wouldn't be able to drive a car and you wouldn't be able to get a job unless you like cleaning stinky toilet bowls or trash barrels and picking up animal poop. If that's the case, then I guess you're all set."

Debbie fidgeted with the box of tissues and waited for Hannah to respond. When she didn't, Debbie continued. "If anyone blabs about that nifty disappearing act you pulled in front of all those people back at the hospital, they'll definitely want to know how you did it. If people find out that the little girl who appeared out of nowhere is missing again, they'll be searching even harder to find you. Maybe you can hide well enough so no one sees you for the next nine years."

Debbie hoped Hannah wouldn't study her logic too closely, since it was about as solid as quicksand. Hannah continued giving Debbie the silent treatment, so she dropped the blasé tone.

"Nothing says that *in time* I can't be your foster mother or even your mother. Believe me . . . I'll keep working at it if you stick around. You of all people should know that incredible things could happen. In a little over a week you've changed my views on so many things." She chuckled and continued, "If I hadn't seen these things with my own eyes, I wouldn't be here right now . . . in Elm Creek for crying out loud!"

Debbie looked around the small room and the enormity of the situation hit her.

"God, we're in Nebraska! We freakin' teleported here!" Debbie gushed. "It's hard to believe, but here we are. Seeing *is* believing. Your mother even wrote it on your bedroom mural . . . *seeing is believing.*"

Hannah rolled slightly on the cot, her attention piqued. "She did? I don't remember that. Where?"

"Well, it actually says something like the ears of men are less likely to believe than their eyes. I know I tortured it, but it's a quote by some Greek philosopher whose name I can't remember. It means people are more likely to believe something if they see it than if they hear about it. Like with ghosts or God . . . or you."

"Oh, I saw that one, but I didn't understand it," Hannah confessed.

Debbie retreated into thought for a few moments and then said, "You know what? That quote gives me an idea. It's a shot in the dark, but I think it just might work if we're lucky." She got up from the chair and moved beside Hannah. "I know I can't make you come with me if you don't want to, but I would love it if you did. I'm not giving up on this. Will you come with me?"

Debbie waited what seemed like forever for a response but it never came. She leaned over, kissed Hannah on the head, and said, "Think about it. I'll be at my house waiting for you . . . if you want."

As difficult as it was leaving, Debbie traveled home.

She got a glass of water from the kitchen and went into her bedroom where The Doobie Brothers rocked on about "China Grove". She sat on her bed and mulled over her options, pulled her iPhone from her pocket and called Essie.

"Where in the hell are you?" she whispered sharply on the third ring.

"And a big hello to you, too," said Debbie.

"I mean it! What were you thinking? Do you have any idea what kind of shit storm you left brewing here? Fortunately, only Doctor Farren and I saw it. He's so amped he's about to fall into convulsions."

"I can imagine. Don't you want to know if I found Hannah?"

"You know I do!" Essie sputtered. "I'm just so goddamned infuriated and concerned. How do we get out of this one? Can you turn down the radio? By the way, how is Hannah?"

"Hey, what happened to your ontological shock theory?" asked Debbie, adding a touch of smart-ass. She pushed the volume slide on her radio down, but not off . . . *never off.*

"Let's hope and pray I'm right! Again, how is Hannah?"

"She's in Elm Creek, but she's fine," Debbie explained. "I think she'll come back soon."

"You think? You didn't bring her back?" Essie asked, sounding aghast.

"Don't worry, she'll be back," Debbie said. "How, pray tell, would I bring her back, anyway? It'd be like catching smoke with a butterfly net."

"I suppose that's true enough," said Essie, sounding a little more collected. "Where are you now?"

"Home. I'd like you to come here, too, if you don't mind. I think I know how to get Marjorie Faulkner to see things our way."

"I'm here and you're home?" Essie said. "Why, thank you Benedict Arnold. Don't you think it's a little late for Marjorie?"

"I hope not, but I need your help," said Debbie.

After a lengthy pause, Essie blasted out a breath and said, "I'll come, but what do I tell Doctor Farren? People are going to want to know where Hannah is."

"Bring Brad along. We need to appeal to his compassion for Hannah's sake. There isn't much we can do about the rest, just hope it doesn't spiral out of control."

"Are you serious?" asked Essie.

"Serious as brain surgery," Debbie assured her and ended the call.

She fell back on her bed, and mulled over the endless scenarios for the night and day ahead. It could be delight or disaster. She rolled to her side and pushed the volume slide on her radio back up. Stevie Nicks and Tom Petty implored each other to "Stop Dragging My Heart Around."

She set her iPhone on the table near the radio but picked it back up and scrolled to the picture she had taken after she had braided Hannah's hair, longing for Hannah's delighted smile to light the screen. Why had she only thought to take one picture? She should have taken a dozen . . . a hundred. She stared at the picture for a while, sighed, shook her head, and then kissed the image on the phone.

"Why you kissing your phone?"

Debbie started and looked around. Hannah's voice was hard to center on; it sounded like it came from everywhere.

"Hannah? Where are you?" Debbie asked, feeling an elation grow that she was afraid to release. The bathroom door swung outward, and Hannah stepped out from behind it, her eyes solemnly locked to the floor.

"How long have you been here?" Debbie asked. She rose and moved to Hannah, who just shrugged in response.

"I didn't hear a pop," Debbie said.

"I got here a little while ago," Hannah said in a dejected voice. "You were talking on the phone. People don't hear a lot when they talk on the phone."

"What a curious observation," Debbie said. She lifted Hannah's chin with a shaking hand. "Let me see you."

A sad frown etched Hannah's face and lined her forehead. Her weepy eyes darted back and forth from Debbie's to the floor.

"You left me there," Hannah said, supporting the accusation with a quivering lower lip. The whole effect was heartrending yet adorable.

Debbie hugged her and said, "I knew you'd follow me."

"I went to Hannahwhere. I looked for Anna, but I couldn't find her anywhere."

Debbie was expecting this. The afterlife was characterized by so many interpretations, but in most of them, life culminated with passage into another realm or dimension. Sometimes passage was delayed, as in Anna's case, but Debbie hoped that there was a fissure or window through which Hannah and Anna could still communicate, but maybe that was too optimistic. *That's why it's called The Big Mystery,* Debbie mused. She wanted to say something comforting to Hannah, but she found herself at a loss for words. Instead, she waited.

"I don't want to be in Hannahwhere if Anna isn't there," Hannah said, nearly pleading. "And I don't want to be anywhere else except here. I want to live here."

"I think we can make that happen," Debbie said. "Again, I can't promise you, but we can try. We have a lot of planning to do when Essie and Doctor Farren get here."

"Doctor Farren's coming here?" Hannah asked, a little glimmer lighting her eyes.

Debbie nodded.

"Did you kiss him yet?"

"That has nothing to do with our plans tonight," Debbie evaded.

"Well, did ya?"

"Not yet," Debbie said, but liking the idea.

"At the school, you said it's a shot in the dark," Hannah said, her tone serious again. "I don't want a shot."

FRIDAY
July 2, 2010

CHAPTER 35

Marjorie Faulkner was reliably punctual and usually in her office by 9:00 a.m., but Debbie wasn't going to tempt fate. Fate had a nasty sense of humor and a keen eye for irony and susceptibility . . . no need offering those enticements. At precisely 10:00 a.m., Debbie led Essie Hiller, Doctor Brad Farren, and Hannah Ariel-Janssen into the DCF office, across the main lobby, and to the door of Marjorie's private office. She gave three solid knocks. Marjorie looked up from her desk to observe the four faces. A knowing yet intrigued expression came to her once she met Debbie's eyes.

"Good morning Debbie, Doctor Hiller, please come in," Marjorie said, and the four of them filed into her office. Marjorie pointed across the hallway. "Would you be so kind as to grab two chairs from the next office?" she asked Doctor Farren.

Essie and Hannah sat as Doctor Farren gathered the chairs and placed them in a semi-curve around the front of Marjorie's faux walnut desk.

"This beautiful young lady could only be Hannah Amiel. Am I right?" asked Marjorie. She extended her hand, which Hannah accepted and firmly shook. "I'm pleased to meet you." Hannah returned a sweet smile.

Closing the door, Debbie introduced Doctor Farren, and then sat beside Hannah.

"There was a message on my phone when I came in," Marjorie quickly said, trying to lead the conversation. "It appears we've had a little mix-up concerning when Hannah was to arrive at her new foster home."

"Yes," Debbie agreed. "Something came up."

"I see. Our prospective foster parents were quite concerned, as am I." She smiled reassuringly at Hannah.

"We're requesting that you reconsider placing Hannah with me as her foster mother," Debbie said. "Doctor Hiller, Doctor Farren, and I are positive it would be in the best interest of Hannah, and it is Hannah's desire as well."

Marjorie closed her eyes for a moment. When she reopened them, they remained composed, but there was volcanic heat behind them.

"Debbie, we've already discussed this," Marjorie said, and then shifted her focus to the two doctors. "I feel it is ethically wrong, and it could be distressing to Hannah if we talk about this in her presence. I'm surprised that both of you agreed to this."

Debbie sat back in her chair and said, "Marge, you're right." She turned to Hannah and said, "I'm sorry, Hannah. We're going to have to ask you to leave, okay?"

"Okay," said Hannah. She was gone from sight in a blink.

Marjorie jumped up and backed against the wall, pulling her chair between her visitors and herself. They all watched her reaction, and Debbie was surprised by how collected she remained, considering what had just occurred.

"Where is she?" Marjorie demanded.

"Gone. Just as you suggested," Debbie said.

"How did she do it? Is it some kind of trick? Is this a joke you're all playing on me? Well, it's not funny."

"No, Marge, this is most assuredly *not* a joke," Debbie said.

"Hannah has the ability to travel," Essie explained. "Astral projection, we thought at first, but it obviously goes well beyond that."

"How is that possible?"

"Who knows," said Debbie. "But she does. You just saw it with your own eyes."

"Hannah's ability makes her quite exceptional, though not totally unique. Supposedly there are more, but I've only seen it twice," Essie said. "They study it deeply at The Monroe Institute, as well as other places . . . mostly colleges. In countries like Peru, for example, shamans claim to have been doing it for centuries. I used to scoff at the idea."

"The biggest danger here is for Hannah," Doctor Farren added.

"She is at risk, especially in her sensitive emotional state. Some people may want to learn her ability . . . maybe fanatics or opportunists. She could become a lab specimen or maybe a hostage, yet her biggest adversaries are her age, innocence, and inexperience."

"Hannah needs someone who understands her capabilities and someone who can teach her and support her. Someone who will not exploit her. We can't be sure that her new foster parents wouldn't do that," Debbie said. "And we're laying it all at your mercy."

Debbie stared at Marjorie as she tried to put everything into perspective. She wasn't doing very well.

"But there are no guarantees. How can you be sure of anyone who finds out?" Marjorie asked. "Even me, for example?"

"I have no idea what you're talking about," Debbie said, looking confounded.

"Must be the pressure at work is getting to her, making her imagine things," said Essie. "I see it quite often in my trade."

"You're clearly fucking nuts," Doctor Farren said.

Marjorie gawked disbelievingly at the people in her office. "I can't believe you're trying to blackmail me," she said.

"Not blackmail, Marge. We want you to see things as they really are and we want to do what is best for Hannah so she can live a better life," said Debbie.

Essie sat forward entreatingly and said, "Consider what she's been through in her nine years. People have lived to a hundred with a fraction of the trauma she's already experienced."

"But how do you know *you* are what's best for Hannah?" Marjorie asked.

"Because," Debbie said. "Been there, done that." Debbie's seat was instantly vacant.

"Oh come off it!" Marjorie barked. "This has got to be a joke!" She looked around as if trying to find the hidden cameras or the guffawing friend or workmate. "Are both of you going to disappear now?"

"Sorry," said Doctor Farren. "Just them."

"This is not a joke, Marge," said Essie. "For Hannah it's quite serious. It's crucial for her quality of life."

With a huge fluttering *pop*, Hannah and Debbie reappeared just to the left of Marjorie's desk, both carrying an armful of flowers in an impressive array of colors. An exquisite and mesmerizing aroma engulfed the office. They moved forward in unison and laid the flowers on Marjorie's desk.

Marjorie slowly moved forward, awed and intrigued by the odd pile of flowers they had spilled onto her desk. She picked one up, held the petals to her nose, and stared silently at the multiplicity of colors.

"What kind of flowers are these?" she asked. "I've never seen anything like them or smelled anything so compelling."

"I haven't the slightest," Essie admitted. She lifted one to her nose and inhaled.

"But they smell like . . . paradise," said Doctor Farren.

Debbie pointed to the flowers and said to Hannah, "You knew about this all along . . . that Hannahwhere *is* physical?"

Hannah shrugged and grinned. "I wasn't positive until last night."

"But, where?" Debbie asked.

Hannah shrugged emphatically and shook her head. Debbie's world tilted a little more. She had a feeling it wouldn't be the last time. She rubbed Hannah's head and then hugged her to her side. Marjorie Faulkner slowly lowered herself into her seat, looking rapt.

"So, Marge," Debbie said. "It's evident I'm the most suitable caretaker for Hannah, wouldn't you agree?"

"I don't want to live with anyone else," said Hannah.

Marjorie Faulkner gently lifted another flower and nodded.

SUNDAY
July 4, 2010

CHAPTER 36

Debbie was not surprised to see Hannah standing beside her bed. It was only her second day in her new surroundings, and if anyone had earned the right to be a little uneasy in the wee hours of the night, it was Hannah. Debbie squinted at the blurred orange numerals on her alarm clock and patted the bed beside her. Hannah, bedraggled in her floral two-piece pajama set, hopped onto the bed and settled in near Debbie. It was 2:34 a.m. and Seal was singing of the honors of being "Kissed by a Rose".

"Hi, pumpkin. You have a bad dream?" Debbie asked.

"No," said Hannah.

"Scared?"

"No."

She studied Hannah, who in turn studied the ceiling, visibly lost in contemplation. Just her presence was a joy and it was all Debbie could do to not grab her and squeeze her. The reality of her was something she hoped would never grow old.

"Good," said Debbie.

The previous two days had gone by in a frenzied flash. Friday she had registered Hannah in school, chose a dentist and a pediatrician—Dr. Farren being the obvious choice—and filled out what seemed like reams of paperwork. Essie and Doctor Farren—who insisted they call him Brad—cleared out the spare room, moving a lot of it into the basement, and even more into the garage to await Monday morning's curbside pick-up. A small mountain of undesignated items waited in a stack in the living room for second evaluation.

Hannah slept on the couch Thursday night, which hadn't bothered her in the least. *Much better than the dumpster*, she had assured Debbie.

Essie donated a dresser and a small desk that had once belonged to her daughter and then her granddaughter. Both were in great condition. She was pleased to see them out of her attic and in use again.

When Debbie called to report the good news to Brandon, he insisted she find a "good" bed with mattress and box spring, and send him the bill. She did buy Hannah a nice full-size bed set, which was delivered on Saturday. (She wasn't sure she'd take Brandon up on the offer, but it was tempting.) Between the generosity of many good people, and Lowe's, Kohl's, The Salvation Army, and a good chunk of Debbie's savings, Hannah had a decent wardrobe and a very respectable bedroom to call her own.

One of the best moments of Saturday evening was watching Hannah finish off two huge helpings of macaroni and cheese, accentuating her bites with small hums and murmurs of pleasure. Debbie used whole grain macaroni, Cabot's Seriously Sharp cheddar, and a light dose of jalapeño pepper. *Sorry, Mr. Kraft, no processed foods here.* Hannah's exuberance upon finding out that Debbie's recipe was nearly identical to Elizabeth Amiel's was hilarious and contagious, and sent an intense jolt of contentment through Debbie.

Hannah was thrilled that she got to choose her own bedding at Kohl's. Saturday night they set up her new bedroom. She marveled at the sheer size of her new bed compared to the hospital bed and even the twin bed she had back in Elm Creek.

"It's weird that I don't have a twin bed anymore, either," Hannah had said to Debbie. After a moment of contemplation, she added, "Am I still a twin now that Anna's not alive?"

"You'll always be Anna's twin no matter where she is," Debbie replied. "I believe Anna's still alive, just not in the same way that we are."

"Like the thinking her? Her spirit?"

"Exactly. She proved it to us in Hannahwhere and Annaplace."

"What about my mom and dad?"

"I'd bet they're with her," Debbie said.

"You know what else is weird?"

"What, sweetie?"

"When I think of Anna, I feel like half of me is gone, but I feel like I'm two times heavier. It's like, the more happy you have, the less you weigh. Does that make sense?" asked Hannah, her words also heavy with sleep.

"More than you'll ever know," Debbie told her. "Do you know that another word for happiness is levity, and that means lightness?"

"I do now," Hannah said and then slowly dozed off.

Sunday morning they planned to touch up the bedroom, and then Debbie would give Hannah a tour of Riverside and share some of the city's history . . . at least what she knew of it. She would then bring Hannah to Hampton Beach. They would walk in the sand, swim, eat fried dough, and watch the Independence Day fireworks. Hannah had never been on a beach, seen the ocean, or eaten fried dough. Debbie loved the thought of introducing Hannah to new experiences, and the anticipation was intoxicating.

Debbie also planned on renting—or buying if necessary—the best digital camera available, bringing it to Elm Creek, and taking numerous high-resolution pictures of the mural in what used to be Hannah's and Anna's bedroom. She knew there were ways to stitch digital photos into one large image, and she had seen numerous online stores that could reproduce images into wallpaper. It wouldn't be like having the original, but maybe she could come close. There was an empty wall in Hannah's room.

If their first days together were any indication of things to come, then it would be blissful, but Debbie didn't carry an illusion that things would be perfect. Hannah would start seeing Essie every Wednesday, tapering off as Essie and Doctor Farren (or Brad) deemed fit. Hannah had had a hard go of it, and there would certainly be times when memories and profound sadness would stagger her. Debbie had seen her teary-eyed and sullen at various moments, but she needed to mourn. It was an essential part of healing.

On Friday, Debbie put a call in to the Kearney Police Department to ask if they'd stored Elizabeth's, Hannah's, and Anna's possessions. It was a distressing thought that the only photographs Hannah might ever have of her mother and sister would be from newspapers and magazines.

"Do you think I'll make any friends here?" Hannah asked, bringing Debbie back to the present. She wasn't asleep after all.

"Of course!" said Debbie, maybe a little too enthusiastically.

"You are the sweetest girl I've ever met. Who wouldn't want to be your friend?"

Hannah shrugged. "Anna and I didn't have many friends in Elm Creek. Actually, we really didn't have any except each other."

"Elm Creek has only nine hundred people in the whole town," Debbie said. "Riverside has more than sixty thousand. That's more than sixty times as many people. I think you'll have plenty of friends, and good ones, too."

"Doesn't that mean there are sixty times as many bad people? Like Travis?"

Damn! Debbie thought. *I'll need to stay on my toes with this girl.* Trying to reassure herself as much as Hannah, Debbie said, "No. Travis was one of a kind, and he's where he belongs now . . . for the rest of his life."

"Am I bad if I say I'd feel better if he wasn't alive?" Hannah asked.

"I don't think so, but if you are, then I'm bad, too," Debbie said.

Hannah shifted closer to her and Debbie draped a protective arm over her. "Why does your ceiling look like that?" Hannah asked.

"That's called pressed tin. They used it a lot in the eighteen hundreds because it's pretty, fireproof, less work than fancy plasterwork, and cheap."

"It's neat."

On the radio, Heart warned them about the guiles of the "Magic Man". Debbie watched Hannah study the ceiling for a while before the realization hit her that Hannah was traveling. She found it somewhat spooky how her eyes stared ahead, absent, yet still present. She'd figured Hannah might still travel, and probably often, either hoping to find Anna or just for the sense of control it must lend to a life that she had so little control over. Debbie was grateful that she was only mentally traveling, and not physically. Not that she could stop either. Hannah being physically elsewhere made her uneasy, and although she had proved herself one hell of a survivor, the protective part of Debbie still felt Hannah would be at risk during those times. The mental traveling concerned her in a different way. She feared Hannah would become obsessed with trying to find Anna, and if Anna had experienced some kind of closure from them finding her body, then this could segue into even larger issues. Of all the uncertainties that she could have imagined herself dealing with in a parenting role, this was never one of them.

"Come with me!" Hannah said. She grabbed Debbie's arm.

"My God! Where?" asked Debbie.

"To Hannahwhere! Come!"

Hannah's excitement was such that Debbie could not help but concede.

They are lying on their backs amid the floral fields. The sun is directly overhead, basking them with buttery rays that feel delicious yet oddly alien to Debbie. A quick, warm gust of wind rushes over them and just as quickly fades. Debbie sits up and looks around, feeling a sense of strangeness yet familiarity. Trees and hills surround the perimeter of the field, except to Debbie's right lies a tremendous body of water, mirror-like, but far larger than before . . . too vast to see the far shores.

"Wow, it's different!" says Hannah from beside her. "I was just here, but now it's different. What happened?"

"I think it's a mix of your place and my place, but even more," Debbie says. "That's Lake Erie."

High in the flawless blue sky an eagle circles, shrieks its greeting, and is quickly joined by another. A diversity of birds weaves through the trees and over the fields. Countless species peacefully share the skies . . . hawks . . . finches. The woods to their left are an amalgamation of trees, sky-high pines, and majestic oaks interspersed with shorter trees draped with shining leaves and laden with blue, metallic-skinned fruit.

Nearer to earth, a familiar red-feathered bird swoops in front of them and lands in the lower branches of a nearby fruit tree. Despite the new flora, Debbie recognizes it as the same tree Anna had lain listlessly in the last time they saw her—also from the mural in Elm Creek.

Chirby-chirby-chirby-djou-djou!

Debbie takes Hannah's hand and helps her up as she rises.

"Cool! Look at the mountains!" Hannah says and points. Long, glassine stretches of green land swell sensually toward the horizon, blending and then merging with purple and gray towers of snow-capped granite. "Why did that happen?" she asks.

"It must be because we're both here," Debbie reasons.

"We were both here before," Hannah says.

"Well, maybe it's because I'm finally accepting it."

"Huh?" says Hannah.

"I'll explain later."

Dismissing it, Hannah shrugs and eagerly waves to the cardinal. *Djou-djou!*

"Look!" yells Hannah, pointing excitedly to the tree.

"What?" asks Debbie.

"Right there!" Hannah starts pulling her toward the tree.

"I don't see anything," Debbie insists, following hesitantly. Apprehension grows within her as Hannah breaks for the tree at full speed.

"It's them! It's Anna and my mom and dad!"

"Wait! Hannah! That's not possible! Your mom can't come here, remember?" Debbie calls, but Hannah is far ahead of her, already near the tree.

When Debbie finally catches up, Hannah is beneath the tree and appears to be talking animatedly, but Debbie sees no one else there.

"Yes," Hannah says. "I am. Uh-huh. I will." She nods and a profound sadness masks her face. She continues, talking through her falling tears. "Okay, Mommy . . . I love you."

Debbie watches the one-sided conversation warily, not wanting to interrupt, just in case . . . maybe. She sees something wavering in the air, like heat rising from pavement, and then it's gone.

Is it possible that Hannah's mother is here? How? Could she not come here in life, but only through death?

"Anna's talking to you," Hannah says to her.

Debbie concentrates on the area where she had seen the wavering, but she sees nothing more.

"I'm sorry, honey," she says. "I can't see anybody."

"Mom says there are no bodies to see. She says to look with your heart, not with your mind or your eyes," Hannah says. She glances back under the tree and asks, "What?" Looking back at Debbie, she says, "Dad says to use a different pra . . . pa . . . speck . . ."

"Perspective?" asks Debbie.

"Yeah, that! He says look like you did back in Lakewood."

Lakewood? Debbie is positive she has never said the name

Lakewood to Hannah or Anna. *How does she know?*

"Use your little girl eyes."

My little girl eyes? Look with my heart? Debbie thinks, and then she thinks *don't think.* She closes her eyes and pushes all thoughts from her mind except for Hannah and Anna and the little girl she once was.

When the sensation begins, Debbie feels heat, direct and intense like a pinpoint of sunlight through a magnifying glass. Miniscule, but growing and blossoming larger, it spreads like warm oil and covers her body. It is heat beyond measure, yet painless, and it swaddles her with serenity.

"Oh my God," Debbie gasps and opens her eyes.

Before Hannah, and through Hannah, Debbie sees the light and feels the heat. There are three sources of light. They are intense at the center and have rays shooting outward like stars. More appear behind them and then right beside her. Debbie looks over the field and out among the trees where hundreds, or maybe a thousand lights in a thousand different hues shine brightly. Some are still, while some move slowly and others dart like birds across the sky. Some move in pairs, some in groups, and many move alone. Debbie understands that these are like the stars from Hannah and Anna's mural.

"Look at them and see them without the conditions life forced on you," says a female voice, emanating from one of the lights near Hannah. "We are all energy. We are all spirit."

It all starts to make sense. Debbie cannot see their arms, legs, or faces, but she recognizes them regardless. She remembers the stars from when she was young like Hannah and Anna, and she would travel to safety. So many travelers, seeking protection and hiding from the pain, like Hannah, Anna . . . and her.

"Anna," Debbie says.

"Hi," says Anna.

Debbie looks again at the many lights. "These are all people!"

"Yes. Spirits," says Elizabeth Amiel-Janssen.

Of course, thinks Debbie, and she recalls the movement of the lights, how some float high in the sky, swooping and spinning like eagles, and others rocket just above the landscape.

"These are all travelers! Are they all flying away—hiding from pain?" Debbie asks.

"Some come here for safety. Some are travelers. Some are not. But all are spirits. Some are crossing over, and others may be caught in between," Elizabeth says.

"Like Anna," Debbie realizes.

"Yes. She had to remain here until this part of her voyage was complete," Elizabeth says. "Now she can move on. You and Hannah have a longer voyage here."

"Mom says we'll all be together again, many times," says Hannah.

"You and Hannah are living a very small part of a forever filled with journeys," Elizabeth explains. "We are all different souls with different voyages, yet we are all connected. This place is just a conduit from one voyage to another."

A light sweeps past Debbie and halts, hovering about twenty feet ahead of her. It shoots back near Debbie, grazing her. She can feel its energy, vital and intense, and she recognizes it . . . the young Middle Eastern boy from the bathroom. He must have followed Hannah there from here. The light rockets away from her like a comet rising into the sky, and then it returns to hover near Hannah.

"He has a connection to Hannah," explained Kyle Janssen's voice. "A linking of spirits like yours and mine. Can you remember?"

And Debbie remembers the very blond boy, flying . . . escaping with her when she, too, would fly and escape.

"Why are they all here in Hannahwhere?" Debbie asks of the other spirits.

"For Hannah, this is her Hannahwhere. For you, it is your Hannahwhere, by however you regard it. It is the same, this haven, for all the others, but viewed through their own consciousness," says Kyle Janssen, Hannah and Anna's father. "There is strength here."

"Why . . ." Debbie hesitates, unsure if her question is appropriate.

"See how conditions hinder you?" says Elizabeth. "You are wondering why I stayed with Travis, knowing what he was. Our bodies make us foolish and weak. Evil is very cunning. He promised to kill Hannah, Anna, and me if I ever left him. I was more afraid of the monster he could become than the monster he was, yet he became that monster anyway. You will do well to learn from my mistakes."

Anna's light moves forward to Hannah and the other two

follow to engulf her. Hannah's mouth moves, but Debbie can hear no words. Hannah raises her arms as if asking to be carried, and for a moment Hannah, too, becomes brilliant light. They blend and become one blazing and pulsing beacon. The light separates into four again, and then Hannah is back, falling lightly to the ground as if in sleep.

The three lights now surround and then flow over Debbie and she again feels the heat surge over and through her. She wants to stay here, within their embrace forever. Somewhere within the light, she can sense Elizabeth and Kyle thanking her, and as Debbie feels herself lowered to the ground, she hears from a place deep, deep within her heart, "I love you, Ms. Coppertop."

They woke, lying in Debbie's bed with the late-morning sun blazing through the window and across their legs. Debbie stretched, and Hannah opened her eyes and smiled.

"You are *so* beautiful, little lady," Debbie said.

Hannah sat up and stretched her arms toward the ceiling. Eyes widening, she pointed happily towards the window.

"Hey, look!" she said.

Outside the window, perched upon a branch of a Japanese quince, was a perfect red cardinal.

EPILOGUE
January 5, 2016

Tecumseh State Correctional Institution was about two miles north of Tecumseh, Nebraska on Highway 50. For Travis Ulrich it was home. He hated his home more and more every day. There was nothing fun about life in prison, that was a given, but as far as prisons went, TSCI (pronounced *tisky* by its residents) was okay. Travis wasn't exactly an authority on prisons, since all he'd ever known of them he had learned from a series of one-night stays at various times of his life. That was before he'd lost it with Elizabeth and her kids.

He was in the eleventh year of his *life without parole* sentence, most of which had been uneventful and even bland years, exactly what most inmates wanted. There had been a bad patch after they had discovered the body of Anna Amiel-Janssen with a huge screwdriver—covered in his fingerprints and DNA—sticking out of her back. You can kill your boss, father, uncle, priest, and even your old lady, but kill your mother or a kid . . . forget it! You're fucked!

Shortly after the discovery, word got out. They gave him his own private room in the Administrative Segregation wing, with its green-and-cream-checkered floors and large steel doors that could double as bank vaults. They said it was for his protection, but they weren't too concerned about it when they turned a blind eye in the showers. They prefer the showers since cleanup is easy. Travis had received a serious ass kicking that left him bloody and bruised, with two broken ribs and minus two teeth.

Travis wasn't a courageous man by any means. He had spent the majority of his life hiding, first behind his mother's skirt and then behind words and actions. He had been small and odd as a child, but had learned from watching his daddy, that small cowards could conceal themselves well behind big talk and erratic behavior, and the only thing he had experienced that was close to courage were the doses of defiance he found in booze and drugs. His defense system was flight, not fight, so it had been a shock to everyone, including himself, that on his first trial release back into general prison population he chose fight.

During mealtime, at the first sign of harassment, it was instantly clear that he was targeted. Travis sprung as if shot out of a cannon and drove the top of his head under George Parrish's jaw. He was immediately buried under a mass of bodies and rewarded with another brutal pounding, but he did manage to sink his teeth into some yielding flesh, eliciting horrendous screams. He still had no idea whose flesh he had latched onto, or the after-effects of his head-butt on Parrish, but he was pleased he had gotten some licks in. He was back behind the heavy gray steel doors in Ad-Seg, right where he wanted to be . . . and he had dodged the showers. More than eight years and three repeat performances later, Travis was labeled a habitual risk and he had become a permanent fixture in Ad-Seg.

Comfort had not been a consideration when they designed the cells in Ad-Seg. They were like walk-in safes with a door, four walls, and two windows, one for observation in case inmates were suicidal, the other looking out onto the endless, flat Nebraskan terrain, cut only by a tall, chain-link fence topped with razor wire. The tile even stopped at the door line. The immovable floor-mounted steel blocks with two-inch square-tube steel rails on which to mount restraints— otherwise known as beds—looked more like industrial tables. They employed no hardware like bolts and nuts, only welds. For Travis it was a fair exchange. Ad-Seg meant safety.

Isolation didn't bother Travis . . . inclusion troubled him. People were bothersome, greedy parasites who only wanted to take. If you wanted anything from them, they only expected more in compensation. Fuck the door, just give him three square meals, four walls—even if they were pink—and a window, and Travis was happy . . . though a bigger window would have been nice.

After lights-out, the only real illumination in his room was the light that came through the window . . . more on the nights when the moon was bright. He could tell by the angle of the moonlight that it was about three o'clock in the morning. He'd been awake for about an hour, which was common. Ad-Seg had a way of messing up a sleep schedule.

Lying on his bed, he stared at the barely visible ceiling and started nodding off, but an unusual sound brought him back to wakefulness. He couldn't place it, but it had a slow, ripping quality to it. Not like cloth, but like a ribbed metallic sound. He waited to see if it happened again and then started to drift off.

Bvvvviiip!

It came from the direction of the little window, which made him think of the mesh screen covering. He got up, moved to it, and peered outside. The small ledge that ran below the window was wide enough to balance on, yet high enough from the ground to be precarious . . . not that he had any way out of there.

Click-tick-click.

From behind him, something had bounced across the floor and hit the side of his bare foot. When he leaned over and picked the object up, confusion and dread washed over him.

"What the fuck?"

He recognized the small piece of wood. It was in the shape of a cartoonish dog holding a plaque with *Travis* written on it in blue ink.

How in the hell did it get here?

Bvvvviiip!

Travis spun towards the window again.

It must be a bird, he tried to convince himself.

He shifted his position, trying to get a better vantage point to see the sides of the opening when a hand dropped down and raked something along the window.

"Fuck!" Travis yelped. He jumped back against the wall in alarm, his heart pounding. It was fast and birdlike, but it had looked like the hand of a small woman. He didn't see what it had used to scrape the mesh. It could have been a rock, a knife, or maybe talons for all he knew, but whatever it was, it was spooky as shit.

He wasn't about to show whoever was out there that they had scared the living shit out of him. He inched back toward the window, figuring if the mesh kept him in, it would keep anything else out.

He looked out the window again, but no one was there.

Then there was . . .

She just appeared, her head downturned, but her eyes peered up through her hair, aiming a demonic gaze directly at him. She floated before the window, and then she settled on the ledge, staring that nasty-ass glare his way. Travis shrieked and again leapt away from the window.

A woman with ghost-white hair.

He didn't believe in ghosts, yet, why else would a fucking albino be floating above a window ledge of an all-male prison at three in the morning?

"Liz?" Travis asked with a quaver in his voice that betrayed his fear.

She didn't answer, but the little bitch's silhouette was still visible on his wall.

Did ghosts have shadows? he wondered, and then it hit him. She looked like a teenager. She was too young to be Elizabeth, but Hannah would certainly be in her teens, wouldn't she? How in the hell did she get inside the yard?

Growling at the top of his voice, Travis scooped water from the toilet bowl, jumped in front of the window, and threw it and the little wooden dog through the mesh.

She wasn't there.

Cold fingernails sunk into the back of his neck, driving such a surge of terror through him that nearly buckled his legs. Travis leapt across the cell, blindly flailing his arms. He backed into the corner of the cell, between the observation window and the exterior window, and looked desperately around the room, willing his eyes to adjust to the darkness. As his vision adapted, she started to emerge from the shadows diagonally across the room from him, those darkness-ringed eyes accusing him.

She vanished. . . and then appeared in the corner to his left. . . and then to his right. . . and then she was gone.

Travis cowered in the corner, pleading for her to leave him alone, appealing to the sun to rise. He waited in the dark silence.

. . . and waited. . . five minutes. . . ten minutes.

She reappeared inches from his face, her eyes boring into his.

"Travisssssss," she hissed, sounding dry as a desert wind.

She disappeared.

Travis catapulted to the cell door, slamming his fists and begging *anyone* to open it. In the hallway beyond his cell door, all remained still and silent. Outside from the window ledge, Hannah watched Travis's breakdown and smiled.

It hadn't been easy finding Travis, but it had been worth it.

ABOUT THE AUTHOR

JOHN McILVEEN is the author of two story collections *Inflictions* and *Jerks and Other Tales from a Perfect Man*. He is the father of five lovely daughters and works at MIT's Lincoln Laboratory. He is well into his second and third novels, *Gone North* and *Corruption*. He lives in Haverhill, MA, with his partner Roberta Colasanti.

Curious about other Crossroad Press books?
Stop by our site:
http://store.crossroadpress.com
We offer quality writing
in digital, audio, and print formats.

Enter the code FIRSTBOOK
to get 20% off your first order from our store!
Stop by today!